KATHRYN KINCAID

Contents

For anyone who has hidden parts of themselves from the world

Content warnings

One of the main characters has bipolar II disorder; there are descriptions of depression, use of self-medicating, and suicidal ideation (past). There is discussion of body shaming (past) and struggles with body image (present). Challenging familial circumstances are also depicted as well as family therapy sessions.

There are on-page depictions of sex/nudity and use of swear words/foul language.

Prologue #1: Zach

Two Years Ago

I SPRINT TO THE hotel's front desk like my life fucking depends on it.

I'll never hear the end of my teammate's chirps if I embarrass myself at my captain's wedding—and as I'm a rookie and the youngest guy on the team, they already razz me enough.

"Restroom?"

The kid behind the desk looks up from his phone with bloodshot eyes. "Down the hall," he says in a bored monotone. He doesn't look much younger than me, maybe a senior in high school. "Third or fourth door on the right. There's a sign."

He says the last sentence like he can't believe I'm this clueless. It's not my fault I couldn't use the one in the reception hall. My teammate was already there, balls-deep inside a woman, thrusting from behind. *Fucking lock the door next time, Lepel,* I shouted before high-tailing it out of there.

One.

Two.

Three.

I count the doors as I run, heaving a sigh of relief when the restroom sign comes into view. It's one of those silly drawings I struggle to decipher when sober, but the guy said the right side of the hallway.

Or was it left?

Right. Left. I flip a coin in my mind, and push through a door on the left into a room with a fancy-looking gold couch I wish I could collapse on. This might be the best men's restroom I've ever been in, clean and smelling faintly like a garden. Then pink flowers on the wall catch my eye, and there's no urinal in sight.

"Shit, it *was* the right," I mutter. Thank fuck no one else is in here.

I book it out of there to the other side of the hall, leaning against the door as I twist the handle. It abruptly swings open, throwing me to the floor of a dark room in front of a shadowy figure.

I yelp, then fumble to my feet and flip on the light. A blond woman sits cross-legged in the center of the room, her maroon bridesmaid dress pooling around her. Bright blond hair frames her head like a crown with loose strands beside her face.

Her friend's wedding reception rages down the hall and she's on the floor of a dusty supply closet by herself. What gives?

Her wide sky-blue eyes meet mine, shocking me back to reality. I've been staring at her for too long.

I spitfire words. "I thought this was the restroom. The guy at the desk said it was. But clearly it's not. Unless you want to step into the hall for a second while I use the bucket back there."

She shakes her head, then takes out an earbud. "What was that?"

I let out a relieved sigh. Take two. "Do you know where the restroom is?"

"I don't work here," she replies with a shrug.

"I know. Your dress makes it obvious." I wave my hand at her. "But I'm lost, and the kid at the desk is high, and I don't want to make a scene and get kicked out of here... can you help?"

She raises one eyebrow. "You want me to go off alone with a stranger to find a restroom?"

I chuckle nervously. "Well... when you say it like that, it sounds sketchy. But it's not. I promise. I really do need to find one, and I've—"

"Did you check the reception hall?" Her words aren't unkind but abrupt, like she wants me out of her hair. A feeling familiar to me.

"It was, uh, occupied. I wasn't sure how much longer they would take—Lepel's got a reputation. And it was awkward catching them, you know? Not an image I'll forget any time soon."

I take a deep breath.

I should leave and find a potted plant to piss in, but my feet won't move.

"I'm Zach, by the way."

She studies me, one finger tapping her cupped jaw, and my face burns. She's so freaking pretty, I find it hard to look at her, to inhale air into my lungs.

When I'm about to start another ramble, she slips the remaining earbud from her ear, secures it in a white container, and shoves it in a small purse in her lap. She climbs to her feet and smooths the fabric of her dress. A slit travels from her right calf to her hip, showcasing a muscular leg, toned and lean. She's nearly a foot shorter than me, but I wouldn't fuck with her.

"I'm Finley."

Finley. It's a nice name, not one I've heard before. Since moving to the US, I've encountered a lot of names I'd never heard in the small Canadian town where I grew up.

"If this is some weird strategy to get me alone," she continues, "you'll regret it. My brothers could have you on your knees in five seconds."

If you want me on my knees, all you need to do is ask.

Thank the hockey gods I keep *that* thought to myself, otherwise Finley would report me, the pervert who cornered her in a closet to talk about restrooms.

"If I were trying to trap you, I wouldn't ask you to leave this room. And if I were trying to pick you up, I wouldn't talk about restrooms."

I don't know what I would say to impress her. I watch my teammates navigate these conversations all the time, like it's easy. It's never easy for me.

Her stern expression breaks into one of amusement. "You make a compelling argument. All right, let's find the men's room before you officially tank this entire interaction."

We're in the hallway now, and Finley points to the next door. "It's out of order," she notes of the men's room before heading toward the reception. She swings right at the fork without looking left to the party and strolls down the next hallway. She stops at the elevator, presses the up button, and steps inside when it opens.

She tilts her head. "You coming?"

I don't hesitate and step in beside her. "Where are we going?"

"The pool," she says as if it's an entirely ordinary answer.

"I might be tipsy, Finley, but I can aim just fine into a small body of water."

"I wasn't suggesting you *pee* in it." She shakes her head, but a trace of a smile forms. "This is the strangest first conversation I've ever had."

"Really?" I grin. "It's fairly normal for me."

"Honestly, I'm not the least bit surprised." The elevator dings as it comes to a stop on the third floor, and Finley steps in front of the door to keep it open for me. She swipes her room card to let us into the pool area, then gestures to the opposite end of the room. "Your palace awaits."

I speedwalk toward the locker room but stop abruptly and glance over my shoulder. "You'll be here when I get back?"

She nods toward the pool, a mischievous glint in her eye. "I'll be swimming."

Finley eases her dress down her torso until she wears nothing but a strapless bra.

Holy shit.

She pauses when our eyes meet but does nothing to cover herself. Not the least bit self-conscious. She has no reason to be, but still, I'm a stranger.

I keep my eyes focused on her face. "Uh-huh," I say dazedly, hoping she'll assume my tongue-tied response is due to alcohol. Not because I'm here with the most beautiful woman I've ever met, and she might be flirting with me.

Or screwing with me.

I scurry away from her. When I come back several minutes later, Finley is floating in the center of the pool, arms spread out. Her dress, undergarments, and shoes are strewn across the floor. I'm surprised she didn't care enough to place them on a chair. But it's not like I know her.

"I've been told alcohol and swimming is a bad combination."

Her head bobs out of the water. "I'm the only sober person in this place. So are you coming in or are you too drunk?"

I hold up a finger. "Tipsy, not drunk."

I undo my belt and step out of my dress pants, tossing them onto a chaise lounge along with my socks.

Finley doesn't divert her gaze. She swims to where I settle on the side of the pool, my feet in the water.

I study her face up close—heart-shaped with featherlight freckles peppering her cheeks and plump pink kissable lips. Her hair's wet, but her makeup remains intact. I swallow hard, praying every thought bouncing around my mind doesn't give itself away in another part of my anatomy.

What does she see when she looks at me? Her beautiful face is frustratingly blank and unreadable.

"So why were you in that closet?" I ask.

She perches her arms on the side of the pool and rests her cheek on them. "Oh, I was lost. I'm *so* glad you found me." Her words drip with sarcasm.

I ignore her attempt at deflection, too curious for my own damn good. "I thought you might be hiding."

"Who would avoid a party?"

"You and me, apparently." I gesture between us.

"Who says this *isn't* a party, Zach?" She kicks off the wall, swimming backward until she reaches the center of the pool, where she treads water. "You going to join me or what?"

I hesitate. I didn't work my way into the NHL only to throw it all away by doing something reckless.

"If you're worried about drowning," she adds while I silently sift through my thoughts, "you should know I can hold my breath underwater for two minutes."

"How does *that* help me exactly?"

"In this situation, I'll be able to reach you if you sink to the bottom." She flashes a suggestive smile. "In other situations... I'll let you use your imagination."

Fucking hell. I cough, choking on nothing other than the image those words bring to mind.

I shrug off my jacket and fumble the buttons of my shirt open. I fling the clothing toward the chair, then cannonball into the water in only my boxer briefs. My body adjusts quickly to the warmer-than-expected temperature.

I shake my head when I break the surface, my hair whipping water in her direction. "I feel safer already."

"If you want safe," she says, "you should stay away from me."

Prologue #2: Finley

Two Years Ago

I've felt nothing all day, a lovely side effect of my bipolar disorder medication.

My doctor said it takes time to find the medication and dose my body needs, but once we discover the right combination, the emptiness will pass. He also said feeling nothing for someone with my condition is better than the alternative.

But after the energetic highs of hypomania, moving through ordinary life is akin to a car stuck in mud. Still not as bad as a depressive episode. During those, everything takes constant, conscious effort, including actions most people take for granted. Getting out of bed. Exercising. Social interaction. I'd argue this nothingness, this sleepwalking through the day, isn't much better.

It took a herculean effort to get through the wedding, hours of hair and makeup, endless conversation with the other bridesmaids, and my sister-in-law Gemma's bubbly personality. I'm happy she's joining our family, and she should effuse happiness on her wedding day, but I still struggle. Watching other guests cry during the vows while I experienced no emotion made it blatantly obvious how different I am from everyone else.

I retreated to that closet so I would stop comparing myself to other people. No one tried to talk to me there. Not until Zach burst through the door, rambling about the restroom in this self-conscious way that made me want to smile for the first time in so, *so* long.

"What makes you *dangerous*?" Zach asks, swimming toward me.

His flirting sends a thrill through me. I like his rambling too. The way my mere presence melts his mind to the point he can't form sentences. I like the way I unnerve him, this cute guy who probably has no shortage of women interested in him. There's a power in it—a sense of control—that grounds me.

"Clearly, I influence you," I tell him with a half smile. "You followed me here, to the pool. Aren't *you* worried about what I might make you do next?"

The water shoves my burdens from my shoulders. I'm free from my family's concerned expressions. From the heaviness of my tired limbs. From the acute awareness my life will never look like it used to. From the fact that I'll always have to deal with something most people will never understand.

I hate self-pity, but I can't stop it. I haven't been able to since my diagnosis, not with the constant reminders of my *otherness*.

"I might like it, I think." Zach's gaze darts away from mine, breaking eye contact first. His nervousness kicks my heart into overdrive. I want whatever this emotion is to swallow me whole. I want a break from the void. I want this adorable boy to make me forget myself.

"Follow me," I say, turning my back to him as I swim to the deep end of the pool.

Climbing out of the water reveals my entire body, especially with these bright lights. Every scar. Every stretch mark. Every tan line. Every imperfection. I should've dimmed the lights, but I didn't bring him here to seduce him. I no longer make plans; I follow the plans other people make for me.

Except no one is here right now telling me what to do. I'm winging it.

Zach won't see me after tonight. If he doesn't like my body, I can leave him in my rearview mirror.

I hear a strong intake of breath as I step off the ladder to the pool deck, but I don't turn around. My steps carry me to the locker room Zach entered earlier where I now stand naked, waiting for him to join me.

The door swings open within seconds, and I'm face-to-face with Zach, wearing soaked black boxer briefs. I swallow hard, taking in every inch of him, from the slight bulge of his biceps to the strong plane of his abdomen. My gaze follows the trail of dark hair beneath his naval, and I eagerly take in the signs of his attraction to me.

He's looking in my direction but not meeting my eyes. Cheeks stained. Pupils wide. One leg bouncing.

"Lock the door."

Zach's eyebrows rise in surprise. "You're sure? I mean... uh, someone could find us."

"Obviously, you could leave instead," I say in a softer tone, though I don't think he will. He followed me in here *hoping* something would happen between us.

When the lock clicks, a wave of satisfaction washes over me. I'm calling the shots. I fucking miss making my own decisions.

"You're..." Zach swallows hard, and his Adam's apple bobs. "Finley, you're so gorgeous."

I haven't craved anyone in months, but a glimmer of desire sparks inside me at the unabashed longing in Zach's expression. I *want* him to bring me back to life.

"And you're hard." I tilt my head and take a step toward him. "What should we do about that?"

"What... um... what do you want to do?" he stammers. It's too damn cute.

A smile blooms on my face, and for the first time today, it's not forced. "I want you to stand against that wall." I motion toward a plain white wall across the room. "Toss some towels in front of you."

Zach wordlessly follows my instructions. After the sixth towel lands on the floor, I stride over and drop to my knees, delighting in the way Zach's eyes widen.

"What are you—"

His words are cut off when I slide his boxer briefs down and his cock springs free. It's the perfect size. Not so large I'll spend the entire time painfully trying not to gag, but big enough to challenge me to take all of him. I want to work for this, to have the gratification of a job well done. I want Zach to remember the woman from the wedding who blew his mind.

The *me from before* would have enjoyed the feel of him between my legs. *A lot*. With the way my mouth waters, hope takes root that I could want sex again someday.

My tongue darts out to lick a path from his base to the tip while my eyes remain locked with his. His hips jerk when my lips reach the head, pushing the tip of his cock into my mouth.

He recoils immediately, his body slamming into the wall. "Shit, sorry, Finley, I didn't—"

"Tell me what you want me to do, Zach."

"W-what?"

I lean back on my heels. "You heard me."

"Finley." He groans, half-pained, half-embarrassed. Maybe he thinks I'm toying with him. But he'll get what he needs as long as I do too. And I need to hear him beg, to know I hold his desperation in the palm of my hand.

I flutter my eyelashes and press my breasts together with my arms. Since retiring from elite gymnastics six months ago, I've gone up a cup size—one of the few perks. Also, my hands no longer sport bleeding tears, and my muscles don't feel like they've been through a meat grinder.

"*Fuck*," Zach curses, his head falling against the wall, his eyes shut. "I need you to—I mean, can you...?"

"Yes?" I encourage.

His eyes open and meet mine, wild and wary. "Please suck me, Finley."

I smirk, rising to my knees. My hand pumps his cock, and I bask in the soft moans escaping his lips. He's not going to last long, not with the way I plan to work him. I've been told my enthusiasm is a massive turn-on... but I haven't done this in half a year, so I'm out of practice.

My lips wrap around his cock, easing him slowly into my mouth while my tongue licks the side of his shaft. His hands land on my wet hair, gripping the crown and undoing my formal updo. *Good*. Every part of today's put-together appearance is a lie.

I want to look like the mess I am.

He groans, his hips surging toward me again. I push him back into the wall, my hands securing him there. He's not determining our pace.

"Stay," I tell him. "Or you don't get to come."

"Yes, sir," he says immediately.

I laugh before I can stop myself.

"Shit. Sorry... I'm so used to saying it—"

I hollow out my cheeks and take him in quickly to cut off his apology. I suspect the reason for his automatic response, and I don't want confirmation. If he tells me he's on my brother's team, I'll have to leave without getting what I came for. I learned long ago not to mess with my brothers' hockey bros.

Zach lets out another curse, a groan pulling from deep in his throat. His fingers brush my cheek, like I'm precious. I can't remember the last time someone didn't treat me like I was breakable, only one wrong move from crumbling before their eyes.

The thought pulls me out of the moment, reminding me how much has changed, how broken I am. The spark inside me still simmers, but it hasn't grown. Maybe my Cinderella night is over, all thirty minutes of it.

I pull back from Zach's cock with a loud smack, then replace my mouth with my hand. It glides easily over him while I sink further to the ground to run my tongue over his balls. I suck one lightly, a stark contrast to the grip of my hand, working back and forth.

"*Shit*, Finley, I'm going to…" His legs spasm.

"Do it," I urge, wanting the evidence of how I've undone him. My tongue resumes teasing, driving him wilder. It's taking effort for him to keep his legs pinned to the wall, but he does it. Like a good fucking boy.

His body jerks, and warmth hits my chest. A first, and I don't hate it.

I kiss the tip of his dick, saltiness coating my lips, then rise to my feet. I could make a dozen wishes—to bring my lips to his, to kiss him until he's hard again, to give myself over to him—but I know I can't get there, and the weight of our mutual disappointment would sink this night.

Zach's eyes remain shut, his chest expanding and retracting as he recovers from his orgasm. Seeing him like this will need to be enough.

"I'd like a rating," I blurt, realizing there's one more way he can satisfy me.

"Fucking amazing," he mumbles, his voice still strained from exertion.

It should be enough to render this usually rambling guy speechless, but I need more. I *crave* more. "I mean a number."

His eyes bolt open, and he watches me clean myself off with a towel. "What? Like out of ten?" Amusement underlines his words, but I'm not laughing.

"Yes." I toss the towel into a laundry bin. "How do you rate me out of ten?"

"Ten," he says instantly, the word filling the cracks in my heart. I like that he doesn't look at me strangely. "Obviously ten. It was the best... *anything* I've ever had. I think I blacked out. If you give me a minute, I'll be good to—"

"I should go." I snatch a clean towel from the rack and wrap it around my body in case someone else is in the pool. My family can't find out where I went during the wedding reception. They'll think this lowering of inhibitions is a symptom of my bipolar disorder.

"I... wait!" Zach says as I unlatch the door. "You don't want—"

"It was nice to meet you."

I turn away from his disappointed expression and walk back into my empty existence.

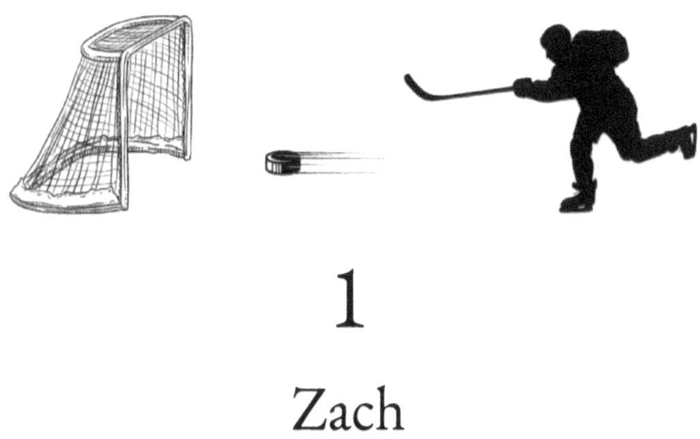

1

Zach

"Briggsy, over here!"

"Can I get your autograph?"

"I love you, Briggs!"

Their shouts rain over me as I exit the tunnel. We're thirty minutes from puck drop, but a sizable crowd already stands at the glass. The second year in a row our season opener is sold out.

Two years ago, during my rookie season, attendance was shit. But with how loud Cole Coliseum gets during games these days, we sometimes can't hear each other on the ice. I wouldn't have it any other way. The energy of the crowd fuels me unlike anything else.

"Hey, guys, thanks for being here." I smack a couple of hands reaching out from the stands as I jog to the ice, stopping short when I see a sign from a young kid.

I WANT TO BE JUST LIKE BRIGGSY WHEN I GROW UP. My jersey number—10—is written on each corner of the poster inside a sloppy star.

I gesture to the sign. "That is so cool."

The boy beams at me with a gap-tooth smile.

"Oh, hey, you look like Addy!"

Lukas Adamek, one of our defensemen, wears a gap in his front teeth as a badge of honor. The kid's cheeks flush as he grips the leg of the man beside him.

"Any chance you want this?" I lift my stick in the air toward him, and his hands dart out to take it. The man beside him grabs the stick, steadying it so the boy doesn't drop it.

The kid stares at it with wide eyes. "Dad! Look!"

"That's amazing, Trev." Then he mouths to me, *Thank you.*

Heat surges in my chest at how easily I make this kid's day. I reacted the same way to hockey players when I was young. I promised myself if I made it into the league, I'd be generous with my time because of the difference it made for me.

I trot back to the locker room to grab another stick. On impulse, I snatch a handful of pucks and throw them to the crowd as I walk down the tunnel. Delighted cheers fill me to the damn brim.

When I reach center ice, Alexei Volkov smirks at me. "Starting early this year?" he asks in his deep Russian accent. His gaze flicks from my face to the crowd by our locker room entrance.

I roll my eyes. "We can afford it."

I have a reputation for tossing too much of our equipment to fans. Everyone does it, and it's encouraged, up to a point.

I'm still amazed every time someone shouts my name or wears my jersey. The guys chirp me about how long I stay after every game—win or lose—to sign autographs. No one drives home with me because of it. Well, that and because I don't exactly have the best driving record.

Matt Harris, our team captain, skates over to us, shooting ice in our direction as he comes to a stop. "Can *you* afford it? I heard if you can't get your Oprah complex under control, it's coming out of your paycheck."

Volk and I stare blankly at Matt.

"Oprah complex?" I repeat.

"For the love of God," Matt groans. "Please tell me you know who Oprah is."

At thirty years old, Matt's in a different generation than me, something neither of us forgets when I fail to understand his references—at least once a day. Volk does too, but he has the excuse of spending half his life in a foreign country. I've reminded Matt I *also* grew up in a foreign country, but he considers Canada an extension of the US since we share a border and a hockey league.

I pick up a puck with my stick and flip it in the air, playing catch like it's a hacky sack. "You mean those fancy concerts?"

Volk winces. "Who's Oprah?"

"Un-fucking-believable," Matt mutters under his breath. "Hey, Princeton!"

Sawyer Jennings got his nickname because—you guessed it—he attended the fancy, rich, smart-people college, unusual for the NHL. He turns and raises an eyebrow. "Yes?"

He's not wearing his helmet yet, so his blond shaggy hair dips below his ears, shining in the lights. He's become one of my closest friends on the team since he came into the league last season.

"You know who Oprah is?" Matt asks.

Jennings sighs, probably thinking we're chirping him over his intelligence again. "Yes, Harry, I know who Oprah is."

Harry, Matt's nickname even though it has the same number of syllables as his last name. It's a hockey thing.

Matt tosses his arms in the air. "And my faith in humanity is restored."

Jennings's brow wrinkles.

I shake my head at him, signaling not to worry about it. "He's old."

Matt whacks me in the butt with his stick.

"Hey," I yelp even though my pads absorb the blow.

"No disrespecting your captain," Matt calls.

I trail Jennings to our bench, where he snatches a water bottle and squirts into his mouth. When he's done, he sprays me, but my eyes close before it hits my face. We do this before every game.

"You ready for the season?" he asks.

"I think so."

He douses me with another healthy stream of water. "What's with the attitude?"

I shake my head, spraying water droplets to the side. "Just in my head."

"About what?"

"I need a good season. It's the last year of my entry-level contract."

I worked my ass off all summer, forgoing time with my family and friends. I'm stronger, fitter, and more skilled than ever. I won't repeat last year's lackluster performance, the dreaded sophomore slump. Disappointing the ownership, my coaches, and the fans is not an option.

Jennings scoffs. "Come on, you're not going anywhere."

My stomach somersaults at the thought of leaving Palmer City, the place I now consider home. I have friends here. An apartment. I like my teammates and my coach. My brand of hockey aligns with the system the Wolves play. I *fit*. I come across as easygoing, but I haven't always felt at home like I do here. I *want* to stay.

"I fucking hope so."

I want a long-term deal with a solid salary to cement myself as part of this team's core. I need to show them I'm worth a multi-million dollar investment.

"Don't hope." Jennings skates by me, bumping my shoulder. "You got this, Briggsy."

Twenty minutes later, I'm on the ice, waiting for puck drop on the opposite side of the face-off circle from Volk. His nemesis, Justin Ward, shoves his shoulder while skating to center ice. They exchange words I can't hear over the roar of the excited crowd, the beginning of tonight's trash talk.

Niko Halonen—a flashy acquisition from the trade deadline last season who centers our line—smirks at Ward. The cocky asshole pushes our patience, but as far as I can tell, he's not a bad guy... unlike Ward, whose favorite part of hockey is to purposefully injure people.

Halo—as the team calls Halonen—wins the face-off and sends the puck to me. Nothing compares to the jolt of adrenaline flaring inside me when the puck lands on my stick. I take off, my skate blades marking fresh ice as I blaze past a defender toward the opposing goal. I pass the puck to Halo and brace for a hit, one of the d-men on the other team checking me into the boards. I'm usually one of the smallest guys on the ice, but it's never held me back.

And it never will.

People have described me as fearless since I was a kid. I wouldn't have made it here if I wasn't.

I shove the guy off me in time to watch Volk slap a shot into the net. The siren sounds to signal a goal, and the arena erupts, generating enough noise to drown out the celebratory song. Volk gestures to himself with raised arms, encouraging the crowd to cheer louder.

I'm grinning as I skate toward my teammates. A goal in the first minute of the first game of the season—there's no rust to shake off. We're picking up where we left off last season, on a mission to win the cup.

"Hell yeah, Volk!" I shout when I reach them, throwing myself into the huddle.

The game is uneventful heading to the third, with both teams buckling down to battle relentlessly. I notch one assist and play solid defense, which will please our coach since he demands we play scrappy.

I hop over the bench onto the ice for my first shift in the third. Matt steals the puck, and I book it toward the opposing goal. His pass connects with my stick in the neutral zone.

If we move quickly, Halo and I will have an odd-man rush, since only one defender stands between us and the goalie.

As soon as I cross the blue line into our O-zone, I zip the puck across the ice to Halo. He winds up for a one-timer, and—

◆○◆

FINLEY

The guy I met two years ago at my brother's wedding is lying unconscious in the bedroom next to mine. He's partially obscured by a half-closed door while my brother, Matt, and his wife, Gemma, settle him into bed.

I suspected he played on my brother's hockey team when we met, but I did everything I could to avoid confirming it.

I never thought I'd see him again.

"Is everything okay?" I push the door further open. I stayed home with my niece, Elodie, so Gemma could enjoy a girls' night at the Palmer City Wolves game. It wasn't a sacrifice; after a lifetime of hockey, thanks to my family, I rarely watch it. And I love spending time with my niece.

Their heads whip in my direction, opening a better line of sight to the bed. Zach's face sports an array of bruises. I hurriedly scan the rest of him, searching for any sign of injury. *Holy hell*. He's changed since I last saw him, now sporting a toned abdomen and muscular, powerful legs. He's not overly built—that turns me off—but he's found a weight room since our hookup. I heave a sigh of relief when I don't find a scratch on him. If it weren't for the bruises, I'd assume he was asleep.

My stomach sinks at their expressions, Matt's pinched forehead and the absence of a smile on Gemma's face. Something bad happened tonight.

Matt sighs in exasperation. "Finley, what are you still doing up?"

I suppress an urge to roll my eyes. My brother doesn't treat me like a twenty-one-year-old adult, and our nine-year age gap means our dynamic won't change. My bipolar disorder diagnosis sent my already protective brother into overbearing territory.

"Watching TV." Like every other night since I moved in with them two months ago, when my parents finally allowed me to attend college out of state.

I'm in the middle of watching a long-awaited love confession between two characters I've shipped for two seasons. How can I possibly sleep before their story ends? I'll pay for it tomorrow when I get up early to train, but it's worth it.

I walk into the room. "Is he okay?" I hope my brother can't hear the waver in my voice.

Gemma studies me curiously. I doubt she missed the sound of my breath catching. She's like a bloodhound with other people's business.

"Zach's fine," Matt replies, turning his back to me. "Go to bed. You need to stay on schedule."

His authoritative tone isn't new, but I haven't adjusted to it. He thinks because I live in his house, he can boss me around, like our parents who have overstepped one too many times. I'm lucky they want the best for me, but their love has manifested by keeping me on a suffocatingly short leash.

Of my immediate family members, I'm living with the one most likely to never understand me. Matt moves through life with incredible ease, making friends everywhere he goes, succeeding at everything he tries. He's captain of the Palmer City Wolves for the fifth year, the youngest captain in franchise history. He married a stunning and kindhearted woman, created the most beautiful baby to ever exist, and lives in a mansion on a hill overlooking the city.

He can't relate to my struggle, which makes it damn hard to be around him sometimes.

Gemma flashes a sympathetic look, one I recognize all too well. She never says a word to contradict my brother in front of me, but I hope she does it behind closed doors. She places a hand on my shoulder and gingerly guides me from the room. "Zach has a concussion, but he'll recover. We'll talk more in the morning, all right? Matt needs to sleep. He hits the road early tomorrow."

"Should *he* be sleeping?" I ask, looking at Zach over my shoulder until Gemma's led me too far into the hallway to see him. I follow her to my room.

"The doctor said it's good for him. Apparently, it's a common misconception you need to stay awake after a head injury. We should periodically wake him to make sure he's okay though." She places her hand on my forearm. "Don't worry, Finley."

"I'm not worried." I turn my back and listen to her leave the room.

I click my show back on, but my heart isn't in it any longer. My mind won't stop focusing on the unconscious guy on the other side of the wall. He was unsure of himself the night we met, but I have no doubt he's changed during the last two years. Zach's a professional hockey player, so women probably throw themselves at him all the time.

I doubt he remembers me.

I'm not proud of our night together, but I'm not ashamed of it either. I understand my condition better, and I know what medication and lifestyle I need to remain healthy. I'm no longer numb, searching for something or someone to fill a void. Still, being confronted with my past isn't easy. I live every day with the fear of returning to a shell of myself.

I must drift off at some point, because the next time I open my eyes, bright sunshine is seeping through the windows. A scribbled note from Gemma greets me on my nightstand beside the digital clock displaying ten a.m. *Shit.* I missed early morning practice, which means I'll get a lecture from my coach.

Ran to the bakery, back early afternoon. Please check on Zach when you wake up. –Gem

I grapple for my phone, but when I unlock it, there are no messages from my brother. He left on his road trip without saying a word to me. It's been two months since I moved in so we're still in an adjustment period, but I can't help noticing how much better Gemma has adapted to my presence.

I slide out of bed, slip on a sweatshirt, and brush my teeth before heading to Zach's room. He lays on his back, tucked under several blankets. If Gemma hadn't told me about the concussion, I wouldn't have guessed it—cuts and bruises are part of a hockey player's uniform.

Before I can second-guess myself, I pull my phone out of the front pouch in my sweatshirt and find the video of last night's hit. Zach carries the puck, moving as quickly as lightning, zipping the puck to another player as they cross the blue line. And then it happens.

Someone on the opposing team wallops him, his shoulder slamming into Zach's face. I wince and my hand lands on my chest. Zach hits the ice and remains motionless for several heart-stopping seconds. He tries to stand and falls. He's crawling toward the bench when one of his teammates hops over the boards and pulls him the rest of the way.

Zach would say it's part of the game, as if getting concussed at a person's place of work is normal. I've heard my brothers and their friends say shit like that my entire life. Maybe this judgment makes me a hypocrite, because my sport also requires a risk to life and limb, but at least no one tries to take me down while I'm executing a tumbling pass during my floor routine.

My fingers smooth back a tuft of Zach's unruly chestnut hair from his forehead.

"What are you doing?"

I jerk my hand away from his face. Kennedy Cole, Gemma's best friend, smirks at me from the doorway. A slash of sunlight illuminates her blue hair. I've always wanted to dye my hair a fun color, but my coaches never allowed it.

"Nothing... um..." I clear my throat. "Just checking to see if he's still alive."

Kennedy moves to the bedside opposite me, worried eyes studying his face. "You might have better luck finding a pulse in his wrist or neck."

"Right. Yeah." I want to evaporate into thin air.

A faint smile graces her face as she shakes her head. "I'm starting to understand why Gemma insisted Zach stay here."

Before I can ask what she means, Kennedy adds, "Gem said we need to wake him up. Did you already do that?"

"I was about to," I say. "I think it makes more sense for you to do it, now that you're here."

Kennedy nods her agreement. "Zachary," she whispers, placing her hand on his shoulder and nudging it lightly. "It's your favorite roomie. Can you wake up so I know you're okay?"

When he doesn't stir, she says his name again, louder, shaking his shoulder a little harder. Not enough for his head to move.

"Say something," Kennedy orders gently.

"This is the second strangest conversation I've ever had," I whisper.

Kennedy tilts her head in question but quickly abandons her thought when Zach's eyelids flutter open.

My breath catches as I stare at Zach's chocolate brown eyes, the eyes I stared up at from my knees, eager to take in signs of his pleasure.

"Oh, Briggsy, you scared the hell out of me." Kennedy grips his hand in both of hers. "How are you feeling?"

"Like roadkill," he croaks.

Kennedy hands him a glass of water. Zach lifts his head to take a swig before falling back to the pillows. He lets out a yawn, his eyes closing for a second before they reopen. He's fighting sleep, but it will take him again soon.

"You look shockingly good for roadkill."

The words fly out of my mouth before I can stop them. I avoid looking at Kennedy but can't ignore the weight of her stare. I can't imagine what she thinks, and I hope she doesn't say anything to Matt or Gemma.

Zach's head slowly swivels toward me, his eyes widening in recognition. "You're even prettier than I remember," he says before his eyes close again, and his chest rises and falls peacefully.

A small smile graces Kennedy's lips. "You're lucky I'm not Gemma."

I lock my expression down. I need to hide how much I like Zach's compliment and our history. I can't risk angering Matt to the point of kicking me out of his house, which would effectively end my secret quest to return to gymnastics.

"I don't know what you're talking about." I leave the room and Zach behind me.

2

Finley

I JOLT AWAKE WHEN someone grips my shoulder to shake it.

Gemma stands beside the chair in the guest room where I fell asleep after Kennedy left. Zach Briggs's temporary room. I now know the last name of the boy from two years ago after watching video of the hit that landed him unconscious.

"Have you been here since this morning?"

"What time is it?" I ask. I muscle into a sitting position and glance at Zach, who's still soundly sleeping.

I didn't mean to fall asleep here. I planned to stay for an hour, wake Zach again, make sure he's fine, then go on with my day. So much for that plan. I can't afford to miss even one workout or I won't make it back into my sport.

"Two," Gem replies. "How long have you been here?"

I clear the sleep from my throat. "Kennedy and I woke him up four hours ago. I was going to do it again, but I must've drifted off. I didn't realize how tired I was."

I regret the words when Gemma squeezes my forearm and asks, "Are you... feeling okay? I know you've been busier than you're used to."

After my diagnosis, my parents forced me to take a year away from school to focus on my mental health. I reenrolled in college last year, taking one class then ramping up to two. This semester, I'm carrying a full course load and work weekend mornings at a café run by Gemma's friends. I like the structure. Before my diagnosis, my life had been highly scheduled to allow me to compete in elite gymnastics and attend high school.

"Never better." I force a smile while answering my least favorite question.

My parents used to hover over my shoulder, wanting to know every grade, how much I slept, the food I consumed, whether I exercised. They allowed me to attend college out of state only because Matt agreed to make sure I stick to the regimen that keeps my brain healthy, monitor my mood, and look for changes in my behavior.

Entering the gymnastics world again is a risk, but it's one I should be allowed to take—a gymnast's shelf life isn't long. If I want a comeback, I can't wait.

Her eyes narrow. "You would tell me if you weren't?"

"Of course," I reply automatically.

Gemma's assessing gaze remains on me. "You're a terrible liar, Finley." Before I can refute it, she continues, "You know you can trust me?"

My chest tightens. I always wanted a sister, and Gemma becoming part of our family is like winning the sister-in-law jackpot. If I didn't know about her devotion to my brother, I might confide in her. No one outside my new gym knows I'm training to compete at the collegiate level. I wish I had someone other than my coach to share with, but I'm too worried it will put my comeback in jeopardy.

"Thanks, Gem." I walk to the hall, already mentally planning how to make up for the lost training time. "I'm going to the gym before dinner, all right?"

Nobody could accuse me of lying. If they want to know *what* gym I visit, they should ask more questions.

"I'm not your brother, Fi. You don't need my permission."

I stuff every last shred of guilt about lying to her deep, deep down. She's gone out of her way to help me adjust to living here, eating dinner with me every night and getting me a job at the Courtside Café. My relationship with Matt will survive this lie. When Gemma finds out, we might not recover. We don't have a lifetime of history together.

She pauses, weighing her next words. "Matt wasn't at his best last night. Zach's like a little brother to him... he was worried, but he shouldn't have snapped at you."

My brother should apologize himself.

"I know. But, um, thanks for saying it."

What would anger Matt more—me lying about gymnastics or me blowing his teammate during his wedding reception? I never want to find out, so I screw my mouth shut.

"Dinner's at six," she tells me. "Taco night."

"I wouldn't miss it."

I work myself to the bone for the next several hours, eating into the time I set aside for an English assignment. Unlike homework, I can't do gymnastics at any time of the day. At least not without worrying my coach. I told Veronica about my bipolar disorder for my protection. She can watch for signs I'm slipping into unhealthy habits, which includes over-training. She gave me the key code to the gym so I can train non-risky elements during off-hours to accommodate other obligations.

I'm strolling into the kitchen, thinking about my schedule tomorrow. With my assignment done, I'm ready to jump back into my TV show with a late-night snack... maybe pretzels or ice cream—

I let out a yelp, my hands flying to my mouth to smother the sound before Gemma or Elodie hear. I fumble for my cell phone, and I turn the flashlight toward the ground.

Zach lays on the floor, cradling his head in his hands. Milk spills from an upturned glass and, I suspect, has soaked his University of Palmer City basketball shorts.

I maneuver around the milk and crouch down, placing a hand on his shoulder, featherlight. "Zach," I whisper.

He grunts something that resembles *dizzy*.

I remember the powerlessness of a concussion. I didn't know I could sustain that injury, but gymnastics is a never-ending education on how a person can hurt their body. It's been several years since I landed short out of a tumbling pass, the impact traveling from my feet to my brain stem.

"Okay." I ease down beside him and lean against the cabinets. I ignore the wetness on my legs. "Keep your eyes closed. We'll stay here until it subsides."

He leans into me, his shoulder pressing mine. He wears a Princeton University shirt, the sleeves roughly cut. I'm in a sweatshirt, so his skin doesn't touch mine, but still, I'm aware of every point our bodies connect. We stay quiet, huddled together for a few minutes.

Zach's breathing eventually finds a steady rhythm. I follow its cadence, my limbs becoming weightless, my mind soothingly quiet. I struggle with falling asleep every night, but here on the floor of the kitchen, partially wet with spilled milk, next to this virtual stranger, my eyes flutter shut.

"So I didn't dream you?"

Zach's words jolt me awake. Does he remember telling me I'm prettier than he remembered?

"Afraid not," I reply.

His head slumps against the cabinet, but at least his eyes remain open. They're a pretty brown, like tree bark in colorful autumn leaves. The two years since we met have muddled my memory of him to the point I couldn't recall his face, but I never forgot the thrill of drawing groans from the back of his throat. My first spark of feeling after my diagnosis.

"Matt Harris's sister... what are the odds?" he murmurs, probably to himself.

I answer anyway. "You met me at his wedding. I'd say the odds weren't terrible." I pause. "Don't tell my brother, please."

"You mean my captain whose house I'm squatting in?" His head swings my way as he laughs, and the movement causes him to grimace. He closes his eyes again. "You don't need to worry. As if anyone would believe me."

Before I can pick at that thread, Zach cracks one eye open. "Did you know who I was?"

I shake my head and swear I see relief cross his features. "If I'd known, I definitely would've told you to go away when you found me."

"Way to kick me while I'm down." But he recovers, one side of his mouth tugging up. "Whatever you have to tell yourself."

I glare at him. We're close enough he can't *not* see me, but he keeps his gaze fixed straight ahead. I ignore his teasing comment like he avoids acknowledging my annoyed expression.

"It's not you. I avoid my brother's friends as a rule."

"Yeah? What bastard made you do that?" His Canadian accent adorably emphasizes the A. I could listen to him stress that A all day long.

Okay. *No.*

Absolutely not.

I do not want to listen to *any* hockey player talk all day.

But he's not like other hockey players. The stupid voice in the back of my mind pushes to the surface.

I'm about to say it's none of his business, but then he flashes his butterflies-in-my-stomach–inducing smile. His light is contagious, and my defenses drop a notch.

I bump his shoulder, but he doesn't move. "Not everything is about a man, Zachary."

A singular chuckle bursts from his mouth. "Not even you can get away with calling me Zachary."

Not even me. Like I *matter* to him.

He grins in the same boyish way as two years ago, except now it doesn't match the rest of him. Something I'm definitely not taking notice of. Not at all.

I turn away from him. I'm not dating this year. And I'd never date a hockey player. Especially not my brother's teammate and friend. *Zach's like a little brother to him*, Gemma said, and I refuse to mess with their relationship. My brother can be a pain in the ass, and he's a coworker Zach can't escape.

Zach and I temporarily live in the same house. I don't need to layer on complications.

"It's Zach, Briggsy, or Ten." Zach clarifies the names he wants me to call him. He's grinning stupidly, his dizziness long forgotten. "Some fans still call me hot-ass rookie, even though it's my third year in the league. Or it was..."

The smile vanishes from his lips, and happiness flickers out of his eyes. Shuttered looks unnatural on him. His vulnerability is the reason I answer his earlier question, revealing more about my history with my brother than I should. I'm crossing a line I drew, but maybe sharing this with him will enforce my boundaries. He can't want to catch my brother's wrath either.

"Matt's always been overprotective of me. I love him for caring, but I wish he'd trust my judgment."

"I have one of those." Zach's tone no longer has its teasing edge. "Melanie's a couple years older than me, but she treats me like she did when we were kids. I told her I'm fine, but she still calls every day."

"Well, you did get absolutely trucked." The words tumble from my mouth before I can consider how he'll react to them. My careful filter doesn't work with Zach Briggs, apparently.

One dark eyebrow raises. "You watched it?"

"I was curious." I shrug. "What do you remember?"

Zach sucks in a breath. "Volk and I were on the ice before the game." Volk, a.k.a. Wolves star Alexei Volkov, Kennedy's boyfriend, and my brother's best friend. "He pointed out this sign in the crowd asking me to a homecoming dance. I showed him one begging him to call the woman a good girl. He gets so riled when I bring up shit like that, so obviously I keep doing it."

Zach laughs, the sound a balm to my worry for him.

"*Anyway,*" he continues, "I remember bits and pieces. Bright lights in the hallway to the locker room. Matt and Gemma in the front seat of the car. And... you."

"*Me?*"

His ears tinge pink. "When you were in my room."

"I remember," I say. "I didn't think you would."

"You have an unforgettable face, Finley."

I smother a smile by leaning into my arm propped, on my tucked-in legs. I'm charmed by this earnest guy sitting beside me. He's unlike any of my brothers' other friends. Whenever one of them risked the Harris wrath to hit on me, they used terrible lines. Stuff they'd said to a thousand girls. Somehow I know—like I know I'm meant to be a gymnast—Zach hasn't said this to anyone else.

"We should sleep." I push myself to my feet. Zach's lips part, but I'm not ready for whatever he might say. "Maybe next time we run into each other, we can both be upright."

I hold my hand out for Zach, and he takes it, warmth immediately zinging up my arm.

"You're saying you don't like being on the ground?" he teases.

My face burns when our gazes clash. I'm hit with memories of him standing in front of me in that locker room, staring at me with such reverence. I look away, wanting to hide from the truth. I don't want him to think it might happen again.

I loosen my grip on Zach's hand, but his remains steady—because of the dizziness or his last statements, I'm unsure. Regardless, I don't resist, soaking in the zap of energy our contact ignites.

I try not to think about what it means.

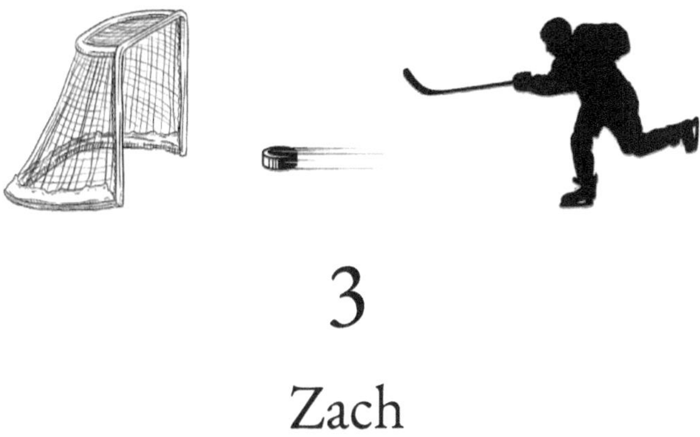

3

Zach

Finley's last name is Harris.

Is that revelation the source of my headache? Or is it the concussion? Probably the concussion, but being attracted to my friend's sister isn't helping the pain. At least he isn't here to see the way my gaze remains glued to the staircase as I wait for her to descend the morning after she found me on the kitchen floor.

How long has she lived in Palmer City, in this house? Matt never said anything about his sister moving in with him, but I haven't seen Gemma or Matt much since they became parents. Still, it bothers me that Finley's been in my city and I didn't know.

"You look like you have a raging hangover." Gemma waves wildly at me as she zips around the kitchen, pulling cooking equipment and ingredients from different cabinets.

"I wish I did," I grumble.

I'm wearing sunglasses and a hoodie to avoid ending up on the kitchen floor again. I don't need Finley's third impression of me to be as embarrassing as the first two. I've never found an explanation for why this incredible woman didn't ditch me immediately after I asked her to help me find a restroom, let alone get on her knees for me. I never told anyone what happened, tucking away the memory of her warm mouth wrapped around my cock, only bringing it out when alone.

Shit. I cannot think about that. I can't think about it *at all.*

Finley *lives* in the room next to mine, and I'll be staying here while I recover. If I think about our hookup, she'll know. I can't keep anything off my face. Last night's tease about her not liking being on the ground made her uncomfortable, and I don't want that for her in her own home.

I don't have a great filter, and when confronted with Finley Harris, it fails 100 percent of the time.

Gemma places a hand on my forearm. "Take it easy. Follow the doctor's orders, and you'll be back on the ice in no time."

The doctor ordered no hockey, no screens, no anything that could hurt my brain. The season just started, and I'm stuck on the sidelines after working my ass off all summer. In a couple of seconds, my opportunity to prove to the team I deserve a deal and last season was a blip vanished. I try not to think about it, because when I do, bitterness consumes me, and I have no outlet for it.

I drop my head to the counter. "I hate this. What the hell am I supposed to do all day?"

Other than dwell on my injury. I'm supposed to begin light activity today, but I can't think of anything more depressing than taking a walk alone without music.

Gemma drops ingredients into a bowl and blends them with a mixer. Her arm sweeps out toward the room next to the kitchen, and she winks. "We have plenty of books."

No one sees me as the kind of guy who'd pick up a book, and they aren't wrong. Reading isn't easy for a person with dyslexia. Gemma wouldn't joke if she knew.

I learned coping strategies when I was younger, but I always find reading to be a challenge. Doing it with a concussion would strain my brain in a way I'm not willing to risk.

The sound of footsteps saves me from having to respond. My gaze bolts to the staircase, and there's Finley striding down to the first floor, her long blond hair swaying in a ponytail. She's wearing baggy forest green sweatpants with "Wolves" written on her right thigh. Her gray sweatshirt sports the same word.

I wish she were wearing my number and last name.

Stop it. If I didn't have a concussion, I would hit myself across the face.

"Good morning, Fi." Gemma's cheerful voice echoes. "Take a seat. Breakfast is almost ready."

Finley's eyes meet mine, and her footsteps pause. She recovers quickly, continuing toward where I sit on a counter stool, but I read every hint of hesitation. She deposits her bag on the floor before taking the chair beside mine.

I've replayed our hookup in my mind hundreds of times, and I still don't know what I did to drive her away that night. I don't even know what I did to attract her attention to begin with. It makes no sense for someone like her to be interested in someone like me, especially if my hockey career works against me. It's my strongest point; if it doesn't sell her, nothing about me will.

Not that I should care about her opinion of me. She's *Matt's* sister.

That fact does nothing to dull my attraction to her, to stop my eyes from snapping to her when she walks into a room, like a damn motion sensor.

"It's good to see you upright this morning." She leans into my space and pitches her voice low so Gemma can't hear.

And *of course* she smells deliciously sweet, like fucking fruity coconut. Because that's how the universe works, dangling what you want but can't have right in front of you.

"It's good to see you," I say.

Her cheeks flush as she pulls back from me, the guy who can't take a damn hint. "So what's for breakfast?" she asks.

Gemma turns away from the stovetop and deposits a plate of waffles in front of us. "I didn't know what you'd want, so I made chocolate chip waffles. Usually a crowd-pleaser." Her eyebrow quirks. "Right?"

My stomach rumbles. After collapsing on the floor last night, I didn't eat anything.

Finley glances sideways at me, a small smile on her face after hearing what sounded like a monstrous beast in my gut. "It's perfect. Thanks, Gemma."

"You sleep well?" Gemma asks Finley. There's a crease between her eyes as she watches Finley take a swig of water.

"Yeah... I mean, who wouldn't? Everything here is nicer than any place I've ever stayed."

The crease vanishes, and Gemma beams. She designed this entire house, and when she gives a tour, she tells everyone where she found every single item. Finley must know this. Is her answer sleight of hand meant to keep Gemma from looking at something Finley doesn't want her to find?

I remember her words from the night we met. *If you want safe, you should stay away from me.*

Finley spears a stack of waffles and plops them on her plate. I watch her carve a bite and bring it to her lips. She raises an eyebrow when she catches me staring.

"What's the verdict?" I ask to deflect from the actual reason I'm watching her. She takes my entire attention any time we're in the same room.

She swallows. "Amazing, as always. I'm going to gain so much weight living here."

Gemma waves a hand at Finley. "As if you have anything to worry about."

I'm glad Gemma said it before I could accidentally make our living situation more uncomfortable. Finley was kind about finding me on the floor last night. I clutched her offered hand like a lifeline, not letting go until we reached our rooms. She waited in the doorway until I settled into bed before retreating to her room, as if she was worried about me. I can't forget it.

Finley shakes her head. "Check with me again in three months." She takes another enthusiastic bite of waffle, as if it's a future problem she's banishing from her mind.

Gemma moves the last waffle to a plate before shutting the heat off. "With the way you work out, I'm not concerned."

"You work out a lot?" I resist the urge to slam my face into the counter. I didn't mean for it to sound like a stupid line.

Finley covers her mouth to stifle a laugh. "I go to the gym."

"You should take Zach with you," Gemma says. She discreetly winks at me, like she's doing me a favor. I worry she's seen something I'm desperately trying to hide, but if she suspected anything between the two of us, she would interrogate me. Gemma loves to meddle, something well-known among our group of friends. I suppose everyone has a guilty-pleasure hobby. "He didn't love my suggestion to read a book."

Finley playfully gasps. "The horror."

"I'm taking Elodie to a playdate this afternoon, but I don't want to leave Zach alone."

I drop my fork onto my plate with a dramatic clang. "I can take care of myself, Gemma."

Gemma reaches over the counter to tap my forearm in a placating manner. "Of course you can." She swivels her gaze back to Finley. "So can you take him to the gym?"

Finley nods toward me. "He looks like he's on the run from the cops."

"I can put my hood down."

Staying here, all alone, for the rest of the day without hockey, Netflix, or video games sounds like my personal hell. Besides, I want more time with Finley.

Finley laughs. "Yeah, because *that's* what looks unusual."

"Sunglasses indoors are cool, Finley."

"It'll be loud," she replies.

Zach pats a pocket in his jeans. "I have earplugs."

Gemma laughs, light and airy. "He'll be fine."

"I don't—"

Gemma cuts her off in a tone that doesn't invite additional input. "It'll be good for you to have company."

Finley goes silent. I see gears turning in her head, but I don't know what worries her. Does she regret what happened between us two years ago? Does she not want to be seen in public with me?

I'm not *that* embarrassing. I play professional hockey with thousands of fans who don't care what I wear as long as they have the chance to talk to me and get my autograph.

"You won't know I'm there," I assure her, because even if she doesn't want to be around me, I can't stop wanting to be around her.

Finley hesitates for an excruciatingly long second. "Can you be ready in thirty?"

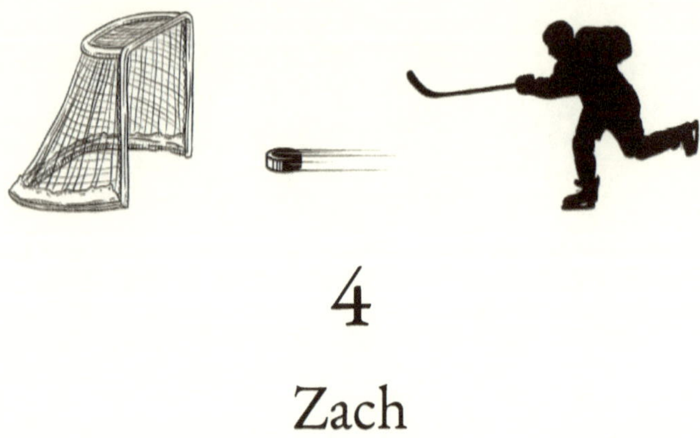

4

Zach

FINLEY RUSHES TO TURN the radio off before the sound blows a hole straight through my head.

"Thank you," I gasp, relief pouring through me. I tried listening to music when I woke up this morning, but my head felt like it had been placed in a blender. "It's been rough sledding these past few days."

"No problem," she says, placing her hand on my seat and turning around to reverse out of the driveway. "I remember how shitty loud noises are the first few days. It's why you should've stayed home."

"Just what I want to do, sit around in silence thinking about how I can't play hockey." Then her earlier words register. "Wait—you said you remember what it's like? Have you had a concussion?"

Finley laughs. "Yep. I've probably been injured more than you have."

"No way," I say in disbelief—not only over her statement, but also how she's able to distract me so easily. Justin fucking Ward ran me down on the ice and ruined my season. I shouldn't be laughing like it's one big joke, the way I treat everything else, but it's nice to take a break from my spiraling thoughts.

Finley shimmies in her seat, sitting taller. "Care to put your theory to the test? I've been injured a lot."

Sitting in the passenger seat beside a smiling Finley, her hair gleaming gold in the sunshine, is surreal. She's lived rent-free in my mind for so long, it's like my dream girl came to life.

"You're on. This will be a short game. Broken finger."

"Sprained wrist," she replies.

"Shoulder tendonitis."

She lifts her hands off the steering wheel and points a finger in my direction. "Had that one too."

I raise an eyebrow. Does she play hockey? Matt has two brothers who play in the NHL. His parents visited a few times when the brothers were playing against each other and invited me to their family dinners... where no one said a word about Finley or alluded to another sibling. What gives?

I shove the question aside and refocus on our screwed-up game. "Bruised rib."

"Sprained ankle." She grins. "I can go all day, Zach."

I suppress a groan. I wish I could suppress the images her words conjure, but no such luck. I get a flash of Finley beside me in bed, blond hair against dark sheets, a flirty grin on her face.

She's screwing with me, right? She has to know how I feel, how she *makes* me feel.

"Split lip. Puck to the face and a punch to the face." I press a finger to my mouth. I'm lucky I haven't managed to lose any teeth, especially with the greasy way I play. "You going to explain what caused your injuries?"

Finley makes a sharp right into a parking lot, and the answer to my question comes into view. She parks in an empty space in front of a massive beige-and-glass building with a sign reading PALMER CITY

GYMNASTICS in thick black caps. Before I can say anything, Finley reaches into the backseat for a backpack and hops out of the car.

I scramble to catch up to her. "Gemma made it sound like you were headed to a gym *gym*."

She stops abruptly, her arm sweeping toward the building. "This is a *gym* gym."

"Is this why you didn't want me to come with you?"

"No one knows I'm training again," she says with a nod, crossing her arms over her chest.

Tension deflates from my chest now I know she's not actively trying to avoid me. But it raises the question of *why* Finley needs to hide her gymnastics from her family.

"I couldn't exactly say no to Gemma without raising suspicions."

"You could've left me on the side of the road somewhere so I didn't learn your secret."

"Talk about a move that would damn me straight to hell, leaving a concussed suspicious-looking dude on the side of the road."

I hold up my hand. "Whoa, whoa, whoa. I'm wearing sunglasses, not a quiver full of arrows."

"A quiver full of arrows?" she repeats slowly. "What century do you think this is?"

"It's a video game thing." I shrug, hating how shit I am at talking to girls. I wish I could skip the flirting and awkward dating stage and move right into a comfortable relationship. I think I'd thrive there. "So you brought me because you don't want bad karma?"

She scuffs the top of her sneaker on the pavement, eyes fixed on the ground. "And... maybe I want someone to know."

A burst of heat fills my chest at the idea she's choosing to confide in me, to share a part of her life she's concealing from those closest to her.

"You can't tell Matt or Gemma or any of your little hockey friends."

Little hockey friends? She can't be serious. Her brother is a giant in a game of giants.

"I won't say anything, Finley. You can trust me."

She scoffs. "I don't even know you."

"You know me a little."

Finley rolls her eyes, dismissing the night I can't forget as if it were nothing. "I'd feel better if we come to an agreement to make sure."

Those words shouldn't sting, but they do. I'm drawn to her. I'd trust her with a secret without hesitation. She watched over me while I slept and recovered from my concussion. I thought it meant she connected with me too. Apparently, she did it out of obligation.

"What do you want?" Finley asks.

"Want?" I repeat.

Evidently around Finley, I word vomit multiple sentences or croak out short phrases.

She clarifies. "From me. There's gotta be a way I can repay you for lying to my brother. I know I'm putting you in a bad position."

I shake my head. "I don't—"

"Zach. What. Do. You. Want?"

As she pouts at me and cocks a hip to the side, all I can think about is kissing her. I want to spend time with her, get to know her. I want her to give me a chance. I shove those desires down because it doesn't matter what I want. Finley is off-limits and she isn't interested in me.

When I hesitate again, she says, "We're not going inside until you tell me."

"Keep bringing me here?" I blurt.

"That's all you want?"

"You remember I told you about my sister? She's worried about me after that hit and how I'll handle being away from hockey. She already thinks I'm lonely so far away from my family, but I'm usually with the team during the season. Now though…"

Her arms drop from her chest and her voice falls an octave. "Are you?"

"Sometimes," I admit, swallowing hard.

She doesn't say anything, only stares.

I bite the inside of my lip to stop myself from word vomiting anything else. Not that I can make myself look any less stupid in her eyes.

"I get that," she says finally. "I promise you'll get bored here, watching me do the same routines over and over."

As if I could ever tire of watching you.

"You *sure* that's all you want?" she repeats the question.

It's not, of course, but it's all I can ask for. It'll have to be enough. "It's better than sitting at home alone," I say instead.

She holds her hand out. "Fine, but if you change your mind because you're bored, you still have to keep my secret, okay? We have a deal?"

I take her hand, flashing back to last night when I held it embarrassingly tight after she found me on the kitchen floor. Her hand in mine brought me safety, and I needed it. She needs to know she can trust me too.

"Deal."

⊰◦⊱

The quiet, empty gym reminds me of the rink when Volk and I practice early.

Fuck, I miss the rink. It's my second day without hockey, and I don't know how much longer I can stand it. The boys play tonight, starting a

West Coast road trip, and I can't watch. I'm not allowed to send them texts either. Damn screen ban.

My life doesn't make sense without hockey. It's as unnatural as I assume Finley's is without gymnastics.

Her eyes light up as soon as we walk in, any worry from our conversation sliding right off her. She warms up on a stationary bike, lost in thought, her gaze sliding around the space, taking it all in.

Minutes later, she dismounts and strides to the floor. It's about fifty feet from where I sit on a couch in an area where gymnasts can watch recordings of their performances. Who knew gymnastics and hockey had this much in common? Massive amounts of injury and hours of studying film.

"You said no one knows you're training again," I start and abruptly stop.

I'm having déjà vu watching Finley undress in the same room as me, like it's no big deal. After years of putting her body on display in her gymnastics uniform, she might be used to it, but I'm not remotely adjusted to seeing her half-naked. I'll always be tongue-tied, in awe of her.

"That's right," she confirms.

Finley kicks her discarded sweatpants into a pile with her sweatshirt, leaving her in a skintight, long-sleeved bodysuit, bright pink at her shoulders and collarbone, darkening to black when it reaches her arms. The elaborate silver design over her chest shimmers as she swings her legs and arms to warm up. Her leg muscles flex with the movements, strong, toned, and devastating. I'm mesmerized.

"It's called a leotard," Finley smirks.

"What?" I croak.

"What I'm wearing," she clarifies. Her shit-eating grin suggests she knows exactly why I'm struggling to form sentences. She runs in place, pushing her knees into the air until they tap her hands out in front of her. "I have more on now than I did when we... went swimming."

I look away, my heart pounding out of control at the memory I've had on repeat since Finley came back into my life. I wasn't sure she remembered.

I don't know where to take the conversation from here, especially with the way she's overwhelmed my body—my palms slick with sweat, my tongue heavy and immovable, my face heating like a furnace.

I clear my throat. "How long have you been away from gymnastics?"

Her movement hitches, her body locking for a second mid-lunge. "Two years."

Huh. That's around the time we met.

Finley sinks back into the lunge, resuming her dynamic stretches. It's a version of our warm-up, except no one is on their knees thrusting their hips in suggestive movements people celebrate on the internet.

"Because of an injury?"

It's a subtler pause this time, but it's there. Finley Harris has shown nothing but confidence since the moment I met her. I like this reminder that she's human, but I hate seeing something ruffle her. Even before she answers, I decide to drop this line of questioning.

"Something like that." She steps one leg forward and sinks into a split.

I swallow hard, turning away from her before the twitch in my pants becomes a problem.

I remain quiet for the rest of her warm-up.

5

Finley

"Do you always look so serious?"

I glare at Zach for asking the question, but it's more playful than angry. He's followed me silently around the gym, watching me intently through the dark glasses protecting his brain, not interrupting. His unspoken respect for my craft tugs at the center of my chest. No one in my life ever questions the difficulty of my sport—it's not like any of my nongymnast friends can flip themselves in the air three times and survive, let alone land upright—but they never understand my sacrifice.

Zach does. It makes me want to know him more, despite the reasons I shouldn't.

"I'm concentrating," I say, lifting one leg in front of me in a pike position and balancing on one foot as I do a full turn. "I have a lot of work if I'm going to have any shot at making the team."

"What team?"

"UPC. It's where I go to school. I'm training for next season. It's a long shot, but my coach went there. She says when I'm ready, she'll reach out to her former coach to see if he'll give me a tryout."

I suck in a breath, readying myself for the first pass of my balance beam routine. It's watered down from when I competed, and I'm still struggling to nail it every time. I raise my hands over my head and take a step, pushing off from the beam to tumble into a roundoff, back handspring, back layout. My feet land on the beam, digging in to prevent my fall, my arms waving to stop my wobble.

I could've done this tumbling pass with my eyes shut before. Now I'm lucky to hold onto the beam for dear life.

"It should be fun, right?"

Zach's question yanks me out of my pity party.

I turn to face him. "It is fun."

"Could've fooled me."

He sees *me* again, like the night of the wedding. I didn't like it then, but I don't mind it so much now. I'm lonely too.

"So what, you goof off and smile all practice long?"

I refocus on the beam, squaring up for my dismount. I complete a roundoff, then launch myself into a somersault with a twist. My feet land on the mat with a satisfying smack, my chest high and proud, arms toward the ceiling. *Perfect.* A simple skill, but executing gymnastics perfectly always gives me a thrill.

"Not the entire time, but... yeah," Zach answers as I walk to him. "It's my job, but I love it too. I want it to be fun."

"Do you think if you were more serious, you'd be better?"

Zach blanches, and I wish I could rewind time to not undercut him. His question hit too close to my insecurity, and my defenses shot up. People once wanted to be around me, to hear what I'd say, see what I'd do. But I'm no longer that person, and I don't think I ever will be again.

The least I can do is excel at my sport. I know what to do to score big, to win, and no one can take that success from me. After losing everything that made me *me*, I need this.

"Maybe," Zach says finally, his features softening into a blankness I've never seen from him before. "Or I could train hard to get into the best shape of my life only to be pulverized in the season opener."

"Shit, Zach, I'm sorry." My toe digs into the mat in an attempt to ease the painful guilt in my gut. "I didn't mean it. Not about you anyway. This is so important to me. I have one shot at this comeback, to prove I can do it, to show everyone who wrote me off they were wrong." *To prove I can have the life I want despite my condition.* "It's serious to me."

"But you're doing it because you love it, yeah?"

"Yeah," I reply immediately. And I mean it. Of *course* I love gymnastics. I remember flipping around my basement as a kid, blasting music and designing routines. Hockey was my family's sport, but my parents couldn't ignore the way gymnastics lit me up from the inside out. I became addicted to how the sport made me feel invincible. I worked hard *because* I loved it.

"I mean, I used to." I drop my gaze to the floor. This ball of pressure inside my chest makes it difficult to relax while I'm in the gym, the way I used to forget the world outside these walls existed. I sigh deeply, words forcing their way up my throat. "I don't remember what it's like to have fun. My life has been very controlled these last couple of years."

There. Unvarnished truth.

I raise my gaze slowly, bracing for his reaction. He's wearing sunglasses but close like this, I can tell when our eyes meet. It's freeing to talk to Zach, who won't pick over my words, looking for a sign I'm unwell.

"That's pretty much my superpower. People tell me all the time I'm the least serious person they've ever met."

There's something beneath his joke, something I recognize because I do it too. I dress up my words, hide the truth of what I actually think, how I'm actually affected.

Before I can figure out how to respond, Zach adds, "I happen to have a lot of time right now. And I'm already around…"

"Okay…" I say, drawing out the syllables, unsure of his point. As he continues to watch me, his meaning hits me. "You want to show me how to have fun?"

He shrugs, gaze darting away. "Why not?"

I can think of oh so many reasons this is a bad idea. When Matt returns from his road trip in two weeks, we'll have to hide our friendship. He won't believe the claim that we're friends, and he might demand I stop spending time with Zach as a condition for living with him. When I was barely eighteen, his teammate, Garrett, made a move on me, and Matt lost his mind when he found out, though the primary driver of his concern was our age difference.

There's also the matter of my jam-packed schedule. I need to focus on school and gymnastics and shifts at the café. I don't have time to have fun.

Fucking liar, my mind whispers. I find time to lie in bed binging TV every single day. It's safe there in my little bubble. One of the reasons I wanted to leave home, though, was to build a life. And a life should include fun.

I study Zach as he watches a couple of gymnasts doing handstand work on the floor. The crease between those dark brows, the strong lines of his jaw, the Adam's apple working in his throat as he swallows. He knows I'm watching him, and he's giving me time to untangle my thoughts.

Since we met, he's never once judged me. Not when I stripped my clothes off to skinny-dip in the hotel pool. Or when I told him to lock the locker room door and stand against the wall.

Not when I told him I didn't know how to have fun anymore.

The real reason I shouldn't accept Zach's offer is obvious—I could *like* him. He might think I have an unforgettable face, but he doesn't know I could never be the kind of person he'd want, at least not long-term. A life with me will never be easy. *I'll* never be easy to love. Relationships are complicated enough without adding my brand of challenges.

Zach turns, cheeks pink, eyes open and vulnerable. Shrapnel pings the walls of my stomach from the explosion of nerves that goes off when our gazes collide.

This doesn't have to be long-term. Zach wants to show me how to have fun. He'll eventually leave Matt and Gemma's house to go back to his hockey career, and all his free time will evaporate. There's a natural end point to protect us both from getting too close.

"Okay," I relent.

Zach's lips stretch into a tentative smile. "And maybe you can show me the ropes on this whole being serious thing?" His foot taps imperceptibly, the top of his shoe moving where it pokes out from under his pretzel-crossed legs.

"You want to be more serious?"

"Nah," he replies, flicking his wrist in the air. "But I'm curious how the other half lives. So what do you say?"

Zach hops to his feet, taking two strides until he's in front of me, and I'm breathing in his scent. It's heady, like the cologne aisle I wander down even when I don't need to buy any products. I stare into his warm, nervous expression—tension lingers between his eyes as his lips form a half smile. He's biting the other side of his mouth, maybe to keep himself from word vomiting like he did the night we met.

If I told him how endearing I found it, would he still try to stop?

"All right," I say. "What do I have to lose?"

6

Finley

WHEN I STRIDE INTO the kitchen the next morning, Zach is sitting in the same spot as yesterday.

His bright eyes track me from the steps to the seat beside him. He doesn't conceal his appraisal at first, but when I move closer, he drops his gaze to the plate of pancakes on the counter in front of him.

"Good morning," I say, tucking a strand of hair behind my ear.

"Hey, Finley."

My stomach lurches at the joy in his voice.

Zach slides the pancakes my way. I usually eat a protein bar before my morning training session, but damn, I can't resist Gemma's cooking. Speaking of...

"Where's Gem?"

"The bakery," Zach answers.

Right. Like every weekday.

I should know Gemma's schedule better than Zach since I live here, but his presence distracts me. She's in the process of opening a second location of A Hidden Gem in the heart of downtown Palmer City, and she's around even less than usual.

I helplessly watch as Zach spears some pancakes and plops them on my plate. Following the same steps I did yesterday with my waffles, Zach applies a healthy spread of butter to each pancake before creating a pool of syrup on the plate. With everything he's dealing with, I'm surprised he noticed my preferences.

I guess I'm eating pancakes this morning.

"I'm surprised you're up," I say, as I cut into the first one.

"You said you had to leave at five thirty."

I swallow hard. I expected the time of my practice to discourage Zach from joining me, not motivate him to get his ass out of bed to prepare breakfast for me. Even if it only involved warming up Gemma's cooking.

"You're supposed to take it easy, Zach."

He quirks a grin at me. "I'm not the one who'll be doing flips, *Finley*. The team doctor says I need light exercise, so this is perfect."

His answer shuts me down. I try to concentrate on cutting my pancakes, but it's impossible to ignore the zing up my arm each time I brush his. I also refuse to move away and reveal how his proximity affects me.

"So what are we up to today?" he asks, turning toward me.

We. I shouldn't like the sound of that as much as I do.

I reach into the pocket of my sweatpants for the list I scribbled last night while watching TV. I wrestled with this strange pact we made once I was alone, wondering if I should tell Zach I don't have time. It's not a lie, but it's also not the real reason I'd choose to back out.

He's put me at ease since the moment I met him. I'm a mouse, inching toward a block of cheese, sure it's a trap, but wanting, so desperately, to be wrong. If anyone else had found me during the wedding reception, I wouldn't have talked longer than thirty seconds. I had been perfectly content sitting alone in the dark. Until Zach Briggs barged into the closet, rambling and nervously laughing while he couldn't tear his gaze from me.

"You made a list?" Zach snatches it from my fingers while I'm distracted by memories.

"It's not—" I say before the paper is ripped from my grip. "Hey—give it back!"

My hand darts toward him, but he deftly avoids my reach, holding the note away from me on the other side of his body. He reads the list, mouthing words for an excruciatingly long time.

His prolonged silence means judgment. Embarrassment creeps into my cheeks, no doubt coloring my skin flaming red.

I wrote the list after remembering Zach has been the most comfortable presence since my diagnosis. I'm not sure how I know he'll accept what I can give without pushing for more or thinking I'm not enough because I hold back. It's the reason I stayed with him the night we met. I needed to bask in the flicker of emotion sparking inside me. I agreed to this silly arrangement with Zach for the same reason. I want to hang onto these feelings a little longer.

Help Zach Do Life

· Learn to cook a recipe with more than
five ingredients

· Load the dishwasher

· Fold laundry (including socks!!!)

· Create a budget

· Work a regular job

"This list is perfect," Zach says as he slams the paper on the counter between us. He flashes a quick grin at me before hopping off his stool and jogging to the desk for a pen. "Just one thing to add."

He hastily writes something in a messy scrawl at the bottom.

• Try college

I blink at him. "You want to know what college is like?"

He shrugs and nods at the same time, sending his shoulders to his ears. "Why?"

"American movies always make college look like the best time of your life."

I cock an eyebrow. "American movies, huh? There's no other reason you'd want to be on a college campus?" He stares blankly, so I add, "It's not an excuse to meet cute college girls?"

"No, no—that's not..." Zach sputters, shaking his head. "It's the movies."

I huff out a laugh, then lean toward Zach and pitch my voice low. "Let me tell you a secret." I'm hit with a wave of his damn heady cologne again and retreat to the safety of my seat. In my normal voice, I say, "Movies lie."

"Not always."

My gaze stays locked on his. "Is that so?"

He nods, his hair shifting enough to catch a glimpse of his pink-tinged ear. A Zach Briggs tell. "Your life can change after a chance magical encounter with a stranger."

My stomach fills with the same fizz as when I'm airbound, flipping and twisting through space. I crave the exhilaration of defying the laws of science, but it unnerves me to experience it while safely on the ground.

I clear my throat, turning back to my cooling pancakes. "Oh, what would it be like to go through life with your optimism?"

"Well," Zach says, tapping a finger on my list, "you're about to find out." He picks his pen up and flips over my note. "Let's make this all official, channel my inner Finley Harris."

I slip off my stool and head to the drawer next to the fridge. While Zach writes his fun list, I take my first lithium pill of the day. Matt insists on keeping the pills beside the fridge in one of those days-of-the-week medication dispensers. I need the lithium to moderate my moods, so I'm not going to skip a dose or chuck the medication. But Matt's an overbearing mother hen, and he periodically checks the security system to make sure I'm not doing something irresponsible.

"I have veto power," I tell Zach, spinning on the balls of my feet one hundred eighty degrees until I face him.

Zach spears me with a grin. "It's like you don't trust me."

"I don't," I fire back, drifting to my seat. "We don't—" I stop myself from finishing the statement. *We don't know each other well*. He'd tell me we know each other better than I'm implying. I don't need the reminder.

Finally, I say, "Trust is earned, Zachary."

"You can trust me, Finley. You'll see."

He tugs my ponytail, a simple tease, but the places it sends my mind are anything but simple. *I can't want you like this*. How do other people handle Zach Briggs and his disorienting earnestness?

"Let me see what torture you have in store for me." My fingers plant on top of the paper and slide it closer. The stomach fizz returns when I see the words he's written across the top of the page.

Make Finley Happy

- Movie marathon and junk food binge

- Midday nap

- Video games

- Karaoke

- Hockey practice

- Road trip karaoke

He hasn't included anything outrageous. My heart swells. He's taking this seriously. I'm determined to go through the activities on my list and give him what he asked. He's going to become a seriously serious person by the end of our deal.

"There's karaoke twice."

A wrinkle forms between his eyes as he holds back a smile. "It's essential for your program."

"My program?" I raise an eyebrow.

He hums his agreement. "The Finley Harris Happiness Project."

"Okay." My tongue clicks as I consider a description of what he wants to accomplish. He claims he wants to see how the other half lives, but I suspect he wants to prove something to whoever doubts him. I've been seeing my desire reflected back at me. "The Zach Briggs Survival Project."

Zach tips his head back, laughing. "It has a nice ring," he says when his laughter subsides. "No objection to my name for yours? I think it's better than the other names I had in mind."

"What other names?"

Zach tosses me a mock-innocent look, wide eyes and parted mouth. I pinch his side, and he twists away from me.

"What other names, Zach?"

I lunge again shifting half out of my seat, which sends him half out of his to escape me.

He holds up his hands, palms facing me. "Okay, okay."

My finger draws a circle in the air, the universal sign to speed it up.

"Crack Finley Harris."

"Like crack *open*?"

"No, your calm veneer," Zach clarifies, "but your way works too."

I point a finger at him. "You said *names*."

"The Indoctrination of Finley Harris to the Zach Briggs Approach to Life." He lets out a chuckle. "It's a little long."

I roll my eyes. "Good luck. I'm *un*indoctrinatable."

"I'll be the judge of that," he says, putting on his baseball cap backward. It's unfair how such a simple move can send my stomach into a tizzy.

Even though there's no chance of anything romantic happening between us—for a whole host of reasons—I might have a little crush. Helpless, really.

And it's this silly little crush that has me looking forward to checking off every experience on our lists.

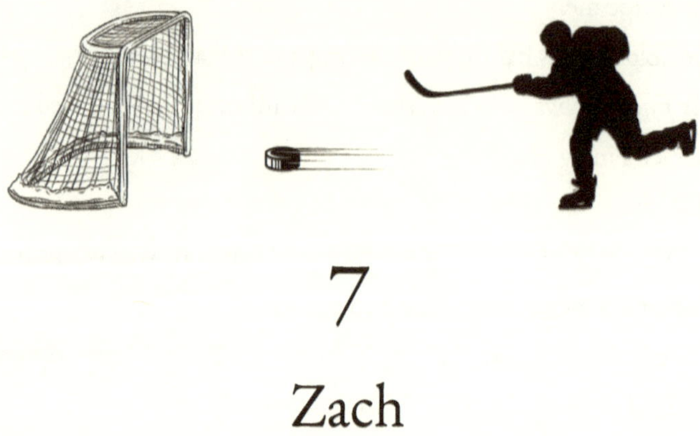

7

Zach

"YOU HAVE GOT TO be shitting me!" The voice booms too loudly, like a ball from a cannon.

The woman across the gym walks toward Finley, her short black hair that barely reaches her collarbone sways as she approaches. She bounces with each step, more energetic than me. And that's saying something.

"Finley Harris, did you bring *Zach Briggs* to my gym?"

Finley doesn't break stride. "Not the first time."

The woman clutches her chest as if she's been struck. "Bold of you to start your sass *before* practice. The first since you blew off your workout."

"That's my fault," I say, stepping up beside Finley. "I don't know if you caught the game Friday—"

"Phoebe—my girlfriend—and I were *there*. The sound when you hit the ice." She cringes over the hit I still haven't seen. I'll watch it tomorrow when my screen ban lifts.

I let out a sigh. "Fucking brutal."

"And then Volk smashed Ward's face in," Veronica continues, her tone filled with glee. "I loved seeing the ice painted with his blood. He's *such* a dick."

Finley's mouth gapes.

Her coach holds out a hand, which I shake. She has a nose piercing—a stud in one nostril—and a single freckle above the piercing. "Damn, man, it's fucking fantastic to meet you. I'm Veronica Lee. I've been coaching this one since summer."

"Veronica was a collegiate gymnast," Finley chimes in. "She holds, like, every record at UPC."

Veronica flicks a wrist at Finley, then promptly changes the subject. "So are you going to explain why you've brought Zach Briggs to my gym?"

Finley walks toward the bike she uses for warm up. "He's recovering and has nothing to do, so he's following me around." She flashes me a goofy smile when she turns back to us. "Honestly, I can't get rid of him."

"I'm sorry," I say. "Which of us has lived in Palmer City longer?"

She pops her hip, resting one hand there. "Are you trying to say I moved here for you?"

"You said it." I shrug, biting the inside of my lip to keep a smile from blooming across my face.

Finley tilts her head, studying me. What is she trying to figure out?

Being around her cranks the voltage on my nerves, but the longer I'm with her, the more comfortable I become with the sensation. And the more comfortable I become, the more I'm my true self, which so many people find to be too much but also not enough.

I want to be enough for her.

Instead of retorting, Finley slips her sweatpants down her legs, her gaze remaining locked on me. The movement strips any shred of bravado I conjured with my last comment.

I swallow hard and avert my gaze.

"Zach's in concussion protocol," Finley answers Veronica's question in earnest. "And I'm his chaperone."

"I can't drive anywhere." I protest Finley's characterization, watching her swing one leg over the bike, propelling herself into the seat. "I'm supposed to be getting back to light activity, so here I am."

Finley winks at me. "Where I can keep an eye on you."

"If you must," I answer nonchalantly, as if the idea of Finley watching me doesn't make me want to simultaneously scream in excitement and vomit all over the floor.

Finley rolls her eyes, then focuses on her warm-up.

"Warm up nice and good, Fi," Veronica calls as she walks over to me. "We'll be doing some conditioning today to make up for lost time." She taps me on the shoulder, head tilting toward the area I stayed in last time. "Come on, Briggsy, let's get you settled. This is gonna be a long one."

"Fine by me." I follow her to the alcove. "It's not like I have anything else going on."

Even if I did, I'd prefer to watch Finley flip through the air and land effortlessly on her feet. I'd prefer to watch Finley, period.

"How long are you gonna be out for?"

"No clue. I'll be reevaluated Friday."

I can't imagine it'll be a quick return to the team, not with the severity of my symptoms. I've had a concussion before, but after a few days of nausea and light sensitivity, I returned to normal. This time is different. I knew it as soon as I woke up and my brain throbbed like a car stereo with its bass too loud. If it wasn't for Finley, I'd spend *all* my time freaking the fuck out about what this means for my career.

Veronica moves the couch from the wall to face the gym floor. "At least Volkov beat him to a bloody pulp. Serves him right. Bastard."

Knowing Ward's in concussion protocol too does little to ease the inferno of anger every time I think about how he ended my season, at least for the foreseeable future.

"I never knew you were this *violent*," Finley says to Veronica from the stationary bike, where she's pedaling faster, further into her warm-up. I didn't realize she was listening.

Veronica winks. "The way I torture you in practice wasn't a hint?"

I'd never dream of teasing my coach, Erik Pomroy, like this. Or I mean, I have in the past, but he never plays along. I never want to play for anyone else though. He loves the sport as much as I do. He wants a win as much as any of us. After one of his intense pregame speeches, I'd run through a brick wall if he asked.

"Hop down and show Zach your best gymnastics."

I take a seat on the couch, resting my arms behind my head and sinking deep into the cushions. Finley's gaze darts over to me, but she says nothing. She dismounts from the bike and walks to the floor to stretch.

Her muscles flex as she moves, displaying the strength required to compete in her sport. Finley places her hands on the ground, then lifts her legs into a handstand. She holds herself there for at least thirty seconds before slowly descending back to the ground, but instead of landing on her feet, she slides into a split. Our eyes meet again because I never stop watching her.

Finley doesn't turn away from my stare, her bright blue eyes electric, the apples of her cheeks pink. Is she *blushing*?

It's probably from the exertion of her warm-up, but dammit if I don't want her to blush from knowing that *I'm* her audience.

Two hours later, Veronica leaves Finley to work on her routines alone so she can focus on other aspects of her job. I'm sitting on a mat next to the bars where Finley swings in ways that shouldn't be possible, but she makes it look so easy.

She's a shooting star of dark blue today with flashes of gold and silver jewels on her chest and abdomen and sheer sleeves that reach her wrists. Every time she releases the bar and grabs it again, an explosion of chalk rains through the air.

"Ready to see something cool?" she shouts.

As if everything I've already seen doesn't fucking mesmerize me.

Finley propels herself around the bar, body straight as a board, again and again until she lets go, twisting and turning before her feet smack the mat. Her face breaks into a devastating smile, full of the same joy that floods me when my team scores a goal. My breath catches, seeing her face light up like this.

So often, she seems subdued, but not here in this gym. Gymnastics might be my new favorite sport because of how happy it makes Finley.

"Do you not want to meet cute college girls because you have a girl-friend?"

Her voice jolts me from my stupor, and I'm a little stunned by her question. She asks as if it were a logical extension of a conversation we were most definitely not having.

When my blank stare goes on for too long, she adds, "Earlier, you said you didn't add the *experience college* thing to the list to meet girls. So are you already with someone?"

Finley fiddles with the grips on her hands while I try not to let my mind run wild with reasons why she might be asking. She walks to the bowl of chalk—clearly, there isn't enough floating in the air around us—and drops her hands inside, concealing whatever prep she does for bars.

I clear my throat, and hopefully all my nerves with it. "No girlfriend."

"Because you're not a relationship guy?"

I'm not following her jumps in logic, but I'm also not entirely sure she's making any. Finley's incredibly skilled at getting answers by rephrasing questions.

"Not for the reasons you're implying." *Or for the reasons I think you're implying, if only I could tell where the hell this is coming from.*

Her gaze snaps to me, and her nose wrinkles. "And what reasons are those?"

I push myself to my feet because it's too strange to talk to her about this while looking up from the ground. "I know what people think when they hear hockey player. It's the same for any young athlete—"

"Young, dumb, and full of cum?" Finley raises an eyebrow, a half smile on her lips.

I laugh, slowly shaking my head. "No one would know how crass you are just by looking at you."

"But *you* know," she says, her half smile turning mischievous. "After all, I'm the girl who let you come on her chest, remember?"

Fuck me. Like I'd ever forget.

I gulp, hard, and it's audible in this empty, quiet gym. My gaze hits the ceiling, as if looking up will stop gravity from sending my blood south.

Finley takes mercy on me. "I grew up with three hockey-playing brothers and their friends. I had no chance to be a delicate little flower." She jabs her finger in the air. "But stop distracting me... you're not in a relationship, and you're not trying to meet cute college girls. Care to explain?"

She jumps to the lower bar, legs out straight, feet pointed. When she catches it, she folds her body in half while raising herself. In a flash, she's perched there, stomach pressed into the bar, legs dangling below her, hands wrapped so tightly, her knuckles turn white.

I cross my arms over my chest and lean against a set of bars beside the one Finley is on. "Because being in a relationship means I can't think only about myself. And right now, I need to be selfish. I *want* to be selfish."

I leave out my uncertainty about dating, period. It's become both easier and harder since I've become a professional hockey player. Growing up short, scrawny, and a total goofball never meant girls scribbled in their notebooks about me. They took more notice as I got older, especially when recognition of my hockey skills increased, which put me in the tough position of judging people's intentions.

I'm not smooth. I stumble and crack weird jokes and overshare. I wish I could skip the dating-around phase and fast forward to living with someone who doesn't mind my idiosyncrasies, who likes them.

Finley jumps from the low bar to the high bar, performing the same maneuver that allows her to rest her stomach on the bar. "Maybe you need someone who understands?"

"That they're less important? Sure, yeah, what a great sell."

My eyes won't leave her, my stomach swimming with nerves while she's so high off the ground. It's ridiculous, coming from a hockey player whose brains were mushed into the ice last week. Still, I can't help but blurt out, "Should you talk while doing that?"

She smirks. "What? This?" She pushes off the bar, swinging her legs for momentum, before rising to a handstand above the high bar. One moment, she faces me, and the next, she switches her grip and turns one hundred eighty degrees. "Maybe you need someone with the same priorities as you."

Finley swings out of her handstand, then does a quick flip off the high bar, and flawlessly catches the low bar. Well, flawless as far as I can tell. I don't know much about gymnastics, but I'm aware perfection is hard to come by in this sport.

"I need a girl who loves hockey and napping and video games as much as me?"

Finley drops off the low bar and turns to me. "Something like that."

"Is that what you're waiting for?"

She barks out a laugh, her head falling back from the force of the apparent hilarity of my statement. "Someone who likes hockey and naps?"

I shake my head, trying to navigate back to serious ground. *Jesus.* The realization that this girl makes me *want* to be serious knocks me on my ass. "Someone who understands you."

"If I were, I'd be waiting a long, long time." She looks away as she brushes errant strands of hair out of her face with the back of her hand.

I don't tell her it wouldn't be so long, not with the way I'm making study of her my main focus. Instead, I say I need water and walk away, putting distance between us before I scare her away.

8

Finley

"So how's my favorite college student doing?" Dr. Warren asks when I join our video chat.

I usually look forward to my weekly check-ins with Dr. Warren, but a ball of guilt sits uncomfortably in my gut at what I'm hiding from her. After my first doctor prescribed a medication that put me into a void of nothingness, she helped me climb out and find my way back to myself, to a life of hope and enjoyment... and sadness and disappointment and anger too.

Good emotions don't exist without tough ones.

"Wait—don't you have a kid in college?" I ask.

Dr. Warren smiles. "That sharp memory will serve you well in school. Let me rephrase, how is my *second* favorite college student?"

I settle deeper into the pillows on my bed, my tense muscles loosening. "Mostly good. Logic is kicking my butt. I didn't expect it to be *math* without numbers, but I'm getting help."

"And living with Matt and Gemma? How's that been?"

I roll my eyes and give an exaggerated shrug. "As expected. I don't see my brother much, because, you know, *hockey*. And when I do see him, he runs down a checklist of questions like the good little babysitter he is. Gemma's cool though. He married up, for sure."

"It sounds like he's concerned about your well-being," Dr. Warren says in the practiced careful voice she uses when she's saying something I might not agree with.

"I suppose, but it'd be nice if he believed when I said I'm fine. If I wasn't fine, I'd tell someone."

Dr. Warren removes her reading glasses and settles them on top of her head. "You remember what we talked about?"

I sigh. My family's concern isn't unwarranted. People with bipolar 2 disorder have longer depressive episodes and higher rates of suicide than most disorders. Even when taking medication, they can relapse. And if they don't take medication consistently, it can become less effective. Dr. Warren has reminded me countless times how important a support system is to staying healthy, and I don't disagree. But my family's version of support has resulted in a micromanagement of every aspect of my life.

"It's hard to recognize early signs, I know, but I'm following the schedule we developed. After this, I'm going to read for fun for my Friday relaxation activity. I know I need to pace myself."

I'm choosing to live in a world with constant triggers. Dr. Warren knows about my rigorous academic schedule and my part-time job at the café, but not my gymnastics. I could tell her because I'm protected by patient-doctor confidentiality.

But I don't; I'm afraid of what she might say.

I trust Dr. Warren. She taught me how to keep myself safe and detect an oncoming episode so I could head it off. It's not an exaggeration to say I owe her everything. She convinced my parents to loosen their grip and let me come here for school. If Dr. Warren doesn't approve of my return to gymnastics, I'd have to revisit the plan. And I don't want to do that. I trust she's sufficiently prepared me.

"That's good, Finley," she says. "I'm proud of you and all the progress you've made."

I swallow hard, trying to keep my emotions in check. "Thank you."

Her words remain with me thirty minutes later as I curl under a blanket on the absurdly comfortable couch to read a sports romance novel. I'm a sucker for these, even if the athletes on the page are nothing like the ones I know in real life. It's nice to pretend.

Ten minutes have passed when the front door of the house opens, followed by the beep of the security system.

"Hey," Zach says, stepping into view moments later.

It's like the universe is poking fun at me, at the declaration I made. *Here's an athlete who's not like the rest of them.*

"Were you driving?"

He shakes his head, his dark hair flopping with the movement. "Nah, one of the athletic trainers drove me. I'm not great at driving on a good day. Best not to chance it."

It's such a minor thing, the way he stresses the A in certain words, but I find it so damn endearing.

"No sunglasses," I observe.

Between my hectic schedule the last few days and Zach working with the Palmer City Wolves trainers, we haven't seen much of each other. I read no fewer than two hundred pages and wrote a ten-page history paper on the Cold War. Add twelve hours of gymnastics and conditioning and eight hours of sleep each night, and I haven't had time to join Gem and Zach for dinner.

Zach poked his head into my room a few times to say *hi* but didn't mention the deal we struck, my questions about his romantic life, or my casual comment about our hookup. I'm on a roll with bad decisions lately.

I'm trying not to read into his standoffish behavior, which is challenging, given my history with men. Not that Zach and I are anything more than friends. Friends who are temporary roommates. Friends who are going to help each other with what they struggle with most. Friends, friends, friends.

"I'm tolerating light better." Zach takes a step into the room, then pauses. "Okay if I join you?"

He's so *nice.* Considerate without being suffocating. How does he manage to chip away at the walls I've carefully built?

"Sure," I reply, which is all the permission Zach needs to hurl himself onto the couch like he's jumping into a swimming pool.

"That must be a relief, getting back to video games and movies and whatever."

His shrug is subdued, which gives me pause. Zach Briggs doesn't usually have low energy.

"I'm not watching much..."

He trails off without explaining. He doesn't have to. I know what it's like to worry about permanently losing the sport you love. The stakes are higher for Zach, whose sport pays his bills. He's been in the league for a couple of years, but he's not set up for life if injury cuts his career short.

I don't need to be a professional to understand the ramifications from an identity and a fulfillment perspective though. Both of us arranged our entire lives to chase the joy of success in our sports, the cheer from the crowds, the high of a win.

Losing can untether you, leave you drifting in a current, hoping to find a port.

I roll my silver ring around my ring finger. "Should we... start on the list?"

His head turns to the side, his dark eyes soft, vulnerable. "Maybe you can read to me?"

I snort. "You want me to read to you?"

He stares, his expression all *Why not?*

"I doubt you want to listen to me read a romance novel."

I'm also unsure I could say some of the words in my book out loud to him, at least not without injecting awkwardness into our dynamic. Friends don't read smut out loud to friends. That's a fact.

"It's also not on the list," I point out, fumbling for an excuse. I'm not a shy person, and I'm not shy about sex... but there's this hesitance I can't explain, discomfort with intimacy that comes with sharing a love story. Something to explore with Dr. Warren one day.

He turns away from me, lifting his gaze to the ceiling as he reaches behind him for a pillow. He wedges it under his head and sighs deeply. "I like your voice, Finley."

My body flushes with heat. No one has ever once told me they like my voice. Guys have commented on my boobs, ass, smile, eyes, and pussy. They like looking at me, tasting me, fucking me.

Zach wants to *listen* to me.

He says statements like these like they're no big deal, as if people talk openly about feelings all the time. He's on his back, eyes shut, waiting for me to read. Not self-conscious about the admission in the slightest.

I want to snuggle against him, wedge myself between his body and the couch cushions. He'd pull me into the crook of his arm, naturally, like he does everything. Kiss the top of my head. Run his fingers over my wrist. Wrap his leg around my ankle.

There wouldn't be a game plan. He's all earnestness and instinct.

Don't change, I pray to whatever is out there. The world needs more men like Zachary Briggs.

I clear my throat. "All right. I just got to the part where she agrees to fake-date this guy on the team who's in love with her. Her ex gets traded to the team they both work for, and she wants him to leave her alone. She doesn't know the guy she's asking to fake-date is already in love with her though. I'm not sure he does either. Not exactly anyway."

I'm rambling like Zach, and by the way his lips tip into a smile, I think he finds it as endearing as I do. Or he's laughing at me for my choice of books, which would seriously put a damper on his appeal.

"People do that?" he asks, his eyes drifting to me.

"Fake-date?"

He nods.

"In books, all the time. It's one of my favorite tropes." When he doesn't say anything, I hastily add, "A trope is a story device—"

Zach laughs. "I know I'm kind of an idiot, Finley, but I know what a trope is."

My cheeks heat. "You're not." I swallow thickly before continuing, unsure why it's suddenly so hard to talk. "You're not an idiot, Zach. You're smart, in ways people don't see—"

He laughs harder. "I've heard this speech before. It's fine. I know my strengths. Or rather, my strength."

Zach thinks he's good at hockey and nothing else. I hate every person who helped form and perpetuate this idea in his mind.

"No, of course you know. I'm sorry, that was stupid. Lots of people don't know about tropes outside the book community. I didn't mean to imply you're an idiot. You're not an idiot, Zach."

The words rush out like a rip current.

"You know people and what they need," I ramble on, my face in full-on flame. "And that's better than solving stupid equations or interpreting poetry. You're the only person who sees *me*."

Zach's laughter subsides into a seriousness most people never see from him, at least outside the hockey rink. His stare burns into me, and he doesn't say a damn word. I've stunned him silent. I don't know what to make of it. Clearly, he doesn't know what to make of me or what I've stupidly blurted at him either.

I snatch the book from my lap, wishing the couch would swallow me whole. "I'm going to read now," I whisper, not trusting my voice to come out steady.

I crack open the book and let the words distract me from what I said. From the intensity of his gaze, I doubt Zach will forget any time soon.

9

Zach

I JERK AWAKE WHEN the doorbell rings and lift to a sitting position with one sharp movement.

"Who's that?" Finley groans beside me. Her head lays perpendicular to where mine had been. She clutches her book in one hand, having drifted to sleep midsentence. She fumbles around the couch, searching for her phone. "What time is it?"

"I don't know," I say, about to go to the front door when it clicks open.

Finley springs to a sitting position, her gaze locking with mine.

"Hello?" Kennedy's voice echoes through the quiet space. "Anyone home?"

"We're in here," I answer.

In the doorway, Kennedy halts at the sight of us on the couch and raises one dark eyebrow. Her arms cross over her chest, a stance I recognize from our time as roommates—when I accidentally left a spatula on a hot pan, burning the plastic and releasing rank fumes in our apartment. Or when I tossed a half-full can of soda into the recycling bin, which spilled everywhere—including over her pants—when she emptied it into the dumpster.

Her eyes narrow on Finley finger-combing her hair into submission. "Whatcha up to?"

I'm well-accustomed to this tone, but it usually comes from Gemma. She likes to insinuate scenarios that don't exist, speaking words to the universe to make them happen. Kennedy's suspicious gaze flicks to me in a scary-good imitation of Gem.

I'm deeply invested in manifesting one of their scenarios into being.

Earlier, when I walked in from my session with a team physical thera-pist, my rapidly beating heart settled after I spotted Finley on the couch. It quickly shifted into high gear again when she flashed the smile that always steals my breath.

She's so fucking pretty, it hurts to stare too long at her. Hurts in a way I like. I can't act on this crush; I also can't help but nurse it.

"Finley was reading to me, and we fell asleep."

Kennedy tilts her head. "I didn't know you like reading, Briggsy."

Because I prefer audio, so I don't have to fight my brain.

She strides into the room, beelining to Finley, and plucks the book from her hand. Her eyes devour the description on the back cover.

There's *nothing* wrong with romance novels, even the ones with smutty covers. My mom's a librarian with an entire bookcase of love stories. She passed her love of romance to my sister, so every family gathering includes an in-depth breakdown of their latest reads—book boyfriends and tropes included.

"You read him *this*?" Kennedy asks, fanning the pages as she waves the book in the air.

"I like it," I say. It's not a lie. I'd enjoy listening to Finley read the side effects off a pill bottle.

Finley's head tips back, laughing. "So much you fell asleep."

"So did you," I retort, then sigh. "It's been a long day."

Those words stun both Kennedy and Finley into silence. I don't want to worry them—there's nothing to worry about, at least not yet. There's more than one path to recovery from a concussion, so the doctor can't say when my symptoms will subside or whether I'm healing as expected.

"How did the doctor's appointment go?" Kennedy asks.

At the same time, Finley says, "We can leave if you need rest."

Once Finley processes Kennedy's words, she adds, "Wait—what doctor's appointment?"

I stand up and shrug. "A check-in with the team doctor, who says I'm fine. I just want to play, and they can't tell me when I'll be ready. Two to six weeks is a long-ass range."

"You should take all the time you need." Kennedy might like watching Volk slam guys into the boards and beat them bloody, but she treats me like a bubble boy, a child needing protection. When we roomed together, she doted on me after games. I liked the attention, liked knowing someone cared about my well-being, but sometimes I question my capability. "The team's off to a good start."

"Yeah?"

"You didn't know? Didn't Finley tell you?" She's fishing for information, and I'm too tired to fend her off.

"I never asked." I've also purposefully not called any of the guys. I don't want them to worry, and it'd hurt too much to hear about every little detail I've missed.

Kennedy snorts. "Too busy reading smut, huh?"

Finley crosses her arms. "There's nothing wrong with smut."

Kennedy flips the book over, her gaze tracing the description on the back cover again. "Trust me, I *know*. Just didn't realize this little firestarter did."

"Little firestarter?" Finley looks to me to explain.

I shake my head, hating that she's about to hear about how I *am* an idiot when I'm trying so desperately to look good to her. "It was *one* time—"

"One time? *That's* your defense, Briggsy?"

I usually don't mind Kennedy's teasing, but tonight, it's forcing an embarrassed flush into my cheeks.

"And you wonder why I'm staying here," I say.

Under her breath, Kennedy mutters something that sounds suspiciously like *Sure, that's the reason*. I hope Finley didn't hear her.

Although maybe I should embarrass myself thoroughly in front of her. She should see me as I am before I get attached. My plan to show Finley how to have fun is going down as one of the worst ideas. If she sees it through with me, I'm the one at risk of getting hurt.

She's beautiful and smart. Athletic, accomplished. And that's only her surface. More time spent with Finley will lead to more incredible discoveries about her. While she'll learn there's not much more to me than a high hockey IQ.

Kennedy tugs me to her side and musses my hair. "Aw, Briggsy, you know I'm kidding. You're the best platonic roommate I've ever had."

I look down at her. "Out of how many?"

"Well, there's—"

I interrupt Kennedy when I spot Finley leaving. "Where're you off to?"

Finley freezes like a deer caught in headlights. "Oh... um. I have homework to catch up on. I didn't mean to fall asleep."

"Afternoon naps are the best, huh?" I ask.

Her lips tip into a half smile. "They have some appeal."

I smile back, suddenly at a loss for words. How does she keep doing this to me?

Finley points over her shoulder, her golden blond hair swaying with the movement. "I should get to it."

"Right, okay. I'll see you later?"

"Uh-huh," she murmurs. "Good to see you, Kennedy."

Kennedy's biting her lip, holding in a smile. "You too, Finley." She waits until the sound of Finley's feet is gone before smacking me in the arm. "Dude." She extends the word for an absurdly long time. "You need to knock it off before Matt kicks your ass."

I head to the kitchen, putting space between us and giving me time to shake off her unsettling words. I keep my back to Kennedy as I snag a soda from the fridge. I know I can't say these words with a straight face. "I don't know what you're talking about."

"Uh-huh."

I spin around, flicking the tab of the can open. "We're *friends*. Matt can't tell us not to be friends."

Kennedy lifts her hands in surrender. "If you say so."

If I had any say-so, Finley Harris and I would *not* be friends. I would've taken the seat beside her and burrowed her into my side. Leaned my head on her shoulder as she read to me, and when it got to one of the sexy parts, my hand would've found its way to the waistband of her pants.

I'd do anything she asked me to do.

But no one needs to worry about a romantic relationship between Finley and me. She chose to leave after giving me the hottest sexual experience of my life. That memory is all I'll ever have of her, and I'm making peace with it.

Friendship with Finley needs to be enough.

10

Finley

My hands push off the vault, using the foam-covered steel to propel my body into a double twisting Yurchenko. I land in the soft pit of foam on my back after nailing the form.

Veronica peers over the edge above me. She's the reason I'm still not landing this skill on the mat. "Much better," she says with more enthusiasm than I've heard all day.

Every preceding vault resulted in critique, from a weak block to crossed legs to an off-center landing. Veronica knows her shit, and I want to trust her to improve my gymnastics, but a skill I've done thousands of times doesn't get my blood pumping.

"Does that mean I can graduate to the mat?"

"Tomorrow."

Finally!

She offers a hand to help me out of the pit. Veronica wipes the chalk I transferred to her hands onto her sweatpants. "Will your boy be joining you tomorrow?"

I glare at her. "He's not my boy."

She flicks her wrist at me. "Boy, guy, man, whatever."

"Aren't you supposed to warn me off guys in case they mess with my training?"

She knows I'm joking because she'd never try to tell me how to run my life. Veronica's coaching style matches my needs exactly. She pushes me hard in the gym, challenging me for perfection and sparking my competitive streak without stressing me. She competed in college, so she understands how to build a training program that won't overwork me but will prepare me for collegiate competition.

She also doesn't want me to focus only on gymnastics. I need balance.

"He brightens up the gym," Veronica says with a grin. She knocks my shoulder as we walk to the floor for end-of-session stretches. "Especially when he's watching you."

"Stop it." I slide into a split, right leg in front, arms reaching toward my foot. I moan softly at the glorious stretch in my quad and calves.

"I promised I'd never lie to you, Fi."

I know the look she means because I've noticed it from Zach before. When I took off my dress and jumped into the pool the night we met. When I stripped down to my leotard in this gym. He finds me attractive; that's all it is.

"Is that right?" I shift to face the opposite leg. "Then can you explain why you're making me vault into a pit for days when you know I've landed that vault hundreds of times?"

Veronica places her hands on her hips. "I need to make sure you're ready."

The words grate. I'm tired of every single person in my life coddling me.

Veronica's tone softens. "I told you we might move slower than you're used to, but I want you to be one hundred percent prepared for any element you do. I don't want you to get hurt and lose your chance to make UPC's team."

"I won't have a shot if I'm still doing moves I mastered years ago," I grumble.

Veronica's eyes narrow. "You don't want to go back to where you were years ago. I need you to trust me."

"I do," I say. "I'm just nervous. I want to make the UPC team so badly."

"I know, Finley. We've got this. It will work out." She walks off the floor toward the staircase and office upstairs. "And bring Briggsy next time. You're more fun when he's around."

The smoke alarm is blaring when I arrive home. Gemma would never burn anything, and Matt doesn't get back from his road trip until tomorrow, which means the man Veronica claims I'm more fun around is responsible for the chaos.

Zach stands in the center of the kitchen, flapping a towel beneath the alarm. Something that must've been food sits atop the stove, burnt to a pile of crisps.

"Oh shit, you're home!" His arm moves faster.

He's already opened the sliding door to the deck. I rush to the wall of windows and hoist them open. By the time I reach the last one, the alarm has shut off.

"Never a dull moment with you, huh, Briggs?"

"I wanted to make dinner. I misread the box. Or I got distracted? I don't know."

His cheeks flame red, but there's no touch of a smile on his face to belie his embarrassment. His chest heaves, which is alarming, given the fitness level required to play professional hockey. I snatch the towel from his hands once I'm close enough. My hands don't reach for him though. I don't know if that's what he needs.

I place the towel on the oven handle and flash him a teasing smile over my shoulder. "What was this supposed to be?"

"It was a bunch of different appetizers." His chest is calming with each passing moment. "I didn't know what you liked."

"You brought *frozen* food into Gemma Harris's house?"

Matt and Gemma bought this house because of the kitchen. It has multiple ovens, some fancy-ass refrigerator that cost like $20K, and enough counter space for multiple cooks to work at the same time. She'd never make processed food, not when she could whip up a fancy schmancy meal in less than thirty minutes.

Zach smirks. "She's not home."

"We can do better than this." My fingers run along the cool granite countertop, moving at the same slow pace as the smile stretching across my face. I am more fun when Zach Briggs is around. "And it's on the list."

Learn to cook a recipe with more than five ingredients.

Zach smiles again, and my chest seizes at the sight. It's been about a week since he reentered my life, but I'm already used to having him around. He'll leave behind a huge hole when he moves out.

At two months into the semester at UPC, I wouldn't expect to have great friends, especially not while living forty minutes from campus. I'm also carrying secrets that automatically put distance between me and anyone I meet. I'm not able to share large parts of myself. I can't talk about gymnastics without disclosing my bipolar disorder. I can't explain why I live with family rather than on campus without sharing it either. It's the lens through which I experience the world.

I hope I'll eventually grow comfortable enough to share this part of myself with someone. For now, I'll hang around with this guy who doesn't push me to answer questions about what the hell I'm doing here and why I'm hiding gymnastics from my family.

"You think we have the stuff to cook something?" Zach asks.

He opens the fridge, peering inside like it's a zoo filled with exotic animals. He examines a shallot, holding it to the light, as if it'll reveal a treasure, before setting it aside. I'm not a master chef like Gemma, but my mom and I cooked dinner together multiple times a week after my diagnosis.

I sidle next to him. "Oh, I guarantee it. Gemma's fridge is always stocked."

We spend the next few minutes sifting through recipes on my phone, cross-checking them with what's on hand. It takes some time, but we settle on chicken parm and collect the ingredients.

Zach stands beside me at the counter, ready to mirror my movements. All is going swimmingly until a slip of his hand nearly takes off his thumb. He drops the knife and retreats to the other side of the counter.

"Here—read me the next step."

Zach resists taking the phone. "That's okay. I can watch."

I laugh. "Don't think you're getting a free pass. You need to learn to follow recipes to cook."

"Unless I'm one of those savants who can cook based on feeling."

Zach scrambles to a rotating spice rack with no less than fifty different herbs and spices. When I first moved in, I pulled a few from the rack out of curiosity but hadn't heard of half of them. I still don't know when the hell to use tarragon.

Zach's rifling through the rack, no doubt looking for something he recognizes. He's less familiar with spices than me and stops when he finds garlic, triumphantly tossing it in the air.

"I won't know until I try," he argues.

I snatch the garlic before it lands back in his hands and place it on the rack. "Zach, we need an *edible* dinner. We can experiment another day, all right? Just read the recipe."

His body goes stock still as we face each other, even more tense than when I got on my knees for him in that locker room. And he was *nervous* then.

"What's wrong?" I ask the question I always hate fielding, but I don't like the idea that I'm the reason Zach is losing his carefree demeanor.

He leans on the counter, his hands gripping the edge, knuckles chalk-white. "I don't want to mess up our dinner. You saw me with frozen food. Maybe you should tackle this without me."

I tilt my head. "If it sucks, we'll order pizza. No big deal. You said you want to cook, so what's the—"

"I have dyslexia."

Something tugs strongly in my chest at the idea that Zach and I each have a secret condition that could change someone's entire perception of us. He carries the same burden as me.

He's braver than me though. Zach's willing to share information that could change my opinion of him. I'd swallow my tongue before telling him my brain requires stabilizing medication. I could never take the gamble, risk changing the way he looks at me with a mixture of adoration and awe.

"I don't know much about dyslexia," I reply, leaning back against the counter across from him. "Do you want to tell me about it?"

"My brain doesn't process visual information like yours does. It takes longer for me to read because I have to take my time. I have strategies…" He shrugs. "They help, but mostly I feel frustrated and stupid."

I want to close the distance between us, but I don't want him to think I'm pitying him.

"You're not," I whisper.

When Zach doesn't say anything, I ask, "Do you want to have the recipe read out loud?"

His eyebrows lift. "You still want to cook?"

What fucking asshole shamed him into thinking someone would walk away after he told them about his dyslexia? I want to maim them.

"We need dinner, don't we?" I cross my right foot over my left, attempting casual despite my internal freakout at the possibility of screwing up this friendship by saying the wrong thing. "And it's on the list, Zach."

He shakes his head. "We don't have to do the lists, Finley."

I offer a little of myself to him. A small part, the only bit I can. "Veronica told me today I'm more fun when you're around."

His grin damn near blinds me. "You talked about me with Veronica?"

I roll my eyes. "She brought you up, Zachary."

He pushes off the counter. "Right."

I hold my phone out to him, a chicken parm recipe open on the screen, I want him to know his confession doesn't faze me. I'd never judge him for it.

"You don't want to read it for us?" he asks.

"Is that what you'd prefer?" I want him to make this decision.

He shakes his head, brown hair flopping onto his forehead. "No, I'd prefer you save your voice for reading those sexy romance novels you like so much."

The knife slips off an onion straight into my finger. It stings, but there's no blood. "You want me to keep reading them to you?"

"I want to know what happens with the fake dating."

I glance sidelong at him. "You do not. You're just waiting to get to the smut."

"I won't lie." He skims his fingertips along my forearm as he walks past. My stomach tumbles. "I'm looking forward to hearing you read those scenes."

"You'll have to earn it, Briggs," I deflect, anything to hide my desire to do more than *read* those scenes with him.

"I'm not afraid of hard work, Finley," he says in a low rumble I'm not used to hearing from him, but dammit, I like it.

I like *him* more than I should. It's all I can think about as we cook together. Each time his body bumps mine. Every time he smiles at me. The joy on his face when he sees the finished meal. That light of his illuminates my life in a way that would've annoyed me once.

Now I ache for him to keep shining it my way.

11

Zach

THE WAY I SPENT the last two weeks with Finley complicates my feelings when I see Matt walk through the front door.

"Hey, jackass," he greets, dropping enormous bags onto the floor like they weigh nothing. His mussed blond hair—I can't help but notice it mirrors Finley's shade—looks as it always does when he steps off the plane after a road trip. "What are you still doing up?"

Matt's seen my odd sleeping patterns on the road, but many players struggle to sleep normal hours because of the constant travel.

"Making up for a lost week of gaming." I sink deeper into the couch cushion and prop my socked feet on the coffee table. "I can only play hockey in video games."

I pause the game and suck in a breath. I need to pretend Finley isn't his sister. It's what I've done for two weeks as I stared at her, flirted with her, followed her around like a damn puppy. Finley didn't stop me. I'm trying not to let hope sink its claws into me, but every time she blushes at a comment I make, flirts back, or gives me her radiant smile, it becomes harder.

Matt plops down on the couch beside me. "How's the noggin?"

"No red flags," I parrot what the team doctor said. My head throbbing if I try to listen to music or getting hit with nausea if I stand up too quickly apparently causes no concern. It's good news, of course, but I need the other symptoms to end so I can play hockey again.

The downside of recovery will be losing my reason to hang out with Finley, but I'll invent another one. With my reputation, no one would bat an eye if I *accidentally* burn my apartment down and need a place to stay.

Matt props his right leg over his left. "How long 'til you're back?"

"Sometime in the next month, if I'm lucky."

He places a hand on my shoulder. "Shit. Man, that sucks."

"Yeah. You guys are on a heater. I wish I was playing."

After finishing my screen ban, I watched highlights from all the games I missed, including Volk hooking off on Justin fucking Ward, which was highly satisfying. I'm flattered by the aggressiveness with which Volk whaled on Justin until blood streamed down his face and spattered the ice. It's not only because of the hit. They'd been rivals for years, even before Volk dated Kennedy, Justin Ward's ex.

"By the way, how's Finley?"

The question drop-kicks my stomach. I peek at him for any sign he knows about us, but his face is relaxed. Why would he worry I crossed an unspoken line when I'm *me* and she's *her*?

"Why are you asking me?"

"Because you can make conversation with a wall. You've been living in the same house with her for two weeks, so unless she told you to fuck off"—he huffs a laugh—"which wouldn't surprise me, I figured you'd be talking her ear off."

I shift in my seat, sidestepping the implied question about how much I've been talking to his sister. "She's fine, I think."

I keep to myself my confusion about what happened between us during his wedding reception two years ago. I want to ask her, but I'm not prepared for the fallout. If she knows I still think about the night that was probably only a blip on her radar, it might freak her out enough to run the other way.

I like her too damn much for that to happen.

"That's good," Matt says with a nod. He picks up the controller, twirling it in the air. "Care for a game before I go to bed?"

I pick up my controller. "You're fucking on."

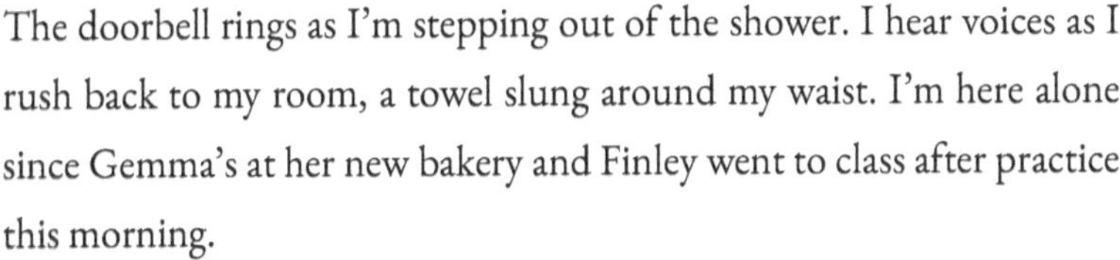

The doorbell rings as I'm stepping out of the shower. I hear voices as I rush back to my room, a towel slung around my waist. I'm here alone since Gemma's at her new bakery and Finley went to class after practice this morning.

"Briggsy?" Matt croons from the floor below. "You've got gentleman callers!"

I roll my eyes and slam the door in response. I dress quickly, and when I reach the top step, Jennings comes into view at the bottom, leaning against the banister. He's reading his phone so intently, he doesn't immediately see me. His blond hair sticks out under his baseball cap.

He turns and flashes a broad smile, blue eyes gleaming. "You look better than the last time I saw you." He holds out a hand for me to slap.

I smack it when I reach the bottom of the staircase. "I still looked better than you ever do, asshole."

Jennings is a pretty boy, and it couldn't be farther from the truth. The combination of smart and good-looking makes him popular with our female fans but he's unfazed by it.

Jennings places his hand on my forearm. "Seriously, dude, that hit was nasty. You doing okay?"

I shrug. "Better than when I was flat on my ass on the ice."

He flashes me a *Be serious* look, the first of many for the day, I'm sure. I ignore it and head toward the noise. I'm not ready to talk about my feelings, to dissect my fears about missing so many games that I lose my chance for a long-term contract with the Wolves.

People view me as loose-lipped and easygoing, sharing my innermost thoughts without thinking. They aren't exactly wrong; I let my thoughts flow out easily, but only the surface-level ones. Anything deeper remains locked down. No one pushes further than the surface, because they assume nothing else exists. Until Finley.

Volk stands from the couch and comes to me when I enter the room. "Good to see you on your fucking feet, Briggsy." He claps me on the back, his version of a hug.

I put a hand on his face, and he immediately swats it away. Faint cuts are still healing beneath his left eye. "Thanks for sacrificing your looks for my honor."

He runs his hand over the scruff on his chin. "Kennedy likes scars."

What would it be like to have confidence in another person's feelings about you? Knowing the parts of you some people consider damaged, they treasure?

Matt rests his hands behind his head. "They do look badass."

"Like he needed anything else to help him cultivate that look," I say, perching on the arm of the couch.

The front door swings open, the security-system chime echoing through the house. I recognize the familiar sounds of Finley's arrival—the rattle of the door, the drop of each shoe hitting the ceramic floor, the jangle of car keys on the metal hook. My heart beats faster with each additional sound, with the anticipation of seeing her.

Volk grips the sides of his collar and pops it out. "Some people just have *it*." He tosses us his signature shit-eating grin, the one fans associate with Volk after he scores a goal or wins a fight.

"Besides Volk getting an even bigger head, whatddya all been up to?"

Matt jerks a thumb at Volk. "We got him to come out for an hour before going back to his room to talk to Kennedy. Princeton, here, had a game-winner against Seattle. And I was the first star in LA."

"Sounds like a great trip." Finley comes into the room, sucking every ounce of air from my lungs.

"I hear you were good while I was gone," Matt says to her.

My stomach tenses at the implication I reported on her. Somehow, he interpreted *She's fine, I think* as insight into his sister's well-being. Finley's gaze meets mine, and I keep my expression carefully neutral. I don't want her to think I'm sharing anything about us with Matt.

"Don't worry, brother, I'm still in school." Her tone remains light, but she crosses her arms over her chest, giving away how much his comment bothers her. "Submitted all my homework on time. Made my bed. Went to sleep before midnight. Didn't kiss a single boy."

I'm damn happy to hear the last one.

Matt lets out a chuckle. "All right. I get it."

"Get what? That you're overbearing?"

Matt stops laughing at Finley's words.

"Imagine having him as your captain," I remark. Finley's eyes snap to me, full of the scary intensity I've seen when she prepares to run toward the vault. "I *have* to listen to him."

"That's rough sledding."

That's my phrase.

And of course Matt, who spends more time with me than most people, notices.

"I don't like the way you're rubbing off on my sister," he tells me.

Jesus Christ. I avert my gaze so Matt can't see the heat in my cheeks.

"Why don't you want him to rub off on me?" Finley asks, her voice sugary sweet. Does she *want* him to suspect us? Or is she mocking my obvious crush on her? When Matt doesn't answer, she adds, "He's your teammate."

Matt doesn't pick up on the innuendo. Thank fuck.

Instead, he lets out a deep-bellied laugh, lurching forward as his body vibrates with laughter. "I don't want you to be like *any* of these jokers."

Finley flips her ponytail over her shoulder. "Then I guess I better leave."

Her gaze catches mine, and our brief eye contact detonates a bomb in my belly. The room remains silent until Finley's steps cease on the stairs.

"*That's* your sister?" Jennings's gaze lingers in the direction Finley went. My blood thrums faster beneath my skin as I imagine Sawyer with Finley. For the first time since I met him, I want to deck my friend.

"Watch it, Princeton." Matt jabs a finger in the air toward him. "If you're as smart as you want us all to think, you'll keep your hands to yourself." He pauses a moment before adding, "You too, Volk."

It's an obvious joke, but Volk gives him the finger. "Fuck off, Harry."

Matt doesn't threaten me. I try not to let it chafe, but I'm stung by this reminder I don't have a legitimate shot with Finley. Her overprotective brother finds the idea so absurd, he doesn't think to warn me off.

Jennings shakes his head, silky blond hair reflecting sunlight from the window behind us. "No, that's not..." His skin flushes darker than the red line, either from embarrassment over saying his thoughts out loud or because he's worried about getting on our six-foot-four captain's bad side. "That's not what I meant."

It's definitely what he meant. I shouldn't resent him for noticing Finley's beauty, but I do. So fucking much.

I've never had one bad thought about the guy. He'd help you move, pick you up from jail, and keep his mouth shut about a secret you told him. He's the teammate you'd trust to date your little sister. He's impossible not to like with his snow-bright smile, vibrant blue eyes, and the aw-shucks way he carries himself.

I don't begrudge it when women approach him in a bar instead of me. But the thought he's a better match for Finley and could charm her if he wanted? It makes me want to drop-kick him.

Jennings suddenly slams a hand down on the arm of the couch, his mouth parted in surprise. "I don't know why I didn't put it together before. She's *Finley Harris*, the gymnast. My sister watches all the meets. Finley was her favorite. She wouldn't stop winking after seeing Finley do it at the end of her routines."

Finley *winking*? It's so ridiculous, I audibly snort. All heads turn my way.

"Be honest. Was it really your sister watching?"

They're the only words I can think of to cover my reaction. The girl who tilts her head and quirks her brow, whose lips rarely rise in a grin. The hardworking gymnast who needs me to teach her how to have fun. She *winked* when she competed?

Jennings chucks a pillow at the side of my head. "Shut up, dude. I'm serious." He focuses on Matt, waiting for confirmation.

Matt's biceps pulse with tension, his eyes glazing over, unfocused. Finley hasn't shared why she's hiding gymnastics from her family, but by the look on Matt's face, it's serious enough he wouldn't think he can trust me—the guy without a serious bone in his body—with it.

"Matt?" Jennings prompts.

"Yep, she was a gymnast. And now she's a college student." Matt's hand clenches in a fist. "Princeton, you will not hit on my sister. She's in no place to date."

He salutes Matt, and there's something sarcastic in the gesture. "Calm down, Cap. You got a beer?"

"Yeah." Matt grits the word. "I'll come with you." He trails Jennings out of the room.

Volk clears his throat. "You need to watch yourself."

The sentence feels menacing in the deep rumble of his accented voice.

"What?" I pretend not to know what he means.

Volk's jaw ticks. "Knock it off, Briggs." His use of my last name instead of my nickname highlights his seriousness. "With your new *roommate*."

I force out a laugh. "Have you seen her? Or are you blind to anyone not named Kennedy?"

Volk scowls; he never likes Kennedy's name to venture too near a dig, joke, or critique.

"There's no way she'd be interested in me."

Volk leans forward, elbows resting on his knees. "Why not? It's not like you're a shlub."

I rub my fists into my cheeks and flutter my eyelashes. "Volk, are you saying you think I'm *pretty*?"

Volk punches my shoulder, and I jostle backward.

"Hey! I have a head injury."

"Can you take something seriously for *once*?"

This common refrain from my teammates, who tire of my boundless high energy, *bothers* me. I stand, exhausted by this conversation, intending to retreat to my room.

"Don't worry, Volky. It's not like I stand a chance."

12

Finley

I SHAKE OUT A cramp in my right thigh, the result of a grueling workout this morning.

Veronica ran me through an hour of conditioning before giving me a "break" to complete my beam routine until she liked the execution of each element. My legs burned by the end, and a bath didn't relieve all the aches and pains, though it did ease some.

"You all right?" Matt asks beside me at the kitchen table, futzing with the computer, trying to launch a video call with the rest of our family.

I shrug. "Fine."

Always fine. If I'm happy, my family worries I'm veering into hypomania, which would eventually lead to a devastating crash. If anything suggests I'm less than fine, they think I need immediate intervention to prevent further damage.

"Gem?" Matt calls. "Are you almost ready?"

"Coming," she answers moments before appearing with Elodie in her arms. Their outfits match, floral patterns and same color headbands. "Sorry about that, she had a last-minute accident."

Gemma settles beside Matt with the baby in her lap, tickling her stomach and sending Elodie into giggles. "It's a good thing you're so cute."

Matt presses a quick kiss to Elodie's forehead, then Gemma's lips. "I love the outfits."

The golden boy found a sunshine girl, and they've never once looked like anything but the picture of absolute happiness. I once thought some of it had to be for show, but it's all real. I'm happy for them, of course, but they set the bar impossibly high.

Matt rubs his hands together. "Here we go."

He clicks the join meeting button, and my family appears in blocks on the screen—my mom and dad beside each other at their kitchen table, my brother Ryan in his car, Charlie in a hotel room. No one could question we're all related, at least not based on our appearances.

"Oh, there's my sweet girl," my mother, Grace, gushes and waves at Elodie. She moves her tortoiseshell glasses from her nose to the top of her head.

Gemma grips Elodie's chubby little hand and guides her to wave at the screen. "El, say hi to Gma."

"What's she been up to?" Mom asks.

"Crawling. All over the place," Matt replies. "And she's getting to her feet on her own. Not long before she's *walking* all over the place."

Charlie laughs. "That's when the real nightmare starts."

No one asks how Charlie's daughter is doing, because they never know the status of his coparenting relationship and don't want to tread on sensitive ground. His daughter, Maura, turned three last month and splits her time between her parents. During the offseason, he sees her more often but not as much as he'd like.

I wish my family shared their struggles like they do successes, but the Harris clan has never been keen on divulging weakness. It's partially why I concealed my unpredictable moods for so long. I thought I needed to push through it after a lifetime of watching my brothers shake off terrible ailments at the urging of our parents and each other.

Even after what I went through, we still don't share. And I can't change it without opening myself up to scrutiny. I'm not willing to risk the future I'm building for an uphill battle to change my familial culture.

My dad, Matthew, Sr., lifts his black coffee cup with the Palmer City Wolves logo into the air. "No, the nightmares start when you're raising three boys born two years apart."

"Oh, hush. I know you miss it," Mom says, her hand dropping to my dad's forearm. "It goes by in a blink, so enjoy it while you can."

Platitude number one of the call.

"Oh, Finley, honey, you look tired." Mom leans toward the camera as if coming closer will give her a better view of me. "Are you sleeping?"

Here we go. "It's great to see you, Mom," I say, ignoring her question. "Dad."

Mom shakes her head, her bob of blond hair fluttering with the movement. Before she cut her hair, people said I looked like a mini version of her. I still see so much of myself reflected back at me—heart-shaped face, sky-blue eyes, long thick lashes.

"Are you sleeping, Bean?" Mom asks undeterred by my attempt to skip the discussion. She's the only one who calls me Bean, a nickname I earned by jumping around so much as a kid.

I slouch in my seat, any hope for a conversation not revolving around my health gone. "Uh-huh. Every night."

She frowns at my dejected tone. "So you're doing well?"

I parrot the answer I told Matt when he returned from his road trip. "I've been submitting my homework on time. Making my bed. Falling asleep before midnight."

I leave out the mention of boys, because romantic relationships are a sore subject for us Harrises after the one I had with Matt's teammate. The summer I turned eighteen, when Garrett came home at the end of the season nursing a broken heart, I was no longer Matt's younger sister; I was a woman he found attractive. He also recognized what no one else did—that I was slowly drowning—and helped me, albeit in a destructive way.

My family didn't like our age gap and how he taught me how to self-medicate. Even if those "medications" helped me get out of bed during bouts of depression and allowed me to push myself to my absolute limits in gymnastics all day. After extensive therapy, I understand how problematic our relationship was but I also know he never meant to cause my downfall.

"That's our little nerd," Charlie says with a laugh. Because he's closer to me in age, we developed a relationship I've never had with Matt or Ryan. Ever the popular kid in school who never took it seriously because he had his eyes set on the NHL, he loved to needle me for being a perfect little student.

"And exercising?" my mom prods, reviewing her mental wellness checklist.

"Jesus, Mom," Charlie mutters.

"You don't need to worry about that," Matt jumps in. "Finley spends a lot of time at the gym."

My mom pinches the skin at her throat. She's about to fire off another question when Dad asks Matt, "Is she sticking to her routine?"

Like I'm not here. My hands fold into fists, nails biting my palms.

"Yes," Matt and Gemma say at the same time. They look at each other, a silent conversation passing between them before Gemma continues. "We eat breakfast before she heads to school and have dinner together every night, sometimes watch a movie if she doesn't have too much homework."

I sigh. "And Matt's got security cameras in the kitchen if you want a compilation video of me taking my pills twice a day. My GPS data will also confirm I've been keeping up with blood and urine labs for Dr. Warren to confirm my lithium dosage is on point."

Ryan pulls in a deep sigh. "I hate to do this, but I gotta run to practice." Of course, the emotionally unavailable brother wants a quick exit from this awkward ass conversation. "I'll see y'all next week."

"Ryan," my mom says, but he's already left the call.

Silence sets in, and my mom eventually picks up where she left off. "We want what's best for you, Bean."

Dad nods beside her like a bobblehead, muttering something I can't hear but would bet money repeats her words.

I remain silent. The less I say, the better. I hate lying to them, but if I don't, I'll never be able to make my own decisions *and* keep my parents in my life. Their opinions on a return to gymnastics are crystal fucking clear. Finding out my secret would drive a wedge between us until I quit again, and I refuse to do that.

"Can we talk about something else?" Charlie asks. I love him for trying to steer the conversation away from me.

"Hell of a game against Dallas, Matt," Dad says, maneuvering us to safe ground. For them.

I have a complicated relationship with hockey. This game ruled over everything else for most of my life. My parents sacrificed their time to take my brothers to practices, workouts, and games, all in pursuit of the elusive goal of playing professionally. I either got dragged along or left with other family members, cutting into my time to develop friendships and hobbies.

Gymnastics gave me purpose, but my parents viewed it as a time-filler for the longest time. When they realized how serious I was about the sport along with my natural talent, their support increased, but the damage was done. I'd known for too long I was fourth in my parents' list of priorities, all because my brothers wore knives on their feet and chased a saucer across a sheet of ice.

"I'll see you at the game next week," Matt says, pulling me out of my thoughts. I missed the entire conversation.

Panic seizes me at the idea of seeing my parents next week. "Wait—y'all are visiting?"

Everyone's gazes snap to me, but no one says anything. I'd let on I hadn't been listening.

"Matt leaves tomorrow for a game in Boston," Gemma replies. Elodie sleeps on her shoulder. Damn, I'd love a nap right now.

My parents have never missed a game any of my brothers have played in Boston since it's only a two-hour drive from our house in Maine.

"We can't wait, dear," Mom says. "I've got my jersey all ready to go."

Charlie scoffs. "Oh, we know, Mom. Matty has always been your favorite."

"That's not true," she protests, but it's a long-played-out topic between my ridiculously competitive brothers, and there's no longer any frustration when she defends herself.

Like the rest of the conversation, her gaze remains on me until the video ends, looking for any sign something is wrong. She won't find one. Because, for the first time in a long time, I'm truly happy and healthy.

I wish I could share with them what's bringing me back to life.

13

Finley

ZACH AND I STOP avoiding each other when Matt leaves. We didn't talk about hiding our friendship from him, but we both kept our distance.

Sitting beside Zach eases the ache of his absence the last several days. But my desire to nuzzle into his side, press my face into his neck, breathe him in during our movie marathon complicates this friendship.

He shifts in his seat as the main characters undress each other on screen. The movie had been building to this for more than an hour, so I'm not surprised the moment lingers, the characters desperate for each other but wanting to make it last, to commit every second to memory.

I'd do the same with Zach.

I glance over at him, and when our eyes meet, he shifts his attention back to the screen. An involuntary sigh escapes my lips as I remember the intensity of his stare two years ago when I was on my knees for him. I try to ignore the flutter in my gut and focus on the movie. But when the man dips his mouth to the woman's boob, Zach takes an unmistakable gulp, and I can't take the tension any longer.

I turn toward him, shifting my legs into a pretzel and nodding toward the TV. "You ever do that?"

Zach's eyebrows hit his hairline. "What?"

"Sex," I clarify, forging ahead.

"Yeah, Finley, I've had sex before."

"It's not that weird of a question." I attempt to ignore the warmth spreading through my body at the idea of intimacy with Zach. "There's no standard timeline. How old were you when you did it the first time?"

The tense lines of his body slacken, and he sinks into the couch, his body tilting toward me. "Eighteen. What about you?"

"Sixteen. And it was terrible. I'm surprised I gave it another shot, honestly."

Zach snorts. "I hope Melinda Hamilton doesn't say that about me."

"Melinda Hamilton," I repeat with a laugh. "She sounds absolutely dignified."

"As opposed to what? Finley Harris? Which sounds…"

"Kicky," I finish his sentence with a grin.

Zach reaches for his beer bottle and raises it to his lips, then pauses. "What was so bad about it?" He takes a swig before lowering the bottle. "Quick off the mark?"

He doesn't hesitate, no stumbling, mumbling, or second-guessing. *Interesting.* Maybe it's the alcohol. His intense eye contact with *that* question intensifies the pounding between my legs. A crackle in the air surrounds us again, and I so want it to ignite.

"I mean, obviously, yeah. He was a teenage boy. But that wasn't it." I grab a cracker from the plate on the coffee table and pop it into my mouth. The drumbeat of my heart sounds in my ears. "I didn't feel connected to him. None of it felt like it was about me, you know?"

Zach clears his throat, shifting his gaze back to the screen. He's quiet for a long moment, mulling over his response. "Is that why you bolted from me?"

Zach Briggs knocks me off guard once again. He's had three weeks to ask about our hookup, the one I cut short because my mind was a mess. When he didn't, I decided it hadn't been as big of a deal to him as it was to me. I can't imagine the DMs waiting for him every time he opens a social media app. Some girl blowing him at a wedding is probably just another Friday night.

"I didn't expect anything—I'd never expect anything—but you led me into the locker room. I thought you... liked me. Then you ran off. Did I do something? Because you could've told me... I would've—"

My spine snaps ramrod straight. Is this what he's thought all this time?

"It wasn't you. I swear, Zach."

He holds up his hand. "You don't have to say that—"

"I still think about that night."

The words rush out, passing every warning sign, ignoring the implications of confessing to him, because I can't stand that I made Zach doubt himself. I'll give him a sliver of truth to reassure him, even if I'm playing with fire by flirting with him under my brother's—his captain's—roof.

His head jerks back. "You do?"

"Why are you surprised?"

"You didn't..." He shakes his head, looking away from me again.

My hand dances, featherlight, across his forearm. He watches, but I don't pull away. "I didn't what?"

"You left after I..." Zach trails off again, his ears turning pink.

I take mercy on him and finish his sentence. "Got off?"

He lets out a nervous laugh. "Yeah."

In all the time I've known him, he's never struggled to find words. The opposite, actually. He word vomits every thought in his mind. But I see the gears turning as he mentally debates his responses. I'm not sure what to make of this deliberate, careful side to Zach. The people in his life have given me the impression he doesn't have a serious bone in his body. Maybe they don't know him as well as they think they do.

He runs a hand through his unruly hair. "Didn't you want... anything from me?"

"I got what I wanted from you," I reply with a smirk. It's a deflection from the information I can't tell him, and it's flirty enough, I expect him to joke back. Instead, Zach's expression shutters, delivering a punch to my gut. The sick feeling causes me to offer him an explanation. "I wasn't myself that night. I hadn't been myself for a while."

Zach's brow furrows. "What does that mean?"

"I was going through something." I try to explain with the scantest of details.

The gymnastics world thinks I tore my Achilles heel and hung up the sport. Because letting people think I tore a vulnerable part of my body is better than the truth. My parent's decision to conceal my condition has made me afraid to talk about my bipolar disorder with anyone unless medically necessary, for fear it will taint how people view me.

"You finding me in that closet was the first time I'd felt *anything* in so long, and I didn't want to let go of it. I thought I was ready for more, and when I realized I wasn't, I left. I hate that you thought you did something wrong because you were exactly what I needed."

You're exactly what I need. A voice in the back of my mind shoves to the forefront. I want to follow the voice's lead, but Zach doesn't need to be burdened with my brand of baggage. I also don't want to complicate his relationship with my brother or mess with his career.

"If you want safe, you should stay away from me," he says suddenly.

"What?"

"It's what you said that night. Is it how you still feel?"

I run my hands over my arms, trying to ease a chill. "It's the truth."

"And you think it's a bad thing?" His hand lands on my knee, a comforting gesture that manages to light every nerve ending in my body. "Safe is boring, Finley. You're one of the most fascinating people I've ever met."

I huff out a self-conscious laugh. "That's because you don't know me."

I launch off the couch, needing a breather from this conversation. Zach won't understand unless I crack myself open and let him see *all* of me. Besides Veronica, he's the only real connection I've made since my diagnosis.

I don't think I could bear losing the way he looks at me, like he thinks I'm worth his time.

<hr>

I busy myself at the kitchen sink, opting to clean dishes instead of facing this conversation, but Zach follows me.

"I want to know you," he says behind me.

When I turn, he's leaning on the counter, any apprehension long gone. Maybe all he needed was a sign this attraction between us—this interest of his—isn't one-sided.

I roll my eyes. "Trust me, you don't."

"Maybe you can let me decide? You might be used to hiding from the people in your life, but I don't want you to hide from me." He breathes in deeply after blurting the words at his usual quick clip. "I want to know you," he repeats, striding toward me.

I refocus on the sink, flicking the faucet on and rinsing a dish. "You're just bored, Zach."

His body wedges between me and the dishwasher, bringing a heat I crave. I miss the press of another person against my skin, the anticipation in my belly during the downshift right before my heart kicks into high gear.

I haven't wanted anyone this close to me before. It scares the shit out of me how much I want to wrap myself around the man next to me. I'm acutely aware of how badly a relationship between us could end.

He breaks the silence. "Loading the dishwasher is on our list."

My arm brushes his as I finish scrubbing the plate. I step to the side, my hands sliding to my hips. It slips my mind that they're still wet from scrubbing dishes, all because I'm staring into the eyes of the guy who makes me question whether I need to hide my heart. I withdraw my hands, reaching for a towel by the sink to sop up the water on my pants and the floor.

"I didn't mean to do that." My face burns, like it's been hit with a wave of four-hundred-degree heat from an oven. There's no way a rare-for-me blush doesn't illuminate my skin.

To his credit, Zach bites his lip, half smothering the amused tilt. I'm embarrassed by the way I lose control around him, that I can't *stop* wanting to be around him despite the discomfort.

He gestures in the air between us. "Is this the first lesson?"

"Stop," I warn in mock outrage, "or you'll talk yourself out of a lesson."

He mimes zippering his mouth before motioning toward the sink.

I can do this. It's just showing him how to wash dishes, for fuck's sake.

"The first step is finding the right playlist," I say, sliding my hands into my back pocket to grab my phone. I choose a playlist aptly named *Hype Cleaning Mix* and the sound of a door opening bursts through the air followed by Olivia Rodrigo's voice and an influx of percussion. "Upbeat songs are a good distraction."

Zach nods appreciatively. "I like it. Much better than the shit they play in the locker room."

"Oh, that would throw me off if I had to listen to a bunch of songs I hate before I compete."

His mouth stretches into a smile that pops his cheeks. "I have selective hearing."

I bump my shoulder into his arm. "Me too. I never heard my family tell me to stay away from gymnastics. What's the biggest thing you've filtered out?"

"That I'd never make the NHL."

"People told you that?"

He shrugs. "No one important. But yeah, a lot of people thought I was too small for the league, worried I'd be pushed around. If I wasted even a second on the doubts, it'd be too much. That's how much of a long shot my dream was. Yours too, eh?"

"It's more likely I'll be struck by lightning or win an Oscar. Something mean girls in high school loved to tell me."

Zach grins. "Good thing you have selective hearing."

I hold up a finger. "I'm not repeating myself, so you better elect to hear what I say, or you'll have no idea what to do."

"I can take direction," Zach says, his voice deeper than usual.

Goosebumps spread across my skin. I imagine that tone in my ear while he's inside me, and heat settles low in my belly.

"I've been told I'm very coachable, Finley."

Holy. Fucking. Shit.

I give myself a moment to internally scream before focusing on the task at hand, moving dishes from the counter to the sink.

I swallow hard, then clear my throat. "Okay. So your first *serious* lesson is the importance of a good rinse."

Zach nods overdramatically, his face furrowed with concentration.

I elbow him in the side. "This was *your* idea."

"What?" he asks with an exaggerated shrug. "This is the face of *serious* Zach Briggs."

I roll my eyes. "Knock it off and pay attention."

He grins, and his eyes light with pure glee. "You always have all of my attention, Finley."

"As I should," I quip, ignoring the swell of emotion his words bring on. Because I can't help but think Zach means them. Literally.

He listens intently as I show him what constitutes a rinsed plate and how to load the dishwasher. Zach's gaze lingers on me through the entire demonstration, its weight branding my skin. But I make it through, grateful to have something other than our feelings to focus on.

"All right, time to put your knowledge to the test." I move to the side to give Zach a clear path to the sink. "Go ahead, show me what you got."

Music continues to blast from a portable speaker as Zach works. Ten minutes later, I stop him after he stacks bowls on top of each other.

"They trap the water in, Finley, so they get a good rinse."

"That doesn't make any sense." I sputter between laughs. "The water can't get in if they're too close like that."

"Maybe I need to watch you again," Zach says.

He grasps my hand, and a flutter of butterflies lets loose in my stomach. He pulls me toward him and spins me until I face the sink, but he doesn't step away. Zach might be considered short in hockey, but he towers over me. Our bodies press together, sending a shiver up my spine. We're not skin-to-skin, but for the way my body reacts, he might as well be touching me beneath my clothes.

"What are you doing?" I murmur.

Zach smells the way he did the first night we met—spicy and musky and cold, like that aisle of men's deodorant and cologne I walk down every time I visit the store.

He drops his head until it hovers over my left shoulder. "Shadowing you. It's the way I learn best."

"Yeah?" My voice comes out hoarse as ideas spring to mind. "Then stay close."

Zach hums low as he inches even closer to me. My voice falters while I explain the importance of avoiding obstructions that prevent dishes from getting fully clean. His hands cup my elbows, and I think this must be it. This is the moment Zach Briggs makes his move.

I let my breath out in an audible rush.

One of Zach's hands grazes mine, calloused skin tentatively making connection. When I don't pull away, he threads our fingers. My entire body alights at this simple touch. I've never experienced it before, and I want to again, over and over. With him.

"Finley, I—" Zach starts to say, but his words cut off when the music ends abruptly.

Both of us whip around. Gemma stands on the other side of the counter beside Kennedy and two friends, Deandra and Brenna. I don't know what Zach was about to say, but I can guarantee it's nothing I want them to hear.

"Well, what do we have here?" Gemma drawls, tossing her purse over the backrest of a counter stool. Her eyes twinkle with mischief as a slow wide smile extends across her face.

"What does it look like?" I say, praying for my jackhammering heart to calm. The beat is in my ears, an insistent *thump thump thump,* continuing to remind me what would've happened if they hadn't barged into the room. "I'm teaching Zach how to do dishes."

A version of the truth works best.

Kennedy smirks. "Interesting. You never cared to learn when we lived together, Briggsy."

Zach's shoulders go rigid, but I'm not sure if it's the reminder of his perceived ineptitude or the implication he's chosen to learn from me. He responds like he doesn't have a care in the world though. "The days of me not having any clue what to do are over. Besides, Finley's more patient than you."

"I bet she is," Deandra mutters under her breath, her bright red lips curled in a smirk. I know her the least well of Gemma's friends since she's got some important job working for Kennedy's dad. She intimidates me with that blunt haircut, severe eye makeup, and fierce stare.

Brenna—my boss at the café—tucks a strand of caramel blond hair behind her ear. "Why don't we let them be?" she says softly, covertly winking at me. I've never liked her more than this moment.

Kennedy turns the speaker back on, and music flares to life. "We'll be outside if you need us."

"Don't forget about the cameras," Gemma says with a smile before leading the group outside.

I'm frozen to the spot. Zach's fingers hook mine, and my breath hitches at the unexpected contact.

"You okay?" he asks.

I shrug one shoulder, reluctant to move my other arm in case it breaks the spell and Zach pulls away. But then, the realization of what we were almost caught doing hits me, and I step back.

Zach snags me by the wrist to keep me in place. "Finley?"

Our gazes lock, and my heart pounds harder with every extension of silence. My mind flashes to the weight of Zach's legs pressed against me, the heat of his body as he crowded mine.

His gaze drops to my mouth and lingers. "Do you want to finish loading the dishwasher?"

I *can't* want this. I'm finding a balance between training, school, and work. My gymnastics improves every single day. All of it is too important to take my eye off my goals, to make room for anything else. I said I'd never date another hockey player. Ever. Not even if my childhood crush, Sidney Crosby, showed up on my doorstep, begging for a date.

And yet, I find myself wanting to surrender to him, to say yes.

"I should do some homework," I say instead. "Big paper due next week."

"Oh." Zach's face sheds every bit of levity, and I curse myself for being the one to do that to him. "Yeah. I get it."

I paste on a smile. "Besides, I think you've got this. You don't need me."

"Right. I'll see you later?"

"Yeah," I tell him, although I have every intention of hiding in my room until I get my emotions under control.

14

Zach

The sound of moans pulls me from a restless sleep.

Sunshine blinds me when I open my eyes to search for the source of the noise. I worry it's coming from my laptop, but my closed computer sits on the chair. It's not coming from this room which means...

My head snaps to the wall I share with Finley. These are moans in real life, coming from *her*.

The realization makes my cock harden painfully, turning morning wood I'd ignore into a situation I can't help but acknowledge. Especially as the sound ratchets higher.

For all of a split second, I wonder if this is an invitation. She's been around less the last few days, since our *moment* in the kitchen. I had been seconds from kissing her when Gemma and her friends walked in and Finley pulled away.

"That feels so, so good," she moans.

My stomach cramps. *Finley isn't alone.* She's with some other fucking person while I lay here getting hard, listening to her soft, melodic moans. *Fuck*.

I hop out of bed, needing to put space between me and the dagger to my heart next door. She doesn't owe me anything, but she could've gone to *their* place and not rub it in my face. Or maybe that's the point—she knows how much I like her and wants to officially close the door.

I sigh deeply, scrubbing a hand over my face.

In the kitchen, I focus on making coffee and cooking scrambled eggs the way Finley taught me last week.

She strolls into the kitchen fifteen minutes later, slipping a sweatshirt over her tank top. "Smells delicious. My cooking lessons are paying off."

"Uh-huh," I mutter, flipping the eggs with a spatula.

"Need any help?"

"I'm good." I could suffocate on the thick tension in the room, but Finley doesn't notice. She scrolls through her phone, lying flat on the countertop. How can she be so *casual*? I clear my throat. "I don't know if I made enough for your guest."

Finley looks up at me, brow wrinkled in confusion. "My guest?"

"Um, yeah." I stare at my feet, shuffling in place. "I heard you... just now."

A flush creeps across her cheeks. "*Just* now or...?"

"Fifteen minutes ago."

"Oh." She sighs as her gaze darts away from me. "I thought you were at the arena this morning."

I shrug. "Didn't feel well. Told them I'd come in this afternoon."

"Right." She clears her throat. "Sorry. I'll be quieter next time."

Next time? Is she fucking kidding me? I'd sleep on a bed of needles to avoid listening to her have sex with someone who isn't me.

"So are they"—my gaze flicks to the ceiling—"going to want breakfast?"

"No, *they* don't eat food." She arches an eyebrow, like she's letting me in on a secret I should find amusing. But I don't understand her hint, unless...

"Wait—are you telling me vampires are real? Because I've always thought—"

"Oh my God, no," Finley shouts through laughter. She wipes away the tears gathering in her eyes. "Zach, I'm trying to tell you there's no one else here. Only my *vibrator*. I'd never bring another guy here."

"Oh" is my brilliant response.

She drums her fingers on the granite. "Best investment I ever made."

"I could tell." I wince, realizing I should've kept that to myself.

"I'm sorry I made you uncomfortable."

"I wasn't... I'm not..." I scramble to respond.

At least not for the reason she thinks. I'll never be able to forget the sound of Finley's moans. I worry my mind will drift there at inopportune moments, when I *definitely* shouldn't think of her coming undone on the other side of the wall. I wish this conversation would end because it's physically affecting me.

Finley scrutinizes me, nose wrinkled, unsure what to make of my answer. "You're not?"

"Nope," I say, popping the P. "It's good it wasn't my concussion or—"

"You thought hearing a moaning woman could be a symptom of your concussion?" Finley's lips quirk into a smile. "Now that would be a medical marvel. Imagine telling that symptom to your doctor."

I'd prefer it over my original fear of Finley hooking up with someone else. But I keep it to myself. She evaded the conversation about my feelings for her before, so there's no point revisiting it and getting hurt all over again.

"We need a sign," Finley says. "You know, in case either of us needs alone time."

My eyes shoot to the ceiling, a long, deep breath escaping my lips to float above my head. I'm going to make an ass of myself in front of the most incredible woman I've ever met.

"Like a secret knock," she adds.

"You don't need to be quiet on my account."

Finley leans her elbows on the counter, her face falling into her open palms. "No?"

"It's your house." I shrug helplessly, unsure how to dig myself out of this hole. She's smiling at me like she's amused, so I do the only thing I can—pivot both literally and conversationally. "You good with eggs and hash browns?"

"Mm-hmm." She hums her agreement as I turn back to the stovetop and prepare her breakfast plate.

⚬

FINLEY

I eagerly take Zach up on his suggestion to watch TV as we eat breakfast, anything to escape the uncomfortable silence.

Zach thought I brought a guy *here*—to my brother's house, to the room next to his. He consumes so much of my brain space, how can he *not* tell? We've flirted consistently, and if Gemma and her friends hadn't walked in on us, I think he would've kissed me. Since then, he's been distant. And now he thinks he means so little, I'd flaunt some other guy in his face?

"What do you want to watch?" he asks casually, as if we hadn't talked about my self-care only ten minutes ago.

He clicks a button on the remote, and the TV comes to life with a show featuring hockey highlights, as if I should expect anything different at my brother's house. I settle on the couch as close to Zach as I can manage without being in his space. My feet curl under my legs, my plate balancing on my lap.

My heart still pounds with equal parts embarrassment and exhilaration. Zach heard me get off this morning after waking up from a dream about us and thrusting my hips into the pillow I hug while I sleep. Waking up that turned-on, desperate to sate desire, isn't an everyday occurrence for me... or at least it didn't used to be.

The timing was perfect because I was home alone—Matt on a road trip, Gemma at the bakery, Zach at the arena. Or he *should* have been at the arena.

"Whatever you want." I shrug, still unsure how to act. Apologizing and making jokes hasn't done anything to dispel the tension. There's one thing that would, but because of the way I pursued him the first time we met, I refuse to rush him now. He has to choose this and be ready to accept the consequences.

"I'd like to watch you."

I choke on my OJ. By the time I speak, my voice has fully recovered. "What do you want to watch me do?"

Zach doesn't look away, and the prolonged eye contact creates a demanding pounding in my core. He chose those words on purpose. He knows what he's doing. And dammit, I need him to make a move before I lose my mind.

"Gymnastics," he clarifies, but there's still a glint in his eye, like he's fully aware of my thoughts.

I gesture around the room. "Here?"

"Nah." He holds the remote to me, nodding toward the TV. "Show off for me, Finley."

Every word out of Zach's mouth dials up the heat flushing my body. I shift surreptitiously as I reach for the remote, trying to shake off the sensations overwhelming me.

Show off for me. I know exactly how to do that. I choose a video compilation of my silver-medal-winning routines at Worlds the year before I stopped doing gymnastics. Zach's eyes are glued to the TV, watching me walk to the springboard beside the balance beam, preparing to mount it. I back dive onto the beam in candle position, feet straight in the air, body wrapping around the beam as if it were the bars. That skill took me forever to master, so of course it's one of my favorites. It also makes me look badass.

The video flips to me preparing for bars.

"You use an excessive amount of chalk," Zach comments.

"Trust me, there's no such thing as too much chalk."

I'm readying for my dismount, swinging around the high bar to build momentum to power the last skill.

"You look so—" Zach starts but I cut him off, not wanting to hear a critique from his lips.

"Thin?" I finish for him.

I can't ignore the differences between that version of me and the one trying to return to the sport. My body changed a lot in the last two years—two cup sizes bigger, three inches taller, hips wider. All terrible for a gymnast. I don't judge the weight of people around me, and I know my perception of myself isn't healthy, but I can't silence the inner voice.

It's easier to toss feathers than a sack of potatoes, a coach used to tell me. It's hard to forget that shit.

"No. I was going to say unhappy," Zach replies, shifting until his body faces me.

"Oh."

His gaze burns the side of my face.

"Finley, you look fucking good." He makes a disgusted sound out of the side of his mouth. "Who put that crap in your head?"

My heart shifts into gear, accelerating from zero to fifty before I can stop it. I can't hit the brakes, and memories flood my mind—the way I'd hold my breath while coaches moved the weights on the two bars of the scale, the audible sigh they'd let out every time, regardless of the number.

Disappointment became what I associated with my body. I didn't believe their hyperfocus on my weight was wrong, only that my body would hold me back.

Gaining twenty-five pounds from bipolar medication made it especially difficult to look in the mirror. I didn't have a gymnastics coach at the time, and internet trolls stopped paying attention to me after I "retired." They weren't there to tell me I looked terrible, but I didn't need their voices any longer. I had my own.

"Finley," Zach says, a careful edge in his tone.

I focus on Zach's words instead of the ugly memories. Hearing him state his attraction so plainly warms the dead place inside of me. His voice drowns out the others.

"Old habits die hard," I explain. "There's been a lot of strides in the sport, but when I was younger, it was pretty damn toxic. And my coaches weren't exactly wrong. It's easier to do certain elements when you're small and light. I've had to change my routines to accommodate changes in my body."

Zach glances back at the TV where the next video in the queue is playing—me at the Olympic Trials not long before my elite gymnastics career ended. The makeup and glittery leotard fooled so many people, but all they needed to do was look closer. If they had, they'd recognize what I see— a girl barely holding it together, burdened by the heaviness of her limbs, exhausted after self-medicating and pushing herself to the absolute brink for the dream she'd always had.

Zach's right. I look *sad*.

"Your routines are cooler now," Zach says after watching me double-pike off the balance beam.

I snort, my hand flinging toward the TV. "My routines are nowhere near as difficult as these."

"Says who?"

"The code of points." When Zach stares blankly, I explain. "It's like the rulebook. The judges use it to grade us."

"Screw them."

"You know, back then I might have if it would've helped."

Zach's brows shoot to his hairline.

"Joking. But I had this desperate desire to win at all costs. I think sometimes I hated the sport as much as I loved it. You ever feel like that?"

"Sometimes." Zach leans back on the couch, shoving his hands behind his head. "I made hockey my entire life, gave up so much for it because I love playing. I enjoy it more than anything else, and sometimes, I resent it for the same reason. Because here I am on the sidelines, thinking about what I'll do if this is a career-ender. I hate how much I need it, you know?"

I nod, his words speaking to a part of myself I don't reveal to anyone. Most people haven't wrapped their life around something, breathing it every waking moment, so they can't relate.

"I know exactly what you mean." I clear emotion from my throat, needing a break from this conversation. "Well, I showed you mine."

Zach scoffs. "You've seen me on the ice." *The clip of him getting concussed.*

"That doesn't count," I protest. "Please?" I flutter my eyelashes, adding a *pretty please* when I'm met with extended silence.

Zach blows out a breath. "Fine. But for the record, I'm not a total pushover who will give in every time you look at me all cute like that. Because I'm not. I'm agreeing to show you this video because watching some asshole take me out on the ice doesn't accurately represent my skill."

I laugh, charmed by his rambling answer. Zach manages to make me laugh, swoon when his smile lights his eyes, and painfully crave him between my legs. A combination I didn't even think could exist.

"Whatever you say, *Calder.*"

"How do you know I won that?"

The Calder Memorial Trophy goes to the best rookie of the year, and the man down the couch from me won it two years ago. Handily. Zach ridiculously downplays his skill. He smiles in a way that has my stomach flipping.

"You look me up, *High-flyer?*"

Heat kisses my cheeks while I run my hand along my jaw. "Oh, are we giving each other nicknames? I've got a few oth—"

Zach's hand lands on my mouth, muffling my words. My body freezes as awareness sparks, my lips tingling from his touch. He doesn't pull away, his hand lingering on my face. I run my tongue along the inside of my lips, fighting the temptation to lick his palm, to push him to break the tension between us.

I swallow hard, becoming more affected the longer our eye contact persists. Zach slowly pulls away from me, but his gaze drops to my lips.

What would it be like to kiss him? I didn't let myself experience it two years ago, but dammit, I want to know now.

He reaches tentatively for my face, his thumb tracing my cheek. I wet my lips, willing him to lean forward.

The alarm beeps and the front door swings open behind us.

Zach throws himself to the other end of the couch, snatching the remote as Kennedy's lilting voice filters through the air. "Briggsy, where are you?"

"In—" Zach clears a croak from his voice and tries again. "In here."

His eyes drift to the screen as he types his name into the search bar. Hundreds of videos pop up, both games and media interviews. Zach's a favorite in the podcast circuit because he couldn't find a canned answer if he tried. The idea of being anything other than his natural endearing self doesn't cross his mind.

It's what I like most about him.

"What are you two up to?" Kennedy's gaze darts between us. It's the first time I've seen her wear anything other than jeans or leggings and a top without Alexei Volkov's name on it.

"I was showing Finley highlights."

Kennedy drops onto the couch between us. There's plenty of room because Zach fused himself to the opposite side from me. She gestures toward the screen. "Let's see it, then we can hit the road."

"You have somewhere to be?" I ask.

Zach looks at Kennedy.

"Where would you be without me? Lunch with my dad, remember?"

"Oh right."

"Finley, you should join us," Kennedy says.

I wave a hand. "I've got homework. And we just ate."

Kennedy sighs and looks at Zach. "Really?"

"Come on, you know I'll eat again."

Zach chooses a five-minute video called *Best Briggsy Moments ON ICE*, which features him faking out a goalie to score, gliding along the boards arms in the air in celebration. It's hard to look away from him on the ice with his talent and the infectious energy he brings to the game.

I understand why he questioned my love for gymnastics when his love for hockey looks like this.

"I'm so glad we drafted you, roomie," Kennedy says with affection and pride.

"Way to show off, Calder. I hope to see you play in person one day."

Zach sports an adorably self-conscious smile when he replies. "Oh, you will."

15

Zach

"You ready for this?" Matt asks when I climb into his truck for my first day of practice since my injury.

Three *long* weeks without hockey.

"You have no fucking idea," I reply with an exhale of breath. "I wish I could *actually* practice."

I'm in the next stage of concussion protocol, so I can skate on my own in a yellow contact-free jersey, which I'll sport for the foreseeable future. It's a tease, getting on the ice but not being able to play. Still, I'm relieved to be one step closer, and that my recovery is moving in the right direction.

"It'll come," he says. "You're back fast for a hit like that."

Matt pulls out of his long winding driveway onto an empty street. By ten a.m., this neighborhood becomes as quiet as the moment before hell unleashes in a horror movie. Kids are in school and parents are at work. I learned the rhythm of this place while on the sidelines.

"Thanks for letting me crash. It would've been hell recovering alone."

He slaps me on the shoulder. "Of course, man. You're family. You know that."

My stomach lurches. If I was a good friend and teammate, I wouldn't hit on his sister behind his back. I'd own the feelings continuing to grow every moment I'm around her. But I know what would happen if I did—he'd cut me out of my life for crossing the line. And Finley would stand by her family. I'd lose them both.

"I want to thank you," Matt goes on as he merges onto the highway. "Gem told me you've been good to Finley. Not that I thought you wouldn't be, but... she's had a rough couple years, and she doesn't know many people here. She deserves good people in her life."

My heart stops beating for an excruciatingly long second before powering back on. "I–I didn't know if you'd be okay with it. You warned Jennings and Volk to stay away from her."

Matt laughs. "I was fucking around with Volk. I'm not sure the guy realizes women other than Kennedy even exist. I warned Princeton because he had that look on his face, and Finley doesn't need any of that shit right now."

I know I shouldn't push the issue and raise his suspicions, but I can't help myself. "What shit?"

Matt hits his indicator and glances over his shoulder before switching lanes. "Guys hitting on her, especially my teammates. She got mixed up with a real asshole in the past. I won't let it happen again. I know it's driving a wedge between us, but I can deal with her anger as long as she's safe."

"Jennings wouldn't hurt her," I manage to force out. *I will never hurt her.*

The vice in my stomach tightens so intensely, I curl into myself.

"Hey, man, you okay?" Matt pulls over to the side of the road to check on me. "I can take you home if you're not ready."

I shake my head violently. His kindness makes the guilt worse. "No, no. I'm fine. I shouldn't have eaten so much this morning, that's all."

His eyebrows draw together. "You sure?"

"I'm sure." I force myself to straighten in my seat and nod toward the road. "I'm good. Let's go. We don't want to be late."

Matt laughs. "Yeah, I don't want to have to discipline you on your first day back."

He cranks the radio as I stare out the window, trying to forget our conversation before I vomit in my captain's car. By the time we reach the arena twenty minutes later, I've managed to compartmentalize everything but hockey, as I've trained to do my entire life. I send guilt to the same place I send pain from injuries and self-doubt after a bad game.

"Well, look who the cat dragged in," Jennings calls when I walk into the Wolves locker room.

"Briggsy!" A chorus of shouts echoes around the room, the voices blending in a wave of resounding support and happiness. And damn, I'm relieved to be back with my hockey family, the guys I get in the trenches with day in and day out, all working toward the same goal.

"Hey, boys!"

Unsurprisingly, the Irish accent of Callan O'Boyle, who we affectionately call Boy-O, hits decibels above the rest of us. He's the hype man every team needs, especially when shit gets hard. I expected to walk into one of his pranks, but he must be worried about me.

"How ye feelin'?" Boy-O asks after I plunk down in my stall. He doesn't look up, continuing to wrap tape around his stick.

I strip off my clothes to change into practice gear. "I haven't been nauseous in a week, which is a good sign."

Hockey players like to follow superstitions, ranging from the clothes they wear to the food they eat pregame to their warm-up routines. I've never focused on that stuff until now. There's more I could say to Boy-O, but for the first time, I'm worried about jinxing my recovery.

"So you're finally going to get out of Cap's hair, eh?" he smirks, stirring shit like usual.

Matt halts a conversation with Volk midsentence to reply. "You all know that's not up to me."

"Exactly why I remain a bachelor," Lepel chimes in from the other side of the locker room. He likes to remind us of his perpetual singledom, as if any of us needs it. I'll never forget the sight of his bare white ass as he plowed into one of Gemma's bridesmaids.

"I'm a good roommate!" I protest.

Volk scoffs loudly, which draws deep belly laughs from the team. They're all aware of the grease fire I started when I lived with him—it would've burned down Volk's house if Kennedy hadn't saved the day.

"At least, I am now."

Volk pauses his locker room exit. "Have you stopped microwaving metal?"

"Shit, I forgot you microwave metal." Matt thrusts a hand through his blond hair, then gives it a firm tug. He's probably imagining his fancy schmancy house burning to a crisp.

I ignore the additional round of snickers from my teammates. I can't wait until I'm no longer the youngest player on this team, and someone else can take the razzing. I won't be the last rookie who microwaves metal, that's for sure.

"For the record, I've never had a problem with it," I say, holding up a finger. "But yes, I've stopped so I won't have to hear your shit anymore."

"I'm glad Kennedy made it out of your apartment in one piece," Volk says. As he walks by, he pats me on the top of my head like I'm a kid who ate his veggies. "For your sake."

I love our camaraderie and the way we tease each other. Having great teammates to watch out for me helps since I'm so far from my family. Still, I can't ignore the scrape against my chest at the reminder of how much of an idiot everyone in my life considers me. Most of the time, I roll my eyes, shake my head, and dish it back.

But not lately. It could be my sensitivity over this injury or the sister of the guy across the room making me want people to take me more seriously. I want *her* to take me seriously. To consider me.

"Glad to hear it," Matt confirms, rising to his feet. He cocks an eyebrow at me. "And how about we stay out of trouble until tonight?"

"Tonight?"

Boy-O leaps to his feet and twerks his ass in my direction. "Time to get down at the Harris house for Halloween, Briggsy."

I hold a hand up to block Boy-O from my line of vision. "Dude, really? My brain can't take any more trauma."

With the conversation in the car and the strange distance between me and Finley, the party slipped my mind. Thankfully, I ordered a costume last month when Jennings told me to, otherwise I'd be going as a ninja (last year's costume) or a pirate (my rookie year). Jennings and I are coordinating this year since we're both going solo, him as a vampire and me as a vampire hunter.

"Get ready for more trauma tonight then," Boy-O says. He finally stops thrusting his ass in my face and heads to the tunnel leading to the ice. "I'm going to be dancing over all of ya!"

Jennings waits for me, slapping hands with everyone as they pass. "Looks like we might need you to stake Boy-O tonight. If this is his energy level now, he's going to be unbearable later."

"You mean you don't want to turn him and live with him for eternity?" I joke back.

With hockey gear on my body again, adrenaline pumps through my veins. I can't wait to skate, even if it's by myself. When we reach the end of the tunnel, I breathe deeply, soaking in the crisp air of the arena.

Home.

"Briggs!" Coach beckons to me with a flick of his wrist from where he stands in the middle of the ice, clad in a dark tracksuit and skates. He's chewing gum with a mildly frightening aggression.

I don't hesitate, zipping over to the coach who intimidates me to this day.

"Coach," I greet as I come to a stop in front of him.

"Good to have you back. You feel ready?"

"More than ready."

He claps me on the shoulder pad. "You'll work with Roy today on your own. If you have any symptoms, you need to tell us. You're too important to this team's future to rush."

"I'm a terrible liar," I blurt out when what I should say is *I'll tell you everything because I'm scared shitless of putting my hockey career in jeopardy.*

Coach is used to me by now, so he's not fazed by my answer. He half grimaces, which is the Erik Pomroy version of a smile. It vanishes quickly as he yanks the whistle dangling around his neck and blows.

The rest of the team skates to us. Every practice starts the same, with a breakdown of our play in the last game and how we'll address issues. By the time he finishes his speech, every guy on the ice would run into the eye of a hurricane if he asked.

I rein in that instinct, the part of me I bring out only on the ice. The fierce competitor who would do anything to win, willing to follow instructions and absorb pain.

But I remind myself it won't be long before I can let it loose again.

16

Zach

LAUGHTER FILLS THE AIR when Jennings and I arrive at the Palmer City Wolves Halloween party, together in our couples costume.

I'm wearing all black from my boots to a long black jacket, and I carry a crossbow in one hand. Jennings painted his face white with bright red blood dripping from his lips and sharp fangs. Every time he moves, his black cape shifts, revealing a flash of blood red.

"No fucking way." Volk shakes his head, a small smile touching his lips. He smiles a lot more now that Kennedy lives with him. "You guys are something else."

Volk's costume matches Kennedy's, a blue-and-white sailor getup that includes a hat with the word AHOY on each of their heads.

"Why do people keep giving him sharp objects?" Kennedy asks.

I point my crossbow at her. "I'm responsible now, Kens."

"That's what you said last year. Do you remember what happened?"

"Nothing that caused permanent damage."

Her hands immediately land on the fake weapon, pushing it down and away from her.

"Come on, it's not real," I say.

She shrugs, replying cheekily, "Better safe than sorry."

"What are your costumes?"

Volk drops an arm protectively over Kennedy's shoulders. "It's *Stranger Things*," he says, like it should mean something. When I only stare, he asks, "Wait—you don't know that show?"

"No…" I say, drawing out the O.

Kennedy nudges him in the ribs. "You had no idea about this show until I forced you to watch it. And then you were always like"—Kennedy drops her voice and puts on her best Russian accent, which isn't *that* bad—"*Kennedy, come over. We need to watch the next episode.*"

"That's not why I invited you over." Volk gives her a lazy grin, enough to force a gagging sound from me.

Kennedy cutely smiles back, the look they exchange speaking a language the rest of us aren't privileged to know.

I fucking want that.

"Come on, guys," I groan.

"What?" Volk plays dumb, exaggerating a shrug and sending his voice an octave higher. "I invited her over to *talk* about the show. Get that trash out of the gutter."

"Mind," I mutter, but Volk ignores me. He always thinks he knows common phrases better than the rest of us, even though English is his second language. *Stubborn pain in the ass.*

Kennedy leans into him, hearts in her eyes as she stares up at his face. "Trash makes more sense."

Volk plants a kiss on her forehead. I turn away, no longer wanting to intrude on their private moment.

Then I see her and lose my damn breath. Finley stands at the kitchen counter, holding a glass to her lips as she surveys the room.

Please be looking for me.

A bright red wig covers her blond hair and stops at her collarbone. A black shirt reveals a sliver of her stomach above black leather pants clinging to her strong legs. The entire outfit emphasizes the muscles she uses to excel in her sport, and knowing that makes the already sexy sight even hotter.

Sufficient words do not exist to describe her.

"This is why you need a girlfriend," Kennedy says, but I don't know why she's saying it.

"What?" I rip my gaze from Finley before everyone reads the forbidden thoughts on my face.

I try to rearrange my expression, but the smirk on Volk's face confirms what everyone's always told me—they can read my every emotion.

"To elevate your life," Kennedy clarifies. Volk's chin rests on her head, his arms draped over her shoulders. Her hands grip his forearms.

"Don't say another word," Matt chimes in as he sidles up to our group. His light-blue denim jacket flutters wide to show off his bare chest and abs. Boxers rise out of his jeans, the white waistband reading *Ken*. "I don't need another year of drama like when you two idiots caused a media shitstorm."

There's a tic in Volk's jaw. Matt knows better than to say anything critical of Kennedy in his vicinity. When they temporarily broke up two years ago for reasons still unknown to me, Volk wouldn't tolerate one bad word about her.

"It was good for the team," Kennedy argues.

"No, the fuck it was not," Matt says, jabbing a finger in Volk's direction. "Every time you two had a... *thing*, he acted like a get-off-my-lawn grandpa. It was exhausting."

"Fuck off, man." There's a subtle warning in Volk's playful tone.

Matt's eyes light up. "Oh, are you still embarrassed about how quickly you became hopeless for her when she still wanted to slug you?"

"Kennedy always wanted me. Even when she found me annoying, she would've—"

Kennedy's fingers brush his lips. "Do *not* finish that sentence if you ever want to see me naked again."

Volk's mouth snaps shut. Kennedy spins in his arms, then lifts herself on her toes to whisper in his ear. His hand immediately finds hers, and I turn away, needing to relieve the ache settling into my chest as I absorb their dynamic, the way they effortlessly flirt.

This time, when I turn back to the kitchen, Finley is watching me. I don't say anything to my friends before taking off in her direction, drawn to her like a defender to the puck. Her gaze remains on me until I stand next to her.

"You look badass," I say in lieu of hello.

"I'm a spy." She kicks one foot back, her leg bending at the knee, sending the weapon of a heel into the air. She effortlessly balances on one razor-thin spike, like she's standing barefoot.

I lean one elbow on the counter and rest my head in my palm. "I'd tell you my secrets."

One side of Finley's lips upturn, and I bowl over in relief. I want to erase the last few days of awkwardness, go back to our comfortable dynamic.

"I think you already do."

"So do you, High-flyer," I reply. "Maybe you're not a good spy after all."

"I'll clue you into a secret of the trade." Finley leans in closer, and I'm hit with a blast of the fruity coconut scent I love. "Sharing a secret is the best way to learn one. It puts people at ease."

I'm grinning like an idiot, I'm sure. I can't play it cool around this girl, even when I try. "Is that so?"

She straightens, then shrugs. "I don't know, but it sounds good. Spies *love* to use their sexiness. Or at least Jennifer Garner did."

I swallow hard. "You'd be a very good spy, Finley."

She goes to tuck a strand of hair behind her ear, forgetting about her wig. Her hand instead drops to her side, fiddling with the gun strapped to her hip.

"Jennifer Garner?" I ask to save Finley from squirming in embarrassment. The insecure part of me loves knowing *I* do that to her, but I never want to make her uncomfortable. Affected, yes, but never unsure she is anything other than perfect in my eyes.

Finley lets out a relieved breath. "From *Alias*. It's *such* a good show. You've never seen it?"

I shake my head.

"Okay, that's unacceptable. I'm making you watch it with me."

"If you insist." *I hope the show is incredibly long and drawn out so I can spend more time with you.*

Finley beams, turning her already beautiful face into a sight that hurts to see.

"So are you going to tell me what you're dressed as?"

I flash the crossbow at her. "You can't tell?"

"Are you an assassin too?"

"Of a kind. It'll make more sense when you see Jennings."

I spot him in the corner and gesture in his direction. Finley walks beside me, my hand on the small of her back to guide her through the crowd.

"Who's Jennings?" she asks.

"Sawyer Jennings, my teammate."

She hesitates long enough for me to notice there's something else going on with her. "You want me to meet your teammate?"

"I want you to meet all my teammates... if you want."

The emotion in those sky-blue eyes does something to me. I'm already a complete goner. She could ask me to do anything, and I'd say yes—as long as it kept her in my company. Her brother might be my friend, teammate, and captain, but the more time I spend with Finley, the less I find I *care*. Which is a massive problem I have no idea how to fix.

"Okay," she says finally.

"Okay," I say, smiling like I scored a playoff goal, and I lead her to my teammate to show off my girl.

17

Finley

DÉJÀ VU STRIKES WHILE I stand in front of my brother's teammate as he tries to impress me.

"As much as I love to play hockey, there's nothing like being on campus. Studying on an airplane with a bunch of smelly dudes is nothing compared to sitting in Princeton's quad when the leaves are turning in the fall."

Sawyer's more understated about it than other hockey players my brothers brought home in the past, including Garrett, who had one goal in mind and attacked like he was on the rush. None have ever tried to charm me by talking about their academic accomplishments, that's for sure.

"Most places would be preferable to a smelly dude plane," I reply.

"True," he says with a laugh. "So what's UPC like? Taking anything good this semester?"

His blue eyes don't stray from my face, like he's interested in what I have to say. I like that about him, even if I chose this costume with distraction in mind, for Zach. The look on his face when he saw me for the first time made every uncomfortable second in leather worth it.

I consider telling Sawyer about my 80s literature class that's made me consider majoring in English, but it's information I'd rather confide in Zach.

Instead, I say, "There's this interesting class about historical events since the 1950s. One of our assignments was to watch *The Big Short* about the financial crisis in '08. I never thought I'd find the stock market fascinating, but it was a good movie."

"Briggsy was talking about that movie the other day. Said he wished everything was explained to him by Margot Robbie in a bathtub."

I roll my eyes. "Of *course* he said that."

Sawyer cocks an eyebrow, as if he's realizing Zach and I are friends. If Sawyer didn't know, does it mean Zach doesn't like me as much as I like him? Am I only a way for him to pass his time while sidelined from hockey?

My stomach turns over like it's filled with curdled milk.

Sawyer props an elbow on the table beside us. "Do you plan to major in history?"

His eyes *gleam*. Women would die for his shade of blond hair, the spitting image of a Ken doll, but I can't find one part of me waking up for him the way I do for Zach.

I shrug, forcing a smile on my face. "What are you majoring in?" I ask to divert the conversation off me.

"Engineering."

"Oh, *come* on," I blurt, waving a hand in his direction. "A professional hockey player who looks like you studying engineering? It's like you walked out of a romance novel."

Sawyer throws his head back, laughing, as one of his hands lands on my forearm. "Speak for yourself," he says. "Hot gymnasts with senses of humor are pretty rare."

I freeze, so shocked to hear him call me a gymnast I don't register the drink being placed in my hand. By Zach. His eyes land on Sawyer's hand still on my forearm. I pull away immediately, but from the glazed-over expression on Zach's face, I know the damage is done.

"Zach," I say, but he's pointing over his shoulder, cutting me off. "I'm going to find Volk and Kennedy. I'll catch ya later, all right?"

My entire body flashes hot, a ball of dread settling in my gut.

Sawyer slowly shakes his head. "You're not available, are you?"

"I suppose those are the deductive reasoning skills that got you into Princeton, huh?" I reply, but my gaze follows Zach across the room to the foyer. I hand Sawyer my drink. "Sorry, but I—"

"No, go get him."

I squeeze his shoulder as I pass. "You're a good friend."

He scoffs. "Yeah, yeah. I know I can't compete with the way you two look at each other."

My blood thrums loudly in my ears as I head in the direction Zach went, maneuvering through the crowd, scanning for him, ducking my head any time I make inadvertent eye contact with someone. I'm about to give up on finding him on the first floor when, finally, I catch a glimpse of his crossbow through an opening in the crowd.

I beeline toward him, driven by the need to fix this.

"Finley, hey," Kennedy greets me. "I love your costume."

Zach's head jerks toward me, his eyes wide. Did he not think I'd follow him?

"Thank you," I reply, motioning between Kennedy and Alexei. "I love *Stranger Things*."

"This one had to be Steve since he has the best hair." Kennedy grips Alexei's arm and exaggeratedly rolls her eyes. "*Speaking of,* we should freshen up."

Volk's forehead creases. "What? My hair looks grea—"

"We'll see y'all later," Kennedy says in a mock-innocent tone, making her intentions clear.

"Upstairs. Five minutes," I whisper to Zach, my gaze flitting to the ceiling.

I don't give him a chance to respond and take off for the steps. Three minutes pass, and I wait for him to appear, hoping he'll gives me a chance to explain.

I heave a sigh of relief when he comes into view a couple of steps from the top.

"You came."

"You asked." He stares at the floor. "So is he the kind of guy you're into?"

"Who?"

He meets my gaze. "You know who I mean. Sawyer Jennings, the guy hitting on you."

My whole world stops.

"But why wouldn't he?" Zach goes on, his chest heaving, distress radiating with every breath. "Why wouldn't anyone take their shot with you? Finley, you're *so fucking beautiful*. Tonight, obviously."

His hand gestures to me lengthwise, his eyes roving over my body, his hungry stare caressing my skin.

"But also in the mornings when you come downstairs and you're still yawning. And when you're doing that ridiculous wolf turn on the balance beam, like it's as easy as walking. You're funny and driven and smart. Who *wouldn't* want you?"

Heat pools low in my belly at his admission, the confirmation his feelings for me match mine for him. I reach for his forearm, wanting to slow him down, to encourage him to take a breath.

But Zach keeps going, "And Jennings... did he tell you that he's working on his degree at *Princeton* while playing in the NHL? He's good too. I bet he'll play top-line with me in a few seasons. And he's nice and a good friend and every girl he meets wants him because he looks like a damn boy band poster come to life."

I take a step forward. "Are you... jealous, Zach?"

He looks away but says nothing.

I take another step closer. "Because if you haven't noticed, I'm not down there with him. I'm up here with you."

"Why?" he asks, his dark eyes never leaving my face. I'm grateful because I want him to see how serious I am. Nothing happening between us is a joke or a throwaway action—not one damn thing since he walked into that stupid closet two years ago and found me on the floor.

"You know why."

He lets out a ragged breath. "Please tell me anyway."

My hand lands on his cheek, featherlight, allowing him to break this spell if he wants. "You're the person I want to be around. Not some guy downstairs. Not anyone else. *You.*"

Zach's hand covers mine as his eyes search my face, as if I didn't deliver him a blinking red sign pointing straight to my mouth. *Zach Briggs needed here.*

But he's wavering, probably for the same reasons I stopped myself from confessing how I felt sooner. His captain is my brother. Dating me will upset his friend and teammate. Attempting to cross the line from friends to something more without knowing how the other person feels is fucking terrifying.

"I want your friend to like me because I want you, Zach."

I might combust if he doesn't kiss me. This man who brought a long-dormant part of me alive, who's supported me while keeping my secret, who pushes me to be the best version of myself, who said the words I've only dreamed someone would ever think about me.

His hand lands on my hip, gripping it tight. "Fuck it."

"It's about damn time," I gasp, the words barely leaving my lips before they're covered by Zach's insistent mouth.

He kisses the way he does everything—at a thousand miles per hour—and it's exactly what I need. My arms wrap around his neck, and I'm pulling him closer, needing the weight of his body against mine. His hands land on bare skin at the small of my back, sending a delicious zing up my spine.

I can't think. I can't think. I can't think.

Every movement happens on instinct—a soft moan escaping when our lips meet, my tongue begging for entrance to his mouth, his hands slipping beneath my shirt, his fingertips skimming bare skin.

"Zach," I murmur, and he pulls me closer, his erection pushing into my abdomen. I break our kiss, raking my teeth across his bottom lip. He shudders, and damn, I want to encapsulate this moment in a snow globe, to set it beside my bed and shake it every night to relive this perfection.

"You want me too."

His head drops back with a slight groan. "You're joking, right?"

"You didn't make a move, so I wasn't sure—"

"You are so far out of my league, Finley." The intensity in his dreamy brown eyes makes me gulp. "I like you. I like our friendship. I didn't want to mess it up. Or all of this"— he points a finger up and twirls it around to indicate my family and living situation—"for you. I know there's something you're not telling me, and I don't want to complicate whatever is going on—"

My fingers trail along his abdomen, toying with the waistband of his pants. "I don't want to think about any of that right now."

"Please don't use me only as a way to forget. I can't take it."

I lay his hand flat on my chest, over my heart, beating like a drum during a solo in a rock song. For him. "This is for you."

Zach's breath catches, and I bask in it, more confirmation I unravel him.

"If we weren't in a hallway where we could be caught," I say, "I'd show you how much I want you."

I guide his hand south, his fingers grazing my abdomen before I settle them above my waistband. I need Zach to relieve me of the thunderous throb between my legs.

"But because I can't, I'll settle for letting you know that when you *heard* me earlier this week..." I swallow hard before continuing. "I was thinking about you."

"*Fuck*, Finley," Zach mutters before he crashes his mouth onto mine again, the momentum pushing me against my closed door so hard, I'm surprised it remains standing.

I'm fumbling for the knob when I hear Gemma's voice. "Finley! Where's my birthday girl?"

Zach pulls away, his eyes glazed with lust. "It's your birthday?"

"Mm-hmm" is all I can manage.

"Why didn't you say anything?" This man plays professional hockey, trains intensely to bust his ass at breakneck speed on the ice for forty seconds at a time, and he's not able to speak without breathing hard right now. Because of *me*. "I didn't get you a gift."

I lean my forehead against his. "This is what I would've asked for."

Zach kisses me again, once, slowly, his tongue working against mine in a way that has me pinching my legs together.

"You'll find me later?" My lips graze his once again. "*Please* find me later."

"This doesn't feel real," he whispers.

I reluctantly pull out of his arms. His fingers weave through mine. I only break our connection because if I'm not downstairs soon, Gemma will come upstairs to find me.

"Don't worry." I give him a sultry smile. "I'll fix that later."

18

Zach

Sunlight assaults my eyes way too soon.

The team Halloween party lasted way longer than I anticipated—longer than I wanted since Finley asked me to find her.

So she could prove to me what happened in the hallway was real. And dammit, I needed the confirmation, to know I didn't dream our kiss. But slipping away to one of our rooms was too risky, especially when my teammates know I never turn in early.

I've never had a reason to want to leave early until last night.

I close my eyes, remembering the way Finley's soft lips slid between mine, tasting like strawberry lip balm. My hands greedily gripped her tight ass, pulling her as close to me as I could. We weren't ourselves last night, at least not entirely with our costumes. Finley wore a wig, so I couldn't run my hands through her sunshine strands like I'd dreamed about. I want to do it today, but I don't know if I missed the moment. If all that remains is regret.

Then I hear her hot breathy moan from the other side of the wall. I wait a beat to confirm it's not in my mind.

My phone dings, and I grope for it with my free hand. The other strokes my dick, both relief and absolute fucking torture, especially when Finley's moans grow louder. What I wouldn't give to make her fall apart.

Finley

Can you hear me?

Me

Yeah

Finley

I went to sleep turned on

Finley

Soaked and waiting for you

"Fuck," I say, fisting my cock harder. I'm thinking of a response when the phone vibrates again.

Finley

Still waiting...

Me

Coming

Me

Shit I mean I'm coming to you

Me

No not *coming* coming. Coming over.

Finley

If you're not here in fifteen seconds you'll be coming alone

I fumble out of bed and down the hall, trying not to rush to show *exactly* how eager I am. She'll know as soon as she sees me. There's no disguising what she does to me in these pants.

It's a miracle she's inviting me to her room. She's too perfect for me to be real. When the other shoe drops, when she moves on, it will be my heart fed through a shredder, crosscut into tiny pieces that can never be put back together.

Still, I knock lightly on her door, waiting for permission to enter.

"Come in already," she calls through a burst of laughter. Every laugh I elicit from her brings me so much joy. "I think we're past knocking, don't you?"

A pair of shorts lays on the floor beside her bed, which means underneath the comforter ten feet away, Finley's naked. Her light blue vibrator sits beside her on the table—it's not intimidatingly big but has an extra arm to stimulate her clit that my cock doesn't have. I haven't worked someone with my dick and my hand before, but if it's what she likes, I'll learn.

"We're alone, right?"

"Matt and Gem are at a playdate with Elodie."

Finley holds up the comforter, inviting me into bed. I stride through the threshold of the room, not stopping until I'm sliding in next to her. We lay side by side, facing each other. Her free-flowing blond hair is mussed, her cheeks pink.

I can't take my eyes off her.

"Hi," she says shyly, such a contrast to her usual confidence.

"Hi," I say back, tucking a strand of loose hair behind her ear. "You look beautiful like this."

Finley's lips quirk. "You mean turned-on? *Someone* kept me wait—"

I can't help it; I kiss her. Finley melts into my arms, kissing me back with the same fervor as last night. She lets out a satisfied sigh when my tongue enters her mouth to tangle with hers. I pull her closer, bringing her leg over mine and squeezing her ass. One of her hands reaches under my shirt, and she runs her fingers over my abdomen, my muscles clenching beneath her touch. Her other hand grips the side of my head, weaving her fingers into my hair.

I'm painfully hard. Close like this, the tent in my sweatpants jabs her center. She repositions herself until she's right over my cock, grinding against it, seeking more friction. My vision blackens from the pleasure, and I'm not even inside her yet.

"Tell me what you want," I murmur between kisses.

She pulls back and her eyes open, blinding me with my new favorite shade of blue. "Your fingers," she says, taking my hand from her face and bringing it between her legs without an ounce of self-consciousness.

"Shit, Finley—" My strangled words are cut off when my fingers easily slide inside her.

She's going to feel so good wrapped around my dick. I close my eyes, breathing in deeply, letting it out slowly, willing my throbbing cock to calm down.

"Zach, what's wrong?"

I keep my eyes shut as I try to talk again, not wanting to see her disappointment or judgment. "I'm not... as experienced as you might think. I want to make this good for you."

Her fingers lift my chin. "Hey," she whispers. "Look at me."

When I open my eyes, the concern in her expression constricts my chest.

"It's already good for me because you're here. Don't stop kissing me, okay?" She places her lips on mine. "And I need you *here*"— she brings my fingers to her clit—"more than anywhere else."

I nearly blurt, *Finley, I like you so much*, but she's not asking me to speak. So I kiss her with every fucking emotion coursing through me. I don't stop, not when she moans against my mouth, or when she writhes on my fingers seeking more pressure, or when her hand strokes my shaft through my pants. I've never been this worked up, needed release this badly. I'm barely holding off my orgasm when Finley's entire body shakes.

She breaks our kiss, throwing her head back. Her voice is breathy and strangled, like she can barely speak. "Zach, I'm *so* close. Because of *you*. I didn't think—"

Her words cut off as she lets out a high-pitched moan.

"Fuck, this is so much hotter than I imagined," I groan.

I'm already addicted to the look of bliss on her face as she rides my fingers, finding her release. Her head turns into her pillow as she cries my name.

My hand lands on the side of her head, threading through her silky strands. "You didn't think what?"

"Hmm?" Her eyes are still closed, her inner walls still convulsing around me. *She's so fucking perfect.*

Reluctantly, I withdraw my fingers, hoping it's not the last time she'll give me the privilege of being between her legs. I think about asking the question again, but with the way she's blissed out of her mind, I don't think she'll respond.

Finley's eyes eventually open, vibrant blue with two wide black irises. She gives me a satisfied smile. "I can't remember the last time I've felt this good."

She shimmies next to me, bottom lip ensnared in the top, gaze on me. "I want to do something for you, if you'll let me."

Finley pulls back the comforter and moves toward the end of the bed. I lift my head to find her sitting patiently between my legs, staring at the tent in my pants. Fuck, I need relief.

More than that, I need *her*.

My head falls back on the pillow, ceding control to Finley, who rips my boxer briefs down my legs. She flings them to the floor, then grips my thighs, squeezing the muscles.

"You're stronger," she says with such reverence in her tone, I have a new appreciation for all those hours I clocked in the weight room during the offseason.

Her mouth slides down my shaft until the head of my cock hits the back of her throat. Her tongue licks up the sides as she slides back to the tip. "As perfect as I remember."

Fuck.

"I'm not going to last long," I choke out.

Her hand lands on my abdomen and traces the skin above my hip bone. "You let go when you're ready."

This woman.

"You are fucking *amazing,* you know th—"

My words cut off as Finley eases my cock back into her mouth. I lose my ability to speak, to think, to do anything other than let tension build. The way her soft moans reverberate against me amplifies the sensation of her mouth, tongue, hand. It's such a turn-on to watch her blond head bob up and down, to know she enjoys wrapping her pretty lips around me.

I don't want this moment to end.

But as I think the words, my hips jerk on instinct, desperate, needing more. She takes me deeper, hollowing out her cheeks to apply the pressure I crave.

"*Finley,*" I warn, but she grips my hips, keeping me in place, silently encouraging me. Her tongue slowly swirls around the head of my cock before she plunges down my shaft again so quickly, I go off like a firecracker, spilling into her mouth.

I'm a fucking mess. She's made me a fucking mess, physically, emotionally.

I've had crushes and puppy love and drunken hookups, but for the first time, I'm consumed by another person. I wake up every morning looking forward to seeing her, to learning more about her, to watching her sail through the air like she's fucking magic. My heart stops in my chest when she laughs at something I've said or when she shows me that gorgeous smile.

I've never been this desperate for another person, never craved their presence regardless of what we're doing.

Finley settles into the crook of my arm, sighing contentedly. Having her in my arms eclipses everything else we did, illuminating the depth of my feelings.

I press a kiss to her hair. "I can't feel my legs."

She laughs, draping her arm across my waist. "I'll take that as a compliment."

"You should." I tilt my head to the side. She's already looking at me, smiling big. I can't not ask the same question I had after our hookup in the locker room. "You don't want my mouth?"

Finley's breath hitches like I've surprised her.

"I do," she replies. "On mine. I *really like* kissing you, Zach."

My mouth breaks into a smile. "Yeah?"

"Like, I could do it all day, and it still wouldn't be enough."

"There's no way I'd survive an entire day. I was barely holding on here... but it'd be a good way to go."

Finley shoves my shoulder.

"I want to take you somewhere," I say. "Can I?"

"You've got me until twelve," she says. "I need to work out this afternoon, plus finish some homework. You can come if you want."

I bite my lip, holding in an *Already did, thanks.* Finley's smiling at me, like she can read my mind.

And I know without a doubt, I'm going to end up loving this girl.

19

Finley

"Where are we?" I ask Zach after he directs me to park anywhere in the lot.

Now that his concussion symptoms have subsided, he can drive but I insisted because... well, I guess *I'm* not ready for it. I avoid the reason for my concern the way I avoid the fact that Zach is my brother's teammate. Both are boulders waiting to come loose as we head down this winding road.

"My apartment," he answers.

He waits for me to exit the driver's door before walking toward a nondescript brick apartment building.

"This is the place you wanted to take me? I think I've given you the wrong impression."

"No, High-flyer," he says, playfully grabbing my waist while I swat at him. "I'm grabbing some clothes before we go where I want to take you. If it means you see where I live to prove I can be responsible, who am I to stand in the way?"

He pauses at the first landing and holds his arm out wide waiting for me to pass him. "Second door on your left."

I pause beside him to whisper, "I bet your neighbors don't know a Calder Trophy winner lives among them."

A laugh bursts from Zach's chest. It's cute the way he laughs, an understated heh-heh-heh he sometimes covers with a hand, as if he's self-conscious about it. The most adorable laugh lines stencil into his reddening cheeks. I don't wait for him to respond and continue to the door marked 124. The doormat beneath my feet reads, *Welcome to the Sin Bin*. I look over my shoulder at him.

"It was a housewarming gift from Volk," Zach explains.

"I like it."

The weight settling in my chest gets heavier once Zach opens the door and invites me into his apartment. His life. Would he do this if I told him the reason I dropped out of the sport I love? The reason my life will always be more complicated than it is for other people?

It's new for me, having to tell someone about my bipolar disorder. My therapist says I'll know the right time, to trust myself, which is laughable given how adept my brain is at lying to me.

During the highs, it tells me I don't need to sleep, that I should do gymnastics at three in the morning. It forgets to warn me my actions have consequences. And then when it sinks into the depths of hell during my lows, it whispers I'm pulling everyone around me down, that I'm a disappointment, that I'd be better off not being here at all.

I shiver, thinking of how low I felt two years ago.

I know the signs of an oncoming episode, but it's not always easy to determine whether something's inane or significant. Like this morning with Zach, I can't remember how long it's been since I felt *that* good.

I'm not talking about the orgasms, which I give myself often. But being around him lights a lantern in my chest, brightening a space that has long been dark. The rush when I kissed him, when his body fused to mine, when he looked at me like I was the greatest gift he'd ever received reminded me of the highs of my bipolar disorder. I'm not sure if this signals the beginning of hypomania or falling hopelessly in love.

I should ask Dr. Warren, but I'm afraid of the answer. Because if I'm entering a hypomanic state, it'll throw off my entire life. It'll mean I'm heading for a crash, the kind that could derail all my progress at school and gymnastics.

"Are you coming in, or...?" Zach stares at me, still standing in the doorway, enveloped in my thoughts.

I take a breath and walk into a normal apartment. It's nice—hardwood floors, a large open-concept space, marble countertops in the kitchen. "I've never had my own apartment," I tell him.

Zach's shoulders relax. "Me neither. Kennedy and I lived here together. She moved out only a month before I was flattened like a pancake."

I can still picture the hit in my head, the way he tried to stand and fell back down, how he had to crawl to the bench. We're both athletes. Injuries come with the territory. But my chest aches remembering how helpless he looked.

Zach continues, "She stayed with Volk most of the time, so I guess I did kinda have my own place, but she took care of a lot, which I need to do now."

"When... are you planning to come back?"

Zach's gaze burns into the side of my face, but my scaredy-cat ass refuses to turn. Part of me wants to stuff it away, to hide from these feelings that keep expanding, but the other part... well, the other part relents, and I rotate my head until I see him. That part of me never wants to look away.

"I honestly haven't thought about it."

"With Kennedy gone, are you going to stay here?"

"I don't know. My lease is up in a couple of months. We got this place during my rookie season, after I officially wore out my welcome at Volk's house."

I prop my elbow on the elevated countertop, leaning into my open palm. "Is that what we call starting a grease fire and running out of the house to let it rage?"

Zach curses under his breath. "If people keep running their mouths, you'll want nothing to do with me."

I smirk. "It *is* a risk you run by bringing me around your friends. But it'll take a lot more than that to scare me off."

His Adam's apple bobs. "Good to know."

I walk further into the apartment, examining the furniture, the decor, the pictures, wishing I could turn this place inside out and find out every little thing about Zach Briggs. I point to the wall with a framed Palmer City Wolves jersey with VOLKOV and the number 42 on the back. "Big Volkov fan, huh?"

"It was a compromise with Kennedy. I can't believe she left it."

I bite my lip, trying to keep my smile in. Kennedy left it here to get under Zach's skin, a favorite pastime of every person in his life. I can't help joining in.

"Yeah? What'd you get in this *compromise*?"

He nods his head in the direction of a long hallway with several closed doors. "I'll show you."

I follow Zach into what looks like a gaming mecca. Bookshelves filled with video games line one wall. The perpendicular wall holds the largest TV screen in existence. Positioned across from the TV is the most comfortable-looking piece of furniture I've ever seen, a cross between a bed and a couch.

And then Zach flips the light switch and fairy lights come alive. He's filled the ceiling with white lights, casting a cozy glow over the entire room.

"Wow," I breathe, spinning once around the room before landing on him again.

He slumps into the doorframe. "Go ahead, call me a nerd. I've heard it all."

I drop onto the couch, and yup, it's so comfortable I might never want to stand again. "Being a nerd is a good thing," I tell him. "If I didn't already think it, this room would change my mind."

Zach's head drops lightly against the doorframe. "Yeah?"

"I think it's cool. I mean, I plan to have an entire room in my house dedicated to the books I love. And it'll be covered in quotes and art."

I let myself fall back into the cushion, reveling in its softness. The bed dips with Zach's weight, and I reach for him, connecting with his hand. He threads our fingers, and my stomach turns over, like the spurt of a blender when it first turns on.

"Zach?" I whisper.

"Yeah?"

I speak the words to the ceiling. "Earlier you said you thought something was going on with me. Why do you think that?"

He swallows hard, his grip tightening on my hands like he's worried I might slip away from him. "You're hiding gymnastics from everyone in your life. You're so good, Finley, and I can tell you love it. The way I love hockey. You wouldn't give it up for nothing. And you're living with Matt and Gem instead of on campus when they can afford to pay for it."

Zach inhales deeply. "That night we met, you weren't okay, were you? I didn't know it then because I didn't know you. You were so confident and sexy. I followed you because I felt lucky you were talking to me. I didn't know something was wrong... and now I feel like an asshole."

I turn to my side and tilt his chin toward me. "Zach, no, that's not... don't put any of it on you. You're right. I was struggling, but there's no way you could've known. I thought I might always be this half version of myself, and then... you were rambling about needing to find the men's room before you pissed in the corner, and... for the first time in forever, I wanted to laugh about something."

Zach groans, throwing a hand over his eyes. "You heard that? I'm surprised you left that closet at all."

"I was so desperate to feel *something*." I let out a slow sigh. "I didn't feel happy at my brother's wedding, then you came along, and I didn't want to let go. I normally wouldn't come on *that* strong—not that there's anything wrong with it—I'm just not usually that bold."

"So did it work?"

I let out a laugh. "You could say so, yeah."

"Why'd you run away?"

"It wasn't you, I swear."

"And you don't want to tell me what it was?"

"Not yet."

"Okay, High-flyer," Zach says, tugging me to him. I nuzzle his side, resting my head in the crook of his arm, breathing in the comfort of his scent. "I'll wait. I'm here to listen whenever you're ready."

I whisper, "I'm glad you found me again."

His fingers trace my arm in a way that tells me he cares. I breathe in deeply, safe, comfortable, happy. "Me too, Finley. Me too."

I'm not used to sleeping against another person, but opening my eyes to Zach peacefully lying beside me warms me to the tips of my toes. There's a faint smile on his face, on those lips I kissed again and again this morning, spurred on by the ever-bright feeling in my chest. One of his hands curls around my right shoulder, the other resting on his chest. I slip my hand into his, moving ever so slowly, not wanting to jostle him awake.

His eyes flutter open, and I soak in their beautiful brown color. Zach offers a sleepy smile when he finds me watching him.

"Hey," he says.

"I see the appeal of naps now."

Zach stretches his arms over his head, his shirt lifting to reveal a swath of toned abdomen and a dusting of dark hair around his navel. "I've taken a lot of naps, Finley, but this one might be my favorite."

I brush a lock of his hair back from his forehead. "You're very good at it."

He laughs softly. "That's me, excelling at those marketable skills."

"Last time I checked, hitting a puck into a net is pretty marketable." I gesture around us. "If I'm not mistaken, it's how you got this sweet setup. Meanwhile, I've only got blood blisters and bruises to show for my efforts."

Zach slips his arm out from behind me and shifts to his side. "What do you want to show for your efforts?"

I haven't said it out loud to anyone. I've barely admitted it to myself, but deep down, I know. Not putting voice to this goal leaves me half-in though. It allows me to give it up, but I don't want to keep living a life where I don't risk anything.

"I want back in," I say, studying Zach, needing to see his reaction. "Getting onto UPC's team is only the first step. I want the Olympics. I want a medal."

Zach doesn't flinch. Doesn't scoff. No doubt creeps into his expression. He continues to stare at me intently, waiting for me to continue.

A nervous laugh bursts from my chest. "I've never admitted it to anyone."

"Why not?"

"I'm past my prime. It sounds ridiculous, but twenty-one is ancient in gymnastics. Eighteen was once considered your last shot, but more women are staying in the sport longer, so it's not impossible but ... still a long shot."

"You want it though?"

I nod.

"That's all that matters then," Zach says. "You think anyone from my hometown thought I'd make it to the NHL? I'd be picked in the first round? I'm five-ten, one hundred seventy pounds. You can throw a stone anywhere in Canada and hit someone whose dream is to play professional hockey. If I'd let myself think about the odds, I wouldn't be where I am now. You have to put on blinders, Finley. You have to believe."

He runs the back of his fingers over my cheek. "I believe you can, not that my opinion means anythin—"

I lunge forward, placing my lips on his, smothering the last words of his sentence. It takes a second before he kisses me back, one arm pulling me to him. He holds me snugly against his body, our lungs expanding and contracting in turn. A heartbeat pulses erratically, but with how close we are, I'm unsure whether it's mine or his.

Eventually, I pull back enough to look him in the eyes. "Your opinion means something to me."

Zach swallows a lump in his throat. I wait for him to speak, expecting a ramble in response to my brazen statement. He remains silent, gazing at me but not in a way I find uncomfortable. I like this opportunity to memorize every section of his face.

Finally, I say, "We didn't go to the place you wanted to take me."

"We'll go someday." Zach waves a hand, shooing my worry away. He acts like we have all the time in the world. I can't help the smile stretching across my face at this promise. "You ready for the gym?"

"Let's go."

When I settle into bed later that night after spending the day with Zach Briggs, that smile is still on my face.

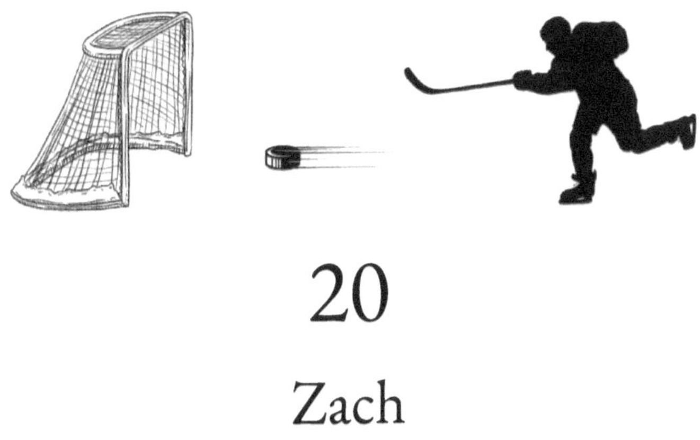

20

Zach

IT'S BEEN A WEEK since the team doctor cleared me to rejoin practices with my team, as long as I wear my bright yellow contact-free jersey.

Everything with concussion protocol moves intentionally slow to protect players, but I'm antsy to play the game I love the way I like. Battling for pucks in the corner. Providing net front to screen the goalie to create a better chance for a shot to go in or to tap in a rebound. Checking guys with surprising force, given my size. Scoring goals on a breakaway. Landing passes on my linemate's tape. Goofing around with teammates. Celebrating wins.

I miss it all.

"You all right?" Jennings asks beside me in the locker room.

We're all putting on gear for a long-held tradition of the Palmer City Wolves—family skate. Families in the stands wait for their players to come out. My genetic family's all in Canada, and everyone in my adopted family is already in this locker room or in the stands waiting for my teammates.

I pull my green jersey over my head, straightening it until it hangs loose over my black shorts. "I'm good. Are *you*?"

Jennings shoves my shoulder, getting my subtle message to stop asking me. I'm on my way back to the game I love and have shed every lingering worry my injury could mess with my career. Instead, I'm thinking about the woman I wish was upstairs waiting for me, the one who occupies every waking thought not focused on my game.

I flick the green pom-pom sitting on top of the black hat on his head. "You got anyone here for you today, Princeton?"

"Actually, yeah," he answers as we head out of the locker room toward the tunnel to the ice. "My older brother's in town. It'll be his first time on professional ice."

"Daddy!" A kid decked out in gear and skates tugs Isak Holm's jersey. He's a winger on Jennings's line and a single dad who went through a nasty divorce in the offseason. "Can we skate together, Daddy?"

He hands his son a stick. "I wouldn't want to skate with anyone else, bud."

"Is this the famous Danny?" Sawyer holds out his hand to the boy for a fist bump.

"Princeton!" Danny says. "Briggsy!"

"Hey, kid," I reply, slapping his hand.

We walk toward the ice at a glacial pace, thanks to Holmie's kid, but soon enough, the crisp smell of ice fills my nostrils and my blood pumps faster. Niko Halonen—the center on my line and the guy brought in to push our team closer to winning the Cup—speedwalks past me after bumping my shoulder without saying a word.

"Hey, jagoff!" I shout, and Holmie smacks my arm, gesturing to his kid. As if he won't hear worse language hanging around the team. "We're walking here."

Halo spins, continuing to walk backward toward the ice. "Places to be, Briggsy."

I'm surprised we all fit in the locker room with his ego. He knocks his stick once on the mat before spinning and gliding across the ice, weaving in and out of my teammates and their families.

"He loves himself entirely too much," Jennings mutters.

"Fu—yeah, he does," I answer, catching myself before I blurt out foul language again.

"Ready, bud?" Holmie asks, holding his arm out toward the rink. The kid ambles along until his skates land on the ice, and he propels himself forward with Holm gliding alongside him.

I'm still laughing at what Jennings said about Halonen when the skaters part, leaving me a clear path to see *her*.

My laugh cuts off, and everyone and everything around me falls away. Finley Harris stands in her skates beside Matt and Gemma in the center of the ice. She's wearing a black Palmer City Wolves hat with ear flaps on each side and a green pom-pom on the top of her head. Her bright blond hair flows down her back over a dark puffer jacket. It's my luck her jacket isn't long enough to cover her ass, which looks incredible in dark-wash jeans.

Jennings claps me on the shoulder, shaking his head as he says through a laugh, "You're so screwed, dude."

"I don't—" I start to object but stop because there's no point hiding this from him. He already knows. Trying to fend off the accusation will confirm it anyway. I've always been shit at lying. "I know. She's so far out of my league."

"And Cap would kick your ass if he knew."

I suck in a breath. "That too."

"What are you going to do?" Jennings asks.

A smarter man would stay away from her. This situation will un-doubtedly end with me alone, watching the woman of my dreams move on after having her fun with me. She wouldn't do it on purpose, she's too good of a person for that. But the novelty will wear off. She'll meet someone more confident, more experienced, more capable of caring for her, and leave me behind.

There's only one way we can end—if she walks away. Because there won't be a day I don't want to be around her.

I wink at Jennings, then skate toward center ice, as if I could go anywhere but Finley's direction. She doesn't see me until I'm halfway there, a smile spreading across her gorgeous face when her gaze lands on me. My skates slide to a stop, spraying her with a bit of ice. Finley doesn't flinch.

"Hey, High-flyer, you didn't tell me you'd be here today."

Finley glances at her brother, but his attention is focused on Elodie in a stroller with a flat bottom to glide on ice. "Matt invited me last minute. Thought it would be a good time for us to bond."

I tug one of the ear flaps. "You look good in my team colors."

Her grin stretches beyond her normal smile while she brings the backs of her hands beneath her chin in a *Who me?* pose and flutters her eyelashes.

"I think you look good in anything," I say helplessly.

Finley leans toward me, dropping her voice. "I shine when I'm wearing *nothing*."

I look toward the ceiling. We're below the scoreboard which reads *Welcome Wolves Families*. "Are you trying to kill me? This is a family event and your brother is standing right there and—"

She places a hand over my mouth, stopping my word vomit. "Skate with me?"

My gaze darts to Matt again, but he's in conversation with our coach. If he wasn't, I'd still make this choice, cross this line, because I can't deny her. I hold out my hands to her. "Let's go."

Finley's head tilts to the side. "I learned how to skate when I was six. I don't know if you know, but my brothers all play in the NHL. They're kind of a big deal."

I keep my hands out to her, waiting. "Tell them you forgot. Besides, you can't risk falling and injuring yourself."

"You'll be my protector?" she asks, placing her hands in mine, sending a zing of energy through me.

I lean in close and whisper, "I'll be the lucky bastard who gets to hold your hand."

The flush filling her cheeks suits her. "I would have never guessed the night I met you that you were such a charmer."

"I'm not." I glide backward while Finley propels toward me. "I'm not trying to charm you. I mean, I *am*, but it's not like I'm trying to play some game or strategize about what might work on you. I'm saying what I honestly think, what I need you to know. If it makes you uncomfortable, I'll stop, I'll—"

"Zach," Finley says, effectively cutting off my rambling. "I like you. I thought I made that clear." She quirks an eyebrow. "Apparently, I need to do a better job convincing you."

I blow out a breath. "*Finley.*"

"I like how you say my name, like I hold some kind of power. And when you call me High-flyer, I remember how you have my back, how you believe in me. You make me laugh, and you care about what I have to say. You get why gymnastics is important to me. You're like this ball of light that's come into my life and made every day better for me. And fuck me, you wear that backward baseball cap so well."

I huff out a laugh, never more thankful the way I prefer to wear my hat does something to her.

Finley's head swivels around, and she drops her voice lower. "Every time I'm in bed, I think about what it was like having you there, how much I want to kiss you again, to have you *touch* me again."

My heart gallops, and it's not only the reminder of our morning in her bed. Of the way she suction-cupped herself to my lips, like she *needed* me to exist. Or the proof of her attraction to me on my fingers when they dipped between her legs. Finley likes *me*, period. Not only because of who I am, but how I make her feel.

I drop my head. "Finley, I'm barely hanging on here. If you say anything else like that, I'm going to haul you to the locker room."

Her eyes spark. "Promise?"

I mutter a curse under my breath.

"Okay, okay, I understand it's not the time. But I... I need you to know I want you around. And you haven't been since like a week ago... and I don't know why."

"Your brother's home."

"You have an apartment where we can be alone, which sounds like it might be something you want."

I grip her hands tighter, pulling her closer to me. "You have no fucking idea how much I want that. But I don't want to push you or have you think it's all I want because it's not. Everything is up to you, all right? My answer will always be yes to anything you ask. I'm happy with whatever we do—or don't do—as long as you're happy."

Finley's smile fades. "We only work if it's good for both of us," she says. With the way, her beaming smile returns, I can almost convince myself I misread her earlier expression. "Though your offer of total control is mighty tempting."

It's not surprising, given the little I know about her life. Choices have been taken away from her, but she's fighting to mold her life into what she wants. I hope she creates a Zach Briggs-size space.

"It's an open offer." I grin, my cheeks hurting, the way they always do around this girl who makes me happier than I thought possible.

Finley's head drops back as she lets out a groan. "I really want to kiss you right now."

"Welcome to my world," I say through a laugh. "I can settle for talking to you."

"*Settle*? Is that right?" She laughs with me, poking my side.

"Sacrifices must be made," I say with an exaggerated shrug.

"I'm about to *sacrifice* you on this ice."

I tilt my head. "Aw, Finley, a temper is so unbecoming."

"Wait until we're alone." Her hands tighten around mine. "I'm going to kick your ass."

"But it's on?"

She snorts. "I mean, obviously, *after* I kick your ass."

I nod. "I'll allow it."

Finley aims for my side again, and I dodge out of the way. "You're lucky I like you, Calder."

Don't I fucking know it.

21

Finley

"WHAT WAS IT LIKE growing up with Cap?" Zach asks as we start another lap—our third? fourth?—at the slow and steady pace he's set.

The reminder of my brother—somewhere on the ice, likely wondering when Zach and I became so close—is unwelcome. But it's necessary to talk about him, because he's a frustrating roadblock we're speeding straight toward.

"Probably your wet dream—the Harris household was hockey central, twenty-four seven. For my brothers and the hoards of teammates who constantly hung around." My dad left our basement unfinished so they would have a space to hang out that was fine to destroy. "It's how I ended up in gymnastics. My parents needed me in an activity to keep me occupied multiple days a week while they carted my brothers around, helping them chase their professional hockey dreams. I think they were shocked when I took to it and had a dream of my own to chase."

"They weren't supportive?"

I shake my head. "Oh no, they were. Once I told them I wanted to go to the Olympics, they supported me as much as they did my brothers.

It meant a lot of split time because my parents can't be in four places at once."

I understood their absence didn't mean they didn't love or support me, or that they didn't want me to succeed. But sometimes, all I wanted was to have someone in the stands cheering for me, to know I wasn't there competing alone.

Zach glances over his shoulder, then maneuvers us around a teammate's family. "My parents worked a lot to support me and my older brother and sister, but it meant they couldn't always be with any of us, too busy providing. Jeff and I often played on the same team because he's only a year older than me. It made it easier for our parents to be there."

"He must be proud of you for making it."

"Sure, yeah. But he's also a little jealous." He shrugs. "I understand it."

If any of my brothers hadn't made it to the NHL, I bet it'd be a similar dynamic. It's never easy to watch someone else live the life you want, even if you're happy for them. Even if you love them.

"I want you to meet them," Zach says, the intensity of his eye contact driving home the sincerity of his words. It's moments like this when I can't believe my luck.

I squeeze his hands. "I'd love to."

He pauses. "Why do you think your parents stopped supporting your dream?" Zach tentatively asks the question that could shatter this moment between us. For that reason, I don't shut down and, instead, push through the ambush of bitterness flooding me.

"They thought it was in my best interest. Which is why I'm hiding it. They still think that."

Zach opens his mouth to speak, but before he can, Alexei Volkov skates up beside him, disrupting us. I've sat at the table with him on more than one occasion when Matt and Gemma invited Alexei and Kennedy over. He didn't intimidate me then but now with his pads and skates giving him extra bulk and height, I'm reminded how he treats anyone on the ice who isn't a Palmer City Wolf as his enemy. After watching Alexei pummel Justin Ward to avenge Zach, let's just say I'd never want to make this man mad.

His eyes bunch together, creating angry creases in his forehead. "You've drawn his attention," Alexei mutters, his gaze flicking to where my brother skates beside Gemma as they push Elodie around the rink.

"We're not doing anything wrong," Zach answers at a normal volume.

I love that he's an open book with his thoughts and feelings. He disarms my fortified defenses in a way no one else has. I've never trusted anyone so quickly, certainly not when it comes to handing over my heart.

"Can I steal her?" Kennedy glides up to me, linking our arms like it isn't a question.

Zach's eyes meet mine, and I mouth, *I'm fine.* He lets go of my hand, leaving me unsteady after I got used to depending on him for balance. It isn't a stretch to tell people Zach and I were holding hands because I need the support.

"Don't worry, I'll keep her in one piece." Kennedy winks at Zach before turning to Alexei. "I'll see you later, babe." Then we skate to the opposite side of the rink from them.

Alexei can't help but track Kennedy, even after dating for two years. I'm betting a Kennedy Cole and Alexei Volkov wedding isn't too far in the future. I'll score an invitation because Alexei is close with my brother, but I'd prefer to be Zach's plus-one.

"So this isn't one-sided?" Kennedy's voice snaps me out of my thoughts.

"What?" I'm stalling to sort out her motive for cornering me. Is she snooping on behalf of my brother? For Volk for my brother? For her best friend, Gemma, who's been staring oddly at Zach and me since he landed in the room next to mine a month ago?

Kennedy drops my arm and spins so she's facing me the way Zach did, except we're not holding hands. Her dark blue hair is stark against the bright white ice. It's one of the most gorgeous colors I've seen, and she pulls it off flawlessly. I'm not surprised Volkov is wrapped around her finger. She's naturally beautiful and can go toe to toe with anyone.

"Don't bullshit a bullshitter," Kennedy says, squaring her shoulders and preparing to confront me. "I lied to myself for a long time about Alexei. And when I stopped lying to myself, I still refused to admit my feelings to him."

I roll my eyes, shifting my stance to match hers. "You've got it all wrong. I have no problem admitting I like Zach to myself or to him. Or you. I like him, all right? Mystery solved."

Kennedy raises her eyebrows, obviously surprised she didn't have to beat it out of me... metaphorically speaking of course.

"When are you planning to tell your brother?"

I shrug. "Zach and I haven't talked about it."

Kennedy laughs. "So you're going the passive-aggressive route, suggesting something is going on in a public setting so you don't have to tell him directly?"

"Skating with Zach has nothing to do with my brother. Or with you."

Instead of my attitude putting her off, she skates toward me and slings an arm around my shoulders. I'm shorter than her, so she easily reaches across me. She smiles wide. "He needs someone like you."

"Someone like me?" I repeat. I've turned into someone desperate for anyone to speak a word about Zach, so I can learn more about him and hear other perspectives on his feelings for me.

"Someone with a mind of their own, who keeps him on his toes and doesn't let him take shit from anyone. Someone who has his back. He deserves more than he thinks he does. I think you'll help him see that."

Her approval means everything. Of everyone in Zach's life in Palmer City, she knows him best. They lived together for more than a year.

"He doesn't know how rare he is," I agree.

Kennedy drops her arm from my shoulder and holds it out wide to encompass the entire arena. "Yeah. He's a star. This fanbase is completely in love with him."

"I'm not talking about that."

She nods slowly. "I know, Finley." Kennedy does a three-sixty spin before coming in closer than before. "Have you told him *everything* about yourself?"

My eyes snap to hers, hackles rising at the knowledge that she knows something I never told her. One of her hands nervously runs through her hair. I hate that Gemma revealed my bipolar disorder, but I have to believe she did it because she needed support. And I can tell Kennedy doesn't want to bring this up. She's doing it because she loves Zach. How can I possibly blame her for that?

I tamp down my instinct to flee.

"I don't know if I could stand him looking at me differently," I whisper, voicing the fear I keep stuffing down. It roars louder the more time I spend with Zach. I'm too invested to play off a negative reaction as anything other than heartbreaking.

Kennedy's brow wrinkles. "You think he would?"

"Not on purpose. Not consciously."

It would be difficult to accept. I couldn't be around him, watching him school his features into acceptance. Because he might want me, but he can't possibly want someone whose mental state could disrupt his entire life in unpredictable ways without much warning.

"It's been a month. Would you have told Alexei?"

She bursts into unexpected laughter. "Not unless my life depended on it. But our story is different from yours, trust me. He wasn't looking at me like *that* quite yet."

Kennedy tips her head toward the other side of the rink, where Alexei and Zach stand against the boards. My stomach hits the floor when Zach's stare collides with mine. He doesn't look away, continuing to hold eye contact, communicating silently how much he cares for me.

"What did you think when Gem told you about my condition?"

She replies without a moment's hesitation. "I thought if there's anyone who could manage a difficult hand, it's the girl who made a four-inch beam her bitch with a Worlds silver medal on the line."

A breathy laugh gushes out of me. "I didn't know I'm in the company of a *fan*."

She holds up her thumb and finger close together, a little space between them. "After my mom died, I spent a lot of time at home. I went through a period watching gymnastics."

I don't know what to say. It's no secret Kennedy's mom passed away tragically, but I have no magic words other than the inadequate *I'm sorry*.

Thankfully, she doesn't expect a response. "Consider this payback for how you helped me. I don't think Zach could learn anything about you that would change his mind. It's not only because he's loyal and unwavering, though he truly is both. I've never seen him look at anyone the way he looks at you, and I've spent a lot of time with him these past couple of years. It's probably why Alexei is over there talking his ear off when he'd rather do anything other than talk about *feelings*."

An anvil drops on my chest. "He's warning him off?"

"Oh, no! Alexei would never do that. We're both team Zinley." I ignore the couple name she gives us when we are not, in fact, a couple. At least, I don't think we are. "Zach's like the annoying little brother he never had, and he's worried. We both are. The concussion had Alexei in a *state*, even though"—Kennedy drops her voice low, saying the remaining words with a Russian accent—"it's hockey and people get hurt."

A familiar refrain in the Harris household.

I grin. "I bet he hates when you talk in that voice."

She beams back. "Oh yeah… so naturally, I make sure to do it at least once a day. I think my fake accent is getting pretty good. He disagrees, but it doesn't stop me."

I can't remember the last time I confided in a girlfriend, not since my gymnastics days. Even then, I was always on guard because my friends were also my competition, and some of them made that abundantly clear. It made for a lonely existence.

"I really like him," I say, the words barely audible over the noise surrounding us. "It's scary how much I like him."

"Aw, Fi." Kennedy wraps her arms around me, and I give into the hug. Mark this off the bingo card of events I never imagined. She's not what I consider the warmest of people, especially compared to the sunbeam that is Gemma Harris. I also don't project the kind of openness that invites friendship. "It scared the shit out of me too. It works out when it should—not because of any stupid thing like fate, but because people step up when it's right."

Her words sooth an ache in my chest I didn't realize was there. An ache from wanting the deep, lasting love story I thought bipolar disorder made impossible. Kennedy's words whisper hope that once would've been reckless to hold onto. Now it doesn't seem far-fetched the *right* someone could care for me despite the challenges I bring.

"I'm here if you ever need to talk, Finley," Kennedy says, placing her hand on my shoulder as we pull out of the hug.

My heart soars at the offer. "Thank you, Kennedy. Seriously."

When I finally tell Zach, when *one day* becomes *now*, I'm going to need her support.

⁌◯⁍

It's hours later, and I'm in my new favorite position for watching TV—tucked into Zach's side, head on his chest, one arm splayed across his stomach. At his insistence, we're watching my favorite show about a precocious high school student who solves paranormal mysteries between romantic and familial drama. I love dissecting the story I love with him, and hearing his opinion of my favorite characters.

Everything takes on new meaning when I experience it with Zach. It's scary, this realization about how his presence enriches my life. After losing gymnastics, I didn't understand who I was anymore. It was with me through every triumph and disappointment. I could mark time based on what I'd been doing in the sport. I never thought I'd have to worry about getting so attached to another person that they could so profoundly affect the way I experience life.

I'd never known real love before.

But as I listen to Zach's steady heartbeat, I wonder if I'm about to find out.

22

Zach

WHEN I WAS A kid, I didn't understand how people who liked each other spent time together without constantly wanting to kiss. It baffled me how they could go about their day with this person, resisting the urge. I'd had crushes, put people I didn't know on unrealistic pedestals, turned them into daydreams, and I knew nothing about relationships.

When I got older, I experienced that pull toward another person, pure lust based on physical attraction. The instinct, the *need,* to be around a person fades quickly when it's all it is. It's all I've ever known.

Until Finley Harris.

I'm insanely attracted to her *and* I never stop wanting to be around her. I'm content forgoing morning naps to hang out at the gym while she practices, mesmerized by her every movement. None of what she does should be physically possible, and yet, she makes every amazing feat look easy.

"What's the gymnastics equivalent of a goal?" I ask while she's taking a break atop the beam.

Her coach, Veronica, left five minutes ago, otherwise I wouldn't risk taking Finley's attention away from the task at hand. Veronica likes it when I'm here, says Finley is more relaxed, but she never hesitates to tell me to shut it if I become a distraction.

Finley turns, arms resting on her hips as she catches her breath. She's done this one pass of flips about fifty times—it'd be hard enough on the ground, and she's doing it four feet in the air with only four inches of wood and leather to balance on.

"I don't know. I guess a stick?"

"A what?"

"You know, *this.*" Finley takes off to the opposite end of the beam, doing a roundoff back handspring before launching herself into the air and flipping twice. Her feet hit the mat with a smack, then don't move an inch. "When we land perfectly still, not taking any steps or shuffling our feet."

She flops down on the chair beside me, the one Veronica used while she was coaching Finley earlier. Veronica peppered me with Wolves questions, wanting to know behind-the-scenes information about my teammates and our training schedule, in between directing Finley.

"How hard is it?" I ask. "To stick your landing?"

She kisses my cheek. "Probably as hard as scoring a goal or making a three-point shot or kicking a field goal. It's why we practice as much as we do. We're building muscle memory."

"Scoring a goal is much harder than any of those things. You know, for the record."

"Oh, of course it is, Calder." Finley's hand lands on my chin, angling it toward her. The breath is knocked out of me as I take in her beauty up close, admiring the light freckle on her face, the gleam in her gorgeous blue eyes, the slight divot in her cheek when she smiles. "Those other athletes ain't got nothin' on you."

"You're such a brat," I say.

Since we're in the gym, I move to pull away, but Finley places her hands on each side of my head to keep me close to her. She kisses me, and I react instantly, my hands going to her hips. I groan when my tongue meets hers, my body demanding more contact. As if she can read my mind, Finley climbs over me, her legs pinning me to the chair, bracketing my hips.

Veronica claps her hands together once, loudly. "*Okay!*"

Finley and I pull apart, lips smacking as loudly as Veronica's clap.

"That's enough of that," Veronica says, "you can straddle the floor or the beam, but not boys or girls while in my gym."

Finley launches to her feet, leaving me with an incredibly obvious tent in my basketball shorts.

"Fuck," I mutter, grabbing her discarded sweatpants from the floor to cover my lap. Finley giggles at my predicament. I narrow my eyes at her. "Laugh all you want, but I doubt this is the only evidence of what happened, Finley."

Her mouth clamps shut.

Veronica heaves a sigh. "You two should go."

"What?" There's no trace of Finley's teasing tone in the word. "I'm not done practicing."

"I can't have you getting hurt because your head isn't in it, and based on what I saw, you're focused on something else. So go deal with... it."

Finley barks out a laugh. "No coach has ever ordered me to hook up instead of practice."

"Just being practical," Veronica says, her back to us as she retreats toward the gym entrance. She has some elite gymnasts showing up to train soon. Usually, there's an overlap between Finley's practice time and the other girls, high school age or younger. "The last thing I need for you to do is injure yourself after I scored you an audience with the UPC coach."

Finley's steps halt. "Wait—what?"

Veronica still doesn't turn around, as if she hasn't dropped news Finley's spent months clamoring for. "Yep. He'll stop by sometime in late January."

"Oh my God. Wait—are you serious? He agreed? To come *here*?"

Veronica hums. "Mm-hmm."

Finley leaps into the air, her hands on her cheeks as she says *Oh my God* over and over again. It's contagious, this joy of hers. My heart is on the verge of bursting on her behalf. She eventually stops hopping around the floor and settles back on solid ground.

"Zach." Tears well in her eyes. "I never..." Emotion clogs her throat, cutting off her words. "I never thought..." She tries again but fails to vocalize the rest of the sentence.

I scoop her into my arms, lifting her off the ground. Her arms wrap around my neck, her mouth pressing against my ear. I breathe her in; she still smells faintly of fruity coconut despite her workout. "I'm so happy for you, High-flyer. You deserve this. You deserve every good thing."

"Thank you," she breathes, her voice still flooded with emotion. I assume she's thanking me for my words until she adds, "Thank you for being here. For supporting me. You have no idea how much it matters to me."

You have no idea how much you matter to me.

"I feel so lucky, so grateful," Finley goes on. "This news means so much more, sharing it with you."

And there goes my heart, pressing into the confines of my chest, damn near bursting with love for her.

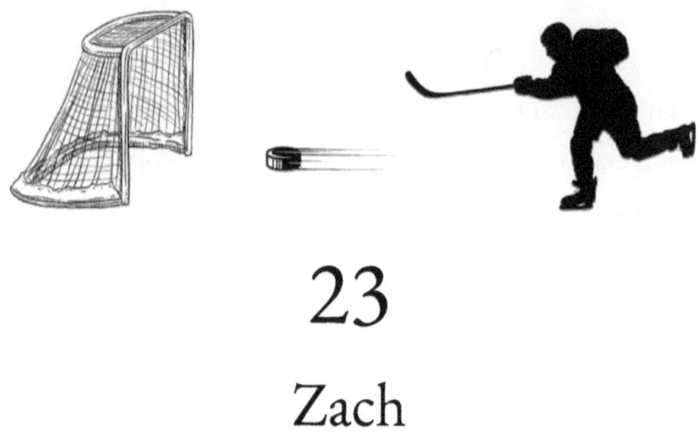

23

Zach

Volk laces my skates, each movement getting me closer to game ready.

Game days are my favorite days. I'm happy to be in the locker room today, preparing to return to the ice for the first time since Ward made me go splat. Matt drove me to the arena, because we live in the same house but also because he thinks I'm anxious. My foot tapping at breakfast had nothing to do with anxiety though; it was pure anticipation. Every nerve ending has been on fire since the moment I woke up, knowing today I'd play in a hockey game on my ice.

And it is mine. I belong on the Palmer City Wolves. I intend to remind management of it at every game for the rest of the season, all the way until I secure a deal to keep me in the place I consider home.

Volk deposits one leg on the floor before lifting the other to lace that skate. I should hate the way Volk and Matt coddle me, like I'm a helpless little kid, but I don't mind it right now. All it does is reinforce they love me like a brother.

"Don't get used to this," Volk grumbles.

It's freaky how well he reads my thoughts sometimes. I suppose living with someone helps with learning how they think. It's how I know the tick in his jaw means something's on his mind. During the dark time when Volk and Kennedy broke up for a few weeks, this dude ground his teeth so loudly, it woke me up from a nap on the plane.

"What's up with you?"

He shakes his head, keeping his focus on my laces.

"You know I'll badger it out of you. You should save yourself the headache."

Volk sighs loudly. "You're a pain in my ass."

I roll my eyes. "You love me."

"Like a puck to the face."

"If you don't want to tell me," I reply, "Kennedy will."

Volk stops what he's doing, and my foot falls to the ground with a thud. "Do *not* tell Kennedy anything. You'll ruin it."

"Ruin what?"

He sucks in a breath. "I'm proposing to her. Tomorrow."

"No shit! You are?" I shout loudly enough to draw the attention of several teammates.

Volk's glare is murderous. He didn't look this intense when I accidentally clipped his side mirror backing out of his driveway.

"Nothing to see here," I try to cover. "Volk was telling me how he's thinking of dying his hair blond. *Platinum* blond. I told him he should clear it with Kennedy since, you know, she's the one who has to look at him, and he doesn't want to piss her off because she's got a temp—"

Volk taps me lightly on the side of my head to cut off the made-up explanation quickly spiraling out of control.

"*Dude*. I just had a concussion."

"You're fine," he says, not the least bit concerned.

I'm about to have my head rocked harder than that on the ice. If I can't take a simple jab, I'm in trouble.

He picks up my skate again and resumes threading laces. "And you'll remain fine as long as you keep your mouth shut."

I mime zippering my lips. "Does anyone else know?"

"Gemma does. She's taking Kennedy to the practice arena—"

"You're proposing at the *practice arena*?"

He lowers my leg to the ground, shifting to his locker to get ready for the game. "It's significant for us... and no, I'm not telling you why."

"Congrats, Volk. This is the best news."

His jaw clenches again. "She hasn't said yes yet."

"You worried she'll say no?"

Volk stares down at his skates, wringing his hands.

I smack the side of his arm. "I barely saw her when we lived together because she wanted to be with you. She's at every game, wearing your jersey. You two are the next Matt and Gemma. Soon, you'll have a little Zach running around."

Volk barks out a laugh. "You think we'll name our hypothetical kid after you?"

"Zachary Volkov," I sing-song. If Volk needs me to be a jackass to get him out of his head, I'll do it. Gladly. I love any excuse to be a brat. "It has a nice ring, doesn't it?"

His response?

He exits the locker room, heading toward the tunnel.

"This conversation isn't over," I call playfully.

I'm excited for tonight's game, so I'm not sure why I'm lingering here. Most of my teammates are already warming up on the ice. It's not the injury holding me back—I've been hurt more times than I can count. I never don't get back up.

This is the first time since coming into the league I've missed games because of injury. And this injury reminded me of everything I could lose.

But I'll be damned if I let fear stop me.

I pull my black jersey over my head, take a deep breath, and sprint down the tunnel until my blades glide on ice. Jennings saucers a pass to me from center ice, and I take it on my stick, heading straight toward our empty net, where a handful of my teammates fire shots.

Jennings skates toward me, spraying ice in my direction. The old guys on our team like to complain we do it too much, but neither of us listens. "It's good to fucking have you back, man."

I hip-check him. "Aw, did you miss me, Princeton?"

"More like our record missed you."

My eyes roll. The team's done all right without me, currently second in the Metro division. The odds of us not making the playoffs are slim, and only people who hate our team would bet against us. Since Volk and I joined two years ago, we've made the playoffs every year—exiting round one the first year but making it to the second round last year. We're building a Stanley Cup team in Palmer City, and every year we get that much closer.

I weave across the ice, stick-handling a puck against an invisible defender. When I reach the other side, I balance the hockey puck on my stick, tossing it in the air, then catching it over and over. Out of nowhere, another stick nabs it.

"Your girl coming tonight?" Jennings asks, balancing the puck on his stick.

I knock into him to send the puck to the ice. "Can you not announce it to the entire arena?"

"Holding her hands during family skate didn't already do that?" he asks. "Cap didn't warn you off?"

"Nope," I reply. Matt didn't say a damn word after Volk told me I'd attracted his attention and not in a good way. "Finley being into me is absurd. Can't say I blame him."

Jennings secures the puck before passing it to me. "Then he didn't see her face. It's obvious she's into you."

I catch the puck and make no move to send it back to him. "It is?" I eat up every confirmation like it's the best damn dessert I've ever had.

"Yeah." He motions around the arena. "So is she here?"

"She said she would be."

"Better show out then, man," he says, telling me something I already know. He knocks into me before heading to the bench.

When I line up on the ice before the national anthem fifteen minutes later, my gaze drifts to the location of Kennedy's season tickets, about ten rows back from center ice and our bench. She's there every game, wearing Volk's jersey, screaming at the top of her lungs. The usual suspects sit beside her—Gemma on one side and Deandra Collins, our communications director, on the other.

The difference tonight? Finley Harris sits beside Gemma. Her lips quirk into a smile, and her sunshine hair flows past her shoulders. She's wearing a Palmer City Wolves winter hat and jersey. Fuck, I hope it's mine. I've never wanted to play a better game than this one—for myself but also to impress her.

Halo taps his stick against my skate. "You ready for me to make you look good?"

Volk groans beside me. Niko Halonen might be one of the best hockey players in the league, but Volk is perpetually exasperated by him. These two guys make sweet music together on the ice despite their clashing personalities. Halo's little comments spark Volk's hotheaded nature, and when that happens, opposing teams need to watch out.

"Let's compare stats in ten games," I reply. "I bet your points per game will go up playing with me."

Halo scoffs but gives me a nod of approval. He wants to win, same as me.

When the national anthem finishes, I take my place outside the circle at center ice, waiting for Halo to win the face-off. Like usual, after the ref drops the puck, he slaps it my way, and the game I've been anticipating for weeks is underway.

24

Finley

MY GAZE LOCKS ON Zach as soon as he sprints onto the ice, and that's where it stays.

He effortlessly floats across the rink with the puck, like he was made to play this game. Growing up, I resented hockey that consumed so much space in the Harris family. Watching Zach zip around the ice with incredible speed, weaving in and out of players, checking them into the boards, sacrificing his body to block shots, gives me a new appreciation for the game.

I'm also falling hard for number ten, not because he's skilled and popular or because seeing him in his element is fucking hot—though all of those are true. I like his soul, the lens through which he sees the world, how he brings out the best in me, the childlike wonder I thought I'd lost.

"Having fun?" Deandra asks from two seats down. The empty two seats between us belong to Gemma and Kennedy, who took off for the restroom as soon as the buzzer signaled the end of the first period.

I swallow hard, trying to school my expression into blandness. "Yeah, it's been years since I've caught a game."

Deandra takes a swig from a plastic bottle of diet soda. "I was surprised when Gem said you'd be here. We're six weeks into the season, and this is the first game you've been to."

After family skate, I expected an interrogation about my relationship with Zach—just not from Deandra Collins. She's been to the house for dinner a couple of times, but we don't know each other well. Not well enough for me to reveal my feelings for Zach.

And yet, she's given me the perfect opening to share what I'm too scared to tell anyone in my life besides Kennedy.

"I want to support Zach. He's had a tough time, as you know."

"You're here for Zach?" Deandra's expression is neutral, but the lack of curiosity in her tone makes me suspect this revelation doesn't come as a surprise to her.

I look toward the ice, where four people wrapped in large plastic bubbles race to win concert tickets.

"Yeah. We've become friends, living in the same place and all."

"Friends?" she repeats, arching an eyebrow.

I want to talk about my feelings for Zach all the time, the way he holds my heart in a vice. I'd love for someone to offer advice because this is all new to me. I used to categorize boys as a distraction from my goals, but Zach has improved my life from the moment he entered it. The problem is the secret I keep from him and the one we keep from the rest of the world, particularly my brother.

"He's hard not to like," I say finally.

She chuckles. "Yeah, you took a shine to him right away."

"What do you mean?"

Deandra opens her mouth to reply, but the arena bursts into cheers as the Wolves charge out of the locker room to warm up before the second period. My breath catches when Zach's gaze scans the crowd briefly before landing on me, and he grins in the self-consciously cute way of his. I give him a quick wave, and Zach's face becomes impossibly brighter.

"Well... hypothetically, if someone headed back to their room during Matt and Gem's wedding because a drunk hockey player spilled wine down the front of their dress, they might have caught quite an eyeful."

"Wait." My head snaps in her direction like whiplash. "You *saw* me and Zach that night?"

She flashes a devious grin, her lips blood red as always. "You wouldn't believe the secrets I know, Finley."

Gemma and Kennedy appear at the end of the row, carrying drinks and snacks, and Deandra and I fall silent. She winks at me, then rises to give them space to return to their seats.

The rest of the game passes in a blink. The Palmer City Wolves pull out an easy victory, defeating their opponent by two goals. Zach got an assist and made several good defensive plays—a solid showing for his first game back. More importantly to me, Zach grinned as he left the ice, happy to be playing the game he loves.

My phone buzzes soon after the game ends. I can't help the smile stretching across my face, knowing I'm his first thought.

Zach

I want to see you

"Finley, you ready?" Gemma stands in front of Deandra and Kennedy, their gazes all on me.

I jump out of my seat. "Oh yeah, sorry."

I start typing a quick response to Zach, but when Gemma tries to catch a glimpse of my phone, I slip it into my back pocket.

"Who's got you smiling like that?" Gemma says in a lilting tone. "You meet someone?"

I nearly blurt a denial, but my face already gave me away. "Maybe. It's new."

The lie turns my stomach, but she's left me no choice. It's a risk to reveal this to her because she might run to my brother, who will tell my parents, who will schedule a mandatory family therapy session with Dr. Warren.

But I'm also tired of hiding myself to make other people's lives easier.

Gemma squeals. "Oh, Finley, I'm so excited for you. Tell me *everything*."

"There's nothing to tell yet."

"Let the girl breathe!" Kennedy jumps in before Gemma can fire off questions. "She'll tell you when she's ready."

Gemma points at me. "I want to meet him."

"I'm sure you'll like him." Deandra gives me a knowing smirk I'm glad Gemma can't see. When Gemma turns toward her, I playfully run a finger across my throat and glare. "Can we go? The guys are waiting for us."

"Waiting for us?" I repeat.

Gemma claps her hands. "We're going out!"

"I think I'm going to head home," I say, pointing vaguely over my shoulder

Gemma ignores me. "We've got a babysitter until midnight, which gives us"— she glances at her watch—"at least an hour to have a drink and sing a song."

I raise an eyebrow.

"Karaoke," Kennedy clarifies, wrapping an arm around my bicep and pulling me to the aisle. In my ear, she whispers, "Briggsy's idea."

Out of view of Gemma's prying eyes, I text Zach back.

Finley

Looks like I'm coming to you

Karaoke is in full swing when we enter the bar, a terrible rendition of "I Will Survive" in progress. Zach added karaoke twice to his *Make Finley Happy* list, so I'm not surprised he suggested this bar tonight.

The boring beige color of the outside building brings to mind the phrase, *Business in the front, party in the back,* because there's nothing understated about the indoor decor of The Final Song. Shimmering streamers line the walls, refracting dim blue lights to illuminate the bar, while rainbow disco lights flash across every surface.

Kennedy's hands land on my shoulders. "Doesn't this place *scream* Zach Briggs to you?"

It's strange for Gemma's best friends to know about my relationship with Zach, but Gemma hasn't said a word. I'd chalk it up to her respecting my boundaries, but after all the matchmaking stories she's told over the years, I know better. Between focusing on her daughter and opening a new location of her bakery, she's had blinders on.

When I don't reply, Kennedy tugs me deeper into the bar until we settle in a large corner booth.

"Anyone want a shot?" Gemma avoids my gaze, knowing I can't have alcohol with my meds.

"I'm down," Kennedy says, sliding out of the booth. "I've got a DD who can carry me upstairs later."

Deandra shakes her head. "I've got a meeting in the morning."

"My dad has made you so focused," Kennedy teases before following Gemma to the bar.

"What does she mean by that?" I ask.

Deandra looks up from her phone. "Cale—Kennedy's father—has a *potential* business deal in the works, so I've been busier than usual. I can't say more than that."

"But you work for the Wolves?"

"For now," she replies, one side of her lips tilting in a coy smile.

A burst of noise pulls our attention to the bar, where a half dozen Palmer City Wolves players approach Kennedy and Gemma. Alexei hauls Kennedy off her feet, and she wraps her legs around his waist, burying her head in the crook of his neck. Gemma hands out shots to Zach, Jennings, and a couple guys I don't know before motioning in our direction. Matt's eyes go wide when they land on me.

"Uh-oh," Deandra says, though the words are devoid of any real worry. I can't see this woman cowering to anything, especially not a man. I wish I had the same impenetrable confidence.

Matt takes five long strides to stand before us. "Finley—"

"I'm being good," I cut him off and hold both hands up innocently. "No alcohol. Deandra's my witness."

Deandra blows out a breath. "Loosen the reins, Harris. She's an adult with a smart head on her shoulders. This is a good test run for you. You don't want to repress Elodie to the point of rebellion during her teenage years. Trust me."

Matt shoves his hands in his pockets. "I was *going* to say I'm glad you could make the game, Finley."

"You played well," I manage to reply despite my shock. No lecture? No order to go home? Who *is* this guy? Because he's not the brother I know. "It's okay I'm here?"

"Of course."

Matt narrows his eyes, as if he didn't expect the question, and I'm not sure why he wouldn't. He knows the rules imposed by our parents, all in the name of keeping me safe. He also agreed to let me live in his house and support my efforts to rebuild my life. Maybe seeing me doing well on my own is proving to him I can take care of myself.

"You want a soda or something?" he asks.

Zach appears behind Matt's bulky frame, placing a glass on the table. "Ice tea, yeah?"

"Yeah," I say, sliding it toward me. "Thank you."

A tap on the microphone causes a burst of feedback before Gemma's voice cuts through the air. "Matt Harris, get your cute butt up here. It's *our* song."

I expect some sappy song that encapsulates their perfect relationship, but instead, an old song about riding a train starts. It's the same one that played when they entered their wedding reception for the first time as husband and wife.

"Excuse me," Matt says with a goofy grin. "Finley, I beg you to keep this to yourself."

"You mean not tell Charlie and Ryan?" I mime locking my mouth shut. "I wouldn't dream of it."

I do one better, opening my phone camera and capturing every cringy moment of Gemma and Matt singing and doing a choreographed dance. My brothers and I will lord this over Matt until the end of time.

Zach sits in the booth beside me. "Hey, High-flyer," he says, then smacks a hand over his mouth.

Deandra smirks. "I know about you and your girlfriend, Briggsy, so you can stop trying to be covert. You're really bad at it, by the way."

I shrug. "She saw us at the hotel pool."

Zach's mouth falls open. "Like you saw *saw* us?"

"You were in the water," she replies with an eye roll. "So you can unclutch your pearls. Not that it'd faze me if you weren't. Once you've seen one, you've seen them all." Deandra scooches out of the booth. "I think I want a glass of red wine after all."

Zach lets out a breath. "She scares the shit out of me."

"I think she might be my hero," I say, laughing.

"You wear our jersey better than anyone else." A contented breath flows out of him when he finds my hand beneath the table. "I love that you were there tonight."

"I've never enjoyed a hockey game so much before."

"Glad I could keep your attention."

How he's looking at me causes me to forget my surroundings and become absorbed in those dark brown eyes.

I drop his hand, moving to run my fingers along his thigh. "I couldn't watch anything else."

Sawyer plunks himself down on the opposite side of the booth, jolting both of us back to reality. "So Zach says you've been teaching him life skills."

"Well hello to you too, Jennings," I reply. "Good game tonight."

"Thanks." He leans forward, resting his elbows on the table, and gives me a cheeky grin full of blinding white teeth. If someone asked me to find the embodiment of "prep school hot," I'd present them with Sawyer "Princeton" Jennings. "Tell me about these life skills."

I glance at Zach who flicks his wrist in Jennings's direction, granting silent permission before taking a swig of beer.

"Well, we took a budget class earlier this week, so Zach now knows people pay for water."

Jennings chokes on his beer. "I'm sorry, what? Say that again."

"Okay, hold on," Zach interjects holding up a hand. "I know people have to pay for water when it's bottled, but you know when you go to a restaurant, water is free, right? I thought it was like that at home since it's something we *need* to survive."

Jennings dissolves in laughter, hitting the table with one hand as he doubles over.

"It's not *that* funny, dude," Zach says, bolting from the booth.

"Zach!" I call, but he moves so quickly, I lose sight of him in the crowd. "Shit, I didn't think he'd get upset."

Jennings's laughter finally sputters to a stop. "He's not. Briggsy doesn't get upset."

He does, I want to protest, but I hesitate a moment too long, and he takes our conversation in another direction. Besides, I'm not sure Zach would want me to say anything.

"Listen, Finley, about the party..."

"I'm sorry I ran off. I—"

"Have a thing for my best friend?" Jennings rubs the back of his neck. "It would've been nice to know before I made an ass of myself, but I understand why you didn't tell me. Don't worry, I won't say anything. I don't want to be the one to break the news to our captain."

I let out a loud sigh. "I wish you would. I don't want to do it either."

"I think you're good for him," Jennings says. "I've never seen Briggsy like this before, and we've gone out a lot. I've seen—"

"I don't need to know," I cut him off, unsure exactly where he's going, but if it puts an image of anyone else with Zach in my mind, I don't want it. "Thank you. He's good for me too."

"Oh, shit, not this fucking song again," he mutters, running a hand over his face. I follow the direction of his stare, and my gaze lands on Zach seconds before he lets out the first line of "Let's Get It Started In

Here" by the Black Eyed Peas. "He plays this every damn day in the locker room."

On stage, Zach struts back and forth, acting out the lyrics, commanding the attention of the crowd singing with him. When he gets to the chorus, he jumps up and down, drawing a few hoots from Wolves players near the bar. He's breathing hard into the microphone when the song comes to an end. The bar descends into applause and catcalls while Zach takes a dramatic bow.

My cheeks hurt from smiling and laughing so hard. "He's unreal."

"That's your boy," Jennings says. "You knew what you were getting into."

"For this next song, I'm going to call some friends to the stage," Zach announces like this is a concert and he's the main act. He turns toward our table. "Don't be shy. I've picked a classic."

Jennings doesn't hesitate to slide out of the booth. Given the lack of resistance, this isn't the first time they've done this. "Finley Harris." He dramatically points to Zach and the karaoke stage. "You've been summoned."

I shake my head. "No one in this bar wants to hear me sing. Trust me. I'm terrible."

Zach motions toward the stage with the hand not holding the microphone. "Don't make me drag you up here."

"Your sensei is calling you to the stage, Finley. Don't let him down."

I blow out a breath, inching out of the booth. "I'm going to regret this."

Jennings locks his arm with mine; he doesn't seem to trust I won't run back to the safety of the table. "Probably, but you'll make a very special boy happy."

I shove him. "You're the worst." When we reach the stage, I say to Zach, "I can't believe you're making me do this."

He hands microphones to Jennings and me. "You're the one who agreed to learn to have fun."

I roll my eyes. "You mean you don't offer all the girls a chance to sing with you?"

"You're the only one."

"You must think I'm pretty special."

All humor falls from his features. "There's no one like you, Finley."

I have ten seconds to bask in Zach's compliment before a 90s hip-hop song, "This Is How We Do It," plays. I start slowly, but it's not long before I'm singing my heart out along with Jennings and Zach, who don't look at the lyrics on the screen.

They also showboat to the crowd, trying to one-up each other over who performs better. The cheers for this second song eclipse Zach's solo effort, but I know it's not for me. Jennings and Zach bow dramatically, then hold their hands in my direction until I do a silly curtsy.

Gemma and Kennedy continue the standing ovation as we approach.

"You would tell me if this"—Gemma twirls her hand to indicate to the three of us—"is a *Challengers* situation, right?"

Kennedy throws her head back, laughing. "Oh my God, Gem."

"What? It's a valid question." Gemma stumbles as she attempts to slide into the booth, and Matt catches her.

"All right," he says. "Time for my wife to call it a night."

Gemma playfully swats him. "I'm fine. It's these stupid shoes."

"Uh-huh," Matt placates her. "We've got to relieve the babysitter anyway. Finley, you ready?"

A boulder of disappointment settles deep in my gut. I don't want to leave Zach, but my mind goes blank when I try to think of an excuse that won't raise suspicions. Especially not after that stupid comment from Gemma.

"I'll make sure she gets home," Deandra says, winking at me when Matt turns to me.

"You want to stay?" he asks me.

It's such a simple question, but for us, whose relationship has been mired by mistrust and resentment, it's significant. I nod.

"All right. If you need anything, call me, okay?"

"I will," I agree.

Matt gathers Gemma into his arms, and she curls into him, all fight leaving her body.

I wait until they disappear out the front door before saying, "Thank you, Deandra. Seriously."

She snatches her wristlet off the table. "Don't mention it. I'm heading out to rest up for tomorrow. Y'all good to get home?"

"I will be as soon as I find someone to come with me," Jennings replies with a panty-dropping smirk. My sympathy to all the men in this bar who have to compete with him tonight.

"We'll be fine," I assure Deandra.

"Give me your phone," she says, holding out a hand. She sends herself a text message. "Now you have my number. If you need anything, call."

Zach leans into me, his head resting on my shoulder. I look around the room, but no one is watching us. Kennedy sits in Alexei's lap, kissing him. A couple of the other Wolves players stand by the bar, entertaining a large group of presumable fans.

I let myself have this.

"What Deandra said earlier..." Zach starts, his voice low, half-muffled by my shoulder. "About you being my girlfriend?"

"She won't say anything."

"I'm not worried about that." His head pops up, and his eyes lock with mine. "I want everyone to know. I *want* you to be my girlfriend. It's just... are you?"

"I don't know," I reply, my lips stretching into a teasing smile. "I've never been asked."

"Come with me." Zach straightens, tugging me out of the booth and guiding me to the exit, his hand on my lower back. I ask him where we're going, but he can't hear me over a group of guys on stage shouting "Mr. Brightside." He fumbles for the keys in his pocket, unlocks his car, then hands them to me.

"You want to leave?"

He opens the passenger door. "I want to talk to you alone."

My heartbeat pounds faster as I walk to the other side of the car and climb into the driver's seat.

Zach faces me.

I bite my lip. "Is everything okay?"

"No," Zach says, shaking his head. "I should've asked you before, but I wasn't sure what was going on between us. I was waiting for you to pull away, but you keep wanting to spend time with me. And I don't want to share you with anyone. I don't want to wonder anymore..." He takes a shallow breath. "Finley May Harris, will you be my girlfriend?"

"It's about damn time," I say, just like I did when Zach finally kissed me the first time. Now we meet in the middle, locking lips, my arms around his neck, his hands holding my waist steady, neither of us wanting to let the other go.

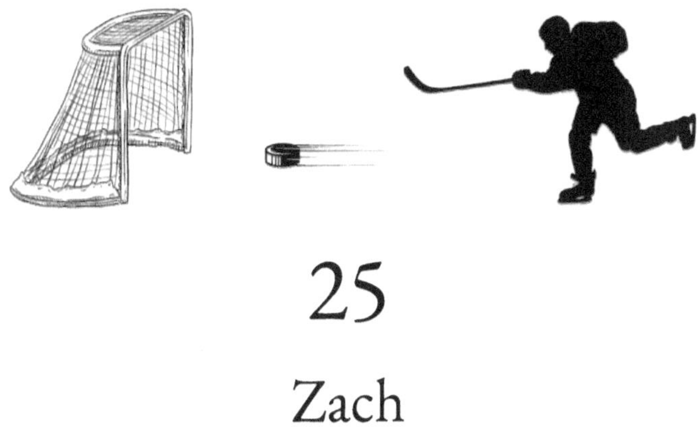

25

Zach

"This was such a good idea," Finley says, using her hand to cover a mouthful of fries.

She sits across from me on the couch in my gaming room, fast food on a tray between us. Because we went wild in the drive-thru, there's enough to feed four people.

I swallow a chicken nugget. "This was *your* idea."

She points at me, mouth still covered. "Exactly!"

I like that we're messy in the same way. Volk had a fit every time he caught me eating anything in his house, especially in my room. Kennedy was a bit more relaxed—something Volk probably hates, but he'd gladly clean up her mess every day for the rest of his life to keep her. I'd learn to clean up my act, my mess, and anything Finley desires to keep her too.

"So you, uh, want to watch a movie?" I ask, flipping on the TV.

She sits up taller, turning toward the screen as I scroll through Netflix. Finley picks up the tray with the remaining food and carries it to my desk. I'm momentarily frozen, watching her move so comfortably around my apartment, wearing black leggings and a thin green tank top that looks incredible with her bright blond hair. She tips her head back while sipping her drink, the long column of her neck on full display.

Finley catches me watching and grins. She comes to me in a flash, dropping one leg to either side of my body, straddling me. "A movie sounds good," she replies breathlessly.

My cock instantly hardens, and I freeze. Finley suggested fast food and hanging out somewhere relaxing. I brought her to my apartment because the Harris house is full of people we're hiding our relationship from. I don't want her to think I set up this entire evening to get in her pants, that sex with her is my end goal.

She sits back on her heels, her weight resting on my thighs. "I'm sorry," she says, tucking strands of hair behind one ear. "I thought it was code."

"No... I, um... I didn't expect—" I sigh, thrusting a hand through my hair. Finley's arms cross over her chest, and my stomach sinks. Can I—for once—say the right words? "Do you want it to be code?"

Finley abruptly stands, her hands still covering her chest. "I'm an idiot. I assumed—"

"I'm not going to talk in code with you," I cut in, standing and taking her hands in mine. "It's not me."

Her gaze bounces to our entwined hands, then back to my face. "I like that about you, Zach." The tip of her tongue darts out to wet her lips, a brief flash of pink. She lets out a deep sigh. "I'm so out of my depth here. I've never had a... normal relationship."

"I don't know what I'm doing either," I admit. "I'm not what people expect from professional athletes. I'm kind of an idiot, sometimes in a way people laugh at, but a lot of the time, they sigh in disappointment. I don't have *experience*, because I've spent my entire life chasing a dream. And I almost always say the wrong thing."

Finley's hands land on my shoulders and push me gently back on the couch. "I like what you say."

She drops back into my lap. I inhale sharply at the contact.

"Yeah? Then I hope you like this." I mold my hands to her hips, kneading the skin with my fingertips. "I want you so badly, I look forward to waking up at the crack of dawn to see your smile. So badly, I'm desperate to be around you. So badly, I'm painfully hard and barely holding it together."

"You are the highlight of my day," she whispers before placing her lips on mine.

There's no hesitation in this kiss. It's the kind of kiss that communicates we both know exactly where this is going. I follow her cues, my lips gliding between Finley's at her quickened pace, tasting her cherry soda. I grip her biceps and guide her off me and onto her back. The vision of her underneath me—hair spread across my blue couch, lips pink and swollen—undoes me. It wrecks me because nothing else will ever compare to the sight.

I lower myself, covering her body with mine, melting into her. My lips worship her neck, sucking softly every place I touch as I move to her collarbone, her chest, until I reach her stomach, lifting her tank top to give me access to her skin. My lips land above her navel, pressing a kiss there before lifting her tank top above her head.

Her hands are on each side of my head, gently tugging my hair toward her. "Not there."

"What's wrong?"

"Oh *come on*, it's not like you can't tell."

I rise off her, thinking I did what I always do and messed up. But her legs dart up to wrap around my waist and keep me in place. I guess there's relief in that, but my mind whirs with possibilities about what's bothering her.

"It's not that dark in here. I know you can see the lines on my stomach. My weight fluctuated a lot when I was younger, and it left me with a permanent gift."

My eyebrows draw together. "I promise I didn't notice. I'm still pinching myself you're here with me."

Finley's breath stutters. My hands land on hers still gripping my head, gently guiding them away. My head ducks to study her stomach. Faint white lines pucker the skin around her navel. *This* is why she's self-conscious? A couple of scars?

I don't need to understand the reason, only that she thought I'd be put off by it.

"Okay, I want to make something clear." My lips drop to her abdomen again, planting featherlight kisses along the lines bothering her. "You are the most gorgeous woman I've ever laid eyes on." I kiss her skin again, lips lingering for a beat. "Every part of you is beautiful. Your bright blue eyes." Kiss. "Your soft mouth." Kiss. "Your legs." My fingers trace her thighs, and she shudders, eyes closing, staggered breath escaping her lips. "I love your strength, it's so fucking sexy."

"You never say the right words?" Her voice is strangled as I kiss my way down her body, savoring this moment I never thought I'd have. "You might need to…" She moans when I take a nipple in my mouth, kissing it the way I did her lips, nice and slow and teasing. "Reassess… that."

I move down her body, my tongue tracing a line over one of the marks on her skin. "I especially love this part of you right here, because I'm seeing *you*. And all I want to do is keep looking. To see more."

She sucks in a breath, her hand reaching for mine, telling me everything she's not saying.

"There's something you should know," she says suddenly.

I look at her face, but she's not making eye contact.

"I don't want you to think it's your fault…"

Her sentence hangs in the air, making me sweat.

"If I don't finish. It's hard for me because of my medication. I don't want you to think it's you."

Her medication? She's never mentioned it before but she's saying it in an offhand way suggesting she trusts me.

"You don't need to worry about it," I say hurriedly.

Finley nervously bites her lip.

I want her to know I'm always here for her. "Do you… want to tell me more? About your medication."

"Not today." She reaches for me, and I take her hands in mine. "I don't want to stop."

"Okay. I'm here whenever you do want to talk."

"I know."

My hand traces her cheek. "I'm not coming unless you are, Finley. And for the record, if I don't, it's okay. We can watch a movie, and this night will be everything I want. Because I'm with you." I kneel in front of her. "Tell me what you need."

Her eyes flutter shut. "Zach, I don't want to waste your time."

"As if a night between your legs isn't the best way to spend my time."

Her eyes open to meet mine, and my stomach explodes with feelings.

"Fuck," she groans, dragging her arm over her forehead. "Why do you have to be so—"

"Annoyingly persistent?"

"Fucking hot."

Her admission stuns me. Finley Harris thinks of me the way I do her. I'm not sure how many times I'll need confirmation of it. I manage to whisper, "Yeah?"

Her head bobs. "I can't remember the last time I was this turned-on."

I roll her leggings down until she's left only in black lace. I trace my fingers up the inside of her thigh until I reach the lingerie, ease it down her legs, and discard it on the floor. Finley opens her legs wide, displaying impressive flexibility.

"I am not fucking worthy," I mutter.

She watches me study her, curious and hungry. The white noise in my mind makes it difficult to process anything, and I focus solely on Finley, gleaming and gorgeous before me. Her chest heaves the closer I move to her center. I need to taste her, to watch her come apart, to hear her moan my name.

"I don't know what I've done to deserve you, but I'm not wasting a single moment you give me. I'm taking my time, High-flyer."

My tongue presses her clit, working back and forth as my fingers slide in and out of her until Finley's sighs become pants. My mouth slides down, my tongue replacing my fingers. I groan, overwhelmed by her sweet taste, her strong tug of my hair, the sound of her panting breath.

My finger circles at the apex of her thighs, the place she told me she needed me most the first time we fooled around. Finley writhes above me, her hands gripping my hair, moaning *hard*. My cock throbs in time to her moans, desperate for release.

I'm cataloging everything I learn about Finley Harris in service to my most important priority—making her happy.

"Fuck, Finley." I sigh against her skin.

Her hands drift to my cheeks. "I'm ready for you."

"Not yet, High-flyer, okay?"

She nods, and my fingers resume working her, alternating pressure and direction, never letting her adjust. Her mouth pops open, eyes clamp shut, hands dig into the cushion.

This image of her sears into my brain, and I know it's a memory I'll return to when I'm by myself. I'm spellbound, out of my mind, acting on pure instinct, unable to form a coherent thought.

"I'm taking too long," Finley sighs in frustration.

Those words draw me back. "No, you're not."

"Zach," Finley tries to interrupt, but I refuse to entertain the idea that she's not perfect, that she's not everything I want.

"Finley, listen."

I rise and climb over her, my knees and an elbow bearing my weight. My fingers slowly trace back and forth along her cheek. Her vulnerable gaze guts me. I hate whoever put these shitty ideas in her head and those who did nothing to dispel them.

"I'm so fucking into this. You have no idea. So please, if it's all right with you, I'd like to get back to my new favorite place."

Finley catches me off guard, pushing up from the couch to capture my mouth. My arms loop around her neck, supporting it as I roll to my side, pulling her with me. We don't break the connection, lips sliding, all while Finley squirms closer. The fruity coconut scent of her shampoo consumes my senses. It's the backdrop to so many of my favorite moments—the first night we met, car rides to the gym, movie marathons on the couch, the first time Finley let me into her bed.

My hand dips between her legs, greedily moving in and out of her, desperate to make her come apart.

Finley sighs against my lips, a strained exasperated sound. "Zach."

Her lips trail down my chin, my neck, igniting me with her slow descent. Her hips roll into mine in languid movements, testing my stamina to the point of pain.

I won't last. I won't last. I won't—

"Finley," I murmur, but she's too focused on her task to register her name.

She reaches for the hem of my shirt, pulling it up my body. My hands cover hers, finally grabbing her attention. Her wide eyes stare at me expectantly. I ease her onto her back, to our original positions. She deserves someone to take care of her. To spend as much time as she needs to finish.

"If you need a toy, tell me, all right?"

I ease my shirt off, sending it to the ground as Finley bites her lip and watches me undress. My belt goes next, the clank of metal echoing in the room as I undo it. I slide my jeans down my legs until I'm left in heavily tented boxer briefs.

"I promise, all I want is for you to feel good."

Her gaze roams my chest and abdomen, before lingering on my crotch. Her eyes drop to my thighs before snapping back to my face. No tinge of embarrassment shows on her features, only a gleam in her eye and a teasing smile on her lips.

"I want to come on your tongue, Zach," Finley says, and fuck if that doesn't do it for me. I want to feel her come against my mouth too. Her handing her trust to me turns me on more. Then my words finally register with her. "Wait—you have toys?"

I shrug, flashing a cheeky smile. "It seemed like you enjoy them." I didn't want to be unprepared if the moment ever presented itself. "At least it's something I heard once. Or *twice*."

"Oh, so you're an authority on what I want—"

Her words cut off when my mouth lands on her pussy. This time, my tongue takes her without hesitation, licking through her center, pressing hard against her clit. I keep it there, rocking the sensitive nerves, while my fingers ease inside her, moving slowly until I find the spot that has Finley's hips bucking off the couch. What I lack in experience, I make up for in attention, memorizing the way Finley reacts to each movement.

"*Ohmygod*," Finley cries. Her hands land in my hair, her thighs squeezing my head, trying to keep me in place, as if I'd go anywhere.

"Zach. Zach. Zach," Finley whimpers, her words breathier with each pant.

She's barely holding on, sweat collecting on her skin, legs quaking on my shoulders. I love seeing her wrung out. And I can't wait for her tense body to collapse. Because of *me*.

My tongue swirls around her clit once more before I suck it into my mouth, my fingers teasing the spot she likes. I secure her hips with my free hand as they try to buck off the couch.

"*Zach*," she moans. "Oh God, oh God... I'm—"

Finley's hips thrust against my mouth once, twice, and then she comes undone. Her moans ratchet higher as she rides out her orgasm, and I stay with her the entire time, wringing out every last drop of pleasure. Once her moans quiet to satisfied sighs, I pull back on my heels.

She slings an arm over her eyes, taking in steadying breaths, her heart rate beginning to normalize. Her hair's an absolute mess from thrashing against the couch.

I'm so unworthy of her, but I can't think of anyone who would be. At least I can guarantee *I'll* treat her the way I know she deserves.

My hand instinctively falls to my dick, rubbing over my boxer briefs, needing friction to relieve the ache. I've never been this turned-on. I'm surprised I didn't unload while face-first in her pussy. Finley might've taken that as a compliment, but if I finish while she lays motionless, I doubt she'll ever want to see me again. I ease onto my feet, ready to take care of myself in another room before I combust and send her running for the door.

"Where are you going?" Finley bolts up, resting on her elbows.

She's so beautiful with her hair askance, cheeks flushed pink, pupils wide. I suck in a breath, knowing I need to say something, but my mind goes blank as I stare at her. Finley's entire body is on display for me, pert breasts, muscular thighs, toned stomach, bare pussy. My balls tighten painfully, I'm unable to keep my eyes off her, even though it's undoing me.

"Zach?" Finley whispers.

When I look back at her, she's got her arms crossed over her chest like she's self-conscious. She thinks I'm trying to sneak away from her.

"Sorry, I'm out of my depth here." I suck in a breath. "You're so fucking perfect, and I want you so badly. But I don't want to rush you. I need to be somewhere you're not so I don't *lose* it in here."

The worried lines on her face melt away, leaving behind the grin I adore. "You're so cute when you ramble."

I scoff. "I'm not. I'm—"

"And you're fucking hot on your knees." Finley pats the space on the couch beside her. "Come here."

My anxiety dissolves instantly when she wets her lips. She wastes no time, swinging one leg over my lap to straddle me once I'm seated. I hiss when her hot center meets my crotch, and she swivels her hips back and forth.

"You're such a good listener," she murmurs.

"Finley." My tone is all warning. I'm about one second from ruining this moment if she doesn't stop writhing on top of me.

"You have condoms, right?" She smirks, fingers toying with the hair at the nape of my neck. "Maybe in the same place as your sex toys?"

"Jeans," I croak.

Finley leaps off my lap and bends over in front of me to snag my jeans off the ground, giving me a view of her spectacularly sculpted ass, a preview of what it'd look like to take her from behind. *Fucking unbelievable.*

"You think so?"

Shit, I must've said it out loud.

She holds out a condom, her smirk still firmly in place. At least she's amused by the way I'm embarrassingly gone for her. "Put that on, please."

I follow her instructions. "Finley, I'm not going to last long."

She twirls the remaining condoms folded together like an accordion. "Good thing we have a lot of these then."

Her knees are back on either side of me. She gazes at my cock, still hovering above me. She bites her lip, a nervous tick, shocking given how in-control she's been about our sexual relationship from the start.

She finally whispers, "I haven't done this in a long time."

The vulnerability in her voice pinches my heart. It sounds like a warning, like she's saying this to head off any concern I might have. For her to think she could disappoint me is laughable. I treasure every single moment with her.

"Do you want to stop?"

"*No.* Definitely not." She lets out a self-conscious chuckle. "I just, um, thought you should know."

"You're in control here, Finley. I can promise you, I will like whatever you do. Don't worry about it, all right?"

"How do you know?"

I push her golden hair behind her shoulders. "Because I'm in love with you."

The words have been rattling around in my mind for weeks. The first time I thought them while watching her do a complicated flip off the balance beam, I tried to ignore them. It was too soon. Sharing every thought in my mind has been a recipe for disaster. I often spew words before I think through the consequences of what I've said. Like right now.

"*Shit*, I shouldn't have—"

Her fingers press my mouth, stopping me from finishing the sentence. "I'm glad you said it."

She's not saying it back, but she's not running away. I heave a sigh of relief that quickly turns into a hiss when Finley grips my cock and lowers herself onto me. We both gasp as she sinks, taking all of me. The slowness with which she moves has me hanging on by a thread, but I'd never rush her. I grit my teeth, working to keep myself together until I'm fully inside her.

"You feel fucking incredible," I whisper.

She tilts her head. "I haven't even moved."

"Trust me, I've noticed," I rasp through a chuckle. A bead of sweat forms on my brow from the effort of not moving her myself. But tonight is on her terms. "You move when you want, High-flyer."

My mouth drops to her breast, sucking a nipple while Finley rocks, using my shoulders for leverage. I groan against her skin, utterly gone for this woman and how much I love her.

"I knew you'd feel *this good*." Her head falls back while she continues to ride me.

I kiss the long column of her neck, sucking lightly, even though somewhere in the far reaches of my mind, I know how dangerous it would be to mark her before anyone knows about us.

Finley does nothing to stop me, only picks up her pace. "You come whenever you want," she murmurs in my ear. "Don't hold back for me."

I tip her chin so she meets my gaze. "I want you to feel good, High-flyer."

"Did you not hear me before? Because in case you weren't aware, the moaning sound means I enjoy—"

My lips silence her, and she sends our languid pace into a frenzy. Finley's hips move quicker, matching the sloppy movements of her lips. It's like the morning in her bedroom all over again, when she said she needed me to keep kissing her. I need it too, desperate to get as close to her as possible. We're fused, her breasts to my chest, my tongue in her mouth, her pussy around my dick, and it's not enough.

No amount of Finley Harris will ever be enough.

"Zach," Finley gasps in surprise. "I might come again."

My hands land on her lower back, pulling her toward me with each thrust of her hips, trying to get her there. Her body shakes in mine. She needs this desperately, and I want to give it to her. I fucking need her to fall apart on my cock.

"Right there," she moans. "Don't move."

I stop, letting her use me the way she needs. She's all choppy movements, grinding against me while I concentrate with a force I usually reserve only for hockey. Her mouth finds mine again, sucking my bottom lip before she rakes her teeth against it. I don't know if I can hold on any longer...

"Oh God." Finley's orgasm slams into her, and she cries out, her moans crescendoing in a call of my name.

Finley keeps moving as she comes down from her high. My hands grip her hips harder, moving them faster, the tingle at the base of my spine building. Fuck, she's so beautiful giving herself over to me like this. It doesn't take long for my body to combust, my nerves catching fire, vision going black at the edges. I collapse backward on the couch, Finley falling with me. She rests her head on my chest, where my heart beats at a speed likely to concern a cardiologist.

"Are you okay?" Finley murmurs. "Your heart is pounding a million miles a minute."

"Is it?" I quip. "Haven't noticed."

It might be my shortest response ever to a question. Finley fucked the words out of me.

Her head settles against me. We lay like this for a long time—Finley listening to my heartbeat, my cock inside her, basking in the aftershocks of her orgasm. The world goes silent around us. It's rare for me to be still unless I'm sleeping, but I'm content. I could be content like this forever, I think.

Eventually, she shifts, gracefully easing off me. "I should..." She gestures over her shoulder with one hand.

"Right, me too." I sit up.

Before she gets too far, I sink my hand into her hair, bringing her mouth to mine again. She kisses me back slowly, tongue slipping inside once before she pulls away.

"Do you have any notes?"

My question harkens back to the first time we hooked up, when Finley asked me to grade her skills. Like with most other jokes, there's truth beneath the surface. I'm not oblivious; I know she enjoyed herself, but I'm greedy and insecure. I want her confirmation.

"Oh, *you* want a grade?" She snatches my shirt off the ground and slips it over her head. It's automatic, like we've done this thousands of times already. She places her hands on her hips. "I happen to remember you finding it weird when I asked."

I shake my head. "Not weird at all, but I felt robbed of not getting to ask you. So what do you say?"

Finley settles her hands on my shoulders, shifting her weight forward to whisper beside my ear. "*More.*"

26

Finley

I CAN'T MOVE A single muscle. Not that I want to while snuggled with Zach.

The man determined to make me come last night snores lightly behind me, one arm around my waist, keeping me secured against him. He wasn't deterred by my admission about medication or the parts of myself I don't like. He didn't push for details, letting me choose when to reveal more of myself.

He said he *loves* me.

But he also doesn't know me completely, because I'm keeping a big secret from him. I didn't tell Zach I love him because it's unfair to dangle the hope of a happily ever after between us when I can't guarantee that ending.

Science doesn't know enough about bipolar disorder. It can't predict whether a depressive episode will emerge from the shadows to overtake me tomorrow, in six months, or not for ten years. Taking care of myself and following my doctor's guidance doesn't mean I'm "cured."

My disorder lasts a lifetime. It's why I need to work up the courage to tell him, even if I might lose him.

Zach shifts, wedging his face between my neck and shoulder. "You smell so good," he murmurs, his hand squeezing my ass.

"Good morning." I sigh, shoving away every worry and giving myself over to Zach.

I reach behind me, fumbling in the limited space between us until his hand guides mine exactly where I want. It's a relief to touch him after the tease of his erection against my back for the last hour.

"Finley," he groans, as I stroke him slowly. His hand snakes around me, heading toward the throbbing spot between my legs. "Are you sore?"

"In the best way possible," I say. "So please proceed."

Zach laughs, his entire chest vibrating my body. "Whatever you want, High-flyer."

His fingers easily slip inside with how much my body demands him. I want to tell him I've never been this content. He makes me feel treasured, desired, *enough*. My heart *hurts* from keeping these intense feelings for him locked away.

But the fear of potentially losing him stops my mouth from opening. I want more time to commit him to memory, in case one day, memory is all I have. Since I can't tell him what's in my heart, I decide to show him.

"Lay back." I release his dick and nudge him back with a thrust of my hips. He falls away, eager for what I offer.

He watches me with heavily-lidded eyes. I love that he doesn't rush me, especially as I'm getting comfortable with our physical intimacy. I kiss him, my tongue pushing into his mouth, tangling with his. His hand lands on my waist, the other winding around my neck, clutching like he's afraid I might slip away.

When I pull back, I lock eyes with him. "Let me take care of you, Calder. Like you did for me."

A sleepy smile plays on his lips. "You haven't called me Calder in a while."

"This setting feels appropriate."

Zach's hands land behind his head, arms jutting to the side. I'm going to make this the best show of his life.

"I'm more excited about this—about you—than any trophy."

I roll my eyes. "Come on. That's like one of the important ones."

I wait for him to laugh, to joke, but he only stares, making sure I don't miss the enormous meaning behind his two simple words. "It is."

I'm so fucking in love with you.

I swallow the words. I want to say them, but I can't do it today. I want a perfect day and night together, memories I can hold onto in case we don't work out.

Because Zach loves watching my gymnastics, I choose to dazzle him, positioning my hands on each side of his body and lifting into a handstand. I rearrange my hands until I've turned one hundred eighty degrees, then lower myself back down to sit on his stomach.

"Holy shit," Zach whistles.

Warmth simmers low in my belly at the compliment, that being myself impresses him.

He places his palms on my ass, fingers digging into my hips. I'm not a connoisseur of penises, but Zach's dick is the best-looking one I've ever seen. It's also the only one to make me come harder than a freight train, though I suspect it isn't entirely attributable to his anatomy. It's also his brown eyes gazing at me like I'm the most interesting sight he's seen. His beaming smile after I land an impressive element at practice.

I've never had this kind of unwavering support. I suck in a breath, trying to process emotions threatening to consume me.

I don't want to lose him.

Tears prick my eyes, but I bite my lip, refusing to let on about my internal conflict. This morning is about *him*.

I turn my head after I've pulled myself together, glancing over my shoulder at the dumbstruck expression on his face.

"You're incredible," he whispers.

I ignore the tightness in my chest, the heat overtaking my body. Instead, I focus on action, dropping my mouth to the tip of his cock, steadying it at the base with my hand, and taking him into my mouth with a torturingly slow descent. With my lips tight around him, I head back up, just as slowly, and swirl my tongue around the head.

"Fuck, baby," he groans in an animalistic tone I've never heard from him.

I pump him once with my hand, gliding easily over him. It's hard to resist the heady sense of power that comes with having him in my mouth and at my mercy. I'm also impatient, snatching a condom from the box we conveniently left beside us. I slip it on before I bring him to my entrance and slam down. Zach hisses a strained *fuck*.

I steady myself on his muscular thighs as I grind against him.

"Finley, you look so fucking hot riding me."

I swivel my hips slowly, basking in his praise.

Zach's grip tightens, and he lets out a strained sigh. "High-flyer, I want you to come with me, all right?"

At my hesitation, he lifts himself to a sitting position.

I gasp at the sudden movement. "What are you doing?"

Zach rests his head on my shoulder and whispers, "Helping." His arm wraps around my body, fingers landing at the spot that throbs for him. "Please don't stop moving."

My hips propel faster, spurred on by the zap of electricity between my thighs.

"That's it." He kisses my neck, stoking the ever-growing blaze inside me. My hips buck against him harder, needing friction to relieve this painful ache consuming my every thought.

"I need more," I say, and Zach's fingers rub my clit slower, applying more pressure.

"Finley..." Zach grits like he's in pain, holding on for me.

"Zach—" My body goes off like a firework, bright lights flashing behind my eyes and heat zipping through my body as my tense muscles go limp with exhaustion.

I'm moving because of Zach, his hands guiding my hips back and forth.

He lifts me an inch off of him, like I weigh nothing before slamming me back down, bouncing me on his dick until his body goes rigid. I push through my exhaustion, taking over, riding him through his orgasm until he collapses back on the couch.

I ease off him, dispose of the condom, snag his shirt off the ground, and toss it over my head. His head tilts, a slight frown forms, and suddenly, I worry we're not on the same page. He said he loves me, but it's not an invitation to shove myself into every facet of his life.

"Do you mind that I keep wearing this?"

"I love it."

A grin stretches across my face. "Great, because I also prefer you without a shirt."

"I'm thinking I don't want this to end."

"It doesn't have to."

"Don't you need to work out?"

"Later," I tell him. I gesture over my shoulder toward the door. "Want some pizza?"

Zach laughs. "Assume the answer to that question is always yes."

I rush toward him, pressing a quick kiss to his mouth. "Be right back."

There's nowhere in the world I'd rather be than half-naked in Zach Briggs's fairy-light–lit game room eating leftover pizza with him.

I return home later that night without Zach. It doesn't matter that I'm a twenty-one-year-old woman and Gemma and Matt aren't my parents, there's still a high probability I'm walking into an interrogation. I need to do it alone.

I take a deep inhale before slotting my key into the lock. The security system welcomes me with a beep. The smell of Gemma's delicious chocolate chip cookies smacks me in the face, and my stomach rumbles.

"We're in here!" Gemma's sunshine voice sounds from the kitchen.

I slip out of my sneakers and drop my backpack—secretly filled with gymnastics clothes beneath a load of heavy school books—by the staircase banister. Gemma stands in her domain, between double ovens and a subzero fridge, plating cookies. She wears an apron Matt bought her for Christmas a couple of years ago that reads, *My Husband's the Only One who gets to Kiss this Chef.*

My brother sits on a stool at the counter beside Elodie's high chair. He beams at the future baby model while she makes an absolute mess of her dinner, spaghetti sauce stuck to her face and strands of pasta in her hair. Gemma sends an air kiss over her shoulder in their direction.

I've walked into a damn Norman Rockwell painting. The two of them shine so bright, it's exhausting.

"Hey Finley," Gemma chirps, holding the plate of chocolate chip cookies toward me. She doesn't step my way, which requires me to

abandon my post at the edge of the room to retrieve one. *Well played.*
"How was your night out?"

I wish she hadn't phrased it that way, highlighting how long I've been gone. I take a cookie from the plate and stuff it in my mouth to give me a moment before answering. I refuse to look at my brother while searching for words so boring, no one will want to ask more. "It was good. Fun."

Gem smirks. "You know you're going to need to do better than that, right, Fi?"

"Where have you been?" Matt interjects.

I muster the strength to look at him, and yep, the smiling guy from a few minutes ago is long gone.

"The library, gym, Chipotle," I rattle off. All true.

After Zach and I ate leftover pizza and had sex again, we watched a movie about a guy who got hit by a car, loses his memory, and mistakes a stranger for his girlfriend. The beginning of every great love story. Around noon, we finally roused ourselves for a workout at his apartment complex gym before I left to study and do a couple of hours of gymnastics. After, I grabbed Chipotle, and we ate in the car while overlooking the city, had sex again, then parted ways.

I've always liked sex—at least I did before my diagnosis—but I've never before needed someone so desperately inside me, again and again. No amount of closeness relieves my craving for Zach Briggs.

"And where did you sleep last night?" Matt presses.

"At a friend's." I casually take another bite of cookie. Nothing to see here. "How was—"

He cuts me off. "With Sawyer Jennings?"

"What? No."

"Then who were you with?"

"None of your business."

Matt's jaw clenches. "If you're screwing around with my teammates, it is my business, Finley. Do I need to remind you what happened the last time you did that?"

"No," I reply, crossing my arms over my chest. "Your teammate preying on me when I was barely legal isn't something I'll forget."

Matt flinches as expected. It's the line I try not to throw in his face because I don't like stoking his guilt over what happened with Garrett. But I have something precious to protect, and all bets are off.

"All right," Gemma says. "Let's not argue in front of Elodie."

"I'm sorry," I tell Gemma, because other than marrying my overprotective brother, none of this is her fault. "I need to do some homework."

"We're not done talking about this," Matt calls to my retreating form.

But my footsteps don't hesitate.

27

Zach

THE TRADITION OF CHRISTMAS Eve at the Callahan's continues this year, bigger than ever.

I haven't spent Christmas with my family since entering the league three years ago, which makes it hard to get into the holiday spirit. The Wolves always play the day after Christmas, so I don't have enough time to fly to Manitoba, and my family isn't able to come to North Carolina. My mom's a librarian with holidays off, but my dad's construction job schedule causes issues. Melanie and Jeff both make their own working hours, but they lose money any time they choose not to work.

It's not only the atmosphere heading into the party that gets me into the holiday mood—decorations covering every inch of the house, a display of Santa and his reindeer on the roof, light-wrapped trees in the front yard, Christmas scents wafting from the house as I approach—but it's also my teammates—my family—waiting inside.

And the woman I've fallen helplessly in love with, whose name flashes on my phone screen as I reach the front door.

Finley

Are you almost here?

Me

Do you have a tracking device on me or something?

I open the front door to the enormous house packed with people. I maneuver my way through the foyer to the kitchen, miraculously not bumping into anyone while scanning the rooms for Finley.

Finley

What are you talking about?

I spot her standing beside the fireplace, her hair glowing in the dim firelight, curls falling over her bare shoulders, splashing onto the top of her dress. The dress hugs her body until it flares out from her waist, the front shorter than the back, showcasing her sculpted thighs. Black boots reach above her knees, tied strings hanging in the back. I swallow hard, managing to make my fingers type a reply to her.

Me

Look to your left.

Finley's scrunched expression smooths when her gaze lands on me from across the room. For a singular moment, it's the two of us—no music, no chatter, no one to distract us—then Finley's head jerks to the right to Kennedy, who whispers something to her and smirks.

Finley

Apparently, we're being too obvious

I love Kennedy for watching our backs, but I also hate that this means I'll likely spend the entire party away from the person I most want to be with.

Me

Any chance I can see you later?

I'm interrupted by a panicked Connie Callahan, our party host, rushing in my direction. "Oh, thank God you're here."

The words don't make sense, but after glancing behind me, there's no one else who she could be speaking to.

"Oh, you're too cute, Briggsy." She rests a hand on my shoulder, like I've seen her do with her kids too many times to count. "I'm talking to you. I need a favor."

"Okay?" I say with a shrug. If I can't spend the night beside the woman I love, I might as well make myself useful. I follow her upstairs to her bedroom.

"Santa bailed on us," Connie says as soon as the door shuts. "But I told everyone he would be here, so if he's not, the kids will think he hates them."

I know what's coming before she says it, but nothing prepares me for the costume she holds up. "Zach, we need a replacement Santa Claus."

I blink. "You want *me* to be Santa?"

I will never live this down with my teammates and friends, not to mention the woman I'm perpetually trying to impress.

"I will *so* owe you."

Can't you ask anyone else? The words linger on the tip of my tongue, but I don't say them because no one else would agree. Connie came to me because I'd never say no, especially not to her kids, whose hockey team I help coach whenever I can. I love her kids and hate the idea of them being disappointed. Imagine the trauma of thinking Santa stood you up.

"Fine," I reply on the exhale of a sigh.

"You're a saint!" Connie thrusts the costume into my arms. "It won't take long at all. A half hour tops. Take some pictures. Hand out presents." She points to the restroom. "I'll wait out here while you change."

Ten minutes later, I walk back into the room, swimming in a costume made for someone bigger than me. Connie stuffs me with pillows to create a belly, securing them to my body with string from the kid's craft table.

I laugh at my reflection in the mirror. "Mason's going to know it's me."

Connie hands me a red velvet bag of presents. "Of course he is, which is why I've bribed him to play along. One hundred dollars gets you a lot of cooperation."

One hundred dollars. Mason Callahan lives a different childhood than mine. My parents didn't have money to throw around, not when they had two kids to send through the expensive sport of hockey. Seeing them bust their asses instilled the work ethic in me that I needed to land my dream. It took grit and sacrifice, and a heavy dose of delusion, to make it to the NHL.

In some ways, the Mason Callahans of the world who have every advantage, are the ones at a disadvantage. They never have to scrap for a single thing in their lives.

"Ready?" Connie asks. She pokes her head out of the bedroom, making sure the coast is clear before holding the door open wide for me. "Go out the front door and come in from the garage. You know the combination still?"

I give her a thumbs-up, then waddle down the steps and out of the house. The combination lets me into a garage full of luxury cars, like the ones my teammates drive to the arena. I'm still driving the same used car I purchased during my rookie season when I was in a pinch, opting to splurge my signing bonus on my family instead. My success belongs to them as much as it does to me.

"Ho! Ho! Ho!" I call in a gruff tone that sounds nothing like me, if I do say so myself.

"Kids!" Connie shouts in fake surprise. "It's Santa!"

Her announcement brings on an explosion of sound as kids sprint toward me, screaming. Connie quickly organizes the chaos, finding a place for me to settle near the Christmas tree. Cookies and milk sit beside my seat, the only incentive I needed to take this gig. She should've led with it.

I scour the room until I find Finley leaning against the kitchen island, one hand over her mouth to smother a laugh, the other gripping a cellphone pointed in my direction.

Yep, never living this down.

After taking photos, Connie opens the floor for questions from the kids, like this is a postgame presser. I answer questions about the North Pole, explain why my reindeer aren't with me, and why I won't lose weight (yes, seriously).

I heave a sigh of relief when Connie coordinates my exit through the garage, to the front of the house, and back upstairs. I head to the guest restroom, not comfortable going into Connie and Rich's bedroom alone.

A soft wrap of knuckles sounds a few minutes later while I'm easing off the costume and unstrapping pillows from my body. "Who is it?"

"It's me."

"Finley?"

I unlatch and crack the door. Finley pushes it open, hands landing on my shoulder to guide me further into the room. She kicks the door shut, waiting for the slam before lunging at me. She moans when her tongue connects with mine, and her hips rock into me.

"I've needed to do that since you walked in."

She kisses me again, hands skimming my torso.

"We can't do this here." But my hands are on her ass, pulling her closer.

She murmurs, "I know." She keeps kissing me as we walk backward until we settle on the lip of the bathtub. Finley pulls her dress up slowly flashing me red lace before descending to my lap.

My hands are in her hair, tracing down her arms, before settling on her hips. "You look so fucking gorgeous, High-flyer."

The door to the restroom swings open. Finley flinches in my lap, and we totter into the bathtub, my hands bracing on the wall to balance us.

"What in the *fuck* is going on here?" Matt stands in the doorway, slack-jawed, staring at his sister straddling me.

I'm frozen, watching the usually amiable face of my captain morph from shock to disgust. His nostrils flare, his hands tightening into fists. With each passing second, I helplessly register a new sign of rage.

Finley doesn't move either. From the way her gorgeous eyes narrow into slits, I don't think it's for the same reasons as me.

"Do you *mind*?" she sneers.

Matt scoffs. "So that's how you're going to play this?"

Fuck. Finley and I hid our relationship from him to avoid this reaction. Some part of me thought underneath his surprise and apprehension, there'd be relief in knowing he trusted his sister's partner to have her best interest in mind.

I never considered my blissful naivety a bad trait until this moment.

"It's none of your business who I date," Finley replies, anchoring her feet on the floor and pulling me to a sitting position.

She makes no move to leave my lap, rearranging herself to be more comfortable—legs crossed over mine, knee-high boots on full display. Her red dress pools around us, but my bare chest is still on display.

Is there a worse way to reveal our relationship than half-dressed and devouring each other during a family-friendly Christmas party?

Matt motions between us with a careless flick of his hand. "Is that what you call this—dating? Is it *also* how you and Sawyer Jennings describe your relationship?"

Finley's hand finds mine, gripping tightly, something her brother doesn't miss. "No. I call *him* my boyfriend's best friend and teammate."

"B-boyfriend?" Matt sputters.

"That's right," she says, exaggerating the A in *that*.

Someone else might see the satisfied smirk on Finley's face and question her motives for being with me, but I know this conflict with Matt and the rest of her family goes much deeper. When we met two years ago, she seemed detached, at least in comparison to the woman I now know. So much about Finley's life still doesn't add up, because there's a missing piece I don't have to explain the seismic shift away from her chosen path.

"You think *he*"—Matt nods in my direction like I can't hear him—"can handle you, Finley?"

I can't remember the last time I felt so small and insignificant. A sinking sensation in my gut tells me I'm about to finally learn what she's chosen not to tell me.

"You don't need to worry about it. It's none of your business."

Matt crosses his arms over his chest. "Wrong on both accounts. You live under my roof, and I'm responsible for making sure you stay on track. *Everything* you do is my business. You have a condition that needs to be managed, Finley. You think *he* can manage it?"

You have a condition rattles around my brain. There's no way the intensity of my stare doesn't prickle Finley's skin, but her eyes remain steadfastly glued to her brother.

"*I* can manage it," she snaps.

Matt rolls his eyes so dismissively, my fist balls at my side. He shouldn't fucking treat her like this. "Yeah, because that went so well last time."

"And no one can grow and learn after a mistake? Forevermore, you'll all consider me a child who needs to be cared for."

"That's not what I'm say—"

Finley cuts him off. "Let's be honest. You don't think anyone can handle my brand of mess. I should do what Mom and Dad want, keep my stress low, live a small little life. Make everything easier on all of you and stop *burdening* you with my existence."

The impact of those words lands on Matt's face like the smack of a puck against the crossbar. He doesn't say anything for a moment. When he finally speaks, his voice is quiet. "Fi, I love you. I want what's best for you."

"I'm tired of being careful. I want to live."

Her voice cracks, shattering my heart along with it. I wrap my arm around Finley's shoulders, wanting her to know she's not alone because she'll always have me. Her turquoise eyes find their way to mine, full of apology.

Matt follows the movement, and it revives his anger. "And living involves hooking up with my teammate, who can barely take care of himself—"

Finley's head whips toward Matt, her tone matching his. "He had a concussion."

"He's not that different without one."

Well, fuck. That hurts.

I beat Finley to the punch, telling Matt, "Dude, you crossed a line."

"*I* crossed a line?" Matt thunders. "You fucked my sister, Briggs."

He's got me there.

I say quietly, "It's not like that."

A disgusted sigh escapes his lips. "Did you tell him?"

He's referring to the mysterious condition I'm apparently too much of a dumbass to understand. This might be the only point the Harris siblings agree on. What other reason could Finley have for keeping something so important from me?

"You didn't, did you?"

Finley leaps off my lap, rushing to her brother. "Matt, don't."

"You know I'm right. It's why you haven't told him. He can't handle it."

"Stop talking about him like that," Finley snaps.

I launch to my feet. "What the hell, dude? I thought we were friends."

"You *fucked* my sister," he repeats. It's the refrain that will allow him to win every argument with me for eternity... if he'll even speak to me after tonight. "You're lucky I'm not breaking your bones right now."

Gemma appears in the doorway behind Matt. "Baby, I can hear you yelling from downstairs. What's going on here?"

She closes the door, blocking the noise from the party and concealing our conversation from prying ears.

"Your husband is out of line," Finley says.

At the same time, Matt replies, "Found these two playing grab ass."

Gemma says nothing, her lack of reaction revealing she already suspected Finley and I were in a relationship.

"Is this why you insisted Briggsy stay with us after his concussion?" Matt asks.

She bites her lip, saying nothing.

The creases in Matt's forehead deepen with each passing second. He asks again, "Gem, is this why?"

"I thought..." Gemma pauses to clear her throat. "I thought they'd get along. She was lonely, babe. I know you see it. And I knew Zach would be lost without hockey. There's nothing wrong with them being friends."

Matt throws his hands into the air. "Dammit, Gemma. When are you going to cut out this meddling bullshit?"

She lets out a sharp laugh. "Well, if it isn't the pot calling the kettle black. You're the one trying to control every aspect of her life and keep her inside a bubble."

"Exactly," Finley says, nodding vigorously at Gemma's proclamation.

Seeing Matt and Gemma argue shocks me to my core. All I've witnessed is steadfast devotion to each other, but here's a crack. Some people might find it comforting to witness imperfection, but I don't like the reminder that the strongest relationships can fall apart if we're not careful.

"She's an adult," I chip in, ignoring Gemma's pleas for us to stop. This conversation has spiraled too far out of control to end now. "It's none of your business."

"I'm responsible for her," Matt repeats his earlier words. "I make sure she's taking care of herself. Something someone should do for you."

"He's smarter than people think," Finley says.

It hurts, hearing her defend me to her brother when I suspect she doesn't believe it. If she did, she would've told me about the mysterious condition that upended her entire life, which has her family so worried.

Matt lets out an ugly laugh. "He abandoned a grease fire in Volk's house. He microwaves metal. He—"

"And you've never made mistakes?"

Matt points at me. "He can barely take care of himself."

I take a step toward him but not beside Finley, because I'm no longer sure we're a team. "If I'm such an idiot, why do I know what she needs better than you do?"

"You think you know what Finley needs? You don't know the first thing about her."

"Matt, stop," Finley pleads in desperation.

"Tell him, Finley. Tell him, or I will."

Gemma utters under her breath, "Baby, it's not for you to tell. You *know* it's not."

Tears stream down Finley's face. "I hate you so much right now."

"This is for your own good." Matt rips open the door; shockingly, it doesn't tear off its hinges. "Hate me if you want, but I'm protecting you."

Gemma glances over her shoulder in the direction Matt stomped. "I'm sorry, Fi. I'll try to talk to him."

"Don't bother," she mutters, staring at the floor. Tears splash her boots.

Every instinct screams to comfort her, to do *anything* to stop her pain, but I can't unhear Matt's accusations. "Is he right? Have you not told me because you think I'm a helpless idiot?"

Finley's eyes meet mine. "What? No."

It hurts too much to stare into the watery blue, so I turn away. "Do you not trust me?"

I barely hear her voice over the music from downstairs. "How can you ask me that?"

"What don't I know about you, High-flyer?"

"I'm not... I'm not ready, all right?"

I nod once, hearing all I need to hear. She's not ready to confide in me even though she knows I love her. It's not like I didn't know Finley had a secret, something to explain everything about her life that doesn't make sense. I told her I'd wait until she was ready, and I meant it. But now, I don't know if she's ever going to be ready.

Not because *she's* not ready, but because I'm me, the guy she teaches how to be a self-sufficient adult. If enough people call your ability into question, eventually you need to consider whether they're right. Maybe Finley came to the same realization.

"I wish you felt differently." I step toward her, leaning in to drop a kiss on her cheek. My lips linger before I dig deep for strength to walk away. "Merry Christmas, Finley."

I wish I felt differently too, because this ache in my chest, it's damn near killing me.

28

Finley

THE SUN FILTERS INTO the gym four hours after I arrive on Christmas morning.

I couldn't sleep last night after the party. Not when I tried again and again to call Zach, only to have it kick over to voicemail every time. He probably shut his phone off, not wanting to deal with me. I still can't stop seeing the sad puppy dog look on his face. I wish he'd lashed out, yelled at me for not telling him what he wanted to know, then I could be angry at him for pressuring me.

Instead, I hate myself.

Once I tell him about my bipolar disorder, everything will change. He might leave me. Or worse, he'll sacrifice himself—his happiness—because he loves me. He might not see it as a sacrifice, but Zach Briggs has the entire world in the palm of his hand. He doesn't need to saddle himself with my complications. I've been selfish not to tell him, to give him the chance to walk away from my mess.

I leap from the low bar to the high, pushing off the balls of my feet and effortlessly catching it. My body propels around the high bar, once, twice, then I let go to complete two layouts before my feet land solidly on the mat.

A slow clap echoes off the gym walls. I turn, my heart in my throat, hoping it's Zach behind me. My stomach sinks to the floor when my brother's glare greets me instead. He leans against the balance beam about fifty feet from me, dressed in matching black Palmer City Wolves sweatpants and sweatshirt with absurdly white sneakers.

"I would've bet any amount of money you snuck out last night to see Briggs, but you've been keeping an even bigger secret."

I cross my arms over my chest. "How did you find me?"

"You're on my phone plan, Finley. I can track your phone. I could've tracked it since you moved in, but I trusted you to stick to the agreement."

I'm such an idiot. All this time, I'd never once thought about this possibility.

Hurt flashes across his features, but it's gone in a blink, replaced by unnerving calm. Matt waves a hand around the gym. "How long has this been going on?"

"Since I was five years old."

"You know what I mean."

I shrug. "It's the reason I came here. Well this, and to escape the house I've been trapped in for two years."

"So you used me."

"What if someone tried to take hockey away from you?" I shout.

"Hockey isn't *hurting* me." Matt matches my tone.

"You're shitting me, right? Injuries are handed out with salaries in your sport."

I shake my head, disappointed he can't put himself in my shoes. Our age difference kept us from being close as kids, but as a fellow athlete,

I expected him to have a baseline understanding of what gymnastics means to me.

"This isn't about me," he says.

"Of course it is!" I throw my arms into the air, chalk shooting out around me. "Everything in my life is about you, and Mom and Dad, and Charlie and Ryan. No one cares how my bipolar disorder affects *me*. How could you when none of you will talk to me about it? It was easier to strip my life of anything that could potentially put me at risk.

"My life isn't my own. My only option was to lie, since no one in this family gives a shit enough to ask me how I'm doing or what I want."

Matt walks toward me. "Finley, do you have any idea what it was like getting the call from Mom when they found you unresponsive in the gym? She couldn't get the words out because she was crying so hard. I thought you were *dead*."

I roll my eyes. "I was asleep."

"You were *unconscious*. That's what they call it when you won't wake up.".

"Thanks for the lesson," I reply. "Did you say everything you need to? I still have another half hour."

"Enjoy it," Matt says. "Because you're going home with Mom and Dad after the holiday. I told them what's going on, and they're very concerned about your well-being."

A scream lodges in my throat; I won't give his smug ass the satisfaction.

"Like I'd expect anything else from you. You're such a brown-nosing golden boy, running to Mommy and Daddy for approval and support, like you have our *entire* lives. I hope their approval is worth it, because after today, you no longer have a sister." I nod toward the doorway before turning on my heel to face the bars. "Don't let the door hit your treacherous ass on the way out."

Then I jump and catch the bar, immersing myself in my routine. If he says anything more, I don't hear it, using my well-honed skills to block out noise and lose myself in my gymnastics.

Zach still isn't answering my calls when I leave the gym. Of everything falling apart in my life right now, I can try to salvage my relationship with him. It's also what I need to fix most. Returning to the gym brought me purpose, but my happiness these last few months stemmed from sharing my life with Zach.

It's pouring rain when I reach his apartment. My legs ache from the rigorous workout, but still, I sprint from my car to his building, taking two steps at a time to his floor. I knock urgently on his door, five loud rasps before I hear him call, "Hold on!"

The door unlatches and swings open, revealing Zach Briggs, shirtless in gray sweatpants. *Fuck me.*

"Hi," I say, wiping rainwater from my brow. "I tried calling."

Zach shakes his hair, water droplets falling to the floor. "I was in the shower."

I raise an eyebrow. "All night?"

"My phone was off."

The stiff conversation hurts, especially when I'm hit with memories of every other time I was in this apartment—joking, laughing, swapping stories, tangling bodies together, sleeping with his arm draped over my waist, pulled snugly against him. A sharp pain settles into the center of my chest at the idea of never having another moment like that.

"Can I come in? I want... I need to talk to you."

Zach steps back, nudging the door open wider. He walks to the main room instead of the game room where we'd spent most of our time. *Message received.* Zach sits on one end of the couch, remaining shirtless. He can't be this oblivious to how seeing him half-naked affects me?

I take the opposite end of the couch, not wanting to cross any boundary he's setting. No matter how much I want his arms around me, I can't lose sight of the reason I'm here. I've hid from him for too long. He deserves the truth.

"What do you want to talk about?" Zach asks after an extended silence.

I tuck hair behind my ear. "I couldn't sleep last night, knowing I hurt you. I want to fix it."

"There's only one way you can do that." He shifts in his seat. "I was fine waiting until you were ready, but then I realized you don't trust me. I'm starting to think you never will."

I lean forward, wishing Zach was close enough for me to reassure him. "That's not the reason. I promise it's not. I've wanted to tell you, but I'm terrified. I've never had this conversation before. I wanted to be sure we were on the same page... but then I cared too much, and your opinion has the power to break me."

Zach's fingers dance across the back of the couch, but he meets my gaze. "Finley, I *love* you. That means I'm here, I have your back. I'd rather break my arm than hurt you."

The words meant to soothe remind me of everything I stand to lose if Zach Briggs leaves my life. He's the rarest of rare—kind, funny, loyal, handsome, talented. I'm one of the lucky few who find a quality man and aren't too oblivious to realize it. Zach's the brave one, putting his heart on the line without confirmation I'll handle it with care. Meanwhile, I keep mine wrapped in barbed wire to remain safe.

I don't deserve you. I think the words but don't say them because it'd be unfair. He'd try to reassure me, and this conversation would take an entirely different turn.

Instead, I say, "I'm going to tell you everything, but I need you to promise not to say anything until I finish. Is that okay?"

Zach lifts one shoulder. "Fine."

I take a deep breath, readying myself to tell the entire story to someone for the first time. "Three years ago, I was training for the Olympics. Everything was fantastic. I'd been performing my routines consistently in competitions. My skills on beam—my best event—were in high demand. The stars were aligning. I thought I'd make the Olympic team.

"But I started to feel different. Not for the first time, but it was worse than before. My parents always said I had a hard time regulating my emotions, not realizing it was a condition I couldn't control.

"I don't know what triggered it or why the change in my mood was more severe than other times in my life, maybe stress or getting older. I didn't want to get out of bed, my body felt drained—both physically and emotionally. I struggled to sleep, and sometimes I had these really scary thoughts."

I shudder as I remember the sheer terror that I might never climb out of that dark lonely hole. I run a hand down my face, surprised it comes away wet. When did I start crying?

"People could tell something was wrong," I go on, "but I didn't know how to explain it, and I wanted to pretend I was fine, so I distanced myself. Sometimes, I didn't want to do gymnastics, the sport I've loved my entire life. It took every ounce of my energy to get through the day. I didn't have anything left for anyone else."

Zach pushes to his feet, comes to me, and settles at my side. One hand lands on my knee while the fingers of his other hand brush tears off my cheeks. He doesn't say anything, giving me time to share my story like I asked.

But he doesn't need to say a damn word for me to know he would do anything to stop my pain right now. It's in the way those soft brown eyes linger on my face, the comforting squeeze of my knee.

All I can hope is this next part of the story won't change his feelings.

"The only person who didn't try to interrogate me was this guy I was seeing casually, my brother's old teammate, Garrett."

Zach's fingers tighten on my leg before relaxing again, the only sign mentioning another guy bothers him. He continues to stare as I talk, his chin propped in the palm he's resting on the couch.

"Garrett gave me pills to help with my energy problem. And they worked great for a long time. Until they didn't." I look away from him, not ready to see judgment. I'd experienced enough of it from my family... and from myself.

"What happened?" Zach's quiet voice breaks through my thoughts.

I clear my throat. "Well, I had a lot of energy. Too much energy. The pills triggered a hypomanic episode. I barely needed sleep. All I wanted to do was work out and do gymnastics. I never got tired. I had this incredible feeling of invincibility. But it didn't last, and the low I felt after..."

I can't say the words, but Zach knows them. His hand entwines with mine, a comforting presence I desperately need.

"Eventually," I continue, "my body couldn't take anymore. My coach found me collapsed on the floor one morning, unresponsive with a slow pulse. I don't remember what happened. The whole night is a blur. I'm thankful I wasn't in the middle of flipping on the beam or swinging on the bars when I lost consciousness. It could've been a lot worse."

"That's why your family is so overprotective? Because of a mistake you made?"

I shake my head. "They're protective because we found out I have bipolar 2 disorder. Since then, my family has solely focused on keeping me healthy—limiting stressors, like college and gymnastics, monitoring my sleep, my diet, my medication. My parents pay for college out of state only because I'm staying with Matt and Gemma. Matt's in charge of making sure I keep to my routine and stay healthy."

A weight eases from my chest, making it easier to breathe. He knows everything now, and he hasn't pulled away. More tears race down my face.

"This explains a lot." Silence blankets the room. Finally, he says, "Can I ask you a question?"

I force a smile. "You can ask me anything."

"How many people know?"

It's not the first question I expect, but that's Zach Briggs, a never-ending source of the unexpected.

"Not many. My family, Veronica. She needed to know so she could keep an eye on me. I didn't tell her... everything."

"Why did you decide to tell me?"

Maybe it's because he's looking at me the same way he did before, despite everything I've told him. Or maybe it's because he moved closer to me with every new piece of myself I shared. I love Zach Briggs, so intensely my chest aches, and I want him to know all of me.

"Well, there are a couple of reasons." I fiddle with the silver ring on my right hand. "You're the best person I've ever met, and I can't stand that keeping this secret was hurting you. I also can't imagine my life without you, and there's no shot at a future if I'm not honest. I've been terrified to tell you for the same reason. It changes things."

Zach tries to say "It doesn't," but I swiftly cut him off.

"It does. I'm never going to be easy to love. It's always going to be hard."

Zach shifts closer, his knee bumping and settling against mine.

"Finley, I've never fallen in love before, so I can't pretend to be an expert on it, but falling in love with you is the easiest thing I've ever done. Nothing would be harder than staying away from you."

A fresh tear falls from my eye, but Zach doesn't sweep it away this time. He holds my hands, anchoring me in this moment, keeping me connected to him.

"*Dammit*," I mutter. "It's *this*, right here, that's turned my entire life upside down. How could I not fall in love with you? Every moment I spend with you lights me up from the inside in a way nothing else ever has."

Zach grips my chin, turning it until I meet his wide eyes. "Did you say you love me?"

There's a tsunami in my stomach, waves crashing one after the other, the longer we hold eye contact. It's unsettling as much as it is thrilling to have everything out on the table between us. There's so much we still need to discuss, but more than anything, I want Zach to know my heart.

"I love you, Zach. For a while now, act—"

His hand slides from my chin to the side of my head and his lips slam into mine, unrelenting in their devouring of my mouth. I'm not sure who moves first, but it isn't long until I'm in Zach's lap, legs wrapped around his back.

His mouth retreats from mine, his tongue skimming my bottom lip as he pulls away. "I'm sorry, did you want to keep talking? I—"

"No, I want this. I want you."

And for the rest of Christmas morning and into the afternoon, I show him the depth of my love.

29

Zach

The smell of delicious baking coaxes me awake.

My hand reaches across the bed, seeking Finley, but lands on cool sheets. I bolt up, needing to put my eyes on her, to confirm last night happened and she didn't run away. My feet hit the floor at the same moment Finley nudges the bedroom door open with her ass because she's carrying a tray with two mugs and a plate full of brownies.

"You ruined the surprise," she says when her gaze lands on me. I'm beside her, reaching for the tray when she pulls it away. Some liquid from the mugs splashes with the movement. "Uh, no, I don't think so, Zach. You're going to have to get back in my good graces first."

I wrap my arms around her waist, leaning into her back and pressing my lips to the crook of her neck. "That can be arranged."

She sighs, and fuck, I can't get enough of the sound. My arms tighten around her while my lips roam her neck.

"You're going to make me drop this." She says the words through a shaky breath.

And that's all it takes for me to harden against her, dick pressing into her back. There won't ever be a moment when I won't want Finley, but with an hour until we head to Kennedy and Volk's house for Christmas dinner, we need to talk. She eases the tray onto the bed, turning until she faces me.

I slip an envelope out of a dresser drawer and hold it out to her. "Merry Christmas, High-flyer."

Her eyes go soft. "You got me a present?"

"It shouldn't be surprising. I mean, obviously, it's fine if you didn't buy me anything since we never talked about it. I won't hold it against you... at least not for long."

Finley grins, snatching the envelope out of my hands. "Of course I got you a gift, O ye of little faith. It's at the house since I didn't know I'd be spending most of the day here."

I tilt my head. "*Didn't* you?" She shoves me playfully, but I grip her hand, holding it above my heart. "Finley, you own this. You know that, right? No matter what happens between us, it won't change."

She collapses against me, enveloping me in a tight hug. "I love you, Zach. God, I want to keep saying it to you, over and over. You're going to get sick of it."

"Trust me, I don't mind."

"I love you," Finley says again, and there's a desperate quality to her voice.

She spins in my arms again, her unbelievable ass connecting with my hardness, ripping a groan from deep in my throat.

"*Someone's* happy to see me."

"Fucking always," I whisper, my chin resting on top of her head.

Finley tears open the envelope to reveal the card I painstakingly searched for. After reading no fewer than thirty cards, I ultimately landed on a winter wonderland picture on the front with a blank inside to write words no other card could sufficiently convey.

Finley clears her throat. "*Finley, I'm shit with words,*" she reads aloud. "*I always say the wrong thing or say too much. So I'm going to keep this simple. The best thing to ever happen to me was stumbling into that closet and finding you.*"

Her eyes quickly dart to mine, and the force knocks me sideways.

"*Thank you for giving me the privilege of being around you, for loving me and my wild mind. I love you more than I know how to say. I hope this is the first Christmas together of many. Yours, Zach.*"

I don't know how singers can stand hearing their intimate private words out loud, being stripped bare, hoping for acceptance. Each second that ticks by without a word is excruciating.

"*For loving you,*" she paraphrases as she turns to face me again. She cocks an eyebrow, trying to joke, but I recognize the shakiness in her voice. "A bit presumptuous writing that before I said it, don't you think?"

A finger taps my chin. "I think it's what we call *manifesting.*"

"No." Her blue eyes snag mine with such determination and sincerity, my breath catches. "You know me. You can read me, unlike anyone else."

My girl diverts her attention to the gift inside the card, away from her emotions. She looks up, her eyes shiny. "What's this? Plane tickets?"

I pull her toward me until she stands flush against me, her head tipped back to hold my gaze. "I can't think of anything I want more than to have you meet my family and friends, to walk through town holding your hand, to show you where I grew up. For my new home to meet my old one."

"Zach," she hums, eyes fluttering shut.

"It's not until after the playoffs. We can change the date if we need to. And if it's not something you're ready for, we d—"

Her eyes open, the shimmering sky blue watching me closely. "This is the best, most thoughtful gift anyone has ever given me."

"But..."

She sighs. "There's something I didn't tell you last night." I hold my breath, bracing for the blow. "Matt found out about the gymnastics, and he told my parents about it... and about *you*. He's sending me home with them tomorrow."

The idea of being separated from her feels like a jagged knife to the chest. "For how long?"

"Until next semester. I'm coming back, even if my parents don't want me to. I don't care if I need to live under an abandoned bridge."

I snort. "And people say *I'm* dramatic."

Finley's eyes narrow in suspicion. "Wait—aren't you worried about seeing my parents today after what Matt told them?"

"I won't let anyone make me feel bad for being in love with you, Finley."

She groans. "Stop being so perfect." When I laugh, she adds, "I'm serious. Because you're making it hard for me to say this next part."

My stomach hits the floor, metaphorically squashed in anticipation of her next words.

"While I'm gone, I want you to think about what I said. A relationship with me will never be easy, Zach. I'll understand if you don't want your future to include an unpredictable partner."

I shake my head violently. "Finley, I'm not going to change my mind."

Her fingers tighten on my shirt, pulling the fabric near my chest taut. "Please... think about it."

"Are you trying to get rid of me?"

"Did it *seem* like I was trying to get rid of you this morning?"

I shrug in an exaggerated way, falling back on my age-old practice of cracking jokes when I can't handle a situation. "Could've been a bang for the road."

"You're an idiot." Finley balls her hand into a fist, then rears back to jab me in the gut. My abs tighten to absorb the blow as if it were nothing.

"So I've been told."

"I want you to be my idiot."

My mouth stretches into an enormous grin, the kind that'll tire my cheeks if I hold it too long. As if I care about that right now. Finley's hand lands on the nape of my neck, fingers running through my hair, overdue for a cut. I nearly moan at the sensation.

"But I need you to be sure—about me, about *us*. So please, will you think about it while I'm gone?"

There's nothing to think about. Even if there were, it's not like my mind can rule over my heart. My love for Finley Harris is too strong to succumb to something as stupid as logic. Finley's expression remains unchanged though. It's important to her, to know I've made an informed decision.

"Fine," I grumble, relenting because she needs it, despite it being the opposite of what I want. "But only if you don't disappear, High-flyer. We'll talk while you're gone, right?"

"We'll talk," she agrees, rising on her tiptoes to plant a chaste kiss on my mouth before collecting her clothes scattered throughout the room.

"You're not going to enjoy the brownies with me?"

She glances at me over her shoulder as she bends to grab her pants. *What an evil flirt.*

"If I do that, we're going to end up being late for Christmas dinner or miss it altogether."

I chuckle. "I'm more than okay with that."

"You know they'll send a SWAT team for us."

She lets my shorts fall to the floor, pooling around her ankles. *Jesus Christ.* Finley makes quick work of pulling on her jeans and stopping my fantasies from running too wild.

"I'll see you there?" I ask.

"You better." Her hand brushes mine as she walks past me to exit the room. "It won't be Christmas without you, Calder."

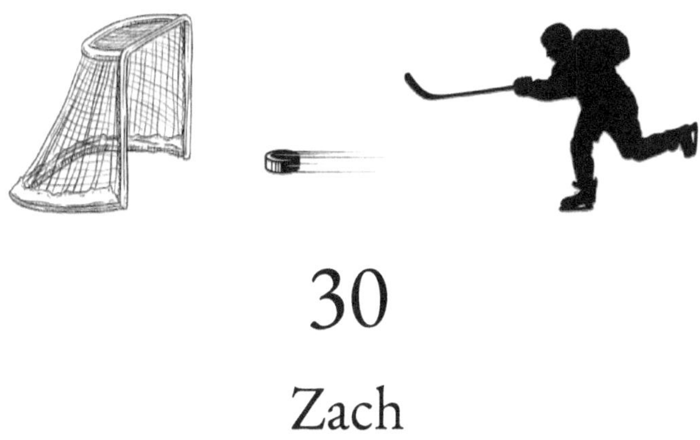

30

Zach

KENNEDY OPENS THE FRONT door a second after the first ring. "Come on in," she sings, holding her arm out to welcome me to her house with Volk, her engagement ring flashing in the light. As if there were any chance she wouldn't say yes.

She shuts the door behind me, then heads to what I affectionately call the Alexei Volkov Hall of Fame, full of a fuckton of trophies, awards, and pictures. It looks like a room belonging to a suspect in Law & Order. I give Volk shit about it, but he's only responsible for half of what's in this room. The other half came from his fiancée, the super fan. I used to pretend I wasn't envious of their relationship, because it meant acknowledging my disappointment I'd never find it.

But Finley Harris found me collapsed on the kitchen floor and changed my entire life.

"I'm surprised you're not in the kitchen," I say, tailing Kennedy into the room to give myself some time before coming face-to-face with the captain who hates my guts.

She puts her hands on her hips over her forest green sweater dress. "*Excuse me?*"

"No," I say through a laugh. "I didn't mean *that*, but this is your party."

She swats the air with one hand. "Oh. I think you're mistaken. This might be"—she sticks one finger in the air and twirls it around—"*my* house, but whenever Gem is in attendance, it's *her* party. It's how I get the honor of hanging out with Elodie."

Kennedy gestures to the stroller where Gemma and Matt's daughter sleeps.

So he's here. That means Finley's parents and her other gigantic hockey-playing brothers are here. *Fucking fantastic.*

"That's one cute baby."

"Of course she is. Did you expect any less from those two?"

Kennedy's hand motions behind her, where Matt and Gemma stand in the doorway, and it takes all my energy not to react audibly.

"Merry Christmas, Zach," Gemma says, stepping forward and opening her arms to me.

Matt doesn't move a muscle—seriously, even his eyes are frozen in place. He furrows his brow so intensely, his stare is more menacing than when he caught Finley in my lap last night. Apparently, he stewed and nursed his anger into a bigger grudge.

"Merry Christmas, Gemma." I step into her hug, relieved she isn't taking Matt's side.

Kennedy's head swivels back and forth, like she's watching an incredibly fast-paced hockey game with both teams flying up and down the ice. "What's with the weird-ass vibe?"

"Nothing," Matt grits out before leaving the room.

Gemma glances at me, sympathy lining her features, before following Matt out of the room. "All the appetizers are out. Dinner will be ready soon."

"Thanks so much, Gem," Kennedy says. "I'd be lost without you."

She's right. We'd end up eating chocolate chip cookie sandwiches from Gemma's bakery if Gemma didn't intervene.

Before Kennedy can interrogate me, I say, "I'm going to find Jennings."

"Uh-*huh*," she murmurs with suspicion, but since she's stuck with the baby, she can't stalk and badger it out of me.

The rest of the guests stand in circles around the kitchen and entertainment room. I spot Volk talking to the team owner, Cale Cole—a.k.a. Kennedy's father—and... *Niko Halonen*? What the hell is he doing here?

"I invited him," Kennedy whispers, suddenly beside me. Her hands rest on Elodie's stroller, where she sleeps soundly. Dammit, she acts quickly. "Your line isn't performing to its potential. All of the talent is there, of course, so it comes down to building bonds and trust."

"I don't know if bringing Halo around more is going to help with that issue. I mean, have you met Volk?"

Kennedy offers a halfhearted shrug. "We'll see. My father carefully vets his roster, so Halonen can't be too bad."

"Justin Ward played on the Wolves for years," I retort, realizing too late I should've let the thought die in my brain.

"Yeah, well, Justin didn't show his true colors right away." Her hand lands on the top of my head, ruffling my hair. "Not everyone is as open as you, Briggsy.

Not the first time I've heard that.

The din of noise in the room quiets when Gemma knocks a knife against her champagne glass. "Dinner time, y'all!"

"We're sitting together," Kennedy says, using her head to gesture toward a table with six seats. There's a parallel table, much longer and larger and another six-seat table beside ours. She leaves Elodie with Gemma before leading me to the table where Volk, Halo, Jennings, and Deandra already sit.

Fucking fantastic, Halo and Volk will snipe at each other throughout dinner.

I don't see Finley anywhere. My phone buzzes a second after the thought, and I relax when I see the name on the screen.

Finley

Hallway

"I'll be right back," I tell Kennedy, already heading in the opposite direction.

Suddenly, a door blasts open, and a hand grabs my forearm, tugging me into the room.

"Hey, boyfriend." Finley's arms slide around me, hands clutching the cotton sweater I wear for holidays. "You look *good*." She rests her head on my chest as I clutch her back. "You smell good too." Her head tips back so she can squint up at me. "Are you trying to impress someone tonight?"

I grin. "There might be someone. She can be a wily one. I wasn't sure she *liked* me at least not until—"

"She confessed her love and screwed you silly?" Finley grins right back at me.

I press a quick kiss to her nose. "So crass."

"You love it."

"I do," I say, my tone turning serious. "Thank you for choosing me."

She bites her lip. Did I get too serious when she wanted to remain light?

"Oh, Zach," she chokes out, her voice saturated with emotion. Finley's hand flies to her chest over the sliver of cleavage offered by her maroon cotton dress, the same color she wore at the wedding. She stunned me that night, but I find her more beautiful now that I know her.

"I don't know the words to describe this feeling in my chest," she says. "I don't know if they exist. I guess I love you is all I can give. I hope it's okay."

My lips land on hers, insistent, hungry, but I pull back, remembering I can't finish what I'm starting, and we already got caught because of our recklessness. "It's more than enough, High-flyer." I suck in a deep breath. "Fuck, it's going to be so hard not seeing you for weeks."

Knuckles rap once on the door. My hand flies to Finley's mouth, covering the response she'd been about to make.

"Who is it?" I call.

"Jennings."

I open the door a crack to Jennings's annoyed expression.

"You're lucky it's me. Your brother is looking for you, Finley."

Finley smooths her hair, finger-combing the tangled ends. "Thanks, Jennings." She gives me a saucy smile, swaying her hips a little as she walks back to the kitchen.

Jennings shakes his head in obvious disappointment, hair flopping with the movement. "Did you learn nothing last night? You're fucking taunting him at this point."

With my head jumbled and my heart ripped open, I'd called him, needing to talk to someone who wouldn't judge me. Except he did.

"I'm not. Seriously, dude, you'll understand one day."

Jennings has a couple years on me, but he's never been seriously in love with someone if he doesn't understand the difficulty of staying away from the person you need most.

"Fuck off," he says but there's no real heat in his words. "Wait for me, and we can go back together."

A few minutes later, I settle in a seat next to Volk while Jennings takes the one on my other side. Everyone has a salad in front of them along with a piece of bread. I immediately bite into mine, hungry for something other than the brownies Finley baked for me this afternoon.

"You two done jerking each other off?" Halo asks from the other side of the table.

"So what if we were?" Jennings fires back in a tone that'd surprise most people. "Would it be an issue for you?"

"Yeah, because we've all been waiting for you to start eating. Meanwhile, this jackass"—he gestures across the table to me with my mouth stuffed to the brim with bread—"sits and eats like it's no big deal."

I chew for another few seconds, then swallow. "That's me, the jackass. At least I'm consistent. I'm surprised to see you here, Halo. Team-building isn't your thing, is it?"

"Ooh, someone's snappy today." Halo leans back in his chair, running his hand over the scruff on his sharp jawline. He directs his gray-blue eyes and charming-ass smirk at Kennedy. "Volkov's girl can be quite convincing."

Volk's jaw grinds. Kennedy's hand dips under the table, heading for his knee—at least I hope that's where it's headed. These two like to get handsy with each other, which is fine, as long as it's not beside me at the dinner table.

"I can be," Kennedy replies. "There's no limit to what I'll do for Alexei."

Halo drops his hands onto his chin. "Aw, ain't that sweet?"

Volk's fist unclenches because, once again, the Alexei Volkov-whisperer intervenes. My gaze drifts to where Finley sits with her family, thankful I have a relationship full of love and support now. As long as Finley allows me to choose her.

Matt catches me staring at his sister and motions to his eyes then points at me. I'm *watching you*.

Volk leans toward me. "You fucked up, dude. I've never seen him this angry."

Volk and Matt have known each other for nearly a decade. His comment spikes my anxiety; Finley and I have a bigger uphill battle than I thought.

"I called it from the beginning," Kennedy jumps in, spearing some salad. "After I saw what she did the morning after his concussion."

"Wait—what are you talking about?"

She straightens. "Oh. Right. Well, you remember when you were unconscious?"

"Yeah. I didn't get hit *that* hard."

The hit caused me to forget a full day, but since then, my memory has been golden.

She swallows her mouthful of salad before speaking again. "You got hit hard enough, Alexei had to defend your honor all over the ice."

Halo snorts from across the table. "Can confirm."

I flip him off. "Kennedy, what did you see?"

"Finley was in your room, checking on you."

"Yeah, so? Gemma told her to."

Kennedy drops her voice, but everyone at this table can hear. I suppose it doesn't matter when the person we need to hide our relationship from already knows. "She was smoothing back your hair with this look on her face... I figured it was only a matter of time."

Finley's been falling for me as long as I've been falling for her. My gaze drifts back to her table and snags with hers, and her smile widens. Matt snaps his fingers in front of her face when he notices.

"Does she know?" Kennedy asks.

I don't need her to clarify the question. *Does she know I love her?* "Yep."

"And she feels the same?"

"Yeah," I say, remembering how she couldn't find the words to adequately describe the depth of her feelings.

Volk shakes his head. "She better be fucking worth it."

"Like Kennedy is fucking worth it?" I challenge.

He curses under his breath. "It's like that?"

"Yeah," I answer immediately. "It is."

"Volkov's been sticking it to the owner's daughter for years," Halo remarks casually before throwing back a shot of brown liquid. "Briggs nailing the captain's sister isn't any worse."

A cacophony of noise bursts from our table. Volk demands Halo fight him outside while I shout for Halo never to talk about Finley like that. Kennedy quips, "And you wonder why you're single."

Halo remains unfazed, continuing to lean back in his chair with that stupid smirk on his face. "I'm single because I *want* to be, sweetheart. These two whipped fools are reminding me exactly why I want to stay that way."

"Everything all right over there?" Matt calls to us, his razor-sharp gaze fixed on me. Does he expect me to answer after he's chosen to ignore me? *On Christmas.*

Kennedy serves as voice for our entire table. "All good."

The rest of dinner I keep my gaze away from Finley, determined not to make this situation even more uncomfortable. It isn't until I'm leaving hours later that I chance a look her way. She glows beneath the lights of the Christmas tree, talking animatedly with Kennedy. I like that they get along so well, and I hope one day, Matt will accept our relationship and not put our friends in the middle of us.

Kennedy nudges Finley in the arm. *I love you*, I mouth when she looks over at me.

I love you too, she mouths back.

I commit this moment to memory, knowing it'll need to last me until she's back in three weeks.

31

Finley

My parents lecture me for the duration of our drive to Maine. Yes, we *drive*. Matthew Harris, Sr. has never been a fan of airports, which would be fine, except his reluctance forces other people into a car for sixteen hours.

Their lecture follows a predictable pattern—an airing of anger and frustration, layering on a healthy dose of guilt before wrapping up with how I need to change.

We've hit Virginia when they finally finish venting their frustration, repeating everything I already know.

"We reluctantly agreed to let you attend college out of state because you promised to follow our agreement," my dad goes on from the driver's seat. "You said you understood the importance and you would make smart choices."

I try to remember they have good intentions, but resentment still simmers. A text from Zach fuels those flames, stoking them higher until they threaten to consume me.

Zach

I miss you already.

"Finley, are you listening to me?"

I drop my phone into my lap and meet my father's gaze in the rearview mirror. My dad grew up with a mother who had undiagnosed and untreated bipolar disorder. She was labeled a bad mother and alcoholic instead. I try to be forgiving with my dad, knowing he experienced the challenges firsthand, along with the consequences when an individual with my condition doesn't receive and follow medical care.

But it's unfair, the way he projects his childhood trauma onto me.

"Yes," I mumble. "I've been listening to you for the last hour and a half."

"Hand your phone over," my dad says, as if I hadn't responded to him. "That way, you'll have no distractions."

I suppress a groan and focus on quickly typing a message to Zach. Who knows when I'll be granted the privilege of my phone again.

Me

I'm counting the minutes until I see you again

Then I click over to my text thread with my brother and blast out an angry message.

Me

I'll never forgive you for not having my back

Then I block him. If he respected me, Matt would've handled this situation with me directly, not ratted me out to our parents, jeopardizing everything I've been working toward.

I place my phone in my dad's waiting palm. I feel sixteen again.

The two people in the front of the car hurt my faith in myself. They're biologically designed to think I hang the moon, but instead, they think I'm not capable of caring for myself.

My mother turns, her head leaning against the seat while she watches me. "Honey, we want what's best for you, you know that."

"I know." I bite the inside of my lip to keep tears at bay. "But Mom, I'm happier now than I've been in years."

"You look tired," my dad says. "Too much time doing flips and staying out all night with your brother's teammate."

"Matthew." My mother says his name gently, but there's an unmistakable warning in it.

"Doing flips?" I repeat. "You mean the incredibly challenging sport of gymnastics? Unless we're boiling down all sports to their simplest form, in which case, your three sons move around on knives, smashing people against a wall. What noble careers they have."

"Same career as your boyfriend," Dad retorts.

"I don't want to talk about him with you."

I lean my head on the window and watch the world zip by. It's how I felt the last two years—stagnant, witnessing everyone else taking steps toward their goals. I'm not going back to that existence, even if it means losing my family. I love them—of course I do—but I can't love them at the expense of my mental health.

"Too bad, because tomorrow we have a session with Dr. Warren."

Fantastic.

⸻◆⸻

My parents and I sit on the familiar green couch in Dr. Warren's office. This couch and I bonded over the years I came here for therapy—daily in the beginning, then twice per week, eventually dropping to weekly.

"It's good to see you in person, Finley." Dr. Warren crosses her legs, resting them on a footstool in front of her. Black frame glasses sit on top of her blond curly bob; she only uses them when taking notes in the book in her lap. "Did you have a nice holiday?"

The weight of my parent's stares burn the side of my face, but I keep looking straight ahead. "It had its moments."

Waking up next to Zach Briggs, for one. He slept with a smile on his face, and I hoped it had something to do with telling him I love him. I could picture every day like that, opening my eyes to see him beside me. I want it so badly, it hurts to think I might lose him. The decision he needs to make about our relationship isn't an emotional one, it's logical. It's why I'm forcing him to think it through while I'm gone.

"What's that smile about?" Dr. Warren probes.

Unsurprisingly, my dad interrupts, impatiently tapping his foot. "She has a secret boyfriend—*another* hockey player—and went back to gymnastics without telling anyone. Unless she told you?"

Dr. Warren shakes her head once. "You know I can't answer that, Matthew."

"I didn't," I say, crossing my arms over my chest and sinking further into the couch.

Dr. Warren slips her glasses onto her face. "Why is that, Finley?"

She waits, poised with her pen pressed to paper to record my response. Omitting details makes me uncomfortable. Lying to Dr. Warren is out of the question. This woman pulled me back from the brink. I owe her so much.

"Because I'm happy, and I didn't want you to tell me I need to give up what I love."

My mom's hand lands on my forearm. "You love him?"

"Yeah, I do."

"You don't know him," my dad protests from the other end of the couch. We've come to therapy dozens of times as a family, and he's never behaved this belligerently. He's angry I lied, sure, but he's fighting every word out of my mouth. I don't understand. "And does he know *you*?"

I turn toward him. "Yes, Zach knows I have bipolar disorder. So does my gymnastics coach, Veronica. And it's thanks to Dr. Warren, I had the courage to tell them."

"Oh, Finley, that's a big deal," Dr. Warren says while scribbling something on her notepad. "I'm proud of you. Can you tell us how those conversations went?"

I cross one leg over the other. "Telling Veronica was easier, because it was transactional, at least at first. I need her to watch out for any signs while I train. I don't trust myself to spot them." Dr. Warren taught me how bipolar disorder could skew my perception of reality. "I put off telling Zach for a long time because I didn't want to lose him."

"Did that happen?"

"No, but I asked him to take some time to think about it without me there to distract him. It's not an easy life he'd be choosing. It's hard to picture my life without him, but I'd hate it more if he jumped in blindly and felt saddled with my baggage, you know?"

Dr. Warren's mouth opens to respond, but my dad beats her to the punch.

"That's not healthy." He looks to Dr. Warren for confirmation. "Attachment for someone with her condition can be dangerous."

"So you want me to live a lonely life? By that logic, I should cut all ties with my family in case 'losing you' sends me down a spiral."

"That's different, and—"

"No," I say. "It isn't."

Dr. Warren shifts in her seat and redirects our conversation. "That's a big statement, Finley. Why don't you tell us about Zach? What do you love about him?"

The tension in my body deflates with thoughts of Zach. "Well, there's the obvious. He's handsome and talented and he has this surety about his life, like he's exactly where he's supposed to be, doing what he's meant to do... but it's so much more than that. He understands me—my life as an athlete, why my sport means so much to me.

"And he's supportive. He came to the gym to watch me train when he was sidelined with an injury. He helped me to loosen up, to stop taking every little thing so seriously. I remembered what it was like to *enjoy* gymnastics, and relax and take things as they come instead of planning every little detail. I like being around him..."

I take a deep breath, exhaustion creeping in with my vulnerability. "He's light, and after being in darkness for so long, it's what I crave—pure, undiluted happiness. He gives that to me."

The room remains silent for ten seconds... fifteen... thirty.

Dr. Warren employs her favorite tactic—silence—to force us to think and speak first.

Mom's the first to break, as usual. "He sounds wonderful, honey. I'm sorry we didn't spend much time with him at Christmas."

"There will be other opportunities, provided he chooses me."

Dr. Warren's brow scrunches. "Why do you think he won't?"

My dad scoffs. "He's a twenty-year-old professional hockey player."

"He's twenty-one," I correct. "And that has nothing to do with it. Zach's the most loyal person I've ever met, but his perspective could change while we're apart."

"Why do you consider yourself such a burden, Finley?"

An involuntary laugh bursts from my chest. "Because I am. Do you have any idea how much gymnastics costs? How much they invested in my Olympic dream, only to watch it fall apart? Then their lives became consumed with my health and caring for an adult child. I hate that they think they need to watch over me."

Dr. Warren turns her attention to my parents. "Matthew, Grace, how does hearing that make you feel?"

"Horrible," Mom chokes out, bringing a finger to dry tears before they fall. "Finley, being a parent never stops... and I don't want it to stop. You—and your brothers—are my greatest joys in life. Nothing you can say or do will ever change that. You have to know that."

Her arm wraps around me, pulling me to her as she squeezes my shoulder. My head rests against hers. All I can think is how lucky I am to have their support, but it also generates a familiar stab of guilt for the problems I bring to their lives.

"Matthew?" Dr. Warren prompts.

"We love Finley, and we want what's best for her. Deep down, she knows that's not what we think."

Dr. Warren tilts her head. "Does she?" She waits for a beat, but my dad doesn't answer. "I'd like to explore this a bit more next time. How does that sound?"

"Good," I say, and I mean it.

My dad holds up a hand. "Wait—we came here to talk about how to get her back on track. We had an agreement in place. She went behind our backs to the sport that almost killed her. And now she's dating another hockey player. We all remember what the last one did."

Dr. Warren clears her throat. "What I'm hearing from Finley is we need to rethink that agreement."

Dad launches out of his seat, raising his arms in the air. "That's bull-shit. These rules keep her safe." He strides out of the office, the door shutting loudly behind him.

My mom places her hand on my knee. "He's scared, honey. He doesn't want to see you hurt again."

I take a steadying breath. "Ironic, right? Since that's what your rules are doing."

"We'll talk this through," Dr. Warren says in her patented calm voice. "I'm proud of you, Finley. You've made so much progress. It's not easy, speaking your mind."

My mom squeezes my hand. It's the first gesture from any of my family that doesn't smother me for as long as I can remember. All I can do is hope Dr. Warren can help us work through this predicament. My family loves me. I don't want to lose them, but I also can't keep living my life on their terms. I need to make decisions and take risks again.

I need them there when I fail *and* when I succeed, even if they don't agree with every choice I make.

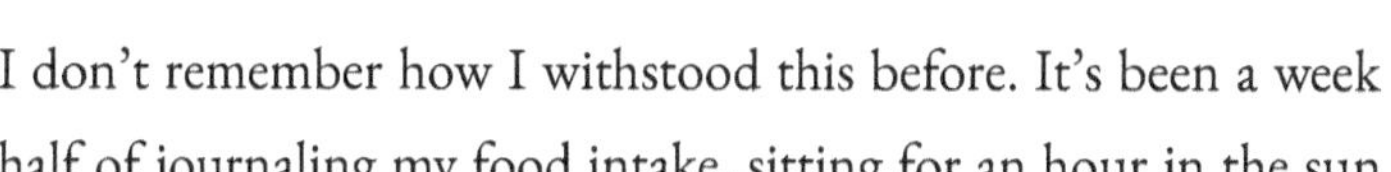

I don't remember how I withstood this before. It's been a week and a half of journaling my food intake, sitting for an hour in the sun while life passes by, and talking to Dr. Warren about my mood. It's plummeted since coming here as I mindlessly follow the routine set for me. But I listen to my parents until I can figure out what to do.

No solutions have come to me yet.

Despite multiple therapy sessions with my parents, we've come no closer to reaching an understanding that would allow me to go back to North Carolina, continue training for gymnastics, and dating Zach. At least not one that involves my parents paying for college, and I've checked—my second-semester payment remains outstanding, so this isn't a bluff.

With exactly zero credit to my name, I'd need a cosigner for a loan. With a corporate accountant and a school principal for parents, our family doesn't qualify for financial aid, so my parents never applied.

Let's not forget that I burned a bridge at Casa Matt, Jr., which means I don't have a place to live.

And I have exactly a week and a half to figure it all out before my life constricts to this meaningless existence for the foreseeable future.

32

Zach

FINLEY PROMISED SHE WOULDN'T disappear, but since going home with her parents two weeks ago, I've barely heard from her.

The logical part of my brain tells me to stop messaging her, to let Finley come back to me when she's ready, but I'm struggling to stay away, especially when she might need me.

Jennings snatches my phone. "If you're debating it this long, it's a bad idea."

My head drops into my hands. "I don't know what to do, man."

"How's this? We demolish those assholes, then get stupid drunk."

He holds the phone out to me, but when I go to grab it, he pulls it away and lifts it above my head. I can't reach it from where I sit by my locker, not when Jennings stands with my phone at his eye level. And I don't want to play along.

Shit. This isn't the attitude I need heading into a game with Justin Ward—the asshole who flattened my head on the ice and ruined the beginning of my season.

"Do you have smelling salts?" I ask.

Jennings claps me on the back. "Now there's the Briggsy I know and love." He leaves the locker room to retrieve them, coming back with the foul-smelling tube of salt that never fails to wake me the fuck up.

I put it to my nose, take a whiff, and let a "Let's go!" fly out of my mouth. Answering shouts chorus around the room from my teammates. They've been giving me little nods all day, the kind they used to give Volk in the hours before we played Justin Ward. The games against our biggest division rival ratchet the intensity, but I suspect today might lift us to an entirely new level.

Volk taps his stick against mine as we line up on the ice for the national anthem. "You ready for this?"

I glance across the rink. Justin fucking Ward stares at me with an insufferable shit-eating grin. I don't care that he runs a charity for underprivileged youth, he's still the biggest piece of shit in the league. The biggest piece of shit I've ever come across, period.

"Fuck yeah, I am," I reply, glaring right back at Ward, tipping my lips in a half smile. That injury shook me to my core, but I'll be damned if I give this asshole the satisfaction of letting it show.

The first half of the first period goes by without a whiff of indecency, but like every other game, the crowd anxiously waits for the inevitable spark to set our hatred aflame. All our games sell out these days, ever since we became a staple in the playoffs, so the crowd roar isn't unique.

The undercurrent of anxiety though? It's not standard.

The game's physical, like every game against this team. There are scrums in front of the net, some punishing—but legal—hits and trash talk exchanged.

But it isn't until the end of the first period that they cross a line.

I'm behind the net retrieving the puck in our O-zone, and I push it out to Volk halfway between me and the blue line. Seconds later, a body slams me into the boards. There's an immediate whistle because the dumbass chose to violate the rules with a ref less than ten feet away. Ward's goon-in-training, Prentiss, throws his arms up to complain about the "bullshit" call.

Ward has his teammates doing his dirty work for him tonight. As the thought crosses my mind, I'm slammed again, with more force this time. My hands come up to stop my head from taking the brunt of the hit.

"How's the head kid?" Ward shouts into my ear.

I don't fight often, but I have a line, and this motherfucker crossed it.

I pop back up—this isn't the first time I've been boarded, and it won't be the last. They'll have to knock me unconscious again to keep me down.

"Never better." I throw my gloves onto the ice, and my blades ease me toward him. "Something you won't be able to say after I beat your ass."

Ward rears back and laughs. "You don't want to fight me, *Briggsy*."

"It's Briggs to you," I say, picking up speed to close the gap between us and shove him. The move catches Ward by surprise, so he loses his balance a little, an annoyance more than a disadvantage.

"All right," Ward shouts, removing his gloves one at a time. "But don't say I didn't warn you."

"Well, fuck," someone mutters fifteen seconds before Niko Halonen decks Ward across the face.

The rink descends into chaos.

Ward charges Halo while Prentiss, who had skated toward the box, comes charging back at me. Everyone is swinging at someone, and the benches empty, every player joining this shit show.

It's a long time before the refs manage to separate us, frantically blowing their whistles, skating from fight to fight. Matt helps them break up fights while their dirty-ass captain—Ward—gets whaled on by Niko. By the time the refs sort out the penalties, Volk, Halo, and I all end up in the box together, while Ward, Prentiss, and another goon—whose only contribution is hurting the opposing team—crowd their sin bin.

"Aw, do you have someone else fight all your battles?" Ward taunts.

"At least people pay to watch me! Didn't these people used to cheer for you? Well, not these people exactly, because you couldn't win a fucking game before Volk and I got here. Listen to them now."

I'm talking too much, and it's unlikely Ward can hear me over the roar of the crowd shouting "Cheaters never win" at him. There's too much adrenaline firing through my veins. I'm hopping up and down on my skates, anxious to charge back onto the ice.

Volk's hand lands on my forearm and tugs me onto the bench. "What have I told you about fighting out of your weight class?"

"Don't start," I mutter, my skates tapping the ground. I don't think I could stop them if I tried.

"I fucking hate that guy," Halo groans.

"Fucking tell me about it." Volk damn near growls the words.

"He's the worst," I agree.

This might be the first time the three of us have all agreed with each other. That's the power of Justin Ward, bonding people over a shared hatred of him.

"How did Kennedy ever date that clown? Someone as *fine* as her settling for *that*."

I wince, glancing at Volk, expecting to see murder in his eyes, returning us to where we started, with Volk and Halo barely tolerating each other. But Volk grins at Halo like they're friends sharing a joke.

"She was going through something."

"That explains a lot. Glad she found someone better."

Volk nods curtly.

My appreciation for the temporary truce between Volk and Halo vanishes when Halo adds, "It wasn't smart picking a fight with him, Briggsy. That asshole has fifty pounds on you."

"You couldn't let me get in one punch?" I lament.

Halo rubs a towel over his sweat-soaked face. "Your punch would have landed you a second concussion this season."

"Is that why you finally have my back? A deep caring for my health?" I twinkle my eyes at him, a gesture he ignores.

"I have your back because you're my teammate, and if anyone fucks with you, they fuck with me. *And* I needed someone to dirty up this face. Can't let Volk walk around with all the bruises and get all the attention."

"He's not your competition," I say.

"It's cute you think that," Halo replies. "Everyone is competition."

I motion between Volk and me. "We're not. We're your allies."

Halo smirks. "Briggsy the Boy Scout, eh?" He mimics my voice, right down to my Manitoban accent. "*Anyway,* what's that thing our fans keep saying, protect you at all costs?"

I gesture around the arena with one hand. "They might start saying it about you now."

The crowd chants Ha-Lo over and over as the screen at center ice replays the fight, showing Halo punching Ward senseless while he shields his head.

Halo scoffs. "I don't need anyone to protect me."

"No, of course not." Volk rolls his eyes, but there's laughter in his tone.

I nudge Volk in the side. To Halo, I say, "Maybe you want someone to have your back, back your play, whatever?"

He shrugs. "My next play is to wipe the floor with these fuckers. You in?"

I hold up my hand to fist-bump him, then turn to Volk.

He rolls his eyes again, like he can't possibly be bothered by this ritual. "You always take it too far, Briggsy."

I crack a smile. "Face it—that's what you love about me."

"I respect it," Halo chimes in. "Sometimes, the situation calls for taking it too far."

"Like right now," I reply with a nod.

When the penalties expire, we charge out of the box, one by one, like bats out of hell. Halo lands a monster hit, which allows Volk to steal the puck and head toward the net. I sprint up the ice, waiting for him to cross the blue line before charging, looking for his pass. Volk fakes out the goalie, making him think he's shooting left, but instead, he slaps the puck to me to score on the open net opportunity we created. I immediately point to Volk but find Halo with both of his arms in the air, celebrating as if it'd been his goal. They skate to me, wrapping me in a hug so wholesome, it'd wreck Gemma's heart. Besides her husband, hockey hugs draw her to our sport.

By the time the third-period buzzer sounds, we've outscored Florida by five goals, three of which came from our line. Kennedy thought inviting Halo to Christmas dinner would create team bonds, but all we needed was for Justin fucking Ward to come to town to align us against a common enemy.

33

Zach

THE FLIGHT TO BOSTON for game one of a four-day road trip involves two and a half hours of travel and a lot of glares from Matt. He's avoided speaking to me outside his official role as my captain. At some point, he needs to move on. Or at least that's what I tell myself.

Matt's been a critical part of me adjusting to playing in the NHL and feeling at home in Palmer City. Matt and Gemma include me in every holiday celebration and countless family dinners. They've helped me figure out adult shit more times than I can count. They gave me a family.

I don't want to think about the possibility of Matt never forgiving me.

I wait until we're off the plane to approach him. His clenched jaw should send me in the opposite direction, but I know he won't come to me. If I want a chance to repair this relationship, I have to make the first move.

"Hey, man."

Matt doesn't look up from his phone.

"I want to apologize. It's not cool that I didn't talk to you first and went behind your back. You've been a great friend and a kickass captain... and honestly, my family. I don't want to lose that, to lose you."

Matt slips his phone into his back pocket and regards me with cool eyes. "Let me get this straight. You're sorry because you lied, but you're *not* sorry for fucking my sister?"

"I told you it's not like th—"

He raises a skeptical eyebrow. "So you didn't have sex with my sister, Zach? After I told you she wasn't in any place to date."

The first name stings. He's never called me that before, ever.

How much easier would it be to tell him no? But since I'm asking for forgiveness for lying, it'd be a stupid fucking move to lie.

"No, I did, but—"

Matt throws up a hand. "I don't want to hear it!"

"I love her. I'm in love with Finley. I'm... serious about her."

He scoffs. "You're not serious about anything."

"Come on, dude. We've played *professional* hockey together for three seasons, and you see me take it seriously. I work my ass off day in and day out. It's fucking insulting to say I'm never serious."

I turn on my heel but hesitate to walk away. If this is my one shot, I need to make it count. "And I'm serious about your sister. I love her. She's my opposite in so many ways, but it's the exact ways I need. She's strong and beautiful and has such a good heart. She's driven and so talented. How could you want to keep her away from what she loves to do? When she's in the gym, Finley lights up more than anywhere else."

"You have no idea what she's been through. You're not the first guy to take advantage—"

"I'm not fucking Garrett. Give me more credit than that."

Matt's eyes widen. "She told you about him?"

"She told me everything, including about her return to gymnastics. Think about why she'd do that, why she's been keeping secrets from you."

He doesn't say a word as I walk away.

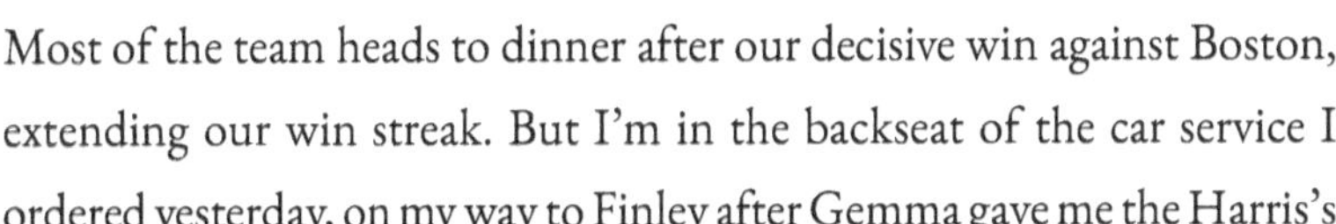

Most of the team heads to dinner after our decisive win against Boston, extending our win streak. But I'm in the backseat of the car service I ordered yesterday, on my way to Finley after Gemma gave me the Harris's address.

It's one in the morning when I reach Finley's childhood home, dark except for one room on the second floor, where dim lights illuminate the window. I'd bet anything it's her room and she's awake binge-watching the show she keeps telling me I need to watch from the beginning with her.

I slip my winter hat on and tighten my coat around me. The North Carolina weather has thinned my blood in the limited time I've lived there. If my family and friends saw me now, they'd petition to revoke my Canadian citizenship.

Me

I'm outside and don't want to ring your doorbell

I wait a few minutes for a response, but like my other messages, it isn't marked as read. Ringing the doorbell and announcing my presence to her parents is out of the question. I pick up a pebble from the driveway, rear back, and toss it in the direction of the window, praying I'm not wrong about it belonging to Finley.

I snatch another pebble, readying to throw at the window again when the curtain flutters, and Finley appears there. Her mouth falls open, and one hand clutches her chest. I wave toward the porch until the curtain flutters shut and Finley disappears from view. I approach the front door, hoping she's on her way to me, otherwise I'll have a miserable drive back to Boston, brokenhearted.

The door eases open as my feet land on the porch steps. Finley pokes her head out, mouth moving but she's speaking so softly, I can't hear anything until I'm beside her.

"Don't make a sound," she whispers directly in my ear as her hand grasps mine and tugs me inside.

The contact sets my skin aflame. I've missed being close to her and so desperately wish we were headed to my apartment to be alone.

"Follow my path exactly so we don't make noise."

I nod, entirely focusing on Finley despite my curiosity about her childhood home. She sucks in a tiny breath when we reach the second floor and tiptoe past a couple of closed doors. I follow her lead, holding my breath until she releases hers after her bedroom door closes.

She looks more gorgeous than I remember in black sweatpants rolled twice at her hips, a thin strip of bare skin showing below a thin white tank. Nothing exists beneath her shirt, giving me a full view of her pointed nipples. My gaze shoots to the ceiling, ripping away from Finley before my brain malfunctions, and I lose sight of what we need to discuss.

"Can you... would you mind putting on a sweatshirt?" I stutter.

"You're good now," she says a moment later, her tone emotionless. No teasing. No laughing. I can't detect one ounce of amusement on her face. I flashback to Christmas, her bright smile at the sight of me awake, gazing at her.

Finley is sitting cross-legged on her bed when my eyes find her again. "You're here."

"I missed you," I say, stuffing my hands into my jeans pockets. She fidgets in her seat, looking at her lap. "I guess you feel differently because you haven't been answering texts."

She sighs. "I haven't had my phone since the last message I sent you."

I sit on the bed across from her, keeping my hands at my sides.

Her chest rises and falls rapidly, visible beneath a baggy gray Harper Cove Elite Gymnastics sweatshirt. She shakes her head, hair swaying into her face, keeping her expression concealed. "You deserve better than my mess. You shouldn't have to deal with this."

"Deal with what?"

Her head lifts, my heart caving in when her watery gaze lands on my face. I hate seeing her like this.

"A *crazy* girlfriend."

I grip her chin lightly with my fingertips, pulling her face to mine. "Never call yourself crazy. You're not crazy."

She swallows hard. "Okay."

"You can't scare me off, High-flyer." I release her chin but keep my eyes trained on hers. "I will never not want you. Any version of you. If you don't want to leave your bed, I'll crawl in beside you. I want to be with you wherever and however you are."

Finley's stare lingers. I nod, silently confirming she heard me correctly. She launches toward me, and I catch her, wrapping my arms around her back, breathing in her comforting scent. Finley takes a staggering breath and tightens her arms around my neck.

"I've missed you too," she says, voice thick with emotion. "But I want what's best for you."

I nudge her back by her shoulders until we're eye to eye again. She needs to see the truth as much as she needs to hear it. "You are what's best for me. I love you, Finley. Don't tell me you've forgotten."

Her fingertips land on my lips, silencing me.

"I could never forget," she whispers before replacing her fingers with her mouth, sucking ever so softly on my lips. I let her do what she wants, remaining still as she moves against me.

All restraint goes to hell when her teeth gently scrape my bottom lip, sending a tingle up my spine.

My hands land on her ass, boosting her into my lap. She lets out a sigh, then kisses her way down my neck while I move her against me, back and forth. The people who rush to the main event seriously miss out. The tease can feel like torture, but it's not something I'd ever turn down.

The thought of people brings me back to myself, to this moment.

"Wait," I say, pulling back from her. I hate myself a little when I see those red swollen lips. "We can't do this here. I don't want your parents to meet me for the first time as your boyfriend like this. They've always been kind to me."

Finley clicks her mouth. "I hate to break it to you, but..."

I groan. "They hate me already?"

"My mom's excited. I told her all about you."

"But your dad's no longer a fan. I get it." I stand, then collapse on the bean bag about ten feet away. "Besides, I know you need to stick to your routine. Lack of sleep can bring on an episode."

Her hands flash at me like two red blinking stop signs. "Wait—have you been talking to *my brother* about me?"

I choke out a laugh. "I *tried* explaining—"

"No, I mean, about my bipolar disorder. How do you know about routine and triggers?"

"I've been listening to a book about it. Some podcasts too. There's a lot of great information out there, especially for loved ones of people with bipolar disorder."

Finley shifts, dangling her legs over the side of her bed. "You read about bipolar disorder?"

"I *listened*," I reply, pointing to one of my ears.

"Listening to audiobooks *is* reading. I don't care what anyone says."

I laugh. "Okay, then yes. I read about bipolar disorder. I want to know everything I can, learn how I can be the best partner to you. That's the bare minimum of what you deserve, Finley."

She's at a loss for words again.

I snatch a book off her bed, turning it over to stare at the cover. The backdrop is a mixture of purple and blue with a blond hockey player holding a brunette skater. "A hockey romance? What *possibly* could have sparked this interest?"

She giggles, clapping a hand over her mouth to muffle the sound as I tickle her. Finley thrashes, but my weight holds her steady. I finally relent when her breath grows shallow, and her hands drop from her mouth to clutch her stomach, in stitches after minutes of laughing.

I flop back on the bed, holding the book out to her. "So are you up to reading?"

Finley props her chin on my chest. "How will you get back?"

"The driver outside. I hired him for the whole night."

"*Zach.*"

"What? I'm paying his daily fee for the next few days."

She tosses an arm around my abdomen. "Can we talk instead? I like the sound of your voice."

I love that she knows me well enough not to ask me to read to her. I would, of course, but it'd be slow and frustrating, especially with how tired I am.

I chuckle. "You might be the only one."

Her head settles in the crook of my arm, twisting a few times before she's comfortable. "I'm okay with that. I don't want anyone else falling in love with you."

"What about me? You're not worried about me falling in love with someone else?"

"Zach Briggs, you're the most loyal person I know. I don't need to worry."

Her faith in me gives me a deep satisfaction like few other things do—scoring a goal, blocking a shot, delivering a sick assist. The belief from my teammates and the roar of the fans build me up. I soak in the validation like a comedian who just made an auditorium erupt into laughter or a stage actor bowing and receiving applause from the crowd. I never expected the feeling could exist thanks to only one person, but it does with her.

She presses a kiss on my cheek. "Tell me a story from when we were apart."

My mind flips through the last couple of weeks, most of which I spent missing her. Then I land on one. "Jennings found this goose in his backyard the other day, and I got a little too close..."

Half an hour later, Finley has drifted to sleep to the sound of my voice.

34

Finley

THAT NIGHT WITH ZACH carries me through the next few days, the final ones of UPC's winter break.

My parents and I avoid the topic of next semester. I'm choosing to operate on the assumption they'll drop me at the airport and share in my excitement about returning to school when the time arrives.

Well, okay, not excitement. Not yet.

"How are you today, Finley?"

Today's session with Dr. Warren includes my parents. She starts every one the same, regardless of whether they're here. It's the equivalent of running chalk over my grips exactly five times each before beginning a bars routine. Regardless, I like the question, especially with happiness coursing through me since Zach made a six-hour round trip to tell me he chose me after playing an *entire* hockey game.

"Great, honestly. I can't wait for the new semester." *To get back to Zach Briggs and my training.*

Dr. Warren cocks an eyebrow. I'm not sure if she's surprised because it hasn't come up before or because she didn't realize our in-person sessions were again coming to an end. But in the span of a second, I realize that's not it at all.

Mom inhales sharply.

Dad says, "You're not going back for the new semester. Finley, you've broken our trust, and as far as I know, you still haven't apologized to your brother or asked if he is open to you living with him again."

I half expect the statement, which is why I took necessary precautions, so I won't need to scramble so close to the next semester. I didn't go back to sleep after Zach left, despite operating on only three hours. My body fueled itself with pure determination as I developed a plan to get back to North Carolina without my family's support, financially or otherwise.

"That's because I don't plan to live with Matt."

"You won't be living with that boy," Dad states.

Mom places a hand on my father's knee, a silent *Let me handle this.* "Honey, why is this the first time we're hearing about this?"

I shrug. "Figured you didn't want to know because you hadn't asked."

"Of course we want to know. It's why we're here with you, talking, trying to understand each other better."

"Huh. I thought we were here because you think I'm reckless and you want Dr. Warren to rein me in."

I don't give my parents a chance to respond, continuing with long overdue words.

"But she never did that. She *facilitated* our discussion. She offered advice. She never laid out conditions. *You* did. And I accepted them, partly because I didn't think I had a choice. I let you convince me to make my life small, and it made me feel incapable. You didn't do it on purpose. You thought you were doing what was best for me."

I tilt my head, looking straight at my dad. "Including you, Dad. I've resented you since my diagnosis. You acted like it was a death sentence and bolted into action to try to fix it. But I don't need to be fixed. I have a condition, something that affects my entire life, but something *I* can manage.

"My bipolar disorder doesn't mean I can't take care of myself, or that I shouldn't have the same opportunities as everyone else. It's a credit to the services you got me that I can say that and wholeheartedly believe it."

Mom cries silently beside me with what looks to be a mixture of guilt and pride. Dad remains silent, mulling over my words. It's more than I told myself to anticipate. The silence stretches into discomfort.

That's when Dr. Warren interjects. "Finley, thank you for being so vulnerable in sharing those feelings with us. Matthew and Grace, do you have anything you'd like to share with Finley?"

"Oh, honey," my mom says with a sigh. "You deserve the world. I want you to be happy and healthy. I'm sorry I ever gave you a different impression."

"Matthew?" Dr. Warren prompts.

"Do you have *any idea* what the call from your mother was like for me?"

He doesn't need to specify which call. My dad had left for work by the time my gymnastics coach opened the gym to find me collapsed on the ground. Mom drove there immediately, calling my dad to let him know what happened after we got to the hospital. I pushed myself to the point of exhaustion and dehydration and was in the depths of a depressive episode, which I'd only managed to push through thanks to the uppers that Garrett gave me. It almost cost me everything.

My father shudders. "I never want another call like that one, Finley. I *can't.*"

"You know the risk is always there, right?"

My tentative question hangs in the air. It's an obvious point, but he needs the reminder. I could have been born genetically perfect, if such a thing exists, or have the powers of Supergirl, and he'd still have to live with the risk of a call like that. It accompanies love. There's no way around it.

"I've taken my medication as instructed every single day. I might not always sleep at the same time each night, but I'm close. And when I don't sleep enough, I nap. I'm an expert napper now, thanks to Zach. He's helped me understand the importance of taking the time to relax. Having fun is as important as working hard."

I go on, "There's nothing else in my life that brings me as much joy as gymnastics"—well, except Zach, but I know better than to say that and send this conversation in a different direction—"and I want to keep doing it in a balanced, measured, *safe* way. I want your support, but I'm prepared to do it on my own. Because it's my life. I'm the one who has to live with my choices."

This is the lightest I've felt in years, with the full truth laid out before us.

"We wanted to keep you safe, Fi," my mom says.

"I know. And I needed your protection at one time, but I don't anymore. I need your support now. The same as you give the boys. Can you do that?"

My mom's hand clasps mine. "Oh, hun, of course I can. But go easy on me as I adjust, okay? It's instinct to protect you."

"I can do that," I tell her with a nod. "Dad?"

He shakes his head, which brings Dr. Warren into the conversation. "Matthew, what would make you more comfortable? Not entirely comfortable, but *more* comfortable than you are right now."

Dad lets out a rough chuckle. "Which is zero, for the record."

"Noted. We're working with baby steps here."

He considers the question while holding eye contact with my mom. A silent conversation passes between them as I wait on pins and needles for his answer.

"Weekly family therapy sessions," Dad says at long last.

"I can do that," I say, nodding profusely.

He points at me. "And I want to talk to your coach."

"Veronica would love that. And you'll like her. She's the healthiest coach I've ever had."

I look at Dr. Warren, who continues to effectively use her silence technique to force us to speak to each other. I'm too afraid to say anything, though, because it sounds like he agreed I can return to school with reasonable conditions.

"Oh, and I'll need to talk to that *boy* too," he adds.

I roll my eyes. "Sure, Dad, you can talk to *Zach,* Matty's teammate, who you've already met a dozen times."

Dad holds out his palm, and I place my hand in it. "I completely approve of him as Matt's teammate, but as your boyfriend... that's still to be determined. I love you, Fi. It takes a special person to deserve you." He squeezes my hand. "There's nothing more important to me in this world than your happiness, your brothers' happiness."

My hand tightens around his for a beat before releasing it. "Thank you for your support." I place my hand on my mom's shoulder. "My life is good because I've had it. I never want to lose you."

"You won't," my mom says, her voice saturated with emotion.

"Kiddo, that will never happen," Dad confirms.

The pit in my stomach that formed when my parents learned I returned to gymnastics and fell in love with Zach finally dissolves, along with the thick tension that surrounded us for years. The tension that kept us distant from each other.

After hours in therapy, I'd like to think we've mastered how to communicate, but it's not so simple. We'll always have to work to keep our relationship healthy.

Just like every other relationship in my life, including the one I have with myself. To find the happiness I've dreamed of for so long, I had to open myself up to hurt, to say what I think, what I need.

And for the first time in a long time, I'm ready to do it.

35

Zach

My knuckles rap against my coach's closed door after practice.

He walked in the direction of his office thirty minutes ago; that's how long it took me to gather my nerve to approach. Erik Pomroy has the respect of everyone in the league, but no one would describe him as warm. He has the textbook definition of a withering stare—unblinking, tense, unnerving as fuck. I've been on the receiving end of that stare many times, and I still can't adjust to it.

I don't like the idea of letting him down, but he's not the most important person in my life. My hesitation to talk to him has nothing to do with the decision I've made. It's the right one, even if no one else will agree, and it's up to me.

"Come in," he calls. Erik sits behind his desk, clacking away on his keyboard, ignoring me as I fidget in the doorway, waiting for his attention. Finally, his fingers lift and he addresses me. "What do you need, Briggsy?"

The question is brusque but not unkind. I'm often on the receiving end of the famous Pomroy stare because I'm rarely to the point, and Erik doesn't like to waste time. Lucky for me, I'm the kind of hockey player he likes—scrappy, unafraid, and hardworking, which buys me a pass for my antics.

I'm hoping that won't end here.

"I need to miss practice Friday."

Erik places his hands behind his head and leans back in his chair. "For what reason? Is it your head?"

"Oh. No, no. My head's good. I mean, as good as it usually is... which I know you probably question—"

He holds his hands up to halt my word vomit.

"It's for my girlfriend, sir."

His thick dark eyebrows raise. "Girlfriend?"

"Yeah," I say with a laugh. "It surprised me too. She needs me tomorrow. I'll accept whatever punishment you think is fair."

Finley finally got her phone back a couple of days ago and learned the UPC gymnastics coach would be at her gym Friday to consider her for his team. Becoming a walk-on athlete at a Division 1 school like UPC isn't common, but Finley's elite gymnastics history plus the recommendation from Veronica, who'd been on the UPC gymnastics team, landed her this chance. Nothing is guaranteed other than this tryout. She didn't ask me to be there, but she needs me.

Erik studies me. Maybe he's waiting to see if I take it back when presented with silence, or whether I'm joking or making an impulse decision I'll regret.

I fidget but say nothing.

"I'll need to healthy scratch you for Saturday's game, and you know the fine."

It's what I expected. There's a pang in my gut at the idea of letting Erik Pomroy or my teammates down.

But the thought of Finley eases the guilty ache in my belly. The idea of not being there for her… well, let's say it brings on literal sickness that wouldn't ever pass. She's more important.

"Yeah, I know. But she's my family now. There are some things more important than hockey."

A brief smile crosses his features, a flash of pearly white teeth, there and gone. "Yeah, there are."

He's long been considered one of the most eligible bachelors in the league, women still clamoring for him like they did when he was on the ice. As far as I know, he hasn't been in a relationship since his divorce though.

"Harris!" Erik shouts abruptly, then motions toward himself with his palm. My stomach plummets; *of course,* Matt is walking past the office at this moment.

"Yeah, Coach?"

I stiffen at the sound of Matt's voice. I keep my back to him, hoping Coach will make this interaction quick.

"Briggsy's missing practice Friday. Says he's got an obligation to his girlfriend. He'll owe the standard fine. And he's not playing Saturday, of course."

There's a long pause. Guys miss practice and games for family emergencies and their kids' births, not for *girlfriends.* Will Matt's curiosity win out over his anger long enough for him to ask me for an explanation?

"All right," Matt says.

He collects fines and keeps them in a safe in his locker. At the end of the season, the team votes on which player embodied the Wolves culture the best through the season, and the fine money affords them a nice vacation. It's essentially a way to honor the toughest motherfucker in the room—the guy who gutted out injuries, who consistently busted his ass, who brought good energy to the locker room. Volk won last year, and he took Kennedy to Spain. Not that he couldn't afford it without the winnings, but still. It's the meaning, the respect of your team, that matters.

Erik nods once, then redirects his attention to his computer screen. "We're good," he says to me after a beat.

"Right," I reply, giving him a salute.

Pictures of his family catch my attention as I shuffle out of the room. Maybe I shouldn't be surprised my news didn't anger him.

I close the door, and Matt falls into step beside me. "You're missing practice?"

"Yep." As much as I want to patch what's broken between Matt and me, I don't stop walking. He dismissed me for weeks, all because I fell in love with his sister. As if it's something I could help.

"For her tryout?"

"She told you?"

"My parents did. You shouldn't miss practice for a *tryout*."

My feet stop abruptly. If this were a 90s sitcom, it's when you'd hear a record scratch.

"Finley's been busting her ass for the last six months preparing for this. It's her dream. You and your family might not approve, but it's what she wants. And she needs me there. So it's where I'm going to be. It's where I'm *always* going to be. Wherever Finley needs me."

Matt stares, his eyes glossy like he's in a daze.

"I think the better question is, why don't *you* give a shit?" I press.

Matt's still got that faraway look in his eyes, but he whispers, "You're serious..."

"What?"

He runs a hand over his chin, and his mouth morphs into a smile. "You're serious about her. You're missing *hockey* for her."

"I'm never going to be like you, but it doesn't mean I'm a fuckup. Finley helped me see that."

His eyebrows raise. "What do you mean, you'll never be like me?"

"A captain. Perfect in every way. Someone people look to for direction. But I'm loyal, and I show up for the people I love when they need me. I'd do the same for you, even though you've been—"

"A dick?" Matt finishes my sentence.

I shrug. "I was going to say turd."

He clears his throat. "My parents told me how important you are to her, and how she credits you with keeping her balanced, something about learning to have fun." He flashes me a smile before his mouth shrinks back into a line. "Finley's always been serious. Maybe it's because her older brothers constantly competed, or because she had to grow up when our parents were spread too thin, focusing on her siblings. I don't know the reason, but I worry about her—the way she single-mindedly focuses on gymnastics, a sport where she spends a lot of time alone."

I stub the top of my sneaker on the linoleum floor. "Do you plan on saying any of this to her?"

Matt winces. "Yeah, when she returns my calls. Listen, I'm not going to lie to you. I'm not wild about you dating her, but I'd feel this way about any guy. It is easier knowing she's with someone who's got a good heart, who will have her back." He lets out a long sigh. "My parents say this is the healthiest they've seen her. So... thank you."

The declaration stuns me silent.

Matt claps me on the shoulder. "If you fuck this up, I will make you regret it though."

"I'd expect nothing less, Harry." I use his nickname for the first time in weeks.

People like to say relationships are tough and it takes work to maintain one. Sometimes, it's described as a sacrifice, but I think that's the problem. When you love someone, putting them first *isn't* a sacrifice. It's pure elation watching the other person's face slip into happiness, to have them laugh and throw their arms around you, to thank you for being there. To know this person needs you, and that they can depend on you.

It's like being someone's teammate, something I have a lifetime of experience with.

I've always loved being part of a team, but calling Finley Harris my partner eclipses the feeling. She matters more than anyone else, *anything* else.

And I'll work every day to show her, to be the best damn teammate she's ever had.

36

Finley

ALL MY HARD WORK comes down to this—one practice, a couple of routines, a demonstration of skills I've practiced hundreds of times in this gym.

Never before in front of the UPC gymnastics coach though.

I barely slept last night, thinking about the importance of today. I insisted on not staying at Zach's because he'd distract me with activities that were decidedly not sleeping. So instead of cuddling up to my boyfriend, I watched the clock beside the bed in Veronica's house, praying I'd drift off. Several painful hours later, it finally happened but it wasn't enough.

A fist pounds on the door. "Finley? You ready?"

"Yep, almost," I call, continuing to take deep breaths, in and out, willing my heart to settle, my mind to calm.

I love everything about competing. All eyes on me. The pressure of the judges. Cheering for my teammates. Chalk in the air. The smack of the mat when I stick my landing. Nothing tops nailing a routine and having the noise of the gym rush back all at once in celebration of my performance.

It'd been years since my last good memory of competition. And today, out there, so much of what helped me thrive as a gymnast will be missing. All that awaits is one man who'll decide if I'm worthy of a second chance and the coach who has backed me every step of the way. I don't want to let Veronica down after she stuck her neck out for me.

And I don't want my gymnastics career to end.

The door rattles again, the knock more casual and less frantic.

"One minute."

But it's not Veronica's voice that answers me. "High-flyer, can you let me in?"

I rip open the door and launch myself at Zach, so thankful he's here. He's not expecting it, but those reflexes of his, honed to perfection by years of playing hockey, allow him to easily catch me. My legs wrap around his waist, my face nestling in the crook of his neck. I breathe in deeply, pulling his heady scent into my lungs. *Home.*

My faculties come back all at once. "Wait—what are you doing here?" I loosen the grip of my legs and find my footing on the floor.

When I step out of his arms, Zach gives me an appreciative scan. "It's so good to see you."

I keep my gaze on him, waiting for an explanation for why he's here.

"What? Am I supposed to play it cool, pretend you don't affect me?"

I roll my eyes. "You didn't answer my question."

Zach's forehead wrinkles. "What was your question?"

"Seriously?" I playfully shove his shoulder, flashing a teasing smile. "You weren't listening?"

"I was. Or I tried to." He shrugs, a sheepish expression on his face. Pink cheeks and an impish smile. "What was the question?"

"I asked what you're doing here." I cross my arms over my chest.

He's supposed to be somewhere else right now. I'd known it and gotten over my disappointment. A few days before leaving Maine, my parents returned my phone, and I received Veronica's texts about the tryout with the UPC coach. I texted Zach first—he's the person I want to share everything with—and he broke the news he had practice at the same time. My heart sank knowing I wouldn't have him in my corner. But I'd never ask him to sacrifice his job for me.

Zach's hands slide into the pockets of his jeans. "I'm here to cheer on my girl while she kicks ass and blows that coach away."

"But you have practice."

"The *team* has practice. I'm excused, and we can talk about it later. Right now is about you. Veronica says you're hiding. What's going on?"

I groan. "I'm not *hiding*. I needed a minute before I go out there and perform the most important routines of my entire career in front of a man who holds my fate in his hands."

Zach points toward the gym. "Don't think about him. Think about this as if it's any other practice when I sat on the sidelines in awe as you flip around like it's as easy as breathing."

One hand drifts to my cheek, his thumb moving back and forth on my skin. "It's me and you out there, all right? And in case it's not obvious, I'm going to love you no matter what happens. I'm so proud of you, Finley. I've watched you balance college and gymnastics and working at the café, and somehow you made time for me and you found a way to manage it all. You do everything so fucking well. Regardless of what happens or doesn't happen, I admire the shit out of you."

His words kick my heart, and like a piñata, my overwhelming feelings for him fall out. I don't realize I'm crying until Zach smooths away my tears. He tugs me to him, and I go willingly, affixing my body to his.

No one has ever said words like that to me. It's overwhelming in the best way possible to know this person will stand by my side whether I succeed or fail. Like I'd do for him.

His fingers trail over my hair, the motion so soothing, that I *relax* for the first time in more than twelve hours.

"I'm so lucky you belong with me," he murmurs.

With him, not *to* him. One word makes all the difference.

"They're going to know I've been crying," I say through a watery laugh, pulling out of his embrace. My hands run over my face, clearing the remaining tears.

"They don't matter, Finley. Only you. And you've got this."

I splash some water on my face, then blot it with a paper towel. Better, but still not great. Good thing I won't be judged on my appearance.

"Thank you for being here, for choosing me. I never thought I'd have this." I motion in the air between us. "I didn't think something as good as *this* could exist."

Zach swallows hard. "Me neither," he croaks, then clears the emotion from his throat before speaking again. "Show them what I already know—Finley Harris is a force to be reckoned with."

I roll my shoulders, taking one last deep breath. "I won't let you down." Zach huffs out a laugh when I wink at him. "Prepare to be impressed."

⊰•◦ ❉ ◦•⊱

"You ready?" Veronica greets me as I stroll into the gym. She stands beside Coach Miller on the edge of the floor, her head barely reaching his shoulder.

I force a smile. My body still surges with nerves. "Absolutely. Sorry for the delay."

Veronica waves a hand. "It gave Coach Miller time to catch up with his favorite gymnast." She winks at me, then pitches her voice low to talk to Coach. "Don't worry, your secret is safe with us."

Zach enters the gym and goes to the alcove, the spot where he watched me train when Veronica ordered him away for distracting me. His presence centers me.

It's me and you out there, all right? And in case it's not obvious, I'm going to love you no matter what happens.

Coach Miller pats her on the shoulder. "I appreciate it." His attention shifts to me. "So, Finley, Veronica speaks highly of you. I saw you compete years ago too. Your gymnastics was always impressive. How long have you been back in training?"

I fight the urge to cross my arms. "Since last summer, but I've been training relentlessly. I'm not back to where I was... you know... before, but I'm confident I will be by next season."

"Are you okay sharing what made you step back from the sport?" he asks.

I appreciate his phrasing, the way he gives me the option to opt out of answering. Last summer, I would've run from this conversation.

I look at Veronica, then Zach, thinking about how telling each of them didn't go the way my mind told me it would. I thought they'd want nothing to do with the "crazy" girl who couldn't control her emotions. But they both stayed. They love me anyway.

And if this coach judges me for my condition—for something I can't help—then fuck him. I will find someone else who accepts me as I am. Because that's what I deserve.

"I needed to focus on my mental health. I have bipolar disorder and had to learn how to manage it. Which I did. I'm healthier than ever, and I can answer any questions you have."

He nods slowly, taking in my explanation. The confession doesn't cause him to drop eye contact or scrunch his face with worry or disgust. "Thank you for telling me, Finley. I value honesty. It's something we need to talk about more if you join the team, but we'll cross that bridge then."

I nod. "Where do you want me to start?"

He gestures over his shoulder. "I'd love to see those famous beam skills."

A genuine smile stretches across my face. "You've got it," I say before striding to the apparatus I'd dominated when competing in elite gymnastics. My other events are solid, but I thrive on that four-inch beam. I mastered it after forcing myself to spend hours practicing difficult skills repeatedly until I defeated the fear of falling.

Veronica approaches while I'm setting up the springboard. "You got this, Fi."

"I know," I tell her, straightening to my full height after placing the springboard in the exact place I need for my mount. "But thank you."

"You don't need me anymore, huh?"

"I'll always need you. You're a huge part of why I know I can do this. So let me show off how good of a coach you are."

She shakes her head, but I glimpse a smile blossoming on her face before she heads back to Coach Miller.

I step onto the springboard, my back to the beam, and breathe in deeply. I take one glance over my shoulder, then raise my hands in the air, and bounce on the springboard to gather momentum for my backflip.

I catch the beam with my arms while my legs remain straight in the air before they drop and I swing myself onto the apparatus.

Zach leans against the alcove wall, his hands clasped together as if in prayer.

I mouth to him, *I love you*.

His mouth forms the words, *Stick your landing*.

I block out everything around me, limiting my vision to no further than each end of the beam. I don't notice the pin-drop silence in the gym, instead focusing on my own voice in my mind as I complete leaps, jumps, flips, and twists, working my way up the beam, then back down it again.

I grin when I land my last flip, readying myself for dismount. Perfection is impossible in this sport, but we strive for it every time we perform. This routine has been pretty damn good. A couple of balance checks, and one missed connection between elements when I paused to gather myself before doing the next flip.

More important than my execution, I'm having fun despite the pressure of this moment. It's something I haven't experienced in *years*.

Cheers break out after I complete a Gainer—a cartwheel into two twists off the beam—my feet sticking to the mat. Zach cheers from the alcove, hooting and clapping loudly, my personal cheer squad. The best one I could ask for.

I turn toward Veronica and Coach Miller; both have wide smiles on their faces.

"Bars next?" I ask.

Every routine that follows goes the same. Mistakes happen, but nothing devastating. On bars, I seamlessly complete a connection from the high to low bar that I'd failed nine out of ten times a month ago. I perform a riskier vault, betting on my training to complete it. The risk paid off, earning me a thumbs-up from Veronica and a cool nod from Coach Miller. Every time I stick a landing, happiness rushes through me because I'm that much closer to my dream.

When my floor music cuts off—my last event—it almost doesn't matter what Coach Miller says. I've fought hard to reach a healthier mental state, clawed my way back into gymnastics, and learned to trust my judgment. Based on the cheers coming from Zach in the alcove and the broad smile on Veronica's face, I know I've made them proud too.

37

Finley

It isn't until Coach Miller and Veronica walk toward the exit that I see an unexpected figure standing in the corner. I glance toward Zach, needing him to confirm my brother stands here when he should be at practice. Zach nods toward Matt, and he mouths, *You got this*.

I heave a sigh, trying to calm my heart, still racing with adrenaline. Not only from the routines I performed but from the news that Coach Miller would like me to join UPC's gymnastics team. I keep repeating his words in my mind, hoping that they'll sink in, that I'll accept the incredible accomplishment and be able to celebrate it.

"Hi." I approach Matt with slow, tentative steps. "What are you doing here?"

"Someone told me this is an important day for you," he says, glancing toward the alcove.

I nod. "It determines the future of my gymnastics career... so yeah, kinda a big deal."

"How did it go?" Matt asks. "I mean, with the coach. I watched the routines—you killed it."

"You watched? What about practice?"

He shrugs. "I want to support you. You've been a part of so many of my important moments, and I've missed out on most of yours. It's why I agreed to let you live with me."

A breath stutters out of me at his admission. Matt and I never talked about me coming to live with him. My parents arranged it, so I never knew how much he chose versus my presence being pushed onto him. Matt was the obvious choice—the brother with a house, a wife, his life completely under control. If I was going to go anywhere, it would be to live with him. But I didn't know if he welcomed the intrusion.

He looks down at his shoes. "I should've told you that, but... you know, it seems stupid to say since you're my sister... but we don't know each other well. I wanted to give you a safe place to live as you move forward. I thought I was doing that—"

"You did, Matt. You're the reason I got to build a life, but when I made choices you didn't agree with you, it was like dealing with Mom and Dad all over again." I cross my arms over my chest. "I can't keep living my life for other people. I can't stop living because it's less for you and Mom and Dad to worry about."

"Finley, I know." Matt holds up a hand. "I know." He runs his hand through his hair, mussing the blond strands. "I've talked to Mom and Dad, and I had a session with Dr. Warren."

"What?" I say. "You did?"

"I've carried around so much guilt for what happened with Garrett."

"Matt, it wasn't your fault."

He waves a hand. "It was. I *blame* myself for it. It's caused me to be overbearing at times."

I snort. "At times?"

"I'm sorry, Finley," Matt says, taking a step toward me. "I screwed up. I was too tough on you, too strict, and more like your chaperone than your brother. I want to change that. What do you think?"

"It sounds nice," I say. "But what does it mean?"

Matt shifts his weight from one foot to the other. "We start over. If you want to come back and live with me this semester, I'd love it. But if it's too much, we can find an apartment so you can live on your own."

I tilt my head. "What if I want an apartment in the same complex as Zach? Would that be okay?"

"Not going to make this easy, huh?" Matt blows out a breath. "But if it's what you want, I can do that."

"Dr. Warren really is a miracle worker," I quip, letting out a nervous laugh. "What I want is to come home to your absurdly gigantic house. It's the first place in a long time I've felt less alone. But I'll only come back if my boyfriend has a permanent invitation." My eyes begin to burn, and I swallow hard to keep my emotions at bay. "I love Zach. We're a package deal."

Matt groans, his head falling back as he looks at the ceiling. "I'm never going to get rid of that kid, huh?"

I punch his arm, and he shoots both hands up like stop signs.

"Kidding. I know he's a good guy, and I like that he puts you first. You deserve it, Finley."

I glance at Zach, whose gaze darts down like I've caught him cheating on a test. I love him so damn much.

"So are you going to tell me what the coach said?" Matt asks.

"I made the team. No promises about how much I'll compete, but I'll have a chance to fight for it."

Matt spreads his arms wide, taking another step forward before pausing. He opens his mouth to say something, but I meet him halfway, accepting a hug from my brother. The golden boy who humbled himself to examine his behavior, to show up here and apologize, who wants what's best for me.

"I'm proud of you, sis," he says as he pulls away. "I'll see you tonight at the house?"

"Tomorrow," I answer, testing the boundaries of this new relationship. "There's someone I want to celebrate with tonight."

"Tomorrow then," he agrees before pitching his voice louder to shout over to Zach. "Be good to her, Briggsy!" He reaches the door and turns back around to add, "Or else."

⊰⊱

I sprint to the alcove as soon as Matt leaves and jump into Zach's arms. He swings me in a circle, clutching me tightly to his body. The movement forces a laugh to whoosh from my lungs.

"You fucking did it, High-flyer," he whispers as he eases me to my feet, his arms still tight against my lower back. "Just like I knew you would."

Like I knew I would too.

I nailed my routines, the ones I'd spent hours practicing in this gym. I'd fallen off the beam, missed the bar, and landed short on my vault countless times, but each time I got up and did it again. It's something people don't understand about successful athletes. The falls and the getting back up time and time again are what allow me to stick my landing when it counts. Like anything else in life, it takes screwing up and fumbling through the dark to find our way.

And it's better when you're not alone, when there's someone by your side on the hard days, encouraging you to keep going.

"Thank you for believing in me." I push onto my tiptoes and press my lips to Zach's mouth, communicating what words are inadequate for conveying.

Because no word in the English language is strong enough to capture how much Zach Briggs means to me, or to properly describe the way my body and mind react to him. The way I covet his presence. But that's okay, because I plan to show him every damn day how much he matters to me.

I'll always fight for him.

As his fingers thread through mine, I don't have a single doubt he'll do the same. We'll face every obstacle together, side by side. When I need someone, he'll be there, and I'll show up every time for him too.

Even when he sets fire to a house and runs away.

Or when I don't want to leave my bed.

And especially moments filled with joy, when we have something to celebrate. Like this one.

For the first time in a long time, I believe these happy moments will exist for me, and there's no one else in the entire world who I'd rather share them with.

38

Finley

Four months later

"You ready for this?" Kennedy asks, as if I'm the one taking the ice for game seven in the second round of the playoffs instead of a doting girlfriend in the crowd.

My heart doesn't get the message I'm not the one about to compete and pounds with an intensity that should alarm me. Since I met Zach Briggs, my heart's gone haywire, acting in unexplainable ways.

It's not only my heart. I'm dressed in a Palmer City Wolves hockey jersey emblazoned with BRIGGS across the back. I let Kennedy, temporarily, color forest green streaks in my blond hair and draw black stripes of warpaint across my cheeks.

I traveled between Palmer City and New York during round one, then to Florida and back for round two, to watch every Wolves game as they charge toward the Cup. It's given Kennedy and me time to focus on our finals, spending hours in a quiet train car for multiple trips. It's also an unprecedented move for me. I've never placed anyone above my own needs before.

"I don't know how you do this," I say.

"What?" Kennedy asks.

"Deal with this... anxiety." I gesture toward the ice, where the Wolves warm up—stretching, slapping the puck into an empty net, playing catch with each other.

I worry for Zach every time someone checks him into the boards or jockeys with him for position in front of the net, something he says I'll get used to. I won't though. Falling in love with him has come with this unexpected *protectiveness*. I want to fight his battles, do whatever's needed to bring out that playful smile of his, make him happy.

Kennedy throws her head back and laughs. "Says the woman who performs acrobatics that could *actually* kill her."

"At least I control the outcome," I grumble. I also train relentlessly with safeguards in place to protect me. And when I step into the UPC gym next season, it'll be me against each apparatus without someone trying to take me down midair.

Her hand lands on mine, squeezing once. "They'll be all right, Fi. Florida knows not to mess with us or Alexei will beat their heads into the ice."

Kennedy says this so casually, like she's commenting on the weather, I almost laugh. Instead, I thank my lucky stars Alexei Volkov has Zach's back out there.

My brother, Charlie, leans forward and rests his arm on top of our seats. He refuses to don Wolves gear out of loyalty to his team, but I'd bet money underneath his sweatshirt, he's wearing Matt's jersey. "You know we can afford a box, ladies."

"With all the food and booze we want," my other brother, Ryan, chimes in. He's got a Palmer City Wolves hat over his buzzed hair, which he claims he only wears to keep his head warm.

I didn't get my stoicism from nowhere, people.

Kennedy smirks. "Well, when *your* teams make the playoffs, we will consider your opinions."

I stifle a snort. People often label strong opinionated women as bitches, but Kennedy doesn't let it stop her from speaking her mind. I'm so glad to have someone like her in our corner.

Ryan opens his mouth, but Charlie raises an arm, halting him. His two hands remain in the air like two white flags before he slides back into his seat. It's better for him; Alexei Volkov takes offense when anyone hits on or insults his fiancée, and these two face him on the ice multiple times a season.

"About time you put those two jabronis in their place." Bertram—the ring leader of the geriatric gambling group at the Courtside Café—leans forward to speak but does nothing to hide his words from my brothers beside him. Bertram's friends and fellow gamblers, Lenny and Oscar, sit on the other side, hooting at the joke their friend made.

"All right, you," Kennedy says. "We're going to be gracious hosts, all right? We're all rooting for the Wolves tonight."

Bertram leans back in his seat, then turns to my brothers. "I grant you a temporary pass. Next season, I'm back to hating you."

Charlie gives a salute while Ryan diverts his attention to the ice.

"These are the seats I shared with my mom," Kennedy whispers to me. I barely hear her over the noise echoing around the arena as the sizzle reel that they play before each game starts on the screen at center ice.

She nudges me forward to reveal a sign I missed on my seat earlier. *In honor of Elizabeth Cole, loving wife, perfect mom, Wolves fanatic.* Kennedy's fingers trace the words as a shadow of a smile sketches over her lips. "She'd like you."

"How do you know?"

"Because she'd be *obsessed* with Briggsy."

"What else is new?" I quip without a millimeter of bitterness. I like being the girlfriend of Zach Briggs, star winger of the Palmer City Wolves, the guy most liked by opposing fans. He *chooses* me, this solid, kindhearted, funny, fantastic guy. For a while, I woke up each day waiting for the other shoe to drop, for him to realize I'm more trouble than I'm worth.

Now I know the guy grinning at me as he lines up on the ice has no plans to go anywhere. Neither do I.

"Finley?" A voice calls a moment before the announcer asks fans to stand if they're able for the singing of the national anthem.

I raise my hand. "That's me," I say, turning toward the source.

And there in the aisle stands Zach's family, who I'd recognize even if Zach hadn't shown me pictures. His mom, Rosie, grins the same way he does, with equal parts joy and gratitude. His dad, Bill, stands behind her, hands on her shoulders to keep her steady. Zach's protective like that too. His brother, Jeff, is Zach's carbon copy, except he has his mom's green eyes. Melanie, his sister, appraises me, her eyebrows knitting together like Zach's when he concentrates. I love them instantly, for every bit of Zach I see in them.

All of us face the flag as the national anthem plays. As soon as it ends, Rosie shouts over the cheering crowd, "Come here, sweetheart!"

I hesitate, not wanting to leave Kennedy alone with her mother's vacant seat.

"I'll take your seat." Deandra appears behind Zach's family, decked out in Wolves gear, the most casual attire I've seen her wear. The fierce winged eyeliner and blunt-cut hair still make her look formidable, but I think she'd give off that vibe regardless of her clothes and makeup. I suppose fighting for a spot in a male-dominated industry will do that to a person.

"Go meet your in-laws," Kennedy whispers, flashing them a smile. "And hurry before you block puck drop. This crowd will yell at you. We'll catch up later, all right?"

"Thanks, Kens."

I move toward Zach's family, sliding past Deandra as she heads toward Kennedy. She whispers, "Good luck," and lightly squeezes my forearm.

"It's so great to meet all of you," I say, raising my voice as the crowd cheers louder. "Here let's—"

Rosie pulls me into a crushing hug, silencing my attempt at suggesting we settle into our seats. "Oh, honey, I've been dying to meet the girl my son won't stop talking about." She pulls back but takes hold of my hands. "I've never seen my boy this happy."

Her words tug the center of my chest, and I swallow hard, determined not to cry in front of Zach's family. I still surprise myself when emotion so easily pushes to the surface. I shoved every feeling down for so long, refusing to let it affect me.

To no one's surprise, dating Zach Briggs has changed that for me. I'll never reach his level of vulnerability, wearing every emotion on my sleeve, but I'm a far cry from the stilted, serious girl who brought him to her gym the first time.

"I've never been this happy," I say through the clot of emotion lodged in my throat.

Bill and Jeff offer me handshakes before exiting the aisle to sit beside Kennedy and Deandra. Melanie makes no move to hug me or offer a handshake, but as we enter the row, she instructs me to sit between her and Rosie. Easier to grill me that way, I suppose. Zach warned me about his overprotective sister and said I shouldn't take her standoffish attitude as judgment against me.

"It's so kind of your brother to pay for our travel," Rosie gushes while we settle into our seats as the puck drops at center ice. "Your parents are here, yes? I want to meet the people who raised such terrific kids."

"That's them," I tell her, pointing over my shoulder toward my parents, who sit on the other side of my brothers.

My parents turn as though they feel my gaze, and I offer a smile and wave. We're still meeting each week with Dr. Warren, slowly building a relationship based on honesty and trust. As long as I'm forthright about my moods and activities, they respect my decisions, even if it makes them nervous. My mom waves back enthusiastically while my dad offers a quick nod before turning his attention back to the ice. He's making an effort despite his hesitance to relinquish control of my safety. I appreciate he's working on it and that our relationship is inching toward a better place as a result.

"I'm Zach's mom," Rosie calls, answering my mom's wave with one of her own. "I love your daughter!"

"But you don't know me," I say before I can filter the internal thought.

Rosie spins back around. "Not as well as I'd like... but, Finley, my son has told me all about you, about how you treat him. The way you put his needs above your own." One hand lands flat over her heart. "Gosh, the way you asked him to think about whether a relationship was what he wanted... it takes a strong person to do that."

Zach knows how much I struggle with telling people I have bipolar disorder. I prefer to do it after I trust them, but I wanted to handle telling his family differently. I wanted them to know me fully, and they couldn't without revealing the condition that affects every day of my life. So Zach told his family for me before this trip, and according to him, they were supportive. I didn't fully believe it until now.

"He told me how you support him," Rosie goes on, "by going to every out-of-state playoff game. Making his favorite foods when he gets home from a road trip, even if you can't wait up because of your schedule." She flings an arm toward the rink. "You love him because of *him*, not for what he can do on that ice. I already see how much Zach's grown since he met you."

I let out a laugh. "He knows how to load a dishwasher now."

Rosie chuckles. "Yes, well. I *tried*, but it took a real incentive for it to stick."

That's what everything in my life feels like now, like it's sprinkled with an extra incentive. Since meeting Zach, my drive toward my goals hasn't changed, but I also want to make him proud. I'm working the same grueling schedule, but something's different within me. There's an extra flicker of awareness that he's beside me, that my wins are his and that his are mine.

"Oh my God!" Rosie shouts suddenly as number ten sprints down the ice on a breakaway. "Go, Zach!"

The crowd hops to their feet as he approaches the net with only the goalie standing between him and a goal. Zach heads toward the goalie's left, but at the last split second, he glides the puck in the opposite direction, giving it a flick into the air. It hits the net, and the siren sounds, followed by the team's goal-scoring anthem and an eruption of cheers through the arena. The camera finds us, bringing our flushed and smiling faces to the screen at center ice as we hop up and down in excitement. Zach and his teammates do their celebratory hugs, driving him against the glass with their momentum. The camera swings to him next, showing his mouth open in a scream, eyes lit, one arm punching the air.

We eventually settle back in our seats, but there's electricity in the air now. The crowd's alive, engaged, and ready for more.

"Well, now that we're all in a good mood." Melanie folds her hands over her lap. "Are you ready for the real test?"

"Mel," Rosie hisses in a mom-scold, but Melanie remains undeterred, her gaze on me.

I motion to myself and give her a teasing grin. "Bring your worst."

Several hours later, Gemma and Matt invite everyone—the Briggs and Harris tribes, Alexei and Kennedy, and Deandra—to their home. As usual, Gemma's armed with enough food to feed an army, including my absolute favorite dessert of hers—double chocolate brownies. With hockey players here and the out-of-this-world taste of Gemma's baking, the food doesn't last long.

Gemma lights the fireplace for purely aesthetic reasons—May is air-conditioning season in North Carolina. She queues up a playlist full of soft- and pop-rock songs from when I was a kid. We scatter through-out the first floor in ever-changing groups.

Jennings, Alexei, and I play a round of Wii Golf. Zach's parents show me photos of him as a kid. In my favorite photo, Zach's covered in cake and icing because he fell into the cake after he and Jeff argued about who'd have the first piece.

When the Harrises all end up in one room, we unsurprisingly break out a deck of cards, ready for any opportunity to compete with each other. Zach's family wanders in halfway through the game, and Jeff gets sucked into it. I watch from the wall as our families blend, competing and laughing and talking, and my chest inflates with so much love, it hurts.

A cool hand slides into mine, but I school myself not to react. Knowing that hand and desperately wanting a moment alone with him. I slide to the doorway, then tiptoe backward until I'm out of the room. Zach tugs me toward him, straight into his arms, securing me against his body. His lips snag mine, kissing me with an intensity that makes me wish we could head back to his place for time alone.

"I missed you," Zach murmurs against my lips between kisses. I can't get enough of his mint taste, his hands gripping my ass, the satisfied moan when my tongue teases his.

"Yeah," I whisper back. "I got the better end of the deal getting to watch you for the last couple of hours. Great game, Calder."

"You're impressed." He's no longer surprised when I express my admiration; instead, there's a quiet satisfaction, an awe.

"Of course." My hand threads through his, always confirming my affection for him, because I want him to believe it without a single doubt. "You're fucking impressive. That goal was *smooth*. Just like that little move"—I gesture around us, referencing the way he deftly pulled me to him—"you did to me."

Zach's face breaks into a shy grin. "You liked that, huh?"

I bite my bottom lip, dipping my head in a slow nod.

"Wanna get out of here?" His head jerks toward the stairs beside us.

My stomach flips over as I think about having him beneath me, my nerves churning like the folding of cream in a dessert. It's the same anticipation that floods my nervous system every time he puts his hands on me or says something sweet, or when I open my eyes in the morning to see him peacefully snoozing beside me with a ghost of a smile on his lips.

Each time, it gives way to an inferno that consumes me, lust an accelerant to my deep love for this man. The one person who made me comfortable enough to let my guard down, to relinquish the tight control over my emotions. I don't regret it, and regardless of what happens between us, I never will. Our love is worth the risk of heartbreak.

Zach and I pause on the steps at the sound of an amused voice ten feet below us.

"Where are you two off to?"

Kennedy stands beside Alexei in the foyer, arching an eyebrow. He smirks, knowing *exactly* where we're headed... and why. He's probably wishing he could do the same with his fiancée.

I pull in a deep breath, trying to regulate my body. "I need to show Zach something in my room."

Alexei snorts. The sound covers the muffled laugh from Zach behind me.

"It's very important," I add, forcing my expression into neutrality. "Can you cover for us? Please?"

"Fifteen minutes," Kennedy says. "Otherwise, I can guarantee you'll have a bunch of guests in your bedroom."

Alexei runs a finger down the length of Kennedy's arm, and she visibly shivers. "Look who's a softie."

"Me?" she jokes, breathless. "I'm not the one—"

Her words devolve into a giggle that echoes around the foyer as Zach and I resume our climb, moving quickly and quietly up the steps, like our feet might catch fire if we linger too long. We're on my bed in thirty seconds, on our sides, legs tangled, lips fused, hands exploring. I remember the first time I invited Zach into this bed, the tentative way he touched me, as if I might evaporate into a figment of his fantasies. It's the opposite of how he's touching me now, his hands moving hungrily down my body, dipping into my leggings.

"*High-flyer*," Zach groans when his fingers push inside me. "You're already ready for me."

"I've had three hours of foreplay, watching you play hockey."

He laughs, more agony than amusement. "I fucking love you."

I push him flat onto his back then swing a leg over him, planting myself over his hard-on. "Show me."

"Our families will hear the bed. Your brother catching us once is more than enough for a lifetime."

"Chair," I say, desperate to have him inside me. "I'll go slow. It'll be torture, but I'll make it worth it. Unless you want to celebrate another way…"

I swivel my hips, drawing a groan from deep in Zach's throat. His hands land beneath my ass, hoisting me into the air with him. I undo his pants as he walks us to my wooden desk chair, taking a seat after his pants drop to his ankles. He shoves my panties aside then lowers me onto his cock, both of us groaning at this euphoric connection. My hips propel forward, then shift back, a tantalizing rhythm grinding my clit against him. It feels so, so good, I can't help but pick up the pace, needing more friction.

His hand covers my mouth, smothering my moan. "Quiet, Finley, or we'll need to stop."

I nod my agreement, and he removes his hand.

"I need more."

Zach tucks a sweaty strand of hair behind my ear. "How about I talk you through it?"

"Words won't—" My voice cuts out when Zach takes my earlobe into his mouth, scraping his teeth lightly across my skin. His other hand migrates up my shirt to tease my hardened nipples, sending a bolt of longing to my core.

"No?" he whispers into the shell of my ear.

My hips buck against him, messy movements until I've found a spot that'll make me explode.

"You're fluttering against my dick. You're close, Finley. *God*, you're close, and—" He mashes his lips into mine but otherwise stays still as I work myself back and forth against him, chasing the breaking point out of my reach. "*Fuck*, I can't hold on much longer. I need you to come with me, babe."

It's the sound of agony in his voice that sends me over the edge, a wave of pleasure cresting at its painful apex before crashing. The tension in my body breaks, spreading a delicious heat through every nerve. I slump into Zach, spent and blissed beyond belief. His hands secure me to him, the pound of his rapid heartbeat reverberating against me. My arms snake around him beneath his shirt, my fingertips running lightly over his skin.

"You good, High-flyer?"

"I could stay here all day," I mutter.

"If we stay in this position, I'm going to get hard again—"

"I know." My head pops off his chest, and I look at him. "Not seeing a problem with it."

"You're tired," he says, halfheartedly.

"You can do all the work next time." I push a kiss into the crook of his neck. "Problem solved."

"I'll need more than the remainder of our fifteen minutes for what I want to do to you."

Slowly, he lifts me off him, but we still manage to make a mess of each other. He grabs tissues from my desk and cleans us up with the carefulness I've come to expect from him. Always so mindful of how he affects me. I don't know how I got this lucky, to find someone who loves me so intensely, as much as I love him.

I handle our relationship with the same carefulness, treating it as if it's breakable, never taking for granted that he's mine.

Epilogue: Zach

One Year Later

PRIDE SURGES THROUGH ME as I watch from the stands as Finley Harris's life changes.

The gymnastics world is seeing what I already know: she's a fucking star. Well, they knew it once, years ago, but her routines in UPC's first regular season meet are putting an exclamation point on the reminder. No one can deny she's back and better than ever.

Finley sticks her landing after doing the flippy twisty somersault off the vault I've seen her practice hundreds of times. She told me once she didn't need to wait for the landing to know whether she'd stick it; she can tell based on how her hands block off the vault.

From the megawatt smile already on her face when her feet hit the mat, I can tell she agrees with the enthusiastic reception of the audience. I'm out of my chair, cheering at the top of my lungs along with them. I sit when Finley's back with her teammates at the beginning of the vault runway.

This first meet is scheduled on a nongame day, unlike most this season. The contingent of us here for Finley goes rows deep, and from the way she glances up at our section every so often, I know how much it means to her to have this support.

It's especially true about her parents, who made the trip from Maine yesterday to spend the weekend and see their daughter compete. They worked to heal their fractured relationships, fighting to get to a healthy place where they can support Finley's decisions.

Jennings leans into me, arms draping over the seat rest separating us. "You're going to be a meme, Briggsy."

Like I give a shit. Other than me, the only person whose opinion holds sway over my actions is Finley. And Coach Pomroy.

I thrust a hand through my hair and flash a silly expression his way. "How does this look? Good enough to be commemorated for all eternity?"

Jennings laughs, but he's also tugging me toward our seats to stop me from making too much of an ass of myself. "Explain to me again how you managed to make someone like Finley fall in love with you."

I flick an invisible speck of dust off my shoulder. "Why? Need tips?"

"Fuck off, man," he replies. "I want to make sure she hasn't been brainwashed into this relationship."

"No need. She loves me as-is, dude."

"It's a fucking miracle," Jennings mutters under his breath.

"Tell me about it."

"Zachary Briggs, don't ever forget you're a catch," Gemma says in an exaggerated mom voice.

Matt scoffs. "No, he's lucky my sister gives this jackass the time of day."

"Hey!" I say, playing into his act.

Matt quickly came around about our relationship when he learned I was willing to miss practice and get healthy scratched for a game to support her. His support has only increased as he's witnessed our relationship grow this past year.

I hope it'll make it easier for him to accept that Finley and I plan to move in together in the not-too-distant future. I mean, after she says yes, of course. After signing my $8.5 million, eight-year contract, I decided to buy a house I could turn into a home, one I want Finley to move into when she graduates college. Buying the right house will affect us both, so I've been putting it off until Finley's part of the equation. And I'll do whatever it takes to make it happen.

Finley finishes the meet on bars, dazzling us with the ease with which she swings and flips and jumps between the low and high bars. UPC wins the meet handily, hopefully the first of many this season. By the time I maneuver my way to the gym floor to meet her, she's talking to a middle-aged female correspondent from the ACC network. Her lips break into a broad smile when she spots me.

The reporter's eyes widen with recognition. "Well, we have another sports star in our midst, Mr. Zach Briggs of the Palmer City Wolves professional hockey team. Come join us, won't you?"

I wave awkwardly to the correspondent but focus my gaze on Finley, seeking silent permission to join the interview. This moment isn't about me, and I don't want it to be. I also don't want to be rude.

Finley lifts one arm, beckoning me to her side. "I can't believe you're wearing that."

I pause to glance down at my T-shirt which reads *Finley Harris's Boyfriend* in bright red font so no one will struggle to see it. "What? It's the title I'm most proud of. I want everyone to know it."

"Aw, how sweet are you two?" the correspondent coos. "Tell me—"

I hold up the hand not wrapped around Finley's shoulders. "I'm sorry to interrupt you, and I know I'm crashing the party. High-flyer, were you in the middle of saying something?"

She flashes me a grateful smile, transferring more of her weight to me. "I was talking about my journey back to gymnastics, and how the key to keeping healthy was finding a psychiatrist who was invested in helping me determine the right medication and lifestyle choices. Like so many people, I was resistant at first, but I'm glad I had people in my life looking out for me when I wasn't in a place to do it myself."

I press a kiss to the top of her head, so proud of my girl for sharing her authentic self with the world.

"Your story is inspiring to many of us chasing dreams," the correspondent says. "You shouldn't give up. You can defy the odds."

"Exactly, but sometimes not by yourself. It's okay to ask for help. It doesn't make you weak." Finley grins, and her pink cheeks puff out adorably. "Okay, now I can answer your questions about us. What do you want to know?"

The correspondent straightens, her posture relaxing after Finley opens the door to personal questions. "Can you tell us how y'all met?"

Finley laughs airily, shifting her wide-eyed stare to me. "Can I tell this one?"

I gesture toward the camera with my free arm. "Go right ahead. You're a better storyteller than me."

Her head tilts. "A more *efficient* storyteller. You're more fun." Finley sucks in a breath. "Zach and I met at my brother's wedding."

"Your brother, Matt Harris, captain of the Palmer City Wolves?"

"That's right," Finley sings.

The correspondent leans forward, hanging on Finley's every word. "That must've been quite the stir?"

"You could say that, but not until they all found out about us."

"Ooh, a secret relationship," the correspondent says.

I lean into Finley and fake-whisper, "We were obvious about it though."

"*We?*" she erupts with glee. "*You* were the one always staring at me from across the room."

"And you know that because you were staring at *me*."

The correspondent steps toward us until she's beside us facing the camera. "Well, I think it's safe to say you two make a wonderful pair, and I'm sure you've gained a lot of fans today. Finley Harris, Zach Briggs, thanks for being here with us."

"Thanks for having us," we both say.

And then the camera cuts off and the reporter says in her regular voice, "Seriously, thank you both for making my job easy today. Best of luck!"

Finley's friends and family wave to us from the bleachers, and I know we'll be with them soon, but I want a moment alone with her before I have to share. I'm grappling for something to say, a phenomenon that happens only around Finley, but she beats me to the punch.

"You're the best boyfriend, Zach."

I shrug, pretending those words don't send a beam of happiness to my chest. "I warned you I'm very coachable, Finley."

She squares her body to me, a playful smile on her lips, and drapes her arms over my shoulders. "Oh, yeah? What else do they say about you?"

"I've got great hands," I say, placing them on her hips.

"Mm-hmm, can confirm," she murmurs. I helplessly watch her mouth form the words. "Shockingly, neither of those reasons are why I think you're the best boyfriend."

I put a finger to my lips like I'm thinking hard. "I skate pretty fast. Oh, and I can make a mean scrambled egg and a passable budget."

"Not those either," she says, her smile fading into seriousness. She puts me out of misery and kisses me. It's not long enough, but it's all I'll get in this setting. "You're the best because you let me pick what we watched last night, knowing I was nervous for today. Because you arranged for everyone to be here to support me. If I fell during every single routine, you'd still look at me like I amaze you. You'd still be proud of me."

She grabs the seam of my sleeve. "And it's because you're wearing this shirt, wanting the world to know you belong with me." Her voice catches, emotion overwhelming her. She pauses a moment before adding, "It's all of those things and none of those things."

I tilt my head. "So it was a trick question?"

She laughs through her tears, dabbing the corners of her eyes. "It's you. If I were to design someone for me, it'd be you."

"You mean you wouldn't change how I *still* don't load the dishwasher perfectly?"

She twists her mouth in fake annoyance. "Be serious."

I kiss the tip of her scrunched nose. "I'll always have your back, High-flyer. It's you and me first, then everyone and everything else. And for the record, it's easy to be your boyfriend. *You're* easy to love, Finley."

She stares at me, one tear rolling down her cheek. I look back, not moving a muscle, enjoying the sight of her. The rest of the world falls away, and it's like we're waking up in bed together, communicating love without words.

And then she throws herself into my arms. I clutch her to me, lifting her off her feet, letting her rest all her weight on me.

It's what we do. It's *why* we work. We take the weight of the other person when needed without fail, without expectation, without conscious thought.

We pick each other up so we can keep going, hurtling toward our dreams. Never forgetting the ultimate dream stands in front of us. This woman wrapped in my arms—my top priority—will never face anything alone again. We'll hold hands through every good, difficult, and wild experience in our lives, as we do now, walking toward our friends and family.

And I'll love every moment with her by my side.

If you enjoyed Stick Your Landing and...

...want more of Zach and Finley, visit my website by scanning the QR code below to sign up for my newsletter and receive a free bonus chapter.

Also by Kathryn Kincaid

Acknowledgements

I can barely believe that this is my third published book. Becoming an indie author has been the most rewarding, challenging, amazing thing I've ever done. Thank you for reading my books, cheering me on, and connecting with me over my stories. I don't have the words to express how much it means to me.

I also want to thank everyone who read *Play Your Part* and showered love on Zach. You're the reason this book exists, and I'm so darn proud it does. As much as I liked writing Zach's love story, I've been equally as anxious about doing his character justice. I loved him from the moment he popped up unexpectedly when I was drafting *Play Your Part*. He deserves everything good thing, and I loved giving that "ending" to him.

Stick Your Landing benefited from the careful read from my incredible beta and sensitivity readers — **AnnaMaria, Becky, Cristina, Hope, Rose, Ashley, Tiffany, Mollie, and Sarah.** I'm always amazed by the insightful, detailed, and thoughtful feedback you share about my work. This book changed in many ways for the better because of you.

Thank you to my **ARC readers** for reading an early copy and providing a review. Sharing your love for the book makes a huge difference for an indie author like me.

To my editor, Rachel Shipp – I love working with you. I always look forward to the editing phase knowing you'll be providing feedback that improves my story. It means so much to know you love my characters. Can't wait to work on the next book with you!

Mary Scarlett LaBerge – thank you for sticking with me on the cover. You took my vague feedback and created this incredible image of Zach and Finley. You make cover design an enjoyable, breeze of a process.

To my parents – you're the best. Thank you for giving me a great life, and for sparking my love for books. None of my books would exist without you.

Mike — every day I'm grateful that you're my husband. And no, it's not only because you'll listen to me spend twenty minutes recapping an episode of a show you hate. Or make my overnight oats even when I ask super late. Or when you act like an idiot to get me to laugh. You're my best friend and I love getting to be my weird self with you. Thank you for listening to me plot out loud, for reviewing my draft covers, and for reading text I'm unsure about. I hope you enjoy the cameo from your favorite character.

About the Author

Kathryn Kincaid writes contemporary romance featuring sports and characters finding the love they deserve. She lives in North Carolina with her husband and four adorable but high-maintenance cats. When she's not working or writing, she spends her free time devouring books, binging TV shows, cheering on the Carolina Hurricanes, and getting her butt kicked at OrangeTheory.

goodreads.com/author/show/31022409.Kathryn_Kincaid

instagram.com/authorkathrynkincaid

amazon.com/stores/Kathryn-Kincaid/author/B0C2K59RGZ

tiktok.com/@authorkathrynkincaid